Dark Art

Mac Logan

Stratagem paperback edition first published 2015

ISBN: 978-1-910166-11-6

'Stratagem' is an imprint of LoganODC.

Author’s Note

During the maturation of Scotch whisky about 2% is lost from the cask through evaporation. The UK Revenue and Customs accept the vanished amount as part of the production process and duty is not claimed. This is known as “The Angels’ Share”.

The Angels’ Share series takes the idea and twists it into a dark criminal conspiracy of self-serving officials, business people, bankers and organized crime. They evaporate money from contracts, drugs and human trafficking. They make money they have no intention of sharing in their vicious, self-serving greed. They’ll kill to protect their revenues.

Eilidh is pronounced “Ay (as in say) Lee”.

Angels’ Share Series

Dark Art, is the second full length novel in *The Angels’ Share* series. The first book, *Angels’ Cut* is available.

These edge-of-the seat thrillers involve crime, corruption, adventure, and mystery as Sam Duncan fights to rescue and protect his capable and feisty sister, Eilidh.

The next book in the franchise, ***Devil’s Due***, will be released soon.

Dark Art

Prologue

'Extreme prejudice is what Americans call it.' The fluent speech bore a slight accent.

Icy, upper-crust English frosted the air. 'We decided to let sleeping dogs lie.'

'We didn't agree, and we don't approve.'

Bloody foreigners. 'Ah, I see.' The chill deepened.

'We must eliminate the danger areas.'

Jumped up bureaucrat. 'We've agreed on—'

'There is no agreement. No ifs. No ands. No buts.' The inflection became more pronounced, forceful.

'Do you know who I am?' Brittle British blue-blooded anger crackled into the phone.

'Of course, you're a powerful and well-connected person.' The silent pause seemed, at first, to be respectful. 'Why don't you answer the door?'

'No one is there.' *Fool!* He allowed himself a tiny snicker. The bell rang.

'There's a present for you. Go and have a look.'

The knight of the realm and Privy Counsellor put his phone on a side-stand, rose slowly and walked from the lounge, into the hall. A small box, wrapped in shiny black paper, lay on the mat. He glanced about, fearful, and moved with some speed back to his seat. He sat with a bump.

'What is it?' He couldn't control a slight quiver in his voice.

'A little treat. Chocolates from Belgium. Trust me, that's all.'

'Chocolates?'

'Chocolates from Bruges.' The foreign laugh hinted at disdain.

'Bruges.' An aristocratic voice squeaked.

'The bearer of gifts could still be in your apartment.'

'*Now see here.*' The fearful British indignation lacked conviction.

'A gift of chocolates … to make a point.'

'How did he get in?'

'I have no idea. It's what people like that do. The package is delivered and the messenger gone. The door is locked and the security chain in its place … no? You're safe.'

'This is outrageous. You've no right to—'

'Listen to me.' A tendril of fear stroked the aristocrat's bladder. 'Duncan will be dealt with. Forget kidnapping, gunfights and crazy chases.'

'Unfortunate decisions.'

'Most unfortunate.' The foreigner slurped saliva. 'Our organization needs no publicity.'

'It won't happen again.'

'No, it won't. We've assigned the task.'

'Assigned the task?'

'Your new leader approves.'

'New leader?'

'New leader.'

'But—'

'No buts. No talk! I don't want to supervise any more … ah … dismissals. Understand?'

'Understood.' The line clicked as the European disconnected. A shaking hand put the phone down. *Shtum.*

A chastened government minister called in a bad attack of flu, switched off his mobile and computer, and poured himself a large glass of Scotch.

1

Cool as a frosty morning. A man ambled into the restaurant past a couple reading the street menu in its gold-crested mahogany case. He inhaled the pleasant, humid aroma of fresh bread, garlic-infused sauces and grilling seafood, paused and gazed around. Diners' heads rocked back and forth as they ate and socialized. The clink of silverware and subdued buzz of chatting folk echoed, warm and convivial. Bursts of laughter sounded and faded like waves on a shore. *There he is.*

A waiter, busy taking orders at a crisp linen-clothed table, questioned him with his eyes. He smiled and inclined his head towards a group of people. A nod of understanding gave permission. He walked over.

Near the window, the man held court at a laden table, surrounded by glasses, bottles and plates of food. He had his back to an earthy Mediterranean yellow wall, inlaid with a scattering of blue and white ceramic tiles showing ancient ships and castles. Pieces of netting hung here and there with multi-coloured glass spheres, oars and gaff hooks supporting the fishing theme.

A happy, somewhat theatrical focus for adulation, the mark waved his fork like a conductor's baton. His two companions laughed on cue. *Grovelling bastards.* The stranger walked over stone-faced. This'll make your day. The pistol wasn't suppressed, the better to terrify the diners.

The thunderous flat bark of the first shot made ears ring, and silenced the talk. The bullet slammed into the diner's upper lip to the right of his nose. Front teeth blew out from a ruined mouth and across to nearby tables, where they tinkled amongst the glassware and utensils.

The exit wound sprayed a fantail of sticky red-orange up the wall. The victim bounced backwards, cheeks flapping. Two shots to the centre of the chest splashed gore on the food and tablecloth. The dying man lurched forward on to his meal. His last jerking sigh bubbled into a plate of linguini, adding a soupçon of bloody foam to a lustrous creamy sauce as his body juddered.

One of the guests leapt up. *No, you don't.* A bullet in the thigh slapped him down, face whitening with shock. A surround-sound of screams erupted. Cutlery clashed and glasses crashed to accompany the terror. Then silence. Nobody moved.

Job done. The killer turned for the door and, unimpeded, walked out into a crowded Poplar High Street near Canary Wharf, London. In moments he vanished, dissolving into a bustling herd of humanity.

* * *

Two minutes after the killing the assassin entered a gent's toilet, removed his blond wig, spat out the mouth padding and threw away the dark jacket. He replaced his white shirt with a red t-shirt and pulled on a baggy, grey hooded training top sporting a Boston Red Sox logo.

A short time later, on the Tube, the killer continued his mission. He dropped his plastic gloves on the tracks when he changed for the Circle Line. Ghost-like hands, they puffed away up the tunnel as air blew in from an approaching train.

2

'It's a shame, but he really had to go.' Jim Thomas said, his Geordie accent sharp as a blade. 'Once he was arrested the dangers were too great to ignore.'

'It's a tragedy, we had such high hopes for him.' The Right Honourable Sir Marcus Attenwood-Leigh MP managed to sound mournful and appear comfortable at the same time.

Gemma Smythsone looked at Kenneth Chen, the banker and new member of the Bizz Board. 'An interesting time to join us Ken.'

'I'm up to speed on the situation Gemma. Nightmare.' Chen nodded his handsome, expressionless, Chinese features.

'Thanks for the use of the room, William.' Smythsone spoke to another new co-director of Bizz, and a Director in UK Counter Terrorism. They were in a secure meeting facility near Kings Cross which provided government quality safeguarding of their conversation, in much the same way their mobile and internet connections were insulated from prying.

'A sad pleasure, my dear.' Bizz director William Wardle's plummy English disclosed an icy indifference to any sadness.

A message pinged into Smythsone's mobile. 'Job done.' Her face stiffened and reality frosted her eyes for a moment.

'One down.' Wardle's voice came from the speaker, voice the same as if he were physically present. 'I have business to attend to. Speak soon.'

'Coffee gentlemen?' Smythsone called the break as Chair. When they stood with their drinks, only Jim Thomas could hold his saucer without the cup rattling.

3

'Where are you, Cal?' DCI Mike Swindon sounded tense. Leaning forward, General Ben Charlton, Head of Agency, listened by the speaker.

'Embankment Station,' Cal said.

'There's been a killing.' Mike said.

'Killing?' Cal Martin thought of Sam and stopped. A pedestrian crashed into him, bounced off his large frame and walked away muttering.

'One of the Bizz amigos, Devlin Forsyth.'

'He should've stayed in jail when we nicked him.' Cal said.

'Too right. The revelations at the meeting won't have helped the Chair.'

'So, they're in ruthless mode.'

'I'll text you an address and contact details for Maybelle Jones.'

'Thanks.'

'Are you armed?' Charlton said.

'Yes sir.

'Better get one up the spout.'

'Will do.'

'We need to protect Ms Jones. Fair chance she's on the list.' Charlton said.

Cal's mobile pinged as he received her work address, phone information and a picture. 'Beautiful big sista, isn't she? Do you think she fell in love with me when we arrested Forsyth?'

'Put your willie away, Chief Inspector.' Charlton said.

'Sorry sir. I'll be about ten minutes.'

'Fast as you can.'

'I'm rushing, willie and all,' Cal said. Mike choked off a snicker. 'You sure she's in?'

'Mike?' Charlton said.

'I've spoken to her secretary,' Mike said. 'Maybelle Jones is in the office and not available. Bloody power stuff, and we're trying to save her life.' Cal kept moving. 'Douglas Fullerton is two or three minutes ahead of you.'

'He's armed and needs back-up ASAP,' Charlton said. 'There are mobile units on their way. They should arrive when you do.'

'Okay, sir, I'm moving. I'll keep you posted.' Cal broke the connection and took the remaining stairs out of Embankment Station two at a time. He jogged along Embankment Place and out across Northumberland Avenue, head turning and body twisting as he searched for a taxi and avoided traffic. The first three in sight were all taken.

For a big man, approaching his fifties, Cal loped along in an easy rhythm, handsome features, similar to a younger Muhammad Ali, unstressed. His broad shoulders, height and athleticism were impressive. The swaying sports jacket concealed his weapon as he jogged.

He trotted along for three more minutes, looking over his shoulder until, at last, a cab heading the other way did a fast U-turn and pulled over.

* * *

'DCI Swindon.'

'I'll be there in five minutes.' The click of a seatbelt engaging sounded through the phone. Cal sat back as pine air-freshener mixed with a scent of leather filled his nostrils. Quite pleasant.

'You're doing fine, mate. The line's still engaged at that fuckin' woman's office.' Mike's voice vibrated with frustration. 'We can't get someone to interrupt her. Still,' a long sigh caressed Cal's ear, 'Douglas is close.'

'He's a good lad,' Cal said. 'I'll arrive soon. Tell the boss I've one up both spouts.' Mike smiled. 'One for him and one for her.'

'Who's the *him*?' Mike said.

'The killer.'

'How do you know?'

'It's always a man. Don't you watch TV?'

'Our intel reports a male,' Mike said.

'See! She's a smart looking woman. I like big sistas. I'll save her, she'll be grateful and the passion will flow. You need to watch more TV, Mike.'

'Time you got your brain out of your trousers and on to the task in hand, Inspector,' Charlton said, unable to hide a twinkle in his dark eyes from Mike. He sat erect, lean left thigh resting on the side of his battered desk. The other leg, relaxed at the knee, dangled a trade-mark, gleaming, black brogue. His tanned bald head gleamed in its frame of short dark hair. The hawk-like nose and thin lipped mouth gave him a desert warrior's profile.

'Want me to take myself in hand, sir?' Silence. 'Sorry sir. A bit adrenal.'

'Of course,' Charlton said, 'testosterone too by the sound of things.' Mike coughed.

4

Sir Marcus checked his watch, nodded to his colleagues and moved to a corner of the meeting room to make the call.

'Maybelle, my dear, could you join me for a coffee?'

'Marcus, this is a pleasant surprise,' she said, voice gushing with an oily mixture of respect and smugness.

'Thank you. I'm out of the House, fresh from a meeting, and we must meet urgently.' The plummy tones were part of his persona. She'd never known him to laugh.

'Can you give me thirty minutes?'

'No, I need to see you straight away. You are the Chair after all.'

'Okay, I'm on my way.'

'I'll be in the coffee shop on the corner by the time you get there.'

She did a quick check and adjustment of her make-up, rose and left her office. Her gleaming black skin and bouffant medium length hair suited her high-cheeked, beautiful face. Her snub nose, full lips and dark almond eyes were arresting. 'I'm stepping out for half an hour, Liza.' She sprayed some Japanese Flower perfume below each ear and a dash on her wrists which she rubbed together.

'You smell wonderful.' Her assistant gave a cheeky smile. 'Anyone dishy?

'Only a knight of the realm.'

'Now there's posh for you.' They both chuckled. Maybelle went to the lifts, her heels clicking on the corridor floor once she stepped off the office carpet on to the tiles. Her red jacket over a bright coloured summer dress was smart and gave her a solid business-like presence. A lift arrow lit with a ping as she entered the foyer. A good omen, she thought. Head held high, the smile on her faced lasted well out into the street.

* * *

Sir Marcus returned to the table. ‘She’s on her way.’ He checked his watch again, ‘timing is everything.’

5

'Just arrived, sir.' DC Douglas Fullerton spoke to Mike Swindon as he paid for his taxi. Forty yards away Maybelle Jones walked on to the pavement outside her office. 'She's just come out!' He accelerated towards her, with a rugby player's athleticism. 'Oh shit! Back-up, sir. I need back-up!'

'Mr Martin'll be there soon.'

'Roger that.'

The radio rustled in Fullerton's jacket pocket as he moved. Tyres squeaked. A horn blew. His shout, muffled by the material, was still clear. 'Maybelle Jones. Ms Jones. Get down! Get down!'

Jones' voice squawked shrill, annoyed. 'What do you think you're doing?'

'Get down! Now!'

Fullerton ran towards Jones and into the line of fire as a man raised a gun. The first shot hit Maybelle in the side, fired from about ten paces. She started to fall backwards. The change from petulant annoyance to shock was almost comical. Fullerton drew his weapon as he ran. The crack of the second shot was more distinct as Fullerton closed with her. The bullet struck high on the right of her forehead. Blood splattered from the wound. Her head snapped backwards. She collapsed spraying blood on to the white zero of a 20-mile-per-hour road marking.

A pedestrian crouched in terror behind the shooter, eyes bulging with panic, his lips framed in a wet-lipped wobbling 'O' of fear. Fullerton couldn't take a safe shot and held his fire. Two bullets slammed into his vest. He stumbled from the impact and fell to the road beside Maybelle Jones. He dragged himself forward on his elbows and covered her unconscious body with his own. A third shot hit his thigh, a fourth entered his chest below the armpit and a fifth punched into his ear.

Eyes wide open Douglas Fullerton's face slapped the tarmac as his breathing stopped. Dark blood oozed from under his curly-hair and bubbled over his lips. Maybelle Jones snored, comatose, life's-blood pumping from her injuries and mingling with her rescuer's.

* * *

The assassin slipped his gun in the back of his jeans and strolled away at a brisk tempo. He wouldn't attract attention. Ten paces and he turned right, walking along the ornamental park railings towards the middle of the square. The trees carried on with their gentle rustling, birds sang and flitted about oblivious to the unfolding human drama. Twenty metres from the corner Cal Martin jumped from a traffic-jammed taxi and raced past him. The gunman knew what he was and smiled. Bloody Filth.

Two turns and a further 200 metres away the killer entered a lane. He removed his beard, threw away the training top and dropped the gun into a skip. Three streets further on, another pair of petrol station plastic gloves went into a waste basket. 150 metres after that he was in a hotel toilet where he'd hidden some clothing in a hand-towel waste basket. Ten minutes later in jeans, a checked shirt and a light sweater, with the wig and prosthetic nose removed, he was heading for Kings Cross.

* * *

At The Agency offices, Westferry Road, Charlton and Mike listened to the wail of police Armed Response Vehicles getting nearer through Fullerton's radio. Cal's steps rushed up gathering volume.

Agitated people rubber-necked as Cal knelt beside Fullerton. One glance was enough.

'Fullerton's dead, Mike.'

'Fuck!'

Maybelle snorted. 'The woman's out of it. Head shot. Still alive, for now.' Cal's words were cool, professional. 'Ambulance fast as you like. Gotta start on her. There's some plods coming.' Tyres squealed in the street. Doors slammed. A constable came over to assist Cal. Three others secured the area.

* * *

Cal worked hard on the CPR. He counted and pumped, listened and worked, until paramedics arrived. Maybelle Jones' blood smeared his lips. The gore tasted metallic. He hoped she didn't have AIDS.

A paramedic cleaned Cal's face with a cool antiseptic wipe and gave him some saline solution to rinse his mouth. Cal spat a pink jet of water on to the pavement, took another swig, slooshed it around his teeth before spraying more fluid out. The flavour of gore was gone, but not forgotten.

'Will you be okay, mate?'

'Yeah. Nice perfume she's wearing.' Cal said.

6

'Why didn't he shoot?' Mike said.

'Good question.' Charlton said. The internal phone rang. He answered, listened and hung up. 'Fullerton is confirmed dead, hit several times. The woman's unconscious and badly hurt. He didn't shoot because some stupid wanker of a civilian wobbled round in his field of fire. Gave his life for a bloody idiot. Brave man.'

Mike's hard oval countenance quivered with shock as tears tried to fall. He clenched his teeth, emotions in check. The skin tightened over the planes of his face. Charlton contemplated him, stone-faced. Mike's rugged frame suited the cream polo shirt and smart jeans. His navy blazer hung round his chair, its collar being flattened as he moved backwards and forwards. Mike stopped, sighed and let his head fall.

'Tough at the top, Chief Inspector. No time for sentiment. Let's get this solved. We have to move fast.'

Mike's enraged eyes held Charlton's for a short time. Understanding followed moments later. He took a deep jerky breath. 'Yes, sir. I'll get a SitRep and find out what we can learn from surveillance.'

'Do that, Mike, I'll handle things after that. Give me a few minutes then get over to the hospital. I'll follow once this is organized.'

'Right, sir.' Mike picked up the phone and began talking in his brisk East End baritone. Five minutes later he was on his way.

* * *

'Mike?'

'Mike's gone to the hospital.' Charlton said.

'If it's any consolation he never felt a thing. He was hit four or five times. One of them went through his head.'

'You okay?'

'I'll cope.' At the scene Cal's face twitched, hidden behind the large hand cupping the mobile phone to his mouth.

'Good,' Charlton said. 'I want to get to the hospital, too, but I can't leave at the moment.'

'How are you, sir?' Cal said.

'Shit happens Cal. We can't prevent it. Mike's shocked. I've got a team to run.' Charlton pushed his reading glasses up his nose and continued to move the mouse and gaze at the computer screen.

'Tough one, sir. I'll head for the hospital. Mike could use a friendly face.'

'Do that.' Charlton ended the call and sat silent for a moment. He took his specs off and rubbed the bridge of his nose, eyes gleaming with menace.

* * *

Cal strode into emergency reception. Mike sat alone pale and distant, a rumpled form, his blazer drooping on hunched shoulders, elbows resting on his knees, head held in his hands.

'Hey, Mike.' Cal took a cheap grey plastic chair beside him. It creaked beneath his bulk.

'Douglas was a good lad.' Mike said. 'I'll miss him.' His face writhed with distress. He stared at the floor once more. Tears splashed his shoes and the scruffy green carpet tiles. His nose streamed, unnoticed, a long strand of mucous stretching downwards in a gloopy, transparent stream until it broke off and splatted on the floor. 'I've got to tell his folks.' A large hand offered a delicate white hanky. Mike took it, wiped his eyes and blew his nose. His professional face returned. The skin on his cheeks twitched before setting into a firm mask.

'I can handle the chat.' Cal's liquid brown eyes offered sympathy.

'No, he's one of mine, it's my job. I wouldn't mind company.'

'I'm with you.'

'Thanks, mate.' Mike's face warmed for an instant before colliding with the present and returning to a distant pale mask.

* * *

Maybelle Jones was being assessed as they spoke. They cut the floral silk-chiffon dress apart with scissors. Two of the nurses said they wanted to cry as they chopped away. Her large body lay flat and splayed out, unconscious, with drips, air tubes and monitors dangling around her. Sexy blood stained French culottes protected her modesty. One sizeable breast sagged against a white blanket the other drooped and wobbled as a medic investigated the wound in her side.

The medical team concentrated all their energy on her. They spoke in quiet, clear and professional tones as they exchanged information and made decisions. A person overhearing them would be reminded of military chat in times of crisis.

Thirty minutes later a neurosurgeon began to explore the inside of her broken skull. The work would go on for nine hours.

7

'Collateral damage is a fact of life, Gemma,' Jim Thomas said, 'nothing personal, some people don't make it home. Pity about the young cop.'

'Right,' her voice stayed flat, 'Maybelle's condition is critical. Head shot.'

'They brought it on themselves,' Sir Marcus made earnest political noises, 'Maybelle was cracking under the strain and going to meet the Chief Inspector on Friday. We couldn't allow it.' He paused and gazed round his colleagues, 'Devlin hadn't covered his tracks after kidnapping the Duncan woman and eliminating the Bain fellow. We've had real pressure over those two from Europe. Our actions, regrettable as they are, reassure our partners.'

'A sad day never-the-less,' Gemma said, 'Truly sad. Now, let's get back to business.'

'Did you say the Europeans want to meet you, Gemma?'

'Yes Marcus. We may have been having a lively time, but they're happy with the earnings.' She smiled and her colleagues joined in. 'Profits make prizes.'

8

The hospital emergency unit buzzed with people. Cal and Mike sat in the police room, fitting into two chairs at right angles around a bashed table. Both of them stared into space, which meant looking at a yellowing wall with a couple of posters and notices. Mike had been quiet for about fifteen minutes. A half-finished plastic cup of coffee died near his elbow. It smelled old with a crinkled scum of greasy solids forming a scabby skin on the chilling liquid.

'You only just missed him, Cal.'

'Yeah. A medium-sized man walked past me before I got to the corner and saw Douglas. It must've been him.'

'Close.'

'… not close enough.'

They went quiet for a few more minutes.

'You did your best, mate. We heard it.'

'The scene is a video in my mind, Mike. The bastard shot Douglas through the head, a deliberate kill-shot. I tasted the woman's blood as I worked on her.' He puffed out his cheeks and rolled his eyes.

'Fuckin' nightmare.' Mike said.

'And we've got to be ready for his parents and their grief, mate.' Cal said.

'I'm not looking forward to that.'

With a knock on the door, a PC walked in. 'Mr and Mrs Fullerton are outside, sir.'

'I'll come and get them.' Mike stood and, before he could move, a large woman entered followed by a slim, fairly short man. Mike and the dead man's mother regarded each other. Her tear-streaked face quivered with distress.

'Say it's not true.' The begging voice echoed from the

depths of a shocked, anguished soul.

'I can't, Mrs Fullerton. Douglas is dead.' Mike's jaw muscles rippled. 'I've seen him.'

'I fed him this morning. Gave him breakfast. We were laughing and talking about the weekend.' Her moist pink eyes still begged Mike to deny the truth, her nose dripped.

'I'm so sorry Mrs Fullerton. He's gone.' The words came out in a ragged whisper. She reached for her husband. They hugged and sobbed, cried and moaned, eyes squeezed shut to keep the evil out. Cal and Mike stood apart. After five minutes a gentle knock at the door admitted two Family Liaison Officers, trained for the pain of loss. Cal and Mike crept out and took seats near the door.

* * *

Two hours passed before a Family Liaison Officer came out. He asked a nearby PC for some coffees and another box of tissues. He turned to Mike. 'Was anyone present when Douglas died?'

'DI Martin.' Mike gestured towards Cal.

'Could you come in for a moment, sir?'

'Of course.' Cal said.

They walked into the room where Fullerton's parents sat at the table. 'This is Detective Inspector Cal Martin. He was with Douglas when he passed away. He tried to save him.'

The mother contemplated Cal. She stood up slowly and walked over to him. Her gaze searched his soul. 'Thank you Mr Martin.' She hugged him gently and he squeezed back. Her husband didn't move, as head in hands he sobbed, locked in a bubble of anguish.

Cal held the mother out from him by the upper arms, eyes searching hers. 'I'm sorry for your loss. Douglas didn't feel any pain, he died instantly and showed huge bravery in the way he handled himself. He's a son to be proud of. If you'll excuse me, I'll leave you to your privacy. If there's anything I can do ...' He walked with gentle dignity to the door and left.

* * *

Ben Charlton spotted Cal across the busy area, back to the wall, his face a wan mask of drained emotion. No Mike. Cal's big frame filled the seat, feet crossed at the ankles, hands slack in his lap, eyes focused on an invisible horizon.

'How are you Cal?'

'Hurting.' Cal didn't look up.

'How's Mike?'

'Hurting a lot worse than me. He's in with the parents.'

Mike came out. He regarded Cal. 'Thanks, mate. Your words and respect helped.'

'Good. We all know the pain of bad news.' Cal said. He shook his head and made eye contact with his colleague.

'Mrs Fullerton hopes we'll attend the funeral with the family.' Mike said. 'You were there. You're connected in her mind.'

'I'd be honoured.'

Charlton engaged. 'How are you, Mike?'

'Finished here, sir. Hoping to go for a drink with Mr Martin and maybe release a little tension.'

'Good idea for the pair of you.' Cal stood and nodded to Mike. 'One thing gentlemen, I need you back on the case by midday tomorrow. We've got some hard yards ahead.'

'Right sir.'

'What about Fullerton's parents, Mike?'

'She and her old man want a few minutes to themselves. The FLOs will take them through to view Douglas, then get them home or wherever. I'm done here.' Charlton gazed at his men. He nodded.

'See you tomorrow.'

* * *

The East Coast Express was a comfortable way to travel. The assassin sat in first class leaning back into his seat, book face down in front of him. The attendant came down the aisle towards him with two flasks in hand.

'Tea or coffee, sir?'

'Coffee please.' It seemed so normal, ordinary. He reflected on the killings. He remembered the dog when he slotted the old

Minister. Maybe he had been a bit vicious with the young cop, but if you're going to play in grown-up games you've got to take the risks. Fuck him. He smiled in a winner's way with no sense of remorse. The attendant grinned back as she placed a cup and sachets of milk and sugar in front of him and held out a small wicker basket of biscuits. He took a couple of shortbreads. 'Thanks.'

'You're welcome, sir.' The brakes released with a slight squeal as the train left York and accelerated north.

9

Gemma Smythsone lay in bed with Sir Marcus.

'Shame about Devlin. He really was trying very hard.'

'Alas, my dear, sometimes trying hard isn't enough. He exposed himself and left a trail we couldn't risk being followed. Bizz is only part of our secretive corporation, a decision had to be made. This'll teach us to handle things more effectively in future.'

'Too right.'

'We have excellent replacements for our erstwhile friends. Kenneth will be a sound partner and help our expansion plans in the Far East. William Wardle has position and power in the security side of things and helpful connections here and there.'

'Wardle is a cold fish.'

'Undeniably arrogant, word is cruel too. Still, he's an operator, Teflon-coated and inside our tent.' Sir Marcus gave a gentle chuckle.

'I tried to tell them, Marcus.'

'I know you did, my dear. Some people simply don't listen ... and have to pay the price.'

'What about Jim Thomas?'

'He's forgiven. Bared his soul, owned past misdeeds, did penance and is solidly with us.'

'So what's next?'

'Kenneth is a great fan of yours, and he'll provide support and oversight in our UK operation. Even our European Chair wants to meet you. He's powerful, focused and hugely well connected. We have corporate plans for you, you know.' She smiled. 'Now, if you'll please make this man very happy for a few minutes, Gemma, we can get on with our day.'

* * *

She stroked him until his erection had achieved maximum, if somewhat squidgy, firmness and took him into her mouth. His breath started to come in gasps and the groan of climax signalled the end of their encounter.

She manufactured happy moaning and slurping noises as he relaxed back on the bed. As he finished she faked a swallow and saw his eyes spark with imagined control. Inside she sneered.

She gave him a titillating glimpse of her lithe body—naked but for stockings and suspenders—as with a wiggle of her pert, muscular derrière she stepped into the ensuite.

It was a tad disappointing to hear a light snore before she was out of sight. In the bathroom she spat out his semen and rinsed with mouthwash from her bag. She didn't shudder, her career advanced, a fine rationale for sexual services to corrupt junior Ministers.

Sir Marcus enjoyed his feels, blow-jobs and the view of her naked flesh. They'd never had proper sex. Maybe he had a 'Clintonesque' defence worked out. She smiled and stepped into the shower tucking her sleek dark hair into a cap. When she came out the pompous old fart was snoring for England.

She dressed in a conservative ochre business suit, with an A-line skirt, off-white silk blouse and matching low-heels that suited her toned calves. She went over to the bed, woke Sir William, gave him a long kiss with plenty of tongue and left for a legal consultation.

His growing recognition of her rising status filled her with joy. Only a few more brief encounters between her and the top. She glowed with good humour all the way into her waiting taxi. A surveillance video recorded her departure and that of Sir Marcus thirty minutes later.

10

The knife thrust forward at a wicked angle. Sam swayed back as the blade slashed across his upper arm. He planted his feet and followed the weapon round as it lacerated the air. He grabbed the shoulder of his assailant and, shifting his right foot, managed to trap the attacker's instep, pull him off balance and throw him backwards. He forced the enemy groundwards where his superior size and strength might make a difference. His breath came in shortening gasps.

His assaulter, tumbling towards the ground, managed a slash to Sam's neck. When Sam fell forwards and on to him he felt the point of the blade dig sharply into his solar plexus. Game over.

He collapsed, expelling a ragged groan and lay unmoving on the sand of Sannox beach, his grey-streaked brown hair ruffled by the wind.

11

'Hello, I was told you'd call,' Smythsone said, she looked at her watch, 6.30 a.m.

'Sir Marcus and Kenneth Chen are most helpful men. I hear things have been somewhat… ah,' he made a slurping sound, 'busy over your way.'

'Yes. A spot of restructuring.'

'Exactly. I'd like you to come and meet us in Brussels.'

'Love to.' The thought of growing power aroused her. The next step in her new career beckoned. 'When should I come?'

'Day after tomorrow, if you can.'

She examined her diary, crammed with appointments as usual. 'Time?'

'Arrive noon in the city centre and depart around three.'

'I'll be there.'

'Excellent.' The sibilance in Xavier's voice made her uneasy. The sound had a reptilian quality. He slurped quietly again. 'Meet you then.' He hung up.

Smythsone clicked on her intercom. 'Jeanine.' she said.

'Yes?'

'Clear my diary for Thursday and book me on a plane to Brussels to be in the centre for 11.30.' She rubbed her hand on the wood, enjoying the cool smoothness.

'Will do. When are you coming back?'

'As near to five as possible.'

'Your itinerary and ticket information will be on your desk shortly.'

'Perfect. Thank you.'

12

Sam sat up. Fine grains of sand powdered his face. He brushed them off. Bright sunlight caught ripples on a restful sea. He relaxed, gasped ragged breaths and gazed at the Devil's Punchbowl, mist easing out of the cauldron like steam from a witches' brew. The magnificent stone spike of *Cioch na h-Oighe*—the Maiden's Breast—nipple erect, towered in the brilliant sky.

'Two each, sir. Fancy one more?' Sam recognized how regular Special Forces training made his opponent less breathless, less sweaty and altogether more ready for another round.

'A kind offer, but the answer is no. I'm knackered.'

'Not bad for an old 'un.' The cheeky grin offered respect and liking.

'Thanks a bunch, I'm at least twenty-five years older than you, and feeling every day of it.' He widened his eyes as he spoke. The soldier smiled in return. Sam took a deep breath, resting his elbows on his crossed knees. His respiration returned to normal with satisfying speed.

'You got me the first two, sir, then age set in.'

'Four is enough and you've made my day, as long as we can forget about the age-setting-in part.'

'You're the fittest oldster I've ever met, sir.'

'You'll get some crawly points for that. But I'm not the fittest oldie. Spar with Peter Waberthwaite. He'll test you.'

'Love to. He's a quiet man.'

'Quiet and effective. I'd lay money you'll have to do more than four or five goes before you get anywhere near him. Have a rest. I'll speak to him and find out if he's interested.' Sam reached across and patted the man's shoulder. 'Thanks for the workout and the training time you've been giving me: I'm honed and toned. I can keep it up now.' The man eyed Sam and smiled. 'The exercise I mean, soldier.' They chuckled, 'I'd better get back to the house.'

* * *

Sam went in through the drying room. The door was high-handled and solid. He walked past hanging jackets and boots in racks. In the kitchen, Tonka stood at the range, wiry muscles and a, medium build. His dark hair short enough to avoid grabbing.

'This early morning exercise will kill me.' Sam said. 'Something up?'

'The shotgun's missing.' Tonka said.

13

Sam's face lost colour. 'What do you think?'

'It's not on the shelf. No one's been around. It was there last night.'

'Wait a moment.' Sam left the room. He was back in moments. 'Everyone's asleep. Eilidh's not in her bed.'

'There's nobody downstairs, I've checked.' Tonka said.

'Everywhere?' Sam said.

'Not the cellar.'

'The watchers?'

'Nothing. You've been outside. The sensors haven't picked up a thing. There's been no movement around the place. She's got to be in here somewhere.'

They exchanged glances and eyed the basement door. Tonka turned off the main kitchen light and switched on a lamp on the tiny shelf beside the range. Sam crossed and eased the door open. A faint wavering glimmer lit the bottom of the stairway. He touched his lip with his finger, took a deep breath and descended with careful, quiet steps.

Once down, he turned, passed the entrance to a small wine cellar and walked back parallel to the stairs. Eilidh was huddled on the floor, leaning against a stack of wood. A candle spluttered on the stone flagged floor beside her. Her eyes were shut. The barrels of the shotgun lay across her body, touching her left ear. Her left hand was on the stock and her right held the grip, index finger along the trigger guard.

'You could have picked a warmer spot to lie down, lassie.' Sam's voice was as soothing as velvet.

Eilidh didn't speak. Her eyes opened slowly and she turned red-rimmed eyes towards him. In a moment the gun pointed at Sam, no waver of the barrels. He'd taught her well.

Both his hands went up, pushing gently towards her with a fanning motion. 'Come closer,' she said. 'You better not be fucking Ned.' Sam move slowly into the light.

'It's Sam. What's with the shotgun?'

'I don't know.' Eilidh's voice was almost a whisper, her mouth twitched. 'That awful man, Ned. I keep sensing him coming towards me. He smelled of manure with a horrid cheesy breath. I've no idea what he looks like. His hands on me. The dark. A kitten. The cold wet toilet. An awful rag stuffed into my mouth.' She cried and didn't resist Sam as he took the gun away. A hand took the weapon, Tonka, silent as a ghost.

'I understand, Eilidh. You're healing.' He sat down beside her and pulled her close. In a few minutes her sobs subsided. 'They took you, you survived. Got out alive. You're safe.'

'It keeps whirling around in my mind. The nightclub, those awful men, the farm smells, the confusion on the way here.'

'Shit happens, Eilidh, I've had the nightmares too. They'll fade and pop back now and then, weaker.'

'I was helpless.'

'Stop it. You're here aren't you? You survived. Stop feeling sorry for yourself, it gets to be boring after a while.'

'What's this? Tough love from a big brother.'

'Love for sure. You don't want the tough bit.'

'Got a hanky, Sam?'

'Nah, why don't you use my shirt? It's well soaked already.' She took the offer and started to giggle.

'I am getting better, aren't I?'

'Yes. You need to push Ned to the side.'

'I can't get him out of my thoughts. He was,' she shuddered, 'horrible.'

'I bet us talking about the swine will make his presence weaker in your head. I mean, problem shared and all that.'

'You think so?'

'I know so. It's helped with some of my own bad experiences. As you talk about them they get less intense.' Karen's searching, ever understanding eyes, came to mind. And being held, loved and somehow forgiven, regardless.

Eilidh hugged him. 'I knew you'd save me.'

'I'm a full service big brother. Why don't you go, clean yourself up and come down for a cup of tea.' She pulled back, gazed at him. 'Only Tonka and I know about this. We can keep it that way if you want.'

'Karen?'

'I may tell her, but won't if you don't want me to unless she's in the kitchen when we get back up.'

'You can tell her. She keeps secrets.'

'Really?' Sam cocked an eyebrow.

Eilidh smiled, got to her feet and picked up the candle. 'I'll be back in ten minutes, the tea better be ready.'

Sam checked his watch. Seven. He stood up and followed the faint light out of the cellar. The shotgun was on its ledge by the door, no sign of Tonka.

14

'Get back here, as-soon-as. Chopper pick-up in four hours. We have trouble and we need a visible vicar. I wanted to give you a few more days. Not possible. Sorry.'

'What's up?'

'Fullerton's dead.'

'Shit!' Sam closed his eyes with a sigh. 'Nice lad.'

'The Jones woman he was trying to protect is critical and in a coma. Another player, Forsyth, was assassinated yesterday lunchtime. Someone's tying up loose ends.'

'It doesn't pay to get in the way.'

'No. Mike's chewed up. Fullerton was in his team.'

'Tough one.'

'Cal arrived on scene moments after he died and saved the other victim. CPR in the street. Mike and Cal met the family and gave them the bad news.'

'Cal will be hurting too, and he's got empathy. He'll help Mike.'

'Yes.'

'I'll get packed,' Sam said. He crossed his legs and leaned back against the chrome rail of the Aga.

'I know this disrupts important family time after your recent adventures. I won't forget. I need you here for the next few days.'

'Count on me, Ben.' Sam ran his fingers through his curly hair.

'See you soon.'

'Right.'

'Oh, one other thing. Bring Waberthwaite if he'll come.'

Sam glanced at Tonka, tilted his head and mouthed 'coming?' Tonka nodded, grey eyes calm and aware.

‘He’s here and he’s coming.’

‘Excellent. Bye.’ Charlton hung up.

15

'It's the deal, love, the promise that made us safe.' Sam backed away.

'You're reliving your youth and enjoying this. Knife fighting in the morning. How many times have I watched you bugger off on some risky adventure?'

'It's the job ...'

'Stop it. Stop it! That bloody, cold, stand up and do your duty crap. I thought we'd left all that behind when you quit the life.'

'So did I.'

'One chance to go back and you're in there, Mr Knight-in-shining-armour.'

'It was for Eilidh.'

'Don't give me the Eilidh rubbish. She's here, safe and you're off to London at old Ben's beck and call. Back into a shooting war.'

'They need me.' *Oops.*

'I need you! The girls need you! Even your bossy old mum needs you!' The volume was up. 'I don't need any more of your repeating bloody nightmares about Tam and Baz being blown to pieces. I've served too bloody much with you.'

Sam stood in front of her, hands up, placatory. 'We've been through a lot.' Their eyes met, 'I'm sorry this hurts you so.'

Karen's lips twitched as angry tears splashed down her hot face. 'I love you lots, you stupid Don Quixote. What am I to do the day you don't come home and that old bastard Charlton comes to tell me how sorry he is.'

'Kick his balls?' Sam's mouth twitched.

Karen grinned through her tears and reached for him. 'This is a hellish, beautiful place, *darling*. No friends, no shopping, no walks without protectors. The girls love it and have new friends in the village. They like being protected. Your dear mum is a pain in the backside after a while. She wants the world in her image and bribes people with excellent food and cups of tea.' They held each other dancing a smooch in a gentle circle.

'It's a tough one, love, we'll find a way to get back to normal. Cut me some slack.' He buried his face in her neck.

'How long have we got?' She felt the tug as his arm raised his watch.

'A couple of hours.'

'Lock the door and do your duty.' She kissed him long and deep.

'Your wish is my command.'

'It's not a wish I want, soldier.'

16

'The criminals are running scared.' The strength of Cal's voice belied his appearance, with his large frame hunched, movement hesitant and alcohol-reddened eyes lacking focus.

'We still need a good picture of what they're trying to cover-up.' Mike's pallid skin gleamed from sweat and a recent shave. The citrus tang of his after-shave smacked the air.

'It must be huge and involve mega-money,' Cal said.

'Loads of dosh and powerful people. I mean, think of the firefight Sam got into. A fuckin' chase half way across Scotland with a horde of aggressive killers on his tail.'

'Lucky to escape with his life. He's a hard man.'

'Yeah and he took a bullet,' Mike said. 'We mustn't forget the way they snatched Eilidh Duncan. That took planning and some clout.'

'Right,' Cal said, 'and the kidnapper is pushing up daisies. Now that was a professional hit.'

'Yeah, and his little helper gets beaten to death by a seriously vicious nutter.'

'Okay, we've got events on the timeline. There must be more strands.'

'Always are.' Mike nodded, eyes screwed-up with the pain of thinking.

'Yeah, and they're killing people faster than we can arrest them.'

'And they killed young Douglas less than eighteen hours ago. They paused, gazed at each other and changed the subject.

'That Tonka's a piece of work too,' Mike said.

'He's been round the block. He and Sam did spook time together.' Cal said.

'So, who and what are we up against apart from: half the

UK Establishment, American mercenaries, our own security people, and every banker, politician, civil servant and criminal within a hundred miles of here?'

'Fuck knows.'

17

They stepped on to the tarmac at Edinburgh Airport. A strong whiff of aviation fuel swirled in the air. The whine of the helicopter became insistent as the rotors accelerated and the Sea King left them. A van waited to drive them to their jet. An hour later they were in the South.

'No City Airport today,' Sam said. 'New route.'

'Variety: the spice of life.' Tonka said.

They crossed the spartan concourse at Luton and caught the next coach to Victoria. As they exited the coach, two of Charlton's security men, ever watchful, hastened them to a people carrier, moving off without delay.

Two small cases lay between the grey leather seats, one contained Sam's Browning in its pancake holster, the other a SIG Sauer P226 nine millimetre pistol with a shoulder harness.

Sam took out the clip. 'Clean and ready to go.'

'Mine too.'

They talked until Tonka told the driver to pull over.

'Invisible from now. See you soon.' He stepped out of the car and into the crowd. Gone.

* * *

Twenty minutes later, Sam walked into the office. A watcher from the other side noted his arrival. Charlton met him as he came through the security door, business-like in a dark suit, crisp white shirt and the ubiquitous regimental tie.

'Bad news, Ben?'

'Could be worse. Maybelle Jones is still alive, but in an induced coma. She's going to be out of things for weeks, maybe forever.'

Sam nodded. 'Give me a moment Ben, I promised Karen to check in when I got here.'

'Of course.'

* * *

Sam sat in an empty meeting room.

'Hi, sweetheart.'

'Safe and sound, darling?' Karen said.

'As can be.' Sam drawled out his calm reassurance. 'Tonka's babysitting me.' He remembered flashes of their parting: her honey blond hair tickling his cheek as she straddled him for a "quickie". The comfort of her fluid weight on him. The loving face, stressed and near to tears when he walked away.

Hugs from the girls and his mother. Tonka urging him forward. The scent of summer sea air, heavy with flowering gorse, as they walked along the sandy path to the pick-up area. As the helicopter rose, he experienced once more the sharp sorrow of departure.

Karen's face filled his mind for a moment. He admired her strength of character and the depth of loving support that overrode the subtle, hollow fear in her beautiful eyes. Her voice called him back to the present.

'How old was the man who died?'

'Twenty-three. Didn't have a chance.'

'Mmm. Remember Fuss's maxim.' She sounded tough.

'Do unto others before they do unto you.'

'That's the one. Promise me.'

'I promise. Bye now.' Sam disconnected the phone, paused and thought about business.

Up north Karen perched on the bed and sobbed her fear into a tissue. After a short while she stood up, rinsed her face and went downstairs, strong and warm for her children, family and protectors.

18

Sitting in silence for a couple of minutes soothed Sam. He sighed and started to tune in. Tonka knocked and entered. 'Tough one for the team,' he said.

'Yeah. An empty space at the table makes it real. The first death never goes away.' Tonka nodded a question. 'Baz?'

'Nice lad. That was a tough action.' Tonka said.

'He did his job. I heard him get it, right behind me, some chunks of frag. He didn't look good. We made eye contact, he waved me on, one of his guys started on him. I never saw him again.'

'I was with him when he died.'

'You didn't tell me, Tonks.'

'He asked if you made it. He admired you, you know. Covering your lot was his mission.'

'Orders is orders.'

'Right, Medevac took you away and it was, what, three years later before we teamed up?'

'Yeah.'

'I told him you were fine, sent your regards. Said you were ordered out for more action.' Tonka's eyes were in the South Atlantic. 'Then he passed away smiling. His head dropped like he'd gone to sleep.'

'He thought I was fine?'

'Right, No point in saying you'd bought it.'

'No. A good lie. Thanks for that.' Sam said.

'Off you went in the chopper. We all thought you'd die.'

'And now we're a team. I've some whisky in the flat. We'll toast Baz tonight.'

'Right. Think of Baz, think of Douglas. That young man gave his life for a corrupt official. No question, he did his duty.'

'Brave man.'

'And it's people like you and me, ugly old fighters, who need to make the difference for our young and inexperienced people.'

'Sure,'

'Is the anger cold?'

'Like ice.'

'Focus?'

'Clear.'

'We've been in the odd hairy scrape, mate,'

Sam nodded, 'Your scrape score's bigger than mine.'

'Maybe.' A nod. 'Maybe not. Our cool and our heart makes us better than the bastards we're up against.' His eyes held Sam's. 'You know the drill. Douglas was a good lad. We chatted once or twice, but he's for later. Now's for surviving. Stay tuned in and wide awake. The bother's just begun.'

'I hear you.'

'Hard yards make us what we are, what we can be. This one is as dirty as it gets, enemies mixed with friends, in our home streets and backyard.'

'You've used up a year's words Waberthwaite.'

'Need every one to get through your thick skull.'

'You're the second person to give me a pep-talk today.'

'Who else?'

'Karen.'

'Wise woman.'

'Yes indeed. Know what she said?' Tonka shook his head. 'Do unto others before they do unto you.'

'Bang on. I'm putting her on my Christmas list.'

'All that manly-words-at-the-breach stuff, and then you go soft on me?'

'Fuck off.'

'Thanks for that,' Sam said. 'Let's whup some ass.'

'What a crap accent.'

Tonka stood and left with a half-smile on his face: the equivalent, for him, of roaring with laughter.

* * *

Sam entered the ops room. The buzz stopped and people gazed at him.

'Hi folks. I'm sorry to be back because of a tragedy.' They nodded and murmured. 'Douglas was our friend. Right now, the usual simple words, we've got to get on with the job and find the bastards who killed him. We need to meet.' He checked his watch. 'Tomorrow morning I think. I'm having a catch up with Mr Charlton in five minutes.'

Charlton nodded. They left together.

* * *

Sam sat at the coffee table to the side of Charlton's large brown desk with its almost Victorian array of blotter, pen stand and black wire filing trays. 'Poor Douglas, Sam. It's hard on the team.'

'Of course it is.'

'I called you back because I need your savvy. Will you do point again?' Charlton's eyes focused on Sam's.

'Remember the Falklands?' Sam said.

'Hmm … that sort of thing. Get good and get used, Sam, ever thus.'

'Visible irritants work in this game. We shook some screws loose when I went walk about, rattled Bill Jenkins cage.'

'And his brothers testicles as I recall.' Charlton shared a smile.

'Right,' Sam said. 'There's no way back from here, right now, Ben. I'm in.'

'Thanks.'

'Karen's finding this situation hard. I want you to swear you'll help me get us back to normal first chance we get.'

'You have my word.'

'One thing, if you do have to go and give her the worst news …'

Charlton's shoulders drooped. 'We must make sure that doesn't happen.'

'Yeah, but if it does happen, be sure to wear a cricket box.'

Sam's wide smile brightened the room. They both laughed.

* * *

'Where are Cal and Mike?' Sam said.

'Hungover, grieving.' Charlton said.

'That's one solution.'

'They're working. Have you had a ponder?'

'Yup.' They settled into a strategic discussion.

19

A night's sleep hadn't made anyone feel better. In Room Two the atmosphere reeked of tension and rage. The team sat at tables arranged in a herringbone around a raised area with seating, a flipchart and projection screen. The strip lighting provided a glow that, combined with light green walls gave everyone a pallor. Ben and Sam walked in, mugs of coffee in hand. 'Sam.' Ben deferred and pointed to the dais. Sam noticed Mike sitting near the front with Cal. He nodded. They responded.

'Thanks, Ben. Anyone got anything they need to say about the shooting of Douglas?' Silence.

After a long pause a young policewoman stood up. 'We'll all miss Douglas, sir.'

'Yes, we will.'

'We want to find the people who killed him and put them away.'

'Yup, and we're working on it'

'How, sir? What do we really know?'

'Fair point. We have basic information, and we're collating it. Eilidh Duncan is recovering. She's less of a basket case every day.' He stood in front of them, six feet one inch of solid muscular man, face tanned and calm, icy blue eyes below somewhat bushy eyebrows. 'We'll be able to debrief her soon.'

'So she'll help us?' A detective of Chinese origin spoke up.

'Yes.'

'What can we do now, before she gets here? We have to do something.' An angry murmur rippled through the team.

'You're annoyed.' Sam nodded. 'On the way down here I thought about Jamie Carron, Eilidh's editor. He mentioned two key things: easing the drugs deliveries and some serious Government contract skimming. It's a pity he's light on detail and contacts. Eilidh kept her key information under her hat as she researched and wrote up her stuff. Carron doesn't know everything, but enough to be pretty excited.'

'He ought to bloody share it,' a voice called from the group.

'Within the constraints of protecting sources, he says he will. We'll put the thumbscrews on him soon.' Subdued laughter trickled round the room. 'Her disappearance involved inside information, files and data. Eilidh can only tell us what she remembers. The drugging and abuse she suffered came close to breaking her mind. Her files are still missing and we hope to recover them soon. If only she'd remember. As I say, the good news is she's getting better. That's the background. Any thoughts before I continue?'

* * *

'We don't know much.' Mike's unhappiness was etched on his hard face.

'Yes and no, Mike, and that provides an opportunity. If we don't know and her editor doesn't know, that's one thing. But, if the criminals who are confronted by this whole thing don't know, you can understand their panic. How do you control the unknown? You try to shut it down. They're making an indiscriminate war, and we're having an unnecessary bloodbath because they made a big mistake: they didn't kill Eilidh.'

'That means her editor could be in danger,' Mike chimed in.

Charlton interrupted. 'You better make a call and get some people to him pronto, Mike.' Swindon stepped out.

'Talk amongst yourselves.' Sam's smile received no response.

Mike returned in two minutes.

'A car is on its way.'

'Thanks, Mike.' Charlton nodded to him as he took his seat. 'Back to you, Sam.'

* * *

'We know quite a lot.' Sam said. 'The hard part is joining the dots. That's where Eilidh's contribution comes in.'

'When's that going to happen?'

'Sooner than you think.' Charlton said. Sam glanced at him.

'Bad people are twitching.' Sam said. 'Look at the last few weeks: Eilidh was kidnapped, the man who set her up had his throat cut, her kidnappers are murdered, people on the periphery are killed and my family was attacked in their hide-away in Ireland. Within a few weeks we know that organized crime, politicians ...

'*No surprise there!*' burst from the group. Some laughter lightened the mood.

'... Bankers ...'

'*Bastards!*' More laughter.

'... Officials ...'

'*Fuckwits!*'

Sam stopped to let the mischief die down, laughing with the team. 'And, we know who some of them are.' He paused, serious. 'Or were.'

'We've seen the faces on the wall, Colonel. Please speculate a little further?' Charlton said. Sam nodded.

* * *

'There's a powerful group of corrupt people across the public and private sectors in the UK and Ireland, who'll do pretty much anything to steal cash from our government. Communications from Grosvenor Square, the US Embassy, led to mercenaries being engaged in the firefight in Scotland. The USA is infected. The transmission was confirmed by the CIA, no less.'

'That big?'

'That big, Mike, and even bigger,' Sam said, 'recent contacts now suggest there are strong links to Europe. The buck starts and stops here, for now.'

'Getting resources committed is hard.' Charlton said. 'Although we have strong backing from Number Ten, we have both security and budget constraints. Cases must be made and secrets kept close.'

'Thanks, Mr Charlton. That leads nicely to our goal, which is to build a detailed model of what we're up against and lay plans to sort it out. The first phase is to gather information and leads, join the dots, and create a structure to build on.'

'That's not just police work, sir,' an attractive young officer, with her blond hair cropped close, spoke up.

'No. It involves spooks, Special Forces, the police, everyone. We will pool and collate information here. Quentin and Indira will expect simple, clear reporting.' Sam said. 'Indira has prepared electronic forms to structure the data and you're expected to use them.'

'Must we?' An older policeman pulled a face.

'Yes, even old fossils like you and me will comply.' Sam winked and nodded. 'Indira is the database expert, any problems, talk to her. Questions?' Silence. 'That's it, folks.'

'Thanks, Sam. As you can hear, we're getting sorted,' Charlton said. 'There should be more people joining over the next couple of weeks. For now, noses to the grindstone, everyone. Thank you.'

20

'What do they know?' Smythsone's stiff face gave nothing away.

'Hard to say, Gemma. Their lid's on fairly tight, but we're working on it.' Wardle's arrogant confidence irritated her.

'Is that it?'

'Of course not. We have plans to eliminate the problem, but it's a political issue, and we, needs must, pull levers, grovel and keep a civil tongue on the right shoes. It'll take a week or two, but we'll get there. Amazing what a little money makes possible.'

'Is there anything we can do short-term?'

'We'll have to see, won't we?'

21

In Charlton's office the lead team—Mike, Cal, Quentin, Indira and Sam met. 'We've got a mole in the police. We don't think it's one of you.

'You checked us out?' Mike said.

'Of course' Charlton said. 'We've reviewed timings, key incidents, internet and telecoms. You all came up clean. We've found a thread leading to a senior officer in the Met and are following it up. We want to know who is leaking to key players on the away team. It's a good opportunity to sow disinformation.'

Mike's mobile rang. He spoke briefly and nodded. 'The editor's safe.'

'How is he?' Charlton said.

'A bit shirty about being guarded. After a spot of chit-chat he understood the danger he's in and accepts the need to be protected for a while.'

'Great,' Sam said, 'but we need to draw out the enemy. Where can we go? Where can we contain them and get some protection in place?' He paused, 'I'm thinking of Bill and Charlie's office. Reactions?' Mike appeared uneasy. 'Mike?'

'We must protect the receptionists at the entrance and any innocents inside, although we don't think there are many, four at last count, and we've been watching for a week now. Above all we must avoid reckless endangerment. I believe we can infiltrate armed officers into the building and protect bystanders.

'We'll secure the place for an hour or so, and use the open door as a trap.' Sam said. 'Can we do that?'

'Yes.' Mike nodded.

'Mike, let's leak a story about the memory stick, along the lines of me going for the information tomorrow via the Neon

Orchid. We believe the other side still have surveillance outside. If so, they'll latch on to me. After that, I want a car to collect me and take me to the Arches. Engage the leak in providing operational support. You can explain we're a bit thin on the ground after losing Douglas. Ask for help. That should keep us safe. I'll go to the Arches with one of your people, but that person needs to know this could be hairy. Tonka will be invisible. We need police along for the show, complete with armour, guns and attitude … and one of those chunky armoured vehicles?'

'Armed Response Vehicle?' Mike said.

'That's right, an ARV. Tonka will identify watchers. If he does, he'll report in. He'll need half an hour for a recce. Then we'll get moving.' Sam said

'Okay, Sam, that gets you moving. What now?'

'Your first leak along the lines of: we think we can collect the data and I'll bring it back here after seeing Bill.' Sam stopped and checked for questions. 'Let's smoke out some enemy. We might shake some fillings loose. The building is a hive of criminal activity, and it isn't heavily populated. We'll take the risk of losing our advantage to protect innocent people.'

They spoke for another half hour and planned how they would handle the different strands. Safety could be the death of them. Sam didn't smile at the thought.

* * *

Tonka and Sam shared a coffee after the meeting. 'Who'd be a cop? Douglas took the hit protecting the public. The man who killed him was a pro. The kill-shots were completely unnecessary.' Tonka's hair bristled with anger. He shared the glint in his eye and a slight edge to his voice with Sam but no one else. His West Midland accent came out, as always, in a soft, almost gentle baritone.

'The rules are different, Tonks, but the aim is the same. Interdict evil people. We're in a war zone in the heart of a huge city. The enemy is murderous. We're trying to draw them out and, if no one shows, we're back to the drawing board. Can they allow us to return to our base believing we've got information to sink 'em? I hope not. I want them to make a move.'

'You're the man with a plan. I'm going out for a while. Fuss has you covered. Meet you at the flat between eight and nine.' Tonka said.

'Fine. Fuss will come back with me tonight.'

'Right,' Tonka sighed, 'I'll give him a second chance. The missus would've liked that. I wonder if he'll do the same for me.'

'It'll work out. You'd better kiss and make up. My life may depend on it,' Sam said, his smile wide. Tonka's eyes brightened for a moment, but his expression didn't change. He glided out of the room.

22

Sam used the thinking time. The mind map flowed onto his pad, helping him structure his thoughts and prepare for action. He sat back, and exhaled a rasping sigh. There was a knock at the door.

Quentin invited Sam into Charlton's office.

'This is going to be risky, Sam,' Charlton said.

'Timing is everything.'

'I want you to brief the people who're doing the protection and all the action at the Jenkins' office.'

'Will do. I need to talk to you privately.'

Quentin stepped out. 'What's on your mind?' Charlton said. Sam shared his ideas for a fall-back if things went wrong. They needed a 'Plan B'. Charlton approved more readily than Sam expected. 'I'll make the necessary arrangements, Sam. After that, we must organize a workshop with the extended team.' That included police, security operatives and communications people. 'We all need to be on the same page.'

'The last call Maybelle Jones received came from an unknown secure line,' Sam said. 'The voice was plummy, upper-crust.'

'We suspect it was Sir Marcus Attenwood-Leigh,' Charlton said. 'He's something of a wide boy by all accounts. He was linked to Devlin Forsyth and Maybelle Jones through that committee thing for the Home Office. He was a sporadic attender at best, with a good reason for attending, as he serves on a relevant committee in the House itself.'

'What do people say about him?' Sam asked.

'Public school bully, frosty, rude to lesser mortals, holds grudges, excellent MP and loved by his constituents. He's a typical narcissistic, power-mad politico.'

'Is there no information on the line? They should know.'

Sam said.

'Maybelle Jones said she was meeting a knight of the realm,' Charlton said. 'The call appeared to come from an internal line. We reviewed the logs and security data. No evidence. We even had the phones fingerprinted. Maybe it's too clean, but we have nothing. Nothing.'

'That's us then, Ben.'

'Right.'

The door opened.

* * *

A medium height, wiry man with a pencil moustache and brilliantined hair walked into Charlton's office.

'Just call me Jackie.' The accent pure Glasgow.

'Why are you here?' Charlton said. The temperature dropped.

'Job done, sir.' He smiled at Sam.

'How so?'

'A wild fucker called Ziggy popped in to finish old Jackie off. He's now under arrest at the local hospital. The mad vicar here doesn't like killin', you understand, the prejudice wasn't too extreme.'

'Quite.'

'He came in swingin' a lump of leaded deer horn, missed me, and the rest is history.' He paused, milking the moment. 'As is his right knee and left elbow. He'll not be runnin' off.'

'Anything else?'

'I don't think he knows much about the big picture. I made some … eh … searchin' enquiries before he was arrested by Mike's lot. He sang the information he'd squeezed out of Jackie. There's more to come, but you've experts for that stuff. Therefore, I'm here to report mission accomplished, and make myself available for duty, sirs.' He winked at Sam.

'Why don't you help yourself to a coffee, Mr Cathel, while we finish up?' Charlton was brisk; visibly happier.

'Very good, sir. Thank you, sir.' Fuss went out.

'Can you use him, Sam?'

'Oh yes. He's here now. He's up for it and exactly what we need. I'd like him involved. Unless someone's got something to say, the ball starts rolling at 09.00 hours tomorrow.'

* * *

Later, over a brew, Sam and Fuss caught up.

'You rubbed Charlton's nose in it.'

'Fuckin' Rupert.'

'Oh stop it, Fuss! You don't need to get up friendly noses.'

'Sorry. But you should have seen his face.'

Sam stayed quiet and, as the silence lengthened, Fuss gave him a stare. 'Fuck you, ya big bloody war-hound.' He stalked out. Five minutes later he returned to apologize. He covered Sam all the way across town to the apartment.

23

At 7.30 pm Jim Thomas arrived home. He used his two keys and opened the door. The security system beeped until he entered its code. He stepped into the flat, turning to close the door, when a tidal force knocked him into the hall. A hand on his collar dragged him upright. Another push bounced him into the foyer. He turned and stared at a balaclava-covered face.

'You *do* know who I am?'

'Yes. And you're going to answer a question or two...'

'And if I don't?'

The man put a knife under his chin, hard enough to hurt but not enough to cut him. 'You'll die.' He felt the jab of a needle in his buttock and he relaxed, in spite of his fear.

His mother, disdainful as ever, watched the interrogation from her position of prominence on the mantelpiece, her dusty picture wedged between two china dogs cavorting in a bright ceramic world of their own.

Stripped to his underpants, his nerve centres and joints were ruthlessly manipulated. God, the pain. He gave up some morsels. He didn't think he'd betrayed much of consequence, but he talked.

After an hour, a distraught Jim Thomas had revealed a few secrets. He was physically unmarked but, at the same time, unmanned. The sharp end, apart from low-key surveillance, lay beyond his experience. It would take a long time to get over the violation. During the past thirty years, he'd never felt empathy for the people he'd handled or used in his line of work. Now he knew: pain, fear, helplessness ... being soiled.

The man left him secured to the bathroom radiator using two of his silk ties. In his sex life he liked to be tied up and whipped, but this was different. The bars on the hot towel rails made him jump in pain when his legs or buttocks touched them. He took twenty minutes to release himself.

Afterwards, he washed his dirty body and disposed of the stinking evidence of weakness. Once clean, he organized personal protection and security. Realising he'd never feel safe again, he shuddered at the memories.

24

Around the time Jim Thomas answered his questions a meeting took place. Eleven armed response police, an inspector, two sergeants and eight constables, assembled in a private conference room near the Embankment. Mike Swindon briefed them, accompanied by Detective Chief Superintendent Lawick. She had invited herself, promising to block bureaucratic interruptions and ensure resource allocation. Mike completed the session then thanked the DCS for her assistance. She walked out with him.

'Anything more you need, Chief Inspector?'

He made brief eye contact and smiled. 'Lots ma'am, but there you go. It's going to be an operational night, and I must get back to the office. See you in the morning.'

Mike's face betrayed stress when he left the building.

* * *

Four different e-mail addresses received a message some minutes after the Embankment briefing ended:

> *Memory stick located. Duncan tasked to secure it. Strong protection provided up to collection point. After that, more fluid. Advise, do not interdict before then. Will notify further intel when known.*

* * *

In Westferry Road, Indira intercepted the e-mail transmission. It would take time to identify the recipients. Quentin was as wide awake as he'd been in years. 'Well, Indira, my dear, don't you just love it when the pieces start to come together?'

Her long, lustrous black hair rippled as she nodded. 'It's what I live for.' Her curvaceous body and beautiful oval face looked positive and pleased in profile. Her delicate fingers flew over the keyboard. She never raised her eyes from the screen.

25

'Nice one, Tonks. What did you get?'

'The new Bizz board for a start. Jones and Forsyth have been replaced.'

'Some golden handshake.' Fuss said.

'By Kenneth Chen, a powerful international banker, and William Wardle, a Section Director in Counterterrorism.'

Sam glanced up after scribbling a note. 'Even more influence than before by the sound of things.'

'Right, you can ask about them and Sir Marcus Attenwood-Leigh, the Junior Minister.' Tonka said.

'That's the whole of the Bizz Board, then.' Sam said.

'Yes. There's also a European Bizz and a version in the USA.'

'Names?'

'Xavier someone or other in Europe. Unclear who it is in the USA. Wardle arranged the mercs in Scotland through a US intelligence contact. Thomas put the government assets after us. They're innocent, according to him.'

'What else?'

'Not much really. Need to know keeps it pretty foggy. One last thing: Gemma Smythsone, the lawyer, is the new Chair.'

'What were you doin' to the poor bastard?' Fuss said.

'Nothing much, mostly a drug cocktail.' Tonka glanced sideways at Sam who nodded. 'Minor bit of pain to get 'im talking, questions and prompts to keep 'im on track. He won't remember much either.'

Fuss stood up. 'I'll get the curry while you debrief yourselves. Lager or wine?' They ordered lager. Fuss went into the kitchen put plates in the oven and left.

* * *

'Once a squaddie …' Tonka raised an eyebrow and gave a half smile.

'We're boring him.' Sam said. 'Anything more on the structure?'

'Nah, but a few more nuggets.' Tonka said. 'Thomas spotted for the Irish assassin who tried to nail you in 1994. You were standing on sensitive criminal toes. Some security people and organized crime on both sides of the divide. He's scared of you.'

'Next nugget?'

'Thomas set Bizz on you, big time. They all hate you now.'

'Can you find out more about Northern Ireland?'

'I'm meeting an old hand tomorrow.'

'Good man.'

'One more nugget, Sam, Bill Jenkins is up to his arse in Bizz, but they're a bit jealous of his power. It may provide a lever somewhere along the line. He wasn't involved in the attempts to kill you, although he did set the Irish killers on your family.'

'No surprises there. He's a complex, capable and vicious operator. His boy, Jason, might make a lever.'

'I'll follow up the Bizz Board with Parker.'

'Sound.' Tonka looked straight into Sam's eyes. 'How far is this going?'

'Between us for now. Let's see what our oppos come up with.'

'Not happy, Sam?'

'Not sure.'

26

At 09.30 the next day, Sam called Bill Jenkins prior to his arrival at the Neon Orchid. Bill took the call.

'Hello, Mr Jenkins.'

'Vicar, what can I do for you?'

'Spare me a few minutes late morning?'

'Tell me more.'

'Mutual interest.'

'I'm out for lunch at one. Drop in any time before then.'

'Thanks.'

* * *

Sam enjoyed a convivial chat with O'Casey over the usual coffee.

'You're not just making a social call, Sam.'

'No, Colm, I'm using you.'

'Tell me no more.'

Sam smiled. 'Your support was greatly appreciated. Without it we may not have got my sister back.'

'The Dublin investors have new leadership. There's less pressure now, and I'm glad we did the right thing.'

'Sounds good. Power to your elbow.'

The niceties went on for twenty minutes. A car appeared for Sam at the front entrance, followed by an ARV. More than one chain of communication started to chatter. Sam's adrenalin surged and his focus sharpened. The men in his vehicle stayed in constant touch with base, their position tracked. They were at the Arches by 10.15 a.m. Sam texted Mike.

tell her

In the next half hour, Tonka spotted two possible surveillance teams and transmitted pictures of people and one vehicle. He remained unseen.

27

An hour before Sam's arrival, police and operatives infiltrated the buildings on either side of Bill Jenkins' office. At the Jenkins' building, the staff were interrupted, shown police ID cards, not allowed to communicate and led to a safe area.

Policewomen became receptionists as civilians were shepherded away to safe areas. All the while, in the way of these things, people complied, stayed quiet and followed instructions.

An operative with IT expertise disconnected external telecoms and patched into the network server. He had a warrant to download e-mails from the past two weeks. Three officers sat at the far end of the reception area, invisible from the window, sweating in the armour beneath their jackets, Glocks held low, the full seventeen shots on board.

With no way into Bill and Charlie Jenkins' offices without battering rams, they waited for Sam to arrive.

28

'Something serious?'

'Yes. Guess who Mike's lover is … the woman he's thinking of leaving his wife for?' Indira said.

'Tell me.'

'DCS Jane Lawick. We just managed to trace some of her recent e-mails and texts.'

Charlton shut his eyes and rubbed his forehead before looking up. 'We are where we are. Mike will have to make a big decision.'

'What about Sam?'

'He'll have texted Mike by now. The show goes on.'

An e-mail was sent ten minutes after Mike received Sam's text and made the call.

SD headed for Jenkins office

Indira notified Sam.

Sam texted Mike.

She sent the email

Arrest her

* * *

Mike stood up in the waiting area and signalled Cal to join him. They went to the Detective Chief Superintendent's door and entered without knocking. Pale and sombre Mike walked over to her desk.

'Jane Lawick, I'm arresting you for corruption and charges associated with criminal activities that will be specified in due course. The initial charge is that you have communicated confidential information to persons engaged in criminal activity, and to the endangerment of police officers and members of the public.' He continued with a formal caution.

She eyed him with a genuine sadness etched on her face

before she looked away. 'How long have you known?'

'Too long.'

Uniformed officers entered with Divisional Commander Mitchell who took over formally.

'My disappointment is hard to express, Jane. Mike notified me of his suspicions and your relationship two weeks ago. You're going down.' He spoke to the constables. 'Take her to the cells and keep her there for the next few hours.' He turned back to the DCS. 'We'll interview you later.'

* * *

Mike sat in his car and wept. His phone rang. It was Charlton. 'You arrested her, well done.'

'She's in the clink. The Divisional Commander has charge of her now.'

'Tough one.'

'You've no idea.'

'Sadly, I do. Integrity has its own rewards, Mike.' Charlton broke the connection and called Sam.

* * *

At Westferry Road, Security noted two boats pulling out from the dock and heading east, they put them under surveillance. On the phone, Charlton said. 'Where are the enemy? Will we catch them?'

'Lap of the gods, for now, Ben,' Sam said. Charlton stared out over the brown water.

'Yes, lap of the gods, Sam. *Not bloody good enough.*' He broke the connection.

29

The ARV left them. The front seat passenger spoke to Sam.

'They've been reassigned to a terrorist threat. We're re-routed to avoid congestion. We'll take the East India Dock Road, up Poplar High Street and round by Millwall. Should add another five to seven minutes to the trip. Sorry, sir.'

'No problem, we're still in good time.' Sam returned to his thoughts. A text came in from Cal:

we've enough evidence to arrest Jenkins

Sam allowed himself a smile of satisfaction.

no action at this time

He leaned back and stretched.

* * *

A large SUV rammed the car at the Wades Place junction. Sam's head bounced off the window leaving him dazed for a moment, blood trickled down his right eyebrow. The vehicle lurched and twisted. Side window glass splashed around the interior. Tyres yelping, the car bounced against the kerb and lurched on to its side. It came to rest pressed up against a wall, wheels spinning.

The driver and his partner jerked and shuddered as they were tasered.

'They live if you cooperate.' An American accent. Sam nodded and hauled himself upright. The door opened, pulled by a solid customer standing on the side of the vehicle. They dragged Sam on to the road at gunpoint, disarmed him and bundled him into a gleaming blue Range Rover. He sat, hands plasticuffed, between two large men, who didn't speak to him. Each held an elbow. They drove off at legal speed.

In ten minutes they arrived at a vast, decrepit warehouse complex near Barking Creek. Two heavies frog-marched Sam across a lumpy weed-broken tarmac surface. Rusty sliding doors about four metres high squeaked open. They entered a vast dark space and walked some fifty metres to a smaller door, in a partition of dirty, magnolia-coloured wood. This led into a corridor with security cameras and cell doors leading off on either side.

Sam could see beds, video screens and more lenses. The place stood empty. At the end of the passageway an oppressive stench of urine made Sam's nose wrinkle. Beyond the toilet another door led into a huge area, with lights suspended from a ceiling he couldn't see. In the distance, storage racks stood taller than the lighting, and loomed up into an echoing darkness.

An Englishman in a navy pinstripe with a plummy accent came over. 'Good afternoon, Colonel Duncan. Or should I say Vicar? There are one or two people you really must meet before you depart to your heavenly father.'

'You are?'

'Wardle. William Wardle.'

30

'Stand down at the Jenkins' office.' Charlton's spoke in a quiet voice. The people who had been taken to safety were released, with thanks and apologies for the disruption to their day.

Bill and Charlie Jenkins came downstairs and enquired what had been going on. They listened, with politeness, to a story about a bomb alert.

Bill thanked the officers for their commitment and concern. He was driven away for lunch in his black Rolls Royce. Charlie followed on a bright red Ducati.

* * *

'Surveillance shows a Ranger Rover. We're scanning number plates and tracing as fast as we can. This could take a while.' Mike paused and spoke to a person near by. '*Fuck!* The number plate is false.'

'What are you saying?' Charlton's hiss of impatience sliced from the handset.

'The Traffic boys need time and a lot of luck.' Mike paused to listen to a murmur in the background. 'We're hanging our hats on them not going too far. Three Rapid Deployment Teams will stand by roughly a mile in different directions from where he was taken.'

'So, when we get a clue we can respond.'

'Right.'

'Thanks.' Charlton disconnected. *Wear a cricket box indeed.* He shook his head.

31

'Some interested parties will be along soon to say goodbye. We'll get you ready for the meeting, shall we?' A punch in the side of the head dazed Sam. 'Think of that as an attention-getter, Sam.' A taser put him on the floor where they removed his jacket, shirt, shoes and socks. Next they secured him.

Sam heard the whispering entry of cars echoing in the vastness of the building. The light was bright where he sat, now stripped to the waist, his hands secured round the front of a chair by looped rope. The position made him bend far enough forward to create a growing discomfort. He managed to raise his head but had to rest after a minute or two.

Wardle contemplated Sam's torso. 'You've seen some action, Sam. The scars are quite communicative. Queen and country, eh? Once a hero …' The echoing sound of voices came towards them. He turned in welcome. From the side, Wardle's features reminded Sam of a praying mantis.

* * *

'Bill, my dear fellow. I have a friend of yours here. Say hello to the Vicar.' Bill's minder, the big man Sam met when he visited the office, stood behind Bill, his hands clasped over his groin. Standing beside Bill, a chubby man around six feet tall, appeared uneasy. A tall grizzled man stood behind him, hands guarding his scrotum.

Bill spoke in a calm voice, eyes watchful. 'Hello, Vicar. Well now… I wondered why you hadn't come by. Now I know, William.'

'Yes. Our source managed to get herself arrested, but an even bigger source kept the picture clear and the tracking operational. Then a simple ambush and we got our man. Duncan was two miles away before the police found the car.

'Good planning, William.' Bill said.

Wardle preened. 'I fear that acting DCI Swindon is going to take the fall for this one. In fact, the Agency will cease to exist shortly. The powerful don't like failure.'

'So why do you want me here, William?'

'To enjoy the passing of this Servant of God.'

'Tough one, Vicar,' Bill said and shook his head. His eyes hardened, 'That's business.'

'Excellent point, Bill, business is indeed business.' He swallowed and his Adam's apple squirmed above his tight pink collar. 'Sam, Vicar, let me introduce you to Len Atwill, he's in the same line of work as Bill. Behind him is his minder, Tom ... that right? Tom?' The man nodded. One of the hard men placed a silenced automatic behind Tom's ear and fired twice. Blood, bone and brain splattered. He fell like a puppet with the strings cut. In a fluid movement, the automatic pressed against the head of Bill's guard, who held up his hands in submission. 'Len, you need to meet your maker, as well as Duncan. Sorry. Nothing personal only business, you understand.' He snorted at his humour and, staring down the bridge of his nose shared a nasty smile.

'Why?' Bill seemed more bemused than fearful, lost in the surprise of the moment.

'Nothing personal, only business. Fantastic line that, don't you think?' Wardle's face became serious, his small eyes glowed with a reddish rodent tinge. 'Len is one gangster too many in London, Bill. He's going to get a seeing to and retire. And you are going to watch, listen and mark well.'

'What's Len done?' Bill said.

'Refused to play ball and got a bit above himself. He's been rather too effective at sticking his fingers in our pie. We don't want a man with capability and connections making off with anything that's rightfully ours. Besides, we've a developing relationship with some of his lieutenants. Not everyone is as loyal as dear departed Tom.' The sharp odour of blood and death scented the air.

'You're going to kill them?'

'Yes. I'm here to ensure Len and Duncan die, and to produce photographic evidence for my senior associates, who want an end to all Duncan's disruptive mischief. A couple of corpses in glorious colour should suffice.'

'Nasty.' Sam said.

'Then, of course, we have a slight problem with your younger sister. The relevance of her information will die with her. Kind of sad in a way, she's lovely and bright. You can't protect her forever.'

'She is protected.'

'Not from me, believe it. She'll have her own photo-shoot.'

Sam stared at him blank faced. 'This'll be the death of you, William.'

'I doubt it. Right now, before you set off on your last great adventure, we want to find out what you know and where her investigative records are. Then it's curtains.' One of the big men waved a machete and smiled menacingly, his acne-scarred face split by a gash of a mouth filled with nicotine stained teeth.

'It was a bluff.'

'Oh yes, Sam, the Jenkins office thing. Good sources you see.'

'I told you, a bluff.'

'I hope that's true, but we're going to have to find out for definite, as I'm sure you'll understand. She'll receive further attention from us in the near future. Let's not waste time on the usual preliminaries. My colleagues are expert in water-boarding. We'll start with Len and, as the Americans say, cut to the chase,' Wardle said. 'You'll have a turn in twenty minutes, give or take. Always good to have time to reflect, don't you think?'

32

'Mr Waberthwaite hasn't returned from the surveillance sir.' Indira's gentle lilting voice soothed despite the situation. 'I'll try to get him for you.'

'Do that.' Charlton paced the floor.

* * *

'Where are you, Cal?' Charlton said.

'Just arrived where Sam was taken.'

'What's Mike doing?'

'Talking to the tactical people.'

'You?'

'I'm a spare, fucking, part.' Cal's anger burst from the phone.

'Ask Mike to stay and liaise. He must keep me posted.'

'I'll tell him.'

'Get yourself back here. There's a helicopter coming. You can go with the home team when we know where Sam is.'

'Thanks sir.' Cal's voice brightened. Charlton disconnected without a word.

33

Another man entered the warehouse.

'Ah, Jim, good of you to join us.' The air of condescension rankled Thomas. 'This'll help you focus and stick with the programme. A mutual friend put in a good word for you. Glad you're still on the team.'

'Thanks for that, William.' Jim Thomas said. His clothes sustained his reputation for untidiness, with a wrinkled dark suit, clashing colours, scuffed dirty shoes, his tie off-centre and not high enough to hide the collar button of his unpressed shirt. His stark nervousness matched his thin pasty countenance. He brushed his lank, grey greasy hair with nicotine-stained fingers releasing a flurry of dandruff.

'And when these brave souls have departed, you can help us display them for a photographic session. Let's prepare Mr Atwill.'

Two of the four men who had brought Sam in came over to Atwill and stripped him to his rather colourful boxer shorts.

'Watch carefully, Bill.' Wardle managed a predatory smile. 'We're going to tie Len to a board, tip it up at an angle, cover his upper half in some coarse cloth and pour water on his face. Can't say it'll be pleasant, but it is quick.' He laughed walked over to Len Atwill, looked down at his groin. 'Nice pants.'

With Atwill secured to the board, Wardle did his cruel work and poured the water. Sam saw signs of sexual arousal as his victim gagged and moaned, jerking against the ropes. One of the assistants caught Wardle's arm and slowed his pouring. He told him in a bland American accent that he shouldn't drown or over-stress Atwill, if he wanted him to talk. On cue, Atwill started to throw up. They removed the cloth. What an impact the man had experienced in such a short time.

'Len, your questions are simple. We'd like the codes for your banks in Switzerland, Lichtenstein and Grand Cayman.'

'Fuck off!' Atwill whispered and glowered, shocked and resolute. They covered him again and more water slurped on to the material. They paused.

'Any second thoughts, Len?'

Atwill talked. Spluttering the codes.

'Now, if you hadn't insisted on keeping these things to yourself, we could have bumped you off like Tom.' He waved a man over. 'Check these.'

'I don't have a Lichtenstein account.'

'Liar, liar pants on fire.' Wardle cackled. 'Off we go again.'

Atwill jerked and strained. Wardle pulled the cloth back. Blood and bile ran down the man's face. 'No ... Licht ... account.' After more persuasion he bawled out a string of numbers. Sequence noted, one of the men made a call.

The account checker listened, smiled and murmured in Wardle's ear. 'Excellent, excellent.' Wardle's cocky grin betrayed no concern. He turned to Atwill. 'Good intel, Len. As for Lichtenstein, I almost believed you. We want to know about other accounts.' He ordered the men to drop Atwill on the floor. With a vicious gargoyle scowl on his face, Wardle stamped on the helpless man's stomach. A gurgling scream bubbled out as Atwill vomited weakly.

The man who had intervened previously spoke quietly to William. 'Oh, silly me, Len. I've made it hard for you to respond.' He stepped back as the tortured man convulsed with shuddering spasms against the restraining ropes. A crackling sound erupted from his chest followed by a choking splutter of blood from his mouth. With a climactic shudder and some twitching Len Atwill died. 'Ah well, Sam. Your turn's come earlier than we thought.'

* * *

'Let's see what you're made of.' Wardle's eyes gleamed.

They grabbed Sam by the arms and held him tight as they cut him from the chair. He resisted being moved to the board:

hard work, the men were strong and knew how to restrain people. A third man came over to help, the one who'd waved the blade, with terrible acne and reeking breath. He sprayed spittle in Sam's face as he talked to him. 'This one's for Tank. You guys killed him in Scotland.'

'You loved him, poor dear.'

'I'm the man who's gonna cut your fuckin' head off. We call it payback. I've seen a picture of your sister. She'll meet me one day, and you'd better believe she'll want to be dead.' He slapped Sam several times. Blood leaked from his mouth and splashed on to Wardle's shoes.

The action stopped momentarily with an unexpected arrival.

34

'In the back of my mind there's a place that's connected to the murders a few weeks ago. Give me some names.' Indira's liquid brown eyes glanced up at Cal from her video screen.

Cal paused and lifted his eyes in thought. He puffed out his cheeks as he thought. 'Lou Armente?'

Indira crunched the name into the system. 'No, he was killed after he took Eilidh Duncan.'

'Jackie Steele?'

More key strokes rattled. 'Not him ... beaten to death, small fry. Fuss Cathel was impersonating him, remember?'

'Stanley Dallie?'

'Died in Spain, one of the van drivers involved in the kidnap—low life.' Cal could see the data file's flashing with SOC photos and fields of text.

'Tommy Bain?'

'Yes.' Her fingers clacked rapidly on the keys. 'Yes. He had a large industrial unit a couple of miles from where Sam was taken.'

'Bingo.' Cal said.

'I heard.' Charlton stood in the door way. 'Let's move. Chopper can't be far away.' Charlton pursed his lips. 'Cal, get Mike moving. Indira, transmit any plans or layout information you can find.' Charlton marched out.

Indira's keyboard responded to the delicate fingers of a virtuoso. Cal's voice murmured instructions in the background. Through the office wall both could hear the time-honoured military communication technique, bellowing, being used to solve the problem of a tardy helicopter.

35

Only one person didn't jerk when Fuss walked in: Len Atwill. His bulging dead eyes didn't so much as blink.

'Nobody move!' But everyone did. The man holding Sam on the right reached for the large knife strapped to his chest. The other grabbed Sam's jaw and started to twist his neck back.

Sam resisted the twisting of his neck by pulling his chin down. He jerked but could not delay the knife being gripped. The blade rasped as it came free. The merc raised the point and swung the blade round his body, aiming at Sam's ribs.

* * *

'A constable at the scene reports shots fired, repeat, shots fired.' The measured tone of Indira's voice belied the anxiety on her face.

'Roger.' Cal put his hand on her shoulder. 'We're out of it, Indira. No chopper and nothing we can do. Can I get you a cuppa?'

'Tea, please, Earl Grey.' Indira let out a whooshing sigh.

* * *

Two near simultaneous blasts from behind Fuss made ears ring. The guards holding Sam dropped straight down in a jerking puff of gore. Their brain matter splattered backwards. Some scalp and blood splashed across Bill Jenkins' silk pinstripe and shining brogues. He jumped back, ponytail waving as if attached to a bucking horse.

A third guard, standing behind the falling men, guessed the shooters wouldn't want collateral damage. He accelerated past Sam, Bill and Wardle before veering to the right. He didn't hesitate as Tonka appeared in front of him. Without breaking stride he lashed his commando-soled boot at Tonka's head in a lightning fast strike. Tonka flowed towards his assailant catching the blow between crossed forearms with a smooth lifting motion that kept his attacker moving forward. He lifted the man high enough to jerk his other foot from the ground.

With his supporting leg airborne the attacker began a textbook circular blow, levering from, and rotating round, the secured limb. Tonka ducked under the kick and accelerated the aggressor's spin before twisting hard against the movement of his assailant's body. A loud crack signalled the knee joint had shattered, followed by juicy popping sounds as tendons and ligaments gave way. A strident scream told of the injury. Tonka let the enemy flop on to the concrete where he lay writhing while Tonka disarmed him and secured his elbows with cable ties, neither gentle nor brutal. As ever, he moved with resolute purpose and efficiency.

Meantime, as the two shot men twitched their last on the floor, Acne-Man jumped forward to grab Sam round the head with both arms, elbows down the line of Sam's jaws. He pressed Sam's face into his sternum and pushed hard, forcing Sam backwards, aiming to fall on to him.

Sam, taken unawares, half-caught his attacker and staggered backwards. Responding by instinct, he fell straight back and twisted. Acne-Man landed underneath him with a startled grunt. He managed to hold on grimly, his ragged breathing signalling pain and exertion. He struck at Sam with his knee and achieved a meaty thump near Sam's navel.

* * *

Wardle picked up a Heckler and Koch machine pistol, making a passable attempt at looking threatening.

'I wouldnae lift that thing to firing position ... William, isn't it? Chances are you're covered. I think I spotted a man armed for fuckwits like your good self.' Confident, Fuss smiled at Wardle.

* * *

Hands still plasticuffed, Sam struggled downwards and sideways before delivering two rapid forward elbow strikes to Acne-Man's testicles forcing him to expel a gurgling scream and release his hold.

Bill Jenkins vomited when he recognized the gelling organic matter on his clothing.

* * *

As Wardle raised the weapon, a red dot appeared on his arm. A tiny plop and a small bloody splatter erupted from his forearm, a bullet from a silenced .22. He dropped the Heckler and Koch and sat down squealing in pain. Fuss picked up the machine gun.

'Some people don't listen,' he said, 'you'll pay attention from now on.'

In the midst of his personal conflict with Acne-Man, Sam went berserk.

36

With Sam's scream of rage, all the tension of the last few days reared up. Only a wild warrior remained. His howl echoed and re-echoed in the cavernous space. He crawled up the man's body and pounded his secured fists like a hammer on the pocked face. Two blows shredded his assailant's lips and a third cracked his cheek, stunning him for a moment. Tonka caught Sam's wrist and cut the plasticuff off.

Exhausted, Sam and his assailant lay intertwined and breathing heavily, like spent lovers. Sam pulled himself free and turned over, with agonized slowness, looking for something on the floor.

* * *

Fuss eyed Wardle who clutched a now bleeding arm. 'Told you, sunshine. Any of you think we should apply a tourniquet?'

'Yeah,' Bill spoke, still shaken by events, 'to his fuckin' neck.'

'Sweet thought, Mr Jenkins. Temptin' too.'

* * *

Sam grabbed at the machete, missing with the first attempt, half catching the handle with his second. At the third go, he hefted the wicked blade, turned, rose to his knees and dropped on to his attacker. A terrifying ferocious energy emanated from him. He pressed his elbow across his assailant's chest, pinning him to the tiles, face wild as a stormy day. Tonka moved forward. Sam waved the blade.

'Don't you fuckin' dare.' The mad light in his eye silenced everyone. 'Whose head is coming off now, you bastard?' The man screamed, too weak to move. Sam slammed the weapon at the meaty part where his attacker's neck joined his shoulder. An almost child-like cry preceded a meaty thwack. Silence.

Sam squeezed his eyes shut, then stared up, vision clearing.

* * *

'They've found injured people and are proceeding with caution.' Cal said. 'It's a big building, sir.'

'Tell them to get a bloody move on. We've got a man in there.' Charlton said.

Cal spoke into his communicator. Indira sat quietly and rubbed her hands together.

* * *

Sam sensed the people staring at him. 'Things are okay, lads. He's still breathing.' He sighed. 'Somebody sort him out.' He locked eyes with Bill Jenkins. 'Well, Bill, who said it's only the truth that'll set you free?'

He moved over to Bill Jenkins, who nodded towards the moaning Sir William. 'Is that what happened to my boy?'

'I expect so. The shooters can't have wanted to kill anyone unless they had to. Little weapons save lives.' Sam said.

'Your people did some damage today. There's bodies everywhere and a tough-guy sobbing over his knee, Wardle moaning about his arm, and an ugly bastard clutching his family jewels and crying like a baby. You scared him big time.' Jenkins said.

'My people? For sure we have one thing in common: Rules of Engagement. According to some people I respect, the main rule is: *do unto others before they do unto you.*'

'They shot my son.'

'He's alive and not too badly hurt.'

A pale faced Jenkins shook his head. 'That's not the point.' He raised his finger and shook it under Sam's nose. 'They shot him.'

'You expect me to say sorry? He threatened my family.' Sam said.

'That's too bad, but it doesn't change things, they shot my boy. *Nobody* hurts my family.'

'Quite.'

'What would you have done?'

'If I'd been there he'd have come home in a coffin.'

They glared at each other: one a lean warrior, the other a pallid, flabby and evil man some inches shorter, his pendulous gut larger than his chest. 'I won't forget this.' Jenkins shook his finger and turned away.

37

Mike Swindon walked in with four armed-response officers in full armour. They all looked jumpy. The corpses lay, heads destroyed. Congealing signs of spray and splatter splotched the floor where they'd been standing. One large size boot print from Acne-Man left a perfect silhouette of gore.

Swindon surveyed the carnage. 'Those two haven't been double-tapped have they?'

'Hardly.' Sam's pale face bore no expression. 'Look like single, aimed shots to me. Must've been weighty rounds.' He nodded his head at Bill. 'In my opinion, as an observer and bystander, whoever did this to them saved lives. I didn't see anyone.'

Fuss said, 'we do have Mr William Wardle on sound and video. I just happened to have a camera and recorded a few things.' His cocky humour took the edge off the horror. He stood with his lean five foot seven frame encased in a leather jacket, black jeans and thick-soled motorcycle boots. His washed-out green eyes sparkled, his bright ginger hair flattened by the motorcycle helmet.

Fuss went on. 'The chap with the fucked knee was apprehended by a gentleman over there in the shadows, who would prefer to remain anonymous. The chap crying over there had a narrow escape from a demented vicar. There's another three people … eh … detained somewhere over there, I think. One or two broken bones and few scrapes, but they'll live. Oh, and that fellow,' he pointed at Jim Thomas, 'his minders are holding up a column, too. They're on the angels' side, aren't they? You'll find them all if you look. There could be more. I may have missed some on my way in to rescue Colonel Duncan.'

Sam said. 'I'm fairly certain neither of these gentlemen fired weapons.' He pointed at Fuss and Tonka. 'You can verify that forensically. It's obvious shooters were active in the vicinity.'

38

The guardians from the Irish encounter relaxed in a barge not a mile from the warehouse with ‘friends’. Their weapons lay in a waterproof container ten feet from the vessel, their shooting gloves already incinerated in a barbecue smoky with meat and sausages.

‘Nothing to it.’ One said. ‘Love the little Ruger.’

‘Righteous.’

‘Sam’s keeping nasty company.’

His friend eyed him. ‘Give me Irish gangsters any day.’

‘That Fuss is a wild little man.’

‘Good sort.’

They relaxed.

After the barbecue, they went out to the pub with two other pals who’d assisted at the warehouse, and the owner of the longboat. They planned to stay available for a few days before going back north.

39

Crime scene secured, Mike separated the survivors for interviewing. Jim Thomas, in his rumpled brown suit, shabby shoes and ancient square-bottom tie, was removed to a central police station.

Sam's clothing was found. He dressed with aching deliberation.

A technician tested Tonka for gunshot residue. Mike released him on the understanding he would attend for interview at Westferry Road later.

Sam and Fuss were taken to separate interview rooms at a nearby police station. They released Sam after two hours.

Bill Jenkins lawyered up and was freed an hour after Sam. He said nothing.

They interrogated Fuss for five hours and released him without charge. Both he and Tonka tested negative for gunshot residue.

William Wardle went to hospital under police escort. After a full diagnosis, his wounds were cleaned and minor surgery carried out.

* * *

Next morning, while the Crown Prosecution Service deliberated over the evidence, Wardle was released on police bail, arm in a sling.

40

Fuss, Tonka, Cal and Sam enjoyed their take-away meal in Kensington. The curry and lager slipped down well. Each of them held a glass of whisky, except Tonka who, on active duty, made do with a mug of tea.

Sam sighed. 'We've had a result. I'm still gutted for Douglas Fullerton.' They sat in respectful silence for a moment. 'Absent friends.' Sam raised his glass.

After a couple of minutes, Tonka said, 'God, following you on the pillion with Wee Jimmy here … now that was hairy, one of the scariest experiences of my life.'

'*Fuck off*. I'm an excellent biker. The fuckin' cheapskates down here wouldn't stretch to a decent pair of wheels.'

Sam smiled and shook his head.

'I'll get over it one day,' Tonka deadpanned. Fuss sighed.

'You were right about the possibility of a fuckin' snatch, Sam. The re-route was the set-up. Worth gettin' some of your people investigatin' that, by the way, Cal. We were fifty yards back when Sam was grabbed. We hid behind some parked cars.'

Tonka picked up the tale. 'Following the big car was easy. The rest was just routine: infiltrate and nobble the sentries; cocky boys, no real support. Wardle made the mistake of having all his best guys with you and Jenkins.'

'How'd you get Freaky and Bilbo to arrive so quickly?' Sam said.

'No problem,' Tonka said, 'Fuss had them on our tail with a mobile connection to me. They were with us before the Thomas guy got to the warehouse. They had other friends outside who nobbled Thomas's minders. Good bit of planning, Fuss.' The fair freckled face beamed and Fuss sipped his dram.

'The bandits hadn't a chance,' Sam smiled.

'None. Disorganized set-up.' Tonka said.

Fuss leaned back, comfortable. 'If they made a stupid move before we were ready, we planned to drop 'em all. That talkative, fuckin' Wardle gave us all the time we needed. I nearly fell a-fuckin'-sleep listenin' to that ugly fucker drone on,' Fuss said. 'Wankers come in all shapes and sizes.'

'The guy who shot Douglas is still at large,' Tonka said.

'I'll be surprised if his killer is ever brought to justice.' Sam frowned, eyes hard for a moment. 'Plenty of stuff'll shake out in the next few days, but I don't think his murderer will be one of them. Why would the Thomases or Wardles of this world admit to involvement in shooting a policeman, along with everything else?'

'Maybe we'll get lucky.'

Sam turned to him and raised an eyebrow. 'Come on, Tonka, it's not like you to talk about luck.'

'You're right. You have to make luck.' The warm West Midlands accent belied the feelings.

'That wee sister of yours is causing a lot of trouble. What the fuck's in her papers?' Fuss said.

'Lots of leads, contacts, direct evidence against the Bizz empire and info about its structure. Valuable intel and a lot of it.' Sam said. He turned. 'You're quiet, Cal, what do you think?'

'Not a lot. When we toasted Douglas, I was back there, I saw him on the deck next to the Jones woman. He had one green and one brown eye you know.' He lapsed back into silence. His colleagues nodded and let him be.

'Poor kid.' Sam said.

* * *

Half an hour later they were reminiscing, laughter and sadness mingled to create a happy wistfulness, and further strengthen the warriors' bond.

41

'William is in a bit of a pickle.' Sir Marcus said.

'The defence lawyers are bullish. The hirelings won't talk. The killers can't talk. Bill Jenkins is on side. The main problem is Duncan, the Vicar.' Smythsone said.

'Can we get to him?' Chen said.

'Not easily, Ken. We'll do what we can.'

'Family?'

'Sewn up tight.'

'Intel?'

'Losing the asset hasn't helped.' Smythsone's competence radiated from her, 'We're working to rehabilitate William, fast as we can. We should get a result soon. I hope we don't have to drop him.'

'If I may say so, Gemma, there are lots of ifs, buts and maybes.' Sir Marcus said.

'We're as on top of this as we can be in such a short time frame, Marcus. We're not in the fantasy world of politics here.'

'Gemma's quite right Marcus,' Chen said. 'In post for a couple of days and you're blaming the past on her.'

'Sorry, didn't mean to ruffle feathers. Just want to get things fixed.'

'No problem, Marcus, but do remember what we are going through. The Agency and their operative Duncan are more effective than expected. Harder too.'

'Of course, Gemma.' Sir Marcus said.

'We've had enough symptomatic relief, I want a solution,' Smythsone said. 'In an ideal world we'd take over the Agency. We need William and a cooperative minister or two for that.'

'The pressure is on.' Chen said.

'The competition is competent, Ken, we have to raise our

game.'

'We must lay our hands on the Duncan girl's evidence,' Sir Marcus said.

'Of course. She and her information need to vanish forever. Do that and our business will run smoothly and make more profit. No more foul ups, no more conflict.'

Sir Marcus smiled. 'At least our goals are clear.'

42

'Europe and the USA?' Sam said.

'Yes. We're dealing with major criminal activity in at least three areas: drugs, human trafficking and government procurement. The people behind this are in with the bricks and have extensive connections, but they couldn't stop a rather beautiful young journalist.'

'I'll tell her you said that.'

'I hope you do, Sam,' Charlton said, pausing for a smile, 'William Wardle has been arrested and charged with multiple crimes and, with any luck, will spend some considerable time behind bars. The video is powerful evidence. We have DCS Lawick, Wardle and Maybelle Jones to sweat, assuming Jones recovers from her injuries. The story against Thomas isn't strong enough, he's been released.'

'What about Bizz?' Cal said.

'As far as we know Thomas, Smythsone and Sir Marcus Attenwood-Leigh stay on the board of Bizz.' Sam said.

'Two down now.'

'I hear Kenneth Chen, international banker, and William Wardle were recruited.' Sam made eye contact with a quizzical Charlton.

'How did you find that out?'

'Sources.'

* * *

The phone rang. Charlton answered, listened and hung up. 'Bill Jenkins requests the pleasure of your company for morning coffee, Sam, in half an hour. Please go and meet him. He may want to share important information after his recent experiences.'

'He's got a lovely receptionist.' Sam wiggled his eyebrows.

'You're as bad as your friend, Cal,' Charlton said. 'That isn't why I'd like you to go.'

Sam winked at him, the scar on his right eyebrow moving up and down. 'Indira, what did our man get from the data pull at Jenkins office?'

Indira shrugged. 'Nothing. The set-up didn't have anything beyond an administrative server for the staff and the diary system.'

'A blank?'

'Completely.' Indira said. 'They must have another setup in Jenkins office proper.'

'Thanks,' Sam said, 'not much of a starter for ten. Bill has information, and, watching the water-boarding and the murder of Len Atwill will have heightened his awareness of ... certain realities. I'd best get over there.'

43

The luxurious office with the massive black desk and gigantic picture window was impressive as ever. Bill stood looking out, his left arm across the base of his spine holding his right arm. He turned as Sam was shown in.

'Better surroundings than last time, Vicar.' Jenkins gestured to a seat across the desk, in front of his massive leather chair.

'I'll say. This is pure luxury.' Sam sat down and watched a subdued Bill seat himself opposite. 'Must have been an instructive meeting for you, Bill.'

'I've nothing to say to you about that.' Jenkins blue pinstripe suit, peach tie and white silk shirt reeked opulence. His chubby face and dark piggy eyes were flinty. His long hair in its tight pig tail rested on his shoulder for a moment. He shook it off with an irritated shrug.

The smell of the coffee enticed. Jenkins gestured to a tray. Sam helped himself to cream from a crystal jug, liquid silk. 'So why the invitation, Bill?' They each held a steaming coffee in a gilt-edged Willow Pattern mug.

'The man who shot Wardle was the man who shot my boy.' Bill was straight-faced as he added two spoons of sugar from a cut glass sugar bowl.

'Your lad's still alive and got a lesson that may add to his chances of survival and prosperity in your world, Bill.' Sam's penetrating blue eyes were direct; his mouth a humourless line.

'Do you know who he is; the man who shot our Jason?'

'Of course not.'

Bill's lips dropped to a scowl in an instant. 'I don't like people shooting my son. He could have been killed.'

'Aye. We all make mistakes.'

'Cheeky bastard.' Anger flashed.

'That's as may be. You sent him over to intimidate my family, or worse. What makes you think I'd help you find a person who helped protect them? The shooter whoever he or she is did a good job.'

'Wasted coffee then.'

'If you say so, but it's nice to see you again, and with good colour in your cheeks.'

'Watch that mouth, Vicar.'

Sam stayed silent, staring at Jenkins without a blink. 'Anything else on your mind.'

'Your people tried to copy our data. Very naughty.'

'News to me.'

'You don't know much for a senior man.'

'All I know is the police caught some criminals, others got away, and there's a big hidden organization watching. I bet you have information that might help to calm things down. I wonder why they gave you a front row seat.'

The sullen expression started to change. 'A complete surprise.' A half smile. 'Even if I knew anything, I'd never grass ... *not ever*. Just the same as you, Vicar.'

'I hope it doesn't come back to haunt you. At least I am protected to some extent.'

'So am I.' The words bounced back like an angry child's.

'Bluster doesn't become you, Bill. That water-boarding wasn't pretty; they reached out, grabbed Len and killed him.' Jenkins paled, eyes like pinpoints in his podgy face. He grabbed the desktop as if to stand up, changed his mind and leaned forward.

'It was you they meant to kill.'

'For sure, but what message were they sending you? What should you take from it?'

'What are you getting at?'

'Who's next?'

'Not me.'

'Len might have said that. What are they telling you? You work with them. Better stay in line, Bill.'

'That's enough. I'm innocent. I know nothing.'

'Pull the other one. It's got bells on.'

'What about the fire power?'

'I couldn't possibly comment, Bill. Pretty awesome though.'

'I don't like cheek.'

'I don't like bullies.'

'I hope your family keeps well.'

'Thanks, Bill. That's kind.'

'Look after them.'

'You, too.'

Bill stood, Sam copied him. They shook hands with an irritated formality. Bill walked him to the reception area, neither of them speaking beyond the formalities. His gaze followed Sam as he opened the door of the car and sat behind the driver.

He turned back into the building and wondered if his fear would ever go away. *Bloody Vicar*.

44

The pier at Brodick on the Isle of Arran was a welcome sight as Sam returned from London. Karen and the security people collected him.

Tonka was away on personal business in the south. Fuss went home after accompanying him to the boat train at Glasgow Central. The two minders, who travelled with him, stayed on the ship to return to their base.

The family circle adjusted, as if he'd never been away. Eilidh seemed better, edgy, sometimes short-tempered. Much improved.

* * *

Karen experienced deep disquiet at Sam's disturbed sleep. She admired the early dawn that first morning with relief.

In a day or two he'd tell her an edited version of the story. For the time being, wide-awake and patient, she absorbed the changing colours on the wall as the sun brightened the world. During the day, she gazed at the mottled colours of bruising on Sam's face and thought about the marks on his body and wrists. It hurt her.

Sam spent a few days playing with the girls, training with the soldiers and hill-walking with Karen who enjoyed the mountains, views and sense of freedom.

* * *

'The team want me to go down and meet with the Bank. They're threatening to reduce our overdraft facility, just when we've committed to expanding the work with a new coaching partner. I must show face. I'll be back soon.' A small business didn't stop because of a violent situation.

'What about protection?' Karen said.

'No need where I'm going. I'll nip down to Prestwick with

cover, pick up the car and get to Westerholm. One engagement after the meeting and I'll return, unless I'm told to do something else. Tonka may catch with me. If he does we'll come back together.'

45

The next morning, Sam was on the ferry from Arran when Pete Molloy phoned to congratulate him on the result of the East End conflict and commiserate about Douglas Fullerton.

They discussed the troubles, the murders of his former colleagues and agreed to keep in touch. Molloy said he was off to London for 'an exchange of views' with a certain Jim Thomas.

* * *

The bank agreed the business plan and a schedule for repayment of the overdraft. After a great lunch with the team, Sam headed south.

* * *

'You'll be Ned.'

'Who the fuck wants to know?' The muddy farmyard was surrounded by a surprising number of buildings in varying states of dilapidation. The open area, where the half-mile long track wound in from the main road, lay cluttered, disorganized and coated in a blend of liquid mud and manure. The stench scoured nostrils and diverted attention from the beauty of the farm's location. The man facing Ned had his rear to the afternoon sun.

'Me!' Ned squinted his eyes at the distorted rubbery face; President Obama stared back.

'Why the fuckin' mask?'

'I want to talk to you about a young woman you had here.'

'Never been a young woman here!'

'A pair of knickers says different.' Ned, a tough bulldog of a man, swung a hard fist at Obama. The blocking of the blow rattled his teeth. Bone deep bruising made him sob with hurt. 'You will tell me what I want to know, or I'm going to bury you up on the fells somewhere.'

'My brother'll be back here soon.'

'No … he won't.' The finality in the remark chilled Ned through the agony.

'It was just a job.' The whine wheedled an apology. The President's face stayed jovial as he punched him hard in the face. His lips split, blood spattered from the burst flesh and swilled from his mouth. 'Jusht a joff.'

'Tell me all about it.'

'I joon't know anyshing.' His mouth was swollen. His speech sounded like cotton wool had been pushed into his mouth. Blood and snot dribbled down his quilted brown shirt front.

'Start talking or die.' Ned didn't hold back. 'Now you can join your brother.' Ned cried and begged. He was dragged to a bed in the barn where his brother lay chained and unconscious. 'A touch of biter bit, I think, won't go amiss.' Ned was pushed down beside his snoring brother and manacled to the bed.

'P'ease. P'ease.'

'I want you to remember one thing when you wake up: confess what you did to the police. Next time I check up, if you aren't in the nick, I'm coming after you, and *you will* be buried up in the fells. No excuses. Nighty night.' He injected a substance into Ned's arm. 'I hope you share the nightmares you inflicted on that poor girl, you sorry, sick bastard.' Ned started to fade and fell back, mouth open, blood dribbling out.

The man in the mask walked away. Silence settled on the farmyard. In the shed where the men lay a little cat jumped on to Ned's chest, and began to clean itself, purring on a comfortable, warm human cushion.

Ned came to awareness, grateful to leave a horror story behind. The police were asking questions as he woke up, dazed and unclear. He told all he knew and confessed. His brother reported a contact with London, and a girl they'd looked after for a short while.

The charges included sexual assault, kidnap and grievous bodily harm. Both brothers made incriminating statements without protest. The local police called Detective Chief Inspector Swindon and provided intelligence.

46

Six in the morning, at Heddon-on-the-Wall, near Newcastle-upon-Tyne, a shape slipped around a silent garden, where the fence line touched the wood off Trajan Walk. The man walked along past several houses before turning on to the path to a particular front door.

The bell ding-donged insistently. A slim, fit-looking male with a crew cut answered the door, eyes sharp. His movement and posture exuded physical confidence.

The man facing him was dressed in a dark parka, jeans and work boots. He aimed a silenced 9mm.

'You found me.'

'Yes.'

'Can we talk?'

'No.' Two silent shots to the head, one in the mouth and the other just under the eye. The man fell full-length in the hall, dead before he was horizontal. A pistol he'd been holding behind his back clattered against a shiny white skirting board.

His killer fired twice more to destroy the heart and then closed the door gently. He vanished silently round the house and into the wood. He was in the south of England before news of the death emerged.

There was no evidence nor sighting of the killer. No leads. After forensic examination, the victim's DNA was matched with two samples of discarded clothing recovered in London. It linked to witness identification and surveillance video evidence of the perpetrator. It was assumed Bizz ordered the killing.

47

On news of the assassin's killing, a conversation took place between an English mandarin and another powerful individual in Brussels: 'The death is troubling. I wonder how they — whoever did the deed — located him.'

'Dissatisfied customer?'

'Could be. On the bright side, there's many more where he came from.'

'Did Duncan do it?'

'Possible. With his track record he's got the bottle. It's hard to say.'

'Perhaps we're best to let sleeping clerics lie.' The pair laughed with conspirators' smugness.

'Why?'

'Why not?'

'Oh very well, play it your way until we can eliminate the threat for good.'

* * *

Back on Arran, Sam was happy. His management team were running the business well. Training with the minders was bringing him to a level of fitness he hadn't enjoyed for years. He had some tasks to attend to.

'Where did Tonka, er … Mr Waberthwaite, learn to fight, sir?'

'Here and there.'

'We had a session before you returned to London, sir. I can't get close.'

'Told you. He's the best I've seen by a country mile, and, believe me, I've seen a few.'

'You're quick, sir, but he's almost slow, always a millisecond ahead of you … never hurried, totally calm.'

'That's him: so fast you're unaware. Good old Tonka. He'll be back in a couple of days, and I'm sure he'll give you some more training, if you want.'

'Thanks, sir. You want to do some more?'

'No, today's been more than fine. I'm off on business. Maybe when I get back, if you still fancy it.' Sam returned to the house and sat down with Karen who was having a cup of tea. She turned as he entered. Her hair was tied up, highlighting her beautiful facial structure — high cheekbones, straight Nordic nose, and characterful slightly square chin — breathtaking. Sam believed he'd been lucky to win her, and even luckier to develop the depth of relationship they shared.

'Hi, gorgeous.' She smiled and tinge of pink flushed her cheeks.

'The warrior returns,' Karen said. 'What have you been up to?'

'The usual: slaying dragons and trolls, snookering wicked witches, and generally spreading good around the land.' He walked to her, stroked her neck and exposed arms with a lightness of touch that made her snuggle against him.

'You're restless, Sammy.'

'Aye. Places to go; people to see.'

'Lovely as Arran is, I wish I could get out of here for a break.'

'I'll remind Ben.'

'Yes please.' He noticed the glint in her clear eyes: pressure, commitment, loyalty and love … the loneliness. He pulled her close and hugged her, holding on without words.

48

'Got a minute, Cal?' The big frame soon filled the door. 'The lead we developed in the north was a good 'un.'

'Excellent, Mike.'

'Hugely cooperative they were. Chained themselves up, ready for arrest.'

'Isn't it wonderful when people see the light, Mike.'

'You know anything about this? I'm wondering if there's been a leak.'

'What would I know? I've been here all the time,' Cal said.

'No idea?'

'None.' He pursed his lips and waggled his head side to side for a moment, thoughtful. 'Hmm, sounds like an act of God to me.'

'Yeah, God. That's it, mate: full, instant confessions, and it ties back to Tommy Bain, God rest the miserable fucker. Even Bill Jenkins got a mention,' Mike said.

'My, my.'

'Yeah, the lads up there say the brothers couldn't confess fast enough.'

'Fantastic.'

'Right. Now about the pretty boy murder ...'

'Give me a mo' and I'll join you.'

* * *

The crime scene pictures were both horrific and routine. Blood sprays splattered up wall. The corpse lay with half-shut eyes, mouth twisted open and tongue lolling out like a slobbering dog.

'Like you said, Mike, Lou Armente never stood a chance. He set Eilidh up and kicked the Bizz thing off.'

'Not pretty. Whoever did him is strong and can handle a knife.'

'Anything from the DNA on Sam's hanky?' Cal said.

'Nah, not so far. You think Charlie Jenkins is good for it?'

'He might be. He's strong and has a reputation with a blade.'

'Why are you picking it up now?'

'I like to spend a half hour, here and there, keeping in touch.'

'Not that long really, just over a month.'

'I interviewed witnesses and they tied Armente to a number of abductions at the Neon Orchid. They've been in and signed their statements. We found some of Eilidh's hair at the scene. The mobile photo ties him to her. We have the bouncer's confession, and the guys with the van, who turned up in the concrete in Spain.'

'Loadsa bodies, big man.'

'Yeah. More to come I reckon.'

'Think so?'

'Just my water, Mike, I had a feeling. This killing tracks all the way back to the Bizz lot.'

'Sam Duncan better be watching his back.'

'He will, especially after the last rumble, and he's got one of the best in the business backing him.'

'Why'd they call him Tonka?'

'Long story.' Cal's face was serious his eyes were somewhere else.

'Don't trust me?'

'Someone as ugly as you is bound to be trustworthy.' A rumbling laugh eased the tension. 'It'll cost you a couple of pints and a curry.'

'It better be a good tale then.'

'Yeah, a stonker, make it three or four pints.'

49

Sam arrived back in the building after a six-day break. He breezed into the reception area, made himself a coffee and headed for Charlton's office. He knocked and entered.

'Good morning, Colonel Duncan.' Wow, kind of formal. A stiff person sat in one of the visitor chairs by the coffee table. 'This is Assistant Commissioner Barclay of the Met.' She looked formal, even in plain clothes: a navy-blue jacket and skirt, white blouse, dark stockings and black flat-heeled shoes. Everything about her screamed Fuzz. Sam glanced at both faces as the AC stood up.

'Morning, sir. Assistant Commissioner.' Sam held his hand out. She ignored the gesture and sniffed.

'The Assistant Commissioner has just arrived and wants to talk to us.'

'Not you, General Charlton ... Colonel Duncan.' Her stiff contralto voice bore overtones of supreme authority.

'Is that your man in the waiting area, Assistant Commissioner?'

'This is a formal visit, Colonel.'

'Why don't you cut to the chase then?' Charlton raised an eyebrow at Sam.

'Excuse me.' The policewoman walked to the door. 'Inspector.' She waved her colleague in. 'You are Colonel Samuel Duncan?' Sam nodded. 'I am detaining you under suspicion of involvement in the murder of William Arthur Crabtree of Heddon-on-the-Wall, Northumberland.' She cautioned him, told him of his right to legal representation and instructed the Inspector to handcuff him.

'Hold on, Assistant Commissioner. Have you a date in mind for this murder?' Charlton said.

'Sunday, 8th June.'

'Can't we handle this here? At least the preliminaries?'

'No. Duncan must come to New Scotland Yard for questioning. The warrant is in order, and I want him now.' Sam winked at her and she bridled.

'Are the handcuffs necessary?'

'In my judgement, he is potentially dangerous and an escape risk.' The smug, almost bullying demeanour seemed designed to provoke an angry response.

Charlton's eyes glinted. 'I will personally deliver Colonel Duncan to you this afternoon. For operational reasons, to do with national security, I insist he stays here until I debrief him.'

'He is in my charge and I must remain with him.'

'What is you security clearance?'

She told him.

'You can't hear what we discuss. You can't remain in my office. Go and sit in the waiting area. When Colonel Duncan has been debriefed you can have him.' She started to protest. Charlton held up his hand to silence her, and pushed a button on his desk top. His two minders came in, nodded to Sam and gave Charlton their attention. 'Escort the Assistant Commissioner and Inspector to the waiting area. Give them a refreshment and stay with them until I tell you otherwise.' The AC started to open her mouth. 'Go.' She went, bright red with embarrassment, even her shapeless mousy hair managed to bristle. But she left.

'She's not happy, Ben.'

'I'm not happy, Sam. Where were you on 8th June?'

'On Arran with half the SAS.'

'Someone in the stratosphere sent that ghastly woman to get you.'

'Nice to be regarded so highly.'

'Quite. I'll get one of Parker's lawyer friends on to this. Sit down and have a coffee.' Ben left the office.

* * *

'The man's a trouble magnet.'

'Are you shocked, Ben?' The phone didn't stop Parker

sensing Charlton smiling.

'No, that's what we need him to be.'

'So tell me your story and what you want me to do.'

Parker listened, asked Charlton to wait five minutes and hung up. He made a call and scribbled some notes. He made another call.

50

Tonka came in with a mug in his hand. 'In trouble, are we?'

'Yes. They think I slotted a man in the North-East.'

'Terrible. And you a pastor.'

'You're taking the piss.'

The craggy face lightened to somewhere south of mild amusement. He touched his lips with his finger. 'I heard the dates just now when I was getting the coffee. Couldn't have been you. That big woman's angry, and she's even less pretty when she's riled.'

'Not exactly an oil painting when she's not riled, Tonks.'

'Nah, but built for it. Large women can rattle the fillings and pop your cork.'

'Voice of experience?'

'Right.'

'Where's the boss gone? He looked pretty pissed-off when he passed me.'

'He's off to get some legal help from Parker.'

'Good man, Parker.'

'Yeah.'

'You'd still be recovering from a hiding if that chubby old lawyer hadn't stood by you.'

'Right,' Sam said, 'but guess who had to do the fighting, and, come to think of it, buy good malts into the bargain.'

'Always worth paying for useful help.'

'Parker's singing for his supper now, all those juicy connections in the City. He's looking into the new Bizz directors. We'll get feedback shortly.'

'As I say worth paying for.'

'Yes. The police want me in connection with a killing when I was on Arran.'

'Glad you're in the clear, mate.'

'They may still take me away.'

'Not the way Charlton was looking. They'll leave in a box more like. Bye.' Tonka turned, moving with silent grace, his dark, neat clothing accommodated easy movement. He was almost invisible by the time he reached the door. The clicking of the lock was the only sound of his departure.

51

Within thirty minutes the AC was back in the office.

'I owe you an apology, Colonel. It appears you couldn't have been involved. We'll look into the source of the information that's wasted everyone's time. I contacted the appropriate authorities. You will not be arrested.' She was brisk, almost courteous.

'Thank you, Assistant Commissioner. No more to be said. I'm sorry your day was disrupted, and I'm glad the matter's resolved.' Sam said. He offered his hand. This time she shook it.

She turned to Charlton. 'Apologies, General.' Frost chilled the air.

'Accepted.' She exited room, her solid shoulders hunched, embarrassment still pink on her neck.

'Won't be too many people she doesn't frighten into acquiescence,' Charlton said.

'No, plenty of weight to throw about.'

'Reputation as a bit of a Rottweiler according to Parker.'

'Not as good looking.'

Sam stood to leave.

'Sit down, Sam.' Charlton's best on-the-carpet voice was quiet and firm—all it needed to be. 'I want to clarify two things and expect full answers.'

'Understood.'

'Do you know anything about the killing?'

'Nothing, Ben.'

'Any suspicions?'

'Yes, now you mention it, but not even strong ones.'

'I'm not interested in weak suspicions. May as well spend time kite flying. We'll not discuss this again.'

'Right. As you say,' Sam said.

'Now, my second question. Where were you on 10th June?'

'Travelling on business.'

'What was your route?'

'Apart from a few minor detours, Ayr to Westerholm, Penrith, over the A66 to Scotch Corner, then back via Newcastle across the A69, back to Westerholm, and back to Arran by the 12th. I arrived here this morning, direct from Glasgow via Gatwick, met by your chaps.'

'What were you doing in the North-East?'

'Making enquiries.'

'What do you know about two criminal confessions made on your line of route?'

'This and that. No one was killed or badly hurt. I hear they confessed.'

'The frighteners were applied.'

'It appears so,' Sam said. 'Is there a problem?'

'Bloody good show.' Charlton's smile almost broke his face in half. 'We'll say no more about this. Some detectives in our team have suspicions.'

'Whoever did it, they ought to be bloody grateful. They're not so good at bringing in witnesses alive.'

'Maybe you should have a word.' Charlton glanced at Sam over half-moon glasses. 'One other thing, Sam: when did you become prescient?'

'Prescient?'

'Clairvoyant, knowing about Bizz, and a few other intelligence matters.'

'Balls, sir.'

'Meaning?'

'Crystal balls.'

'Go on.'

'That's how it's done,' Sam said, 'sometimes information comes to me.'

'Nothing to do with one James Thomas needing guardians?'

'Guardians can be useful, sir.'

'Your clarity has no beginning, Colonel.'

'As you say, sir.'

'Now, let's have a brew and do some real business.' Ben opened a file. 'You've got travelling to do. Good skiing in the season where you're going.'

'Sounds interesting.'

'One needs to be careful when going off-piste.'

'Always.'

52

A large man by the Customs post made eye contact. Swarthy, with collar-length wavy black hair, he looked formidable. The jeans and tee-shirt showcased a tough body, slabbed with muscle and battered, rugby-playing features to match. A smart black jacket dangled over a meaty shoulder from the man's left index finger.

* * *

The big frame eased away from the wall and walked over. 'Sam Duncan, working again … welcome to Nice.' The handshake was almost violent.

'Mo, how's the wild man of Provence?'

'Quietening down as I mature. The bar awaits.'

'A Ricard for old times' sake?'

'Oui, maybe more. I get a driver now.' Maurice Cassanet smiled and parodied his importance, lifting his right hand in a royal wave.

'Wine of the country.'

'Lead on, *Monsieur le Directeur*.' Sam's pronunciation was flawless.

Cassanet nodded. His rolling stride ate the distance towards a corridor with a no-entry symbol at eye height. They entered the well-lit, grey-walled passage, went on for thirty metres and stopped at a solid looking door with keypad entry. Cassanet tapped in a code and the door opened outwards. Inside, two black dressed officers were ready with submachine guns.

Video panels showed the area around the doorway and down the passage in both directions. The guards had seats. Mo showed his credentials and Sam's passport. They were scanned. Both received a green light. Next, Mo walked up to a line and stared at a camera, another green light.

'Sam, could you please do the same.'

Sam complied. The green light came on once more.

One of the guards swiped a card and pressed a button beside the reader. A door opened and they went through.

'Formal stuff, Mo.'

'We take our borders seriously.'

'I thought you'd walk me in.'

'Once upon a time, my friend. Not now. No exceptions.'

'Who gets the record?'

Mo smiled. 'No one. My code diverts the record to my little agency. Our entry is recorded as the law demands and can be produced later, if required. The evidence is on our system and no one else's.'

'Only in France.'

'Nowadays, there's nothing more suspicious than a walk-through.'

'So, now where?' Sam said.

'Pastis.'

'Here?'

'How about Cabris?'

'Fantastic.'

'We can talk on the way in my armoured chariot.' They walked into a covered area. A silver Citroen C6 waited for them. The driver took Sam's bag. Mo and Sam settled in the back of the car, which accelerated quietly out of the building into the airport traffic and westwards towards the motorway and the Provençal hills. 'Remember the chapel on Des Hautes Ribes?' Mo said.

'How could I forget?' Sam said thinking of a steep and narrow twisting lane and the aged building with the little shrine on the dry stone wall, partially hidden by gnarled olive trees.

'We will operate from there.'

'Good set-up.'

'The best. Excellent security.'

'Yeah, and the invisible old road.'

'A parallel opportunity. What better way to get bread and

exercise? The guards loved keeping up with you on the morning run, you tartan tear-away.'

'I remember.'

'Safety, *mon ami*, in a beautiful place.'

'So, Mo, what's our time frame?' Sam said.

'One day for us, then Fogarty later this afternoon. The Germans and Dutch meet us tomorrow in Le Mas, and our Yankee after that. '

'Why Le Mas?' Sam said.

'No eavesdropping. The northern types always want to be off the beaten track. There's a special restaurant.'

'Okay.'

'The Yankees are on board, but our governments like us to be a little European, so we must have meetings. I talk things through with you first. You summarize, I summarize, we agree.' Mo shrugged and raised his large hard hands in a Gallic shrug. 'We discuss with the Germanics, and they go home to think about things.'

'The Germans, Dutch and the Belgians.'

'Same region, same attitude.' Mo shrugged. 'Actually, these guys are okay to do business with, they're switched on, clued up and just a tiny bit stiff.' He paused and patted his pocket. 'Excuse me, my phone.' He pushed a button and lifted a small device to his ear. 'Oui. Oh it's you, you damn Yankee.' He leaned across to Sam. 'Fogarty.' He listened, spoke, listened some more. 'Okay, Bob. He'll brief you after tomorrow. I'll tell him.' He held the mobile in front of him and pushed the disconnect button. 'He sends his regards. We'll talk to him tomorrow when we've finished meeting with the others. 'Now it's pastis time.'

'A pastis or two, a light lunch, a glass of wine, a brandy, a noisette ... heaven.'

'I'd forgotten about the noisette. Wonderful coffee.'

'A perfect Provençal café, monsieur.' Mo pretended disdain.

'Naturally, how could I suggest anything less?'

Mo tapped his driver on the shoulder. They drove up a small

dual carriageway to the roundabout where they turned back towards Grasse and pulled over. The doors unlocked as they stopped in an avenue of trees. Leaves rustling in a warm breeze on the Boulevard du Dr Belletrud, Cabris.

They stepped out of the car and moved quickly into the maze of streets. Sam gazed around.

'We're covered, Sam. Just like your family.'

'You've had quite a briefing, Mo.'

'The best. Charlton is clear and complete.'

They walked round to the terrace and over to L'Auberge. A table was reserved. The pastis arrived in a schooner, already turning milky, with an ice cube and a small curved carafe of iced water placed beside each glass. They eased back in their seats and relaxed with a sigh. Across the cobbled and narrow road a pavement full of tables did brisk business. A scent of bread from the bakery was in the air.

'*À votre santé*, Sam.'

'Yours, too.'

They settled in for a pleasant afternoon. Thunder rumbled in the distance. 'Not for us I hope.'

53

In Strasbourg a secure telephone winked. A chubby bronzed hand picked it up. The manicure was perfect and the gold cufflinks were an elegant, unobtrusive display of wealth.

'Xavier.' The phone settled next to pursed, fleshy lips. The sibilant English rang icy, clear and abrupt. The dark eyes in the chubby face glinted. He concentrated. 'They've sent Duncan to France.'

'So, the Brits are talking to the French. Why are we scared?' He listened some more.

'Action is down to the London people. As agreed, the decision is hers, Ms Smythsone is both beautiful and tough.' The voice rambled on and he rolled his eyes.

'The situation in London was crazy. Me? I'd be careful. We are well concealed. There is no risk unless we react. Think of the UK problem as a farce, plain and simple,' Xavier said.

Xavier paid attention as the voice droned on. His face turned pink with frustration. Beads of sweat appeared on his forehead. 'How many times must I say this? They don't know too much, they don't know enough ... not enough!'

The voice increased in volume. 'You're not being very helpful.'

He sat back squeezing the handset. 'I am being helpful, I'm being clear and factual.' He slammed the phone down, grunted as he tried to swallow his rage. He shook both fists in front of his chin, face screwed up.

* * *

Five minutes later, Xavier rested his chin on his hand and doodled on a pad near the phone. Panic lost games. It was to do with success. The closer they got to the politicians the more unhelpful weaknesses were nearer to the surface: anxiety, hasty action, half-truths and deceit, cover-up, and, vengeance … with more he hadn't thought of. He sighed, half-smiled and shook his head. Pragmatism. He must be pragmatic.

The nature of the business structure meant inherent weakness. He might despise the flawed and craven people who made him wealthy, but he wouldn't show it. He picked up the phone.

'Sorry if I was annoyed there, I'm so concerned about our project. I've thought some more. We must support the majority in this, I defer to the judgement of the group.'

The voice on the other end was almost affectionate. 'Of course, we're all in this together.' The smile in his tone might have enthused the speaker, but Xavier's eyes remained gelid.

His next call was to one of the real leaders. After sharing his thoughts he leaned back once more, his pristine white shirt smooth against his chubby body, the dark blue silk tie, like all his attire, a gentle understatement of wealth and power.

54

'Meeting without the Yanks makes life easy.' Mo smiled and spread his large hands wide. The meal combined fresh produce and culinary skill, the wine perfect and the coffee in its little cup a delight and with a finger of good brandy on the side. 'When we communicate with Bob Fogarty we'll have an accord. His absence is timely. He will agree in the usual way. You know ... some rude words, a little weight thrown about, and then we're kissing cousins.'

'With your skills and a Ricard or two, we'll all be eating out of your hand. Where do I sign?'

'Lovely thought, sweet-cheeks.' Sam grinned. He loved the tough Frenchman's fluency and irreverence. 'Don't get your hopes up. This is Europe. Since when did we Froggies or the Cloggies get on with the Krauts? Or les Rosbifs get on with the Froggies? Or les Ecossais love les Rosbifs?'

'Shall I go home now?'

'Of course not, my hairy caber-tosser.' Mo started to laugh. 'We are about to unite Europe.' He paused and his face stiffened into serious mask. 'The most corrupt old whore in the world.'

'Do I detect a touch of cynicism?'

'I'm no cynic. This situation is truly evil, vicious and growing like a cancer.'

'Yup.'

'Your boss, General Charlton, told my boss about your adventures in the last weeks. The events and story are similar to some suspicions we have in France, people died. Then we find the Germanics share almost identical concerns, not through normal channels, of course—we don't trust them—but through discrete and honest contact between our invisible anti-corruption agencies.'

'Sponsored at the top political level.'

'Ugly and powerful, like our beloved president.'

Sam laughed. 'Okay, so we're anointed by our leaders. Doesn't make it safe.'

'No, Sam, but we get access and leverage.'

'An *entrée* without friends is worthless.'

'Of course.'

'How do we know who our friends are?'

Mo thought a moment. 'Past experience and present situations.'

'Perhaps a better question: how do we know who our enemies are?'

'Associations, opportunity, connections … there are always those. Also, the places unexpected blockages come from.'

55

The conversation and intel exchange lasted until the early hours.

At 06.00 Sam ran up the old road for bread in Cabris and bought three loaves. Three minders jogged with him at a slight distance. A large SUV ran slowly up the new road parallel and above him.

The woman at the counter looked up. 'Ah, *monsieur*, you are back.'

'Excellent memory, Madame. It's been eight years.'

'I never forget a handsome face. Are you glad to be back?'

'Yes, I love this place, it has such beauty, just like the bakers.' She laughed, blushed, reached over and patted his hand. She gave him his bread.

'Thirty years ago I might have believed you.' She searched his face, her fine brown eyes moving from side to side then up and down. 'We could have made beautiful music, as the Americans say. Now, I enjoy memories and an occasional glance from my old man.' She rolled her eyes and tossed her head. 'Still, I love him.'

Sam blew her a kiss, wished her goodbye and jogged back down the hill.

Breakfast comprised a coffee-filled bowl with bread, butter and jam. The crunchy pleasures and scents of the food, and a nearby lemon grove, elevated the experience. Warm sunshine dappled the table below rustling leaves. It all served to relax and enthuse them. They talked business, interlaced with memories of shared risk and camaraderie.

'Big day today. We need some serious discussions and decisions. Martijn Van Venendaal and Fritz Rosenkrantz will meet us in the mountains in four hours. The Belgiques are to liaise with Martijn.'

'And Bob?' Sam said.

'Fogarty called. He's on a related investigation in New York. He wants more involvement later. I have discussed things and he agrees with our take. He says if you disagree with me we can get back to him, otherwise okay.'

'A private chat?'

'Nothing sneaky. He phoned after you set off. You ran all the way up to Cabris, my excellent bagpiper?'

'Of course. No Gauloise for me, mon gros choux.'

'You dare call me a fat cabbage, you unsophisticated heathen.'

'A thousand pardons, your nobleness. Forgive my error.'

'We French overlook so much from you boring northerners: *faux pas*, rudeness and no pastis worth having.'

'Tough one.'

'You have just enough time to fuck yourself before we get down to business.' Sam went for a shower laughing.

* * *

'We're going up to Sainte-Vallier and towards Thorenc, over the winding passes in the hills. Such beautiful country – rock, pine and alpine vistas set against an azure sky.'

'Brings back memories: loads of scary driving.' Sam said.

'We'll be careful today.' Mo nodded. 'No heroics. We need to survive to fight a real evil. Take your gun.'

'When are the others due?'

'They are on the way. We should arrive about the same time. The restaurant is booked and secured for us alone.'

'I'm honoured.'

'Of course, imagine the cream of European crime-busting eating wondrous rustic food. Unthinkable except here in France.'

56

In the hills above Le Mas, the big Citroen came clear of some trees and out along the edge of a precipice around five kilometres from the village, moving at a steady pace in the hands of an expert driver.

A gunship rose over the escarpment, identified and took the car out in less than twenty seconds. The first rocket blew the engine and front wheels off. The second destroyed the passenger compartment in a welter of blood, steel and flame. The third and a fourth completed the destruction.

A storm of metal and body parts blew over the cliff, to sail down into the void below the road. Debris whistled into trees The chock-chock sounds of shrapnel slicing off branches were followed by a silent fall into the chasm, or small pieces dangling in disarray, attached by strands of bark and wood.

Job done, the chopper dropped backwards over the ridge, before arching its muscular back and tilting forward to race down sparsely inhabited valleys, emerging many miles away. The lethal machine landed at a quiet military base above Ventimiglia in Italy.

Hardly anyone saw the gunship. It would be hours before the authorities made the connection between it and the precision assault … except for some happy planners, criminals, civil servants and business people.

* * *

'So much for your scepticism, Xavier,' a senior European official crowed into the phone. 'Colonel Sam Duncan and Directeur Maurice Cassanet are history, and no collateral damage.'

'Congratulations, Anton.' Xavier allowed a warmth of tone he didn't feel. 'One can't be correct all the time, and you called this one right. I commend you.'

The executive talked with triumphant energy. 'Blew the bastards off a mountain. The police still haven't worked out what happened. Our team is already safe and back in Italy.'

'What can I say? Thanks for being so firm, and delivering a result.'

'An obstacle removed and the Londoners in our debt. All will be grateful.'

'Yes.' Xavier paused. 'These are hard people we fight. I hear the Smythsone woman does a good line in gratitude. Maybe you should drop in and have a cuddle.'

'I wish.'

'Wishing is fun.' Xavier said.

'What else is on our agenda?'

'You decide, now you're on a roll.'

'Maybe some more tidying up.'

'Anyone in mind?'

'Hmmm, yes. I'll need your backing.' He talked through his plan.

'Lopping off senior heads is preferable to murdering lots of minor players. I give you my support.' Xavier stroked his lip; pragmatism was essential. 'I think killing an entire family to make an unrecognizable point was stupid and liable to create the wrong sort of energy in the investigation. I did not support that.'

'Okay, I agree. I'll push the other buttons.'

'I hope you don't need an Apache for this one.'

'No, no. Discretion and precision is all.'

'It's a shame about the Duncan man. I'd like to have met him, questioned him, found out what made him tick.'

'He's gone. May he rest in pieces.'

'Fine. Anything else?'

'No. I'll take care of business.'

57

'Any doubt, sir?'

'None, Mike. Their car left the road in rugged country, assisted by high explosives. They think rockets: blown to pieces and blasted over a cliff. Not much left of the occupants.'

'Sam's family?'

'We're awaiting more detail. This is especially sad for his family, who've been having a tough time as he's worked this case. We can't notify them until we get the forensics, which we expect later today. The car was where it was due to be, when it was due to be there, and a clear target for the enemy.' Charlton's pallor expressed his feelings. 'As I learn more, I'll tell you.'

The silence in the room lay heavy; a shroud of shock and disbelief.

'Where's Tonka?' Cal said.

'Search me.' Cal stood up and left. Mike followed him out. Shocked eyes watched them go.

'On the chin, we have to take it on the chin. Pick ourselves up and get on with it.' Charlton exited and the quiet became a loud buzz of conversation. Outside, Cal sat on a chair stone-faced, Mike alongside him, uncomfortable; nothing to say.

58.

The drive up the hills was as pretty as ever as they followed the route of the D5 up and down. The trip along the gorge had been spectacular until an unexpected turn. 'What's going on, Mo? We just passed the road to Le Mas and we're heading towards Saint Auban.'

'Well spotted, Sam. I forgot to tell you. We're worried about leaks, even in the safe house. We are going somewhere else for lunch. A car like this left for Le Mas as we passed through some trees a few klicks back.'

'That's why you stopped for a pee.'

'Oh, *mon brave*, you are such a deductive detective for a military man with a brain of solid muscle. We have a totally safe restaurant to meet in, and the Legion guarantees our safety.'

'You must be worried.'

'The deaths of two people I have known and worked with in the last three weeks.'

'Painful.'

'Yes. Now we are safe. We are getting things nailed down, and if we didn't need to get together we wouldn't be meeting at all.' Mo's demeanour had changed. 'Things will be better in a couple of weeks. We must complete our investigations. The political flack and barriers are an embarrassment. The corruption stinks.'

'Yes, I've experienced some of that in my time.'

'You killed people in London and Scotland?'

'Mercs.'

'Mmm. It may get worse before it gets better.'

'What about Giselle and the kids?'

'Corsica with her uncle, under guard.'

They drove down to Saint Auban and went right, through

the tunnels and onwards to a small bar and restaurant at Briançonnet. The streets were narrow, khaki and bright with sunshine.

'So much for fine-dining.'

'Good food doesn't need stars from self-styled experts. This will be fantastic. You'll praise me forever after this.' The car stopped. 'Let's move briskly, my friend.' Inside, two men stood up beside a table and came over to shake hands. Fritz and Martijn. After the pleasantries they sat down, ordered pastis and went straight to business. The bar was wood-lined and spacious. To the far side a wide terrace looked out over the hills. A scented breeze of pine and flowers kissed the air. The patron came over with the drinks.

* * *

The talks were energetic and wide-ranging. Alcohol eased reticence and intelligence flowed. The meal was an excellent duck in plum sauce, served on rustic stoneware, supported by superb, brightly coloured vegetables, a smooth local wine and wonderful fresh bread. A slender young waitress provided service with polite attentiveness. Her carriage, figure and fresh beauty were admired.

As the exchange went on, threads started to emerge, with links into Brussels and Strasbourg. While the London killings seemed to close off some lines of enquiry, they legitimized the investigation and connections were teased out. The reports from each country highlighted common ground and suspicions. The mood was positive.

'So, we think there is a European equivalent of the British Bizz.' Fritz said. 'The structure is similar. Your sister's investigation gave us a clue, and we've uncovered some junior collaborators. There are a few good people who are supplying intel.'

'Where do they convene?' Sam said.

'Western Europe, mainly Brussels and Strasbourg.' Martijn said. 'We are identifying the membership just now and will have details within the next couple of weeks.'

Fritz became serious and deferential. 'Directeur Cassanet, we have consulted within the group and would ask you to take the lead on interdicting …' He smiled 'EuroBizz.'

'Okay, I'll do it.' Cassanet said. 'Sam Duncan will be assigned to assist me when needed.' Sam nodded and tried not to smile. Cassanet could fly a kite.

'Agreed.' Martijn said, and Fritz nodded.

Cassanet's driver came in, whispered in his ear. Cassanet excused himself. He returned an unhappy man. 'The blind worked … but not for two of my people. The car, a duplicate of mine, was blown up on the route to Le Mas.' His face broke and he shed a tear.

'Are we safe here?'

'Oh yes. Our work must be finished, and then we'll get you home. You gentlemen,' he indicated Fritz and Martijn, 'leave by road in two hours, a plane is coming to take you north from an airfield about an hour from here. Sam, we go by helicopter. The police have notified your death to London, routine thoughtlessness. Perhaps it's an opportunity. I will contact Charlton when we get back to Nice.'

* * *

They landed at Nice Airport. The helipad was surrounded by soldiers and black uniforms. They went into a meeting room. A lean officer entered, stood at attention and briefed Cassanet in staccato French. Mo nodded, asked questions and turned to Sam.

'It was the house steward at the chapel. We took the building apart after the attack; found some evidence.' He sighed. 'The man has been looking after the place for five years. Now, of course, he's disappeared. He betrayed our complete trust. I want to know how they got to him. Two of my boys, Sam, *two of them*: wives, children, families.'

'Hard to bear, Mo, losing people is the worst thing.'

Mo took a deep breath, pulled himself up to his full height, exhaled and gazed into Sam's eyes, nodding. 'Our meeting was good. We have strong ideas. Go communicate to your boss.' He handed Sam a pen drive, 'these codes keep our communications secure. Personal communication only.'

'Of course.'

'We have arranged a special passport for now. You are dead as far as the world is concerned. Your family won't have heard anything yet.'

'I hope not, the last time something like this happened, Karen thought I was dead, the shock cuts deep. Bizz murdered an old friend by mistake.'

'Oooolala. You will leave Nice with an excellent tan, which I have arranged for you. Your hair colour will lose the grey. We don't think you're in immediate danger, but we'll stay on the safe side.'

'Thanks, Mo.'

'Until the next time, *mon ami.*' Mo gave Sam a bear hug, 'Rombout will take care of you.' The driver nodded, picked up Sam's bag and waved him to follow. Cassanet walked away, the droop of his shoulders oozing pain.

59

'What's it like to be dead, Sam?' The sitting area reeked of modernity and leather. The reception space enjoyed good lighting, with the other nooks more subdued and private. The bustle of people walking in with the rattle and click of wheeled cases couldn't be avoided.

'Surreal, Ben, absolutely surreal.'

'You and Waberthwaite will go off the radar for a while. The family's briefed, Karen is concerned, but I managed to speak to her before the newsflash.'

'Thanks for that.'

'She is upset.'

'It'll be good to get back and reassure her.'

'Yes, go back north to grow a beard, change the profile of your hair … whatever it takes to be different.'

'Understood.'

'A chopper will collect you in half an hour. Now, tell me what you and Cassanet agreed, plus helpful background.'

60

Sam stood quiet, hidden beneath the sodden trees. Water trickled down his neck. He didn't move, relaxed into the moment. Memories returned of other times: silent watching, stealthy movement, aggressive action.

* * *

The Narrows at the bottom of Strangford Loch, Northern Ireland, bubbled and swirled as the Strangford ferry pushed its way against the tide, drifting with practised skill and accuracy on to the concrete ramp at Portaferry, opposite the hotel. He checked his watch 20.35.

Fresh from the ferry, the large estate car entered the drive and scrunched to a stop on the granite chips. A big man eased himself out of the seat with a grunt and, limping slightly, walked up to the entrance of the property near Windmill Heights. He unlocked a security keypad by the door. An amber light winked. He entered a code and the colour turned green. With a scraping click he fitted his key to the lock, walked into the porch and shut the outside door. He followed a secure locking-up routine and, finally, set the external alarms.

He took off his damp raincoat and hung it on the first brass hook in the vestibule, then stepped into the house, paused and yawned with an extravagant spread of his arms, collecting letters and flyers from the container. The glass-paned door to the hall swung smoothly on well-oiled hinges and closed behind him with a sharp click. His next step was into the kitchen, his movement followed quickly by the raucous bubbling of a busy kettle as he finished scanning the mail. A scent of cafetière coffee wafted around.

The doorbell rang, sounding for nigh on two seconds under a strong press. Mug in hand the man opened the door, the security chain rattled.

'Evening, Pete.' Molloy gazed at the figure and heard the Scots accent.

'Do I know you?'

'Aye, we've met once or twice. We spoke at Belfast International a few weeks back. You called me the other day. We first met when a man tried to kill me.'

'Step closer to the light.' The man moved forward.

'In the name of the wee man, Sam Duncan. You're dead accordin' to the news. What're you doin' here?'

'Wanted a chat, Pete.'

'You didn't call.'

'Dead men don't, do they?'

'This can't be official.'

'Well, slightly ... sort of ... but not highly visible.'

'Will you be showin' up on the security logs?'

'Nope.' A shake of the head. 'I hope not.'

'Come in.' Tension grew as Molloy went through the locking procedure once more.

'Any chance of a mug?'

'Sure.'

'White, no sugar,' Sam said.

They walked into the kitchen together. An arthritic hip made Pete Molloy limp around as he brewed the coffee. His hands shook as he poured the milk. He had a pale, nervous cast to his face and returned Sam's scrutiny.

'I nearly shit myself,' Molloy stared at his visitor. 'What are you doing here, scaring the bejesus out of an ageing cop?'

'We need to talk, Pete.'

'So it appears.' An angry light in his eye. 'Want a towel?'

'In a minute.' Sam dripped on the stone-tiled floor.

'Can't let me out of your sight?' Pete said.

'Not yet.' Sam leaned against a black marble work surface.

'I'll ask again ... is this official?'

'*-ish*.' Sam said.

'What's *-ish* mean?' Molloy's face coloured with annoyance

'Deniable.'

'What about normal channels?'

'This isn't a normal situation.'

'Is there a problem?'

Sam gazed round the kitchen, at the cupboards and fittings, then locked eyes with his host. 'Depends on your answers.'

'Am I safe?'

'I hope so.'

'What's on your mind?'

'1994.'

'Orin O'Reilly? The man you killed.' Sam nodded as Molloy said, 'I'll never forget that, watching the action unfold and being helpless as it happened. So bloody fast, so deadly and here you are, a fuckin' ice-cold killer ... supposed to be dead, and drinkin' my fuckin' coffee.'

'It's not about him, Pete, more to do with you and your presence. No accident.' Sam sipped his coffee.

'Something bothering you?'

'Yup, I've an itch to scratch.' Sam shared a bleak smile. His half-grown beard and now longer curly hair, both black, had changed the shape of his head. A deep tan highlighted his blue eyes.

'Questions then?'

'One or two. I need clarity.'

'And if you don't get answers?'

61

'Cassanet survived. They were in separate cars.' Xavier smiled and turned his head sideways. 'Can't win them all.'

'We nailed Duncan for the Smythsone woman.'

'Careful, she's joining the European Board.'

'After all the trouble in the UK?'

'She'll fix it.' Xavier paused and smirked at the phone, 'or die in the attempt.'

62

'Pushed your panic button yet?'

Molloy half-smiled. 'No, but I've been thinking about it. Ask away.'

'May I sit down?'

'Of course.' Pete Malloy waved a hand at the kitchen table and wheel-back chairs. 'Now what do you want to know?'

'Why were you there, Pete?'

'Surveillance.'

'On who?'

'You, Sam.' Molloy paused and looked at Sam. 'For Christ's sake! Stop dripping all over the bloody floor. I'll fetch a towel.' He went into a cupboard beside the range and came up with a big bath towel, which he tossed to Sam. 'Been waiting long?'

'About an hour and a half.'

'Fly in?'

'Chopper, came in nearby and linked with a local team.' Sam rubbed his hair and neck. 'Boy, that's better. Thanks.'

'I'll lend you a jumper.' Pete left and went upstairs. Sam could hear him tramping into a room, opening drawers and returning. 'There you go.' Sam pulled the sweater on and found himself looking at the business end of an automatic.

63

'Contacts in Belfast will eliminate a key link to the past.' Smythsone said. 'Jim has convinced me we need to wipe out this important connection to Duncan.'

'Why should we do it? We expose ourselves yet again. And it's a senior policeman' Chen said.

'We can disguise the killing as sectarian.' Smythsone paused and sipped her coffee.

'Share the rationale with me.'

'Peter Molloy witnessed Jim's complicity in a failed assassination attempt on Duncan about eighteen to twenty years ago.'

'Old stuff.'

'An entire detective team was eliminated, Duncan was the last in line, and only surviving member.'

'Still … old stuff.'

'There are apprehensive people who have been milking the system over there with security, banking and commercial links.'

'Criminals.' Chen said.

'Aren't we all?' Her smile cracked Chen's impassive demeanour. He smiled back. 'One or two of them were our founding fathers.'

'Where's the benefit?'

'Pulling Jim Thomas properly into our orbit. He has knowledge and connections world-wide. This particular part of the past is haunting him. He offers strategic relevance.' She shrugged, 'I don't care about … don't really want to do more strong-arm stuff.'

'I'm not happy, but I understand your thinking now. I'll report my support.'

'That's important and helpful, Ken, thank you.'

'Let's hope it doesn't backfire.'

64

'Feel safer now, Pete?'

Pete nodded. 'I've questions of my own, Sam.'

'Fire away … not literally, please.'

'Stand up and lean against the table.' Sam did as he was told. Molloy frisked him, always keeping the gun pressed to his head. He didn't find a weapon. 'What brings you here?'

'Comprehensive trail-covering by evil people.'

'Those murders in London?'

'Yes. Those and some other stuff that won't make the news. We believe there may be, shall we say, murderous activity elsewhere.'

'So, you didn't come to kill me.'

'Ah, no. I want information from you. I want you alive.'

'Am I in danger?'

'We think so.'

'Soon?'

'Mmm.' Sam nodded.

'You haven't a gun.'

'Not in here.'

'Outside?'

'Yes. We're covered.'

'You're not alone?'

'No,' Sam said.

'What's your plan?'

'Get you out of here tonight.'

'Just like that?'

'Just like that. We hope we're ahead of the game, but a signal went to some bad people about twelve hours ago. You're the bullseye.'

'So?'

'Pack the essentials: laptop, notes, stuff you need. We leave in ten minutes.'

'I've more questions.'

'Not right now, Pete.'

'When?'

'When we get to Howth. We've just enough time to catch the last ferry to Strangford.'

'I've got to make a choice?'

Sam checked his watch. 'You have eight minutes, matey, then I'm out of here.'

65

'Our people report action at Molloy's house.'

'Action, sir?' Mike Swindon said.

'Duncan and Waberthwaite linked with a team by helicopter near Newcastle, County Down. They went to Portaferry via the Strangford Ferry. The pair of them arrived at the house and waited for the man. Sam gained entry. That's the most recent update.'

Charlton's phone blinked. He listened. 'Thank you.' He looked up. 'Two men have been apprehended.'

'Arrested?'

'There can be a difference when it's operational, Mike.'

Cal nodded. 'The rules are different, mate.'

'Different?'

'There aren't any. We're talking paramilitary killers here. Some of them are pretty competent.'

Charlton said, 'we don't know what resources they'll deploy. It's risky.'

'It's the job, Mike.' Cal said.

'And if it goes tits-up?' Mike said.

Cal's eyes held Mike's. 'The people on the ground play it by ear.'

'They're pretty good at it,' Charlton said. 'We've had just under twelve hours from the tip-off.'

'It seems pretty hairy to me.'

'It is. We used to say, scary-hairy.' Cal looked at his watch. 'They've got fifteen minutes to get the job done.'

Mike rested his forearms on his knees and gazed at the floor. 'Pressure.'

'It's what they train for.' Charlton said. 'Piece of piss.'

Cal laughed. Mike scowled at him.

66

'Shit. This is hard!'

'The good news is you don't have family. No loose ends. So get a bend on. Move! Bring any sailing gear you've got, too.'

Pete nodded. 'Ready in a couple of minutes.'

A text pinged into Sam's phone. 'Right,' he said.

Pete hurried upstairs. He was back in moments with a small carry-pack. 'Underpants and toilet stuff. Laptop at the front door. I've got some deckies, sweaters and other sailor stuff.'

'Excellent.'

'Should I bring my weapon?'

'Why not.'

'A bottle of Bushmills?' Molloy said.

'Essential. More than one, if you like.' Sam smiled at him. 'I've just had a text.'

'And?'

'Some bad guys got here twenty minutes ago.'

'How many?'

'Two. They're out of it.'

'Just like that?' Molloy said.

'Yup. They came to kill you. This is hardball. I'm hoping they only sent two to do the job, because you shouldn't have been expecting trouble.'

'No.'

'A car might be waiting, but it's hard to tell without compromising ourselves. We'll do that well enough when you drive us to the ferry.' Sam said.

'What's all this about?'

'Money and loose ends.'

'It's not political then?'

'Political, commercial and public sector, too. Just a

moment.' Sam sent a text. 'Let's get moving.'

Lights off, they crept from the house. Molloy reset the alarms and headed for the car. A hand took his cuff as he neared the parking place tugging him gently back. He jerked and a calloused hand covered his mouth to silence him. He could see Sam five paces away staring ahead, concentration on his face.

67

'Molloy's on board.' Charlton looked up from his mobile. He sighed. 'They're moving out, heading for the ferry.'

'It's the scary-hairy part.' Cal said. 'You have to move. If they've second guessed you, it's fireworks.'

'The support is very low profile. We really don't want to use them unless it's absolutely necessary,' Charlton said. 'Too many spooks spoil the plot.' They winced *har-har-har*.

'What the boss is saying, Mike, is they're on their own. They're covered but you can't do everything. For two or three minutes they will be unprotectable on a dark, rainy night …'

'Christ!' Mike said.

'Good friend to have.'

68

'I'm with Sam.' The voice was calm, strong. 'There's a van about twenty yards up the road, not friendly. Wait here while I deal with it.' He moved off, silent, and vanished in the gloom. Sam stood beside Pete.

'He says he's going to deal with a van.'

'Right. He'll do that.'

'What made you come?'

'Do you know a Francine Callaghan?'

'She's a cousin.'

'Her old man's connected to a paramilitary outfit.'

'Yes.'

'Family bond is strong, she heard things and made contact through a person who's connected to our work.'

'And?'

'You'd have been dead about twenty minutes ago if we hadn't acted.'

Molloy was silent for a moment, playing with dirty knees and a runny nose on the divided streets of old Belfast. Francine …

* * *

Then the man was back. He glanced at Sam. 'Sorted.' He checked Molloy's car for booby-traps.

'Let's move,' Sam said.

They got into the Mondeo. Five minutes later, they were parked in a space near the slipway. They watched the lights come closer as the ferry fought the current and swung in towards the shore.

'Let's go.' Sam and Molloy shared the luggage between them. 'Leave your keys on the front wheel. The car will be safely home by morning.' Tonka, hands free, crabbed backwards behind them.

'Any dead?' Sam spoke to his minder.

'One,' Tonka said.

'They'll be tidied away,' Sam said.

The ferry ramp clanked on to the slipway.

'Tidied up? *For fuck's sake!* It's a fuckin' nightmare, so it is,' Molloy said.

'But you're alive, and you'll be safe. Experienced man like you, I've got some work that needs doing.' Sam said.

They walked onto the ferry. Tonka faced the road, almost invisible at the left hand railing and crouched slightly. A squall of rain swirled in a spotlight.

69.

'What's he got under the coat?' Molloy watched Tonka and marvelled at his poise.

'Mini assault rifle.'

'Unreal.'

'I wish.' With a sounding of the alarm, the ramp raised. Sam sighed with relief as the vessel cast off. 'Right on time.'

At the slope on the other side a dark car and a Range Rover waited just past the steps at the slip. The two other passengers left, heads bent to the downpour, oblivious to anything else. Sam, Tonka and Molloy entered the big car. Two men followed from the side, and another man came down from the main road.

'No action this side, sir.' The driver had a Liverpool accent. 'No further vehicles or people detected at Portaferry. The clean-up is going as planned.'

'Thanks. Good job. Seamless,' Sam said. 'Let's find a good chippy on the way south.'

'We'll manage that, sir.' The driver smiled. They left Strangford, with Tonka already asleep in the front seat.

'Take a rest, Pete. I think you'll need it.' Sam was asleep in moments. Molloy shook his head and watched the sleepers.

No sleep for him, as his mind raced and his world changed forever.

70

Four hours later, dressed in holiday sailors' gear, they boarded a yacht near Howth.

'Been a while since I've been on the coast road, and now I've to climb aboard a yacht and sail for my life.'

'Best we could do at short notice, Pete,' Sam said.

'How very covert of you.'

'Right, Pete, and we aim to stay that way. Know anything about sailing?'

'A bit.'

'John is the skipper. He'll keep you busy, after we leave. Coffee, anyone? Dram?'

* * *

Two days later they arrived in North Devon. A helicopter took them from a deserted beach to a safe country house.

'That's you then, Pete,' Sam said.

'Long way round.'

'Yes, a quiet route and under the radar.'

'Sneaking around, typical bloody spookery.'

'You've bared your soul, I've submitted a report. You'll be joining us for a while, either for your protection or as an active member.'

'Make mine active, Sam.'

'Excellent, I've got a whiny, angry, camp journalist for you to befriend and pump for information.'

'Jamie, the man you were telling me about.'

'Yes, he's angry, rude and needs a spot of sorting.'

'Leave him to me.'

'He should be up at the house. Make yourself at home.'

'Thanks.'

'See you soon. I'm off,' Sam said. 'The boss will handle

your welcome.'

'And you?'

'Places to go, people to see.'

'Ben Charlton wants to meet you. We hope to get you off the killing agenda, but it may take a while.'

'And if not?'

'There's worse places to stay.' Sam said.

'Right. I suppose I should say thanks.'

'No thanks required.'

Sam walked away. The chopper flew off as soon as he boarded.

* * *

'They're out.' Charlton shared a rare smile. He produced a bottle of Malt and three glasses. Quentin sat smiling with him.

Indira appeared at the door wearing a bright white smile. 'Excellent news, General Charlton.' He waved the bottle at her. 'Only the most tiny of drops, sir.'

He added a finger nail's depth and passed it to her. 'Active friends, Cheers.'

They sipped. Indira started spluttering and making faces. They laughed.

71

A middle-aged couple stepped from their terraced house into the street.

'What's with you, love?,' the husband said, 'you've been off colour for days.' The warm tones of his Belfast accent sounded loud because of increasing deafness.

'I don't know how to tell you something.' Her serious, handsome face showed strain instead of her habitual warmth and character.

'You've not been having an affair with the postman?' He laughed as he punched the key button and the car doors unlocked.

'Stop being silly, Tomas, I'm trying to tell you something important.' She entered the passenger seat beside him.

'I need to get us moving, but I'm all ears.' He put the key in the ignition. He's not really listening.

'I overheard Tom Gourlay say Pete Molloy, my cousin, is due to be killed.'

He didn't turn the key. 'Sorry you heard that. It's a sad business.'

'It's an evil business, Tomas, and has no place in these times.'

'You don't understand, Frankie, some things have to be done. This is one of 'em.' He glared at her and reached for the key again.

'I told them, Bren.'

'Told who?'

'Pete's colleagues. They put me in touch with a man in London.'

She watched her husband turn white as a snowfield. 'Do you know what you've done?' He turned the ignition key by reflex.

The car started and settled into a brisk idle. He puffed out a trembling sigh.

'I played in the street with him from when I could toddle. It's only because of your evil connections that we haven't seen him for twenty some years.'

'We're dead. They'll work it out and come after us.'

'I couldn't tell you yesterday, you were so angry and aggressive.'

'Sorry about that, love. It's not how I want to be.'

'We can have witness protection.'

He sat back and sighed, lowered his head. 'I can't, you and the kids will become an example: no mercy. It's not God and the Cause anymore. These are evil gangsters, and I'm connected to them.' He stopped the car.

'Go back in the house. I've got some people to see.'

She started to weep. 'They'll not listen, Bren.'

'I'll get their attention. Get in the house.'

She watched him drive away, certain she'd done the right thing, stomach churning with fear for the future.

* * *

They called the meeting as a matter of urgency. Three men sat at a table in the small room at the back of the bar. Tomas Callaghan arrived slightly late, unusual for him. He turned to hang up his coat.

'You shouldn't keep your betters waiting, Tomas.' The mouthy bastard was the worst sort of fuckin' bully. The other two laughed.

'You'll wait no longer then.' Callaghan turned round with the Uzi and put a burst in the man's chest. Blood, bone and cloth erupted from both sides of the man's body as he and his chair went over backwards.

Brendan emptied the magazine into them a burst at a time, they all fell. As the dust settled in flecks on the blood on the floor, he leaned back against the wall and cried.

He laid the hot weapon on a table and sat down on a chair. 'You've had my soul, but you can't have my beautiful wife, you bastards, or my kids.'

When the police arrived he was waiting for them, hands in plain view. He'd never talk, never ever. His text to a senior player said it all:

hands off

72

'Blew them away?' Molloy's shock punched out of the earpiece.

'Said it's the only way to protect his family.'

'Even with witness protection he's probably right. Tell me about him.'

'Hardest of the hard. Good family man. Old school paramilitary and gangster.'

'Why are you alive after the team was wiped out and they tried for me?'

A long silence seemed to squeeze the line. 'You think there might be more than they didn't want to kill a policeman?'

'Yes. Francine confirmed it in an interview. She's bargaining for him, trying to justify herself. He intervened for you back in '94.'

'Please don't contact her, Pete.'

'Why not?'

'He's a lever,' Sam said, 'and in solitary for his protection until arrangements can be made to move him somewhere safe.'

'And?'

'We'll remand him to a UK mainland high security prison ... make him hard to visit for a while.'

'And?'

'It'll add pressure. He knows stuff we want.'

'What about her, Sam?'

'She saved your life. She couldn't tell him what she'd done until he had no options but murder and threat of telling what he knows. Now she'll pay the price for keeping you alive.'

'For betrayal.'

'Yes, for loving a cousin.'

'This is the worst fuckin' sort of hardball.'

'Wrong, the best sort. She got what she wanted. He proved

his love for her. You're alive. She has to cope with a big change.'

'This is cruel. You're not just a killer. What are you like?'

'I'm a soldier. We're facing an evil enemy. We get you out with minutes to spare. These people will kill us quick as look at us. An attack helicopter against a car in France for goodness' sake. Four men sent to kill you in Ulster. Gangsters after my family in Galway. A harum-scarum car chase in Scotland with mercenaries and UK operatives. Waterboarding and murder in London a couple of weeks ago … Need I go on?'

More silence. 'Sorry. You're right, it's frightening.'

'You have Charlton's word we'll try to protect Francine and, if he can, in a while they'll get her old man out of jankers and into a new life.'

'I need to think.'

'Fair enough. You've got until I get back in a week or so to decide.'

'On what?'

'Whether you're an associate or a full team member.'

'Either way I'm safe.'

'Of course. The choice is between safe boredom and risking your life, fighting evil and never getting recognition.'

'Thanks.'

'How's friend Jamie?'

'Comin' round. Hard work.'

'Kick ass and get names, dates and content, Pete.'

'What did your last slave die of?'

'Lead poisoning.'

73

'That sister of yours is coming along well.' Charlton said. The bearded man in front of him, dark-skinned and black-eyed. He wore a reefer jacket with a light blue polo-neck and sat upright in a chair by Charlton's desk.

'Yes, Eilidh's getting better every day.'

'Quite a feisty person by all accounts.'

'Always. Can't have a Mum like ours and sit on the fence.'

'We want to debrief her. The Yanks want a shot as well.'

'Where is she, Ben?'

'That's not a friendly light in your eyes, Sam.'

'We're pros. She isn't.' He waved his finger at Charlton. 'Not bloody cannon fodder like yours truly.'

'Of course not. She's well covered.' The door opened and closed behind them, Sam didn't turn, eyes locked on Charlton.

'You're getting round to telling me she's in London.'

'Yes.'

'Where?'

'Here.'

Sam turned and stared into beautiful blue eyes. 'Not funny, Eilidh. It's dangerous.'

'I know, Sammy, but I'm not a wee sister any more.' She looked down at herself and held out her hands, rotating and inspecting them. 'I'm sort of a destroyer to your battleship.'

'Staying here?'

'In a small flat with access to the gym and so on. We've changed her appearance. She will not contact friends.'

'Boring but necessary,' Eilidh agreed. 'You want me to grow a lush beard like Sam, Ben?'

'That won't be required. Skin, eyes, hair colour and cut will do.' The humour in Charlton's eyes niggled.

'You look so different, big brother,' Eilidh said. Sam grunted.

'Eilidh, would you please excuse us.' Charlton's business face switched on.

'Give him his marching orders, Ben. He needs discipline.' She left, laughter tinkling like wind chimes.

74

Sam snapped alert as the landing gear banged on the runway. Some trip. The subway to baggage reclaim rattled and shook from Terminal N to the main Terminal at SeaTac airport, near Seattle.

At last, the doors opened on to the platform. Sam almost reacted to a powerful push from the side. A large woman dressed in too-tight lilac Lycra rushed past him. The adrenal surge of the contact kept him alert as he walked across to the escalator. In moments, three steps behind and below, he gazed in awe at the powerful, shiny cellulite-dimpled buttocks of the hasty woman. He couldn't help smiling at the quivering energy as she bounced from foot to foot with unrestrained urgency.

A voice from above cut in. 'Hi, Haggis.' Sam gazed up into a craggy, rosy cheeked face.

'Hey, Foggy.' The smile could be heard in the tone.

Once off the moving stairs, the two met. The handshake was followed by a hug. 'Let's get your bags, tough guy, then we'll shoot the breeze over a couple of margaritas.'

'Sounds like a plan, cowboy.'

Five minutes later, they left the carousel with Sam's battered old Samsonite case. The large woman waited for her bag with a sour face. In minutes he and Fogarty exited the multi-storey car park and onto the freeway heading for West Seattle. The engine rumbled with V8 authority. 'I thought you'd have given up the game by now, Foggy.' Sam said.

'No fuckin' chance. One too many divorces. Besides, the work is way too much fun.'

'Fun?'

'Yeah, fun. I get to do exciting things, live on expenses and meet crazy people like you.'

'It's been ten years since we teamed up.'

'Good team,' Fogarty said.

'Aye; good and tough.'

'Nature of the business. Not everyone cuts it, but we did. And only a year since our last few days together. What a gorgeous woman your wife is.'

'She's had some recent experiences she could have done without.'

'Sorry to hear that. Is she okay?'

'Not bad, but the threat is ever present. And there's the kids.'

'Nightmare.'

'Yes.' Sam's voice was almost metallic.

They turned off the freeway, looped on to a ramp and headed for Arbor Heights. The conversation stopped as Fogarty manoeuvred, restarting when he had made the right turn up the hill.

'Like old times, Sam.'

'Yeah, but closer to home.'

'I hear you. So why are you involved?'

'The price of protection.'

'That all?'

'Not entirely. I'm ashamed to say I'm enjoying it.' They stopped at the lights on the crest at 35th Avenue South-West, and turned left with the green light.

'In the blood?'

'Kind of.'

'We've done some good over the piece.'

'I suppose we made something of a difference, but we didn't stop the real bad guys,' Sam said.

'Maybe this time, buddy.'

'That's why I'm here.'

'I spoke to your boss, Charlton. You've been in a shooting war.'

'Aye,' Sam said.

'Bit hairy.'

'Right.'

'So talk to me, you poor excuse for a spook.' Fogarty went quiet.

Sam outlined the story so far. 'The attack in France hammered the comfort zone. This corruption thing permeates Europe. Then Charlton told me how the good old U-S-of-A uncovered a similar phenomenon.'

'What are we talking about?'

'Cooperative corruption, public and private sector with tendrils and connections across the West.'

'A fuckin' conspiracy,' Fogarty said.

'Exactly. And they don't mind killing people.'

'They didn't get you, buddy.'

'No.'

'Word is they took your sister.' Sam nodded. 'You got her back, right?'

'A bit rough,' Sam said, 'but she's safe.'

'So what's with these guys?'

'They want it all. They're driven by greed. They get access. They're becoming utterly ruthless. People are dying.'

'How did you find them?'

'I didn't. When things kicked off they found me and mine. Eilidh got on their tail about eighteen months ago. She's something of a reporter. She built a list of informers.' They turned right and followed a quiet road down towards a bend.

'So at least you have insight and information.'

'Potentially, for sure. At the moment she's recovering from rough treatment. She has lots more to give, but it's tricky. They took her, abused her and she ended up with a mind like a pound of mince.'

'Your man Charlton said something about that, and a web of bad people.'

'Murder, extreme violence, kidnap … not much they won't do. And they'll get better at it.'

'They're getting organized?'

'Sure. Now we know of them they resent it. Imagine, for

quite a while they've been getting away with taking what they want, when they want. They have resources, contacts and can misuse bona fide intel as they choose. The French thing is an example. They tried to take out a group of lead investigators, me included.'

'What stopped them?'

'Foresight and paranoia on the part of one cute Frenchman.'

Fogarty said. 'Is he still on the team?'

'Yes. Digging away with an angry German and an even angrier Dutchman, who don't like the crosshairs. The threads point at a European connection.'

75

The car followed a tree-lined drive, cluttered with flowers and bushes, to a brick-surfaced parking area outside a sizeable wooden house in a quiet neighbourhood. Sam saw a glint in the woods and ducked by instinct.

'No need to duck, Sam. We're here and that's a guard.'

'Hidden guards shouldn't be seen. Nice looking place, Foggy.' He looked and took in the wide area in front of an attractive rambling house.

'Safe and secure.'

Sam puffed out his cheeks. 'That's what the French said.'

'Fuck you, Scotchman.' Fogarty paused and gave Sam a mock fierce stare. 'Let's get inside.'

The door was solid wood. Once open the alarm tone bayed until switched off. Sam listened to the beeps as Fogarty worked his way round the keypad.

'Follow me, my Scots friend.' Fogarty walked Sam through a wooden-clad reception area with pictures, plants and brightness from a skylight, and on to an open staircase. 'Up the stairs, second on the right.'

Sam strode up admiring a couple of photographs on the wall: one a sunset, the other a jagged mountain range with a turquoise lake in the foreground. On the landing he turned down the passage and into a spacious room, with a settee, rug, desk and chair, plus a wall of cupboards. The walk-in bathroom had a spacious wet-room shower and a stack of towels on shelves. The toiletries were comprehensive and, on the back of the door, a huge white towelling robe hung ready for use.

Sam unpacked, wincing as he accidentally knocked the healing wound in his side against a cupboard handle. He stripped off and enjoyed a hot, well-pressurized, torrent of water. After a vigorous towelling he dressed in fresh clothing: shirt, jeans, socks and trainers. Last, he slipped his pancake holster and Browning into the small of his back. He felt clean as he went down the stairs.

'Don't you trust us to take care of you?'

'You, you scrofulous old fucker, with my life. The rest of the world … not so sure.'

Fogarty laughed. 'What about your man, Waberthwaite?'

'Him? He gets me to save his sorry ass from time to time.'

'Really?' Tonka said. Sam hadn't noticed him walk in.

'Good trip?'

'Okay.'

'We well protected then?'

'Not bad.'

'Whadaya mean not bad?' Fogarty butted in. 'Fuckin' state of the art, you Limey cocksucker.'

'You're short of a long-rifle, and your police presence is dozy.' Tonka provided calm, clear information.

'You've looked around?'

'Yup. Not much else to do after I got here.'

'A bit sweeping, don't you think?'

'Could have said more. Check out the bumper on that car. What do you see?'

'A sticker.' Fogarty picked up some binoculars. 'Yankee, go home!'

'Dozy.'

'You stuck it there?' Tonka nodded. 'Dozy.'

Fogarty coloured. 'I'll tear them another asshole.'

Sam laughed. 'Peace on earth, Foggy. The key point is we're more vulnerable if we don't know our vulnerabilities.'

'Okay.' The right side of Fogarty's mouth lifted in a lopsided smile. 'What do you propose?

'Put the commander and Tonka together. Let them walk through our security, colleague to colleague.'

'You got it.'

Tonka and Fogarty went off to make introductions. Sam

headed upstairs to call Karen. 'Hi.'

'How's Bob?'

'Irascible as ever. He'd send his love if he knew we were talking.'

'Give him mine. Alice broke her leg this morning.'

'God! How badly?'

'She's got a painful fracture of the tibia just below the knee.'

'What happened?'

'She was playing on the boulders beside the house and fell. Jeannie is upset because they'd been horsing around and she feels partly to blame. The pain Alice went through shocked Jeannie.'

'How's the prognosis?'

'Plaster cast and full recovery. No surgery needed. They're keeping her in until this evening for observation.'

'Poor Al. Give her my love.' They talked on for twenty minutes in their intimate, best-friend way. Chat over, Sam went back downstairs.

* * *

'Your pal Tonka knows his onions.' When Fogarty sounded respectful you could bet he had something to respect.

'Yes, he does.'

'You know him well?'

'Since the Falklands.'

'Only soldiering?'

'Maybe more.'

Fogarty shared a thoughtful glance. 'When your boss, Charlton, said "No Tonka, no Sam" he wasn't fuckin' kidding.'

'He doesn't kid.' Sam shook his head. 'He wants me alive. Cuts and bruises are okay. Dead isn't.'

'I'm starting to feel what you Brits would call a slight chill. *You* show up with a fuckin' minder.'

'You'll not find a better guy for keeping us safe. If we get to fighting you'll be glad he's around.'

'Bit old isn't he?' Fogarty said.

'Younger than you.'

'Okay, okay ...'

'He's still bloody good. He's had my back recently through some gritty stuff.'

'If Charlton wants you alive, there's an obvious corollary, somebody wants you dead.'

'Wrong.' Sam said.

'How so?'

'*Loads* of people want me dead.'

'Over here?'

'You can bet on it. This is the land that invented extreme prejudice.'

'This'll make the travelling around a sight more fuckin' interesting.'

'Awareness is all, and at least I'm officially deceased.'

'The conference venue isn't far from here.'

'Nice road,' Sam said.

'You been this way before?'

'Once or twice.'

'Work or pleasure?'

'I've got family in Vancouver, and friends in Seattle.'

'Who in Seattle?'

'You, ya dumb shit, for one.'

'Watch your mouth.' Sam saw the pleasure in Fogarty's eyes.

'Sorry, I didn't mean to use offensive language.'

'We don't do offensive language in Arbor Heights.'

'Right.'

76

Five people met in a secure room in an EU office block near The Palace of Europe, Strasbourg. The fittings were more luxurious than London. The usual refreshments and snacks were available. Xavier, Gemma Smythsone and three others: a senior member of the IMF, Justine Corlay; an American billionaire, Jack Samson; and a top German security official, Kurt Lederer.

'That business in France was clinical, Kurt. Anton loved your support.'

'Thanks, Xavier.'

'A tidy piece of work,' Smythsone said. 'You accomplished what we could not, one bird with one stone. Time for a quieter life.'

'Sad about Cassanet escaping, still, a quiet life sounds excellent.' Xavier spoke, the sibilance of his voice went well with his reptilian eyes. 'A real pity about your colleagues, Gemma.'

'We couldn't guarantee their discretion. With Forsyth's arrest and involvement in the security breach, his position became untenable. And to discover Jones was to be interrogated by the Met, with her petulence and bluster, didn't bear thinking about.' The ruthless beauty spoke with calm objectivity. 'Someone had to make the call.'

'Will Ms Jones recover?'

'Unlikely. We daren't do more at the moment. We're keeping tabs on the situation. She's still in a coma.'

'What did Kenneth Chen make of this?' Xavier pressed his steepled fingers together in front of his mouth. Behind him wood panelling framed his head. His fleshy lips glistened.

'The bankers agreed the necessity without dissent. The work was arranged by Jim Thomas.'

'Kenneth says he's a good man.' The American spoke with a cultured, warm voice.

'Yes,' Smythsone said. 'He's an excellent fixer. Duncan's death eased his concerns considerably.'

'Who ordered the assassination of the assassin?' Xavier said.

'Not us. Neither Thomas, Marcus nor William know anything. The police have drawn a blank. Intelligence has no idea. We put it down to a grudge in the killing community.'

'A loose end,' Xavier said.

'What do you suggest?' Smythsone remained calm, frosty.

'Nothing. Invisibility from now on is the solution.'

'Agreed.'

'One last thing, Gemma,' Xavier gazed at her, his lizard eyes unblinking. 'The Northern Ireland policeman, what happened to him?'

'He vanished.'

'A hit requested by a colleague in Belfast via London, and sanctioned at a more senior level of the Consortium. I did not agree, but assented. The four men, *four men*, sent to do the task disappeared. No trace.' Smythsone paled.

'Jim requested it and I agreed,' she said, 'Ken discussed it and backed the hit.'

'So we can't blame you.' Xavier's lips twisted up at the side and his moist pink tongue lolled from the corner of his mouth. His power chilled her. His mocking smile made her skin crawl. 'Welcome to the Board. You, Jack,' the American nodded to her, 'and Justine are in the Hotel de Ville. I suggest you settle in, read the papers and we meet again in the morning.'

The meeting ended. The large German and the IMF woman, Justine Corlay, stayed behind with Xavier. Smythsone left with Jack, who was most courteous and friendly.

She let her sexuality do the talking in the car, enough to interest, but not too much. She wanted to assess the lie of the land. Justine radiated power and a certain sense of earthiness she couldn't quite make up her mind about.

77.

The restaurant was Tex-Mex with good beer. Outside, security was barely visible. An attractive woman led the three of them to a pleasant table in the far corner. She went through a memorized list of specials, took an order for drinks and left.

Half an hour later the steaks were going down nicely when four fairly large men came over. The front man had a red nose and plenty of alcohol on board. 'You boys are sitting at our table.'

Fogarty practised his civil tongue. 'I'm sorry, sir. We're nearly done.'

'We want it now!'

'You have a reservation?'

'Don't need one. We want this table.' Alcohol, testosterone and stupidity gleamed from piggy eyes.

The waitress came over, embarrassment on her face. 'Please, gentlemen, our guests are having a pleasant meal. Can I show you to another table?'

'No. This is the one we like, so BUTT OUT.' The shout made her flinch and step back.

Sam felt an adrenalin rush. He turned from the unfolding drama … to an empty chair. Tonka made for the bully.

'Treat the lady with respect and go away, mate. No more warnings.'

'A fuckin' Limey! I mighta known.' Tonka gazed at him. The hard guy took a swing and ended up falling into his three friends, who caught him and pulled him away.

'Nice one, Tonks.'

'Apologies, guys. This is not what we'd expect in Seattle,' Fogarty said.

The waitress came over. 'Gentlemen, I'm so sorry. Those

men are from out of town and getting somewhat lively.'

'No problem, ma'am.' Fogarty smiled at her. 'We'll finish up soon and leave.'

'Where's the restroom, love?' The waitress told Tonka who got up and went across to a door in the wall opposite. The angry man followed him fifteen seconds later.

The server came back. 'Will your friend be okay?'

'You can count on it, ma'am.'

'Everything'll be fine.'

Tonka returned rubbing his hands, picked up his knife and fork and continued eating. No one said anything. The man's friends went into the toilets and came out looking confused and talking. The meal finished pleasantly after a dessert and coffee. When they asked for the bill the waitress spoke to Tonka.

'Sir, did that man cause you a problem in the restroom?'

'No, love.'

'His friends are concerned about him.'

Tonka nodded. 'I'm sure he's fine. Maybe he's lost.'

Bill paid, they left.

In the car as they drove up the hill, Sam spoke up. 'Okay Tonka, put us out of our misery.'

'I helped him channel his aggression into a cupboard for toilet-cleaning equipment. He's sleeping inside it. Give him a couple of hours to wake up and he'll be fine.'

'No broken bones, bleeding or anything else?'

'No.' Tonka didn't even smile.

'Screw him!' Fogarty laughed. His fillings and inlays gleamed as he snorted.

78

After dinner, they began the conversational dance towards an energetic bout of sex. Jack turned out to be a more than adequate lover. He knew the buttons to push, enjoyed give and take, and shared genuine pleasure with a resolute passion. At one point she gave herself over to the stimulation, lost in waves of sensation.

They slept after two hours of breathless, sweaty bliss. Smythsone awakened as the dawn started to colour the sky. Jack's hands explored her body. A moist tongue caressed her neck and she responded with a light touch, pressing her hand gently between their bodies and stroking him. Soon they were engaged in a passionate embrace.

When finished, they dozed. Smythsone lay and thought about the financial probabilities ahead until sleep overtook her.

In the morning Jack said. 'You're fun to be with.'

'You, too.'

'You might as well know Justine and I are an occasional item. It's important to remember one thing, if it comes to the crunch, the business always wins.'

'I'm not sure I completely understand.'

'Okay. You fucked Devlin Forsyth and, when circumstances dictated, you had him killed. That's why we promoted you. Mistakes happen, and we accept that. Generally, there aren't consequences for a screw-up. We only ask for learning and no repetition. Where someone becomes a risk we watch and, at some point, when we're concerned enough, we mitigate the threat.'

'I understand, and accept the need for…' she searched for the right word, 'pragmatism.'

'Excellent! I knew you'd get it. Now, if you don't mind, I'll breakfast alone and catch up on some business. I think we're going to be strong friends.'

'Likewise,' she said, and kissed him on the forehead. She pulled on her dress, picked up her undergarments from the leather Chesterfield settee, and grabbed a lone stocking from a candle-like wall light. She ran her fingers along the wall as she made for the door. The flock wallpaper made her skin tingle. She turned and waved as she left Jack raised his hand in farewell and returned to his reading.

In the shower Smythsone felt powerful, and part of a much higher level in 'the Corporation' as they called it. She walked across the room, switched on the TV and, stood by her unused king-sized bed, working out the remote control. A few presses of the channel button and she was with the BBC.

She sat down and, after a moment, smiled, confident she'd go even farther in this wonderful world of business and more. She enjoyed a sense of scary excitement.

A knock at the door and a maid entered with a tray: croissants, butter and jam with fresh, excellent coffee. *Life is good.*

79

'He's a character.' Fogarty handed Sam a coffee. 'Stuffs a warlike drunk in a cupboard.'

'Best of the best,' Sam said.

'Coming from you, praise indeed. Does he always vanish like that?'

'Yes. He's gone walkabout. Met your guys, didn't he?'

'Sure.'

'He works the security angle constantly when we're on the road. He gets on with it and I feel safe.'

'Okay Sam, tonight sees the jet lag and the hospitality finished. You're here to learn and share. We have three days to prepare a joint report for our masters. We're expecting new arrivals, all here by morning, and then it's down to business.'

'Someone else? Charlton didn't brief me in on that.'

'I guess he wouldn't. She should be here in less than an hour.'

'It'll be good to have a she around.'

'Right,' Fogarty said. 'Tell me about France.'

* * *

Forty-five minutes later people entered the house. Muffled voices echoed. Feet on the stairs. Doors opened and shut. Floors creaked. A toilet flushed.

A lengthy stride came towards the archway. A large African Brit walked in.

'How do you do,' Cal said.

'Hey big man,' Sam said. He stood up, they hugged. 'Can you keep a secret? I'm Calum.'

'I'm part of the information exchange, Calum. They need a police input, so here I am. Charlton told me when I left for the plane.' Cal grabbed Sam in a bear hug.

'That leaves me.' A lean woman, medium height, close-cropped dark hair, dusky skin and amber eyes walked in. She smiled at Sam.

'You?' Sam's eyes widened.

'I'm as safe here as anywhere else, Calum. Any way it's my jigsaw!' Sam walked over and gave her a long hug.

'The world's a dangerous place for us right now. I need to think about things.' The flash in his eyes cooled the smiles on the faces. The air stayed frosty when he left the room.

80

'Calm down.' Charlton made placatory noises.

'Come on, Ben. Why is she here? She was safe in London.'

'She's safe with you.'

'Pull the other one.'

'Right, I can tell we're not going to agree. Let me explain things to you in words of one syllable. Eilidh is remembering. To her, Arran is like a prison. We've had a thorough psychiatric and psychological assessment as recently as two days ago. The time in the US gets heads together and shares intel. Who has key knowledge, central to this whole thing? Your sister.'

'Why send her out here?'

'Why not? She's an adult. She's getting better. She's desperately concerned for you, your family and how you've been dragged into this.'

'Come on, Ben. You have kids.'

'Stop the emotional stupidity. I have a job to do. We are on the trail of a major criminal conspiracy which costs us hundreds of millions of pounds a year. Include the USA and Europe and we're talking billions.

'Okay,' Sam said.

'The money isn't going into education and welfare. It's being stolen. The trail mustn't go cold. We need what Eilidh knows and the strength of good investigators. The Yanks are right behind us and sending top people. Europe is coming along. The French episode shows how close we're getting to the cabal, and the assets they bring to bear to harm us.'

'Okay.'

'Where you are in Seattle is a particularly secure area. Calvin Martin took a protector role on the way over, that's your job now, Calum. The military will fly you back. I'm doing everything possible to protect her, and you, and get the job done.'

'Okay, Ben.' Sam's sigh hissed from the phone. 'I hear you. She's a strong-willed lassie. Right now she's doing a righteous thing.'

'And, she has experienced the dark and dirty side of this business as well, and she's still up for it.'

'True. I suppose I've got to accept things as they are.'

'I spoke to your wife about this. She understands and agrees. I can do no more.'

'Thanks.'

'We knew you'd fight this tooth and nail. Better a fait accompli.'

A big inward sigh echoed, followed by, 'Yeah.'

'Not much different to your chat with Molloy. So get with the programme.'

'Will do, sir.' Sam shook his head and hung up.

81

The knock at his door was barely audible. He opened and met Eilidh's concerned gaze. She blinked back tears. He pulled her into the room and pushed her gently into a seat beside a small table.

'I had to come.'

'I understand. Please don't go getting yourself killed.'

'Fat chance of that with you, Tonka and that man Fogarty around.'

'What about Cal?'

'He's too much fun to be a killer.'

'Like me?'

'You know what I mean.'

'Yeah.' *Ouch.*

She held up a memory stick. 'Guess what this is!'

'Your notes?'

'No, the summary I gave to Jamie, my editor. My memory is coming back.' She drifted away and her eyes lost focus. 'Sometimes the man Ned crashes into my head, and I feel his hands and cruelty.'

'Ned, I hear, has been found, and is under arrest.'

'Go on.'

'Best ask Cal. He's the policeman.' Another knock at the door and Tonka walked in.

'Dinner's ready.'

82

The American team moved in during the day and with them Fritz, Martijn and Mo.

In the morning, large dark MPVs arrived about every five minutes. Three people entered each one and left followed by an unmarked car.

Fogarty and Sam would travel with Eilidh.

'The Secret Service is supervising this. The President wants results and no interference with the good guys.'

'So protective resources are in place?'

'Sure are. We're heading down to a secure building about half a mile beyond the restaurant we ate in last night. We're safe as can be here. All arrivals and departures are low-key. We've got three days. Comm-links are being set up for each-way data transfer.'

'Big show,' Sam said, 'what's to go wrong?'

'Just about anything, Sam.' Fogarty didn't do irony. 'You're as familiar with this world as I am.'

'The enemy is bound to get a whiff.'

'Yeah. I think we're okay right now. Five days is running near the edge for me.'

'Risk, reward. A big attack is too high profile.' Sam's voice was cool and serious. 'In their shoes, I'd take pictures and track people. I'd find levers and intel. Divide and rule. I'd turn anyone I can, and kill folk who stray from safety.'

'This is a tough business.'

'It's a dark art, buddy, *a dark art*.'

'Here comes Eilidh. She's lovely.'

'Isn't she? Time to lighten up.'

'Hi, Eilidh,' Fogarty spoke with genuine warmth.

'Hiya, sleep well?' Sam said.

‘I slept fine until a sparrow farted and today’s agenda grabbed my mind. Is this what they call hardball?’

‘No, love, it’s the warm-up. You’ve had a wee flavour of hardball. I hope you’re not around if we play it.’ Sam turned away so she couldn’t see his fear for her. ‘Car’s here. Best be off.’

83

The meeting ran on. 'Fritz Rosenkrantz left Berlin yesterday. We tracked him into the USA, and he disappeared,' Xavier said, his wet lisp making his words juicy.

'Nothing unusual. Spooks often disappear for meetings.' Jack's voice oozed calm.

'The Dutchman went, as well.'

'So?'

'They are survivors of the French situation, wrong place, right time,' Xavier said.

'You think there's a link?' Gemma said.

'Maybe.'

'Where is the Dutchman?'

'Vancouver,' Xavier said.

'They might not be together.' Jack said.

'I'm concerned. A policeman from London went over to the USA around the same time. He is involved in our case. He vanished at Newark. Three people with connections, however tenuous, travelling in a similar timeframe makes me edgy.'

'What action are you taking?' Gemma said.

'I have spoken to a colleague in America. We are awakening an asset in the US Secret Service,' Xavier said.

'When do you expect news?'

'One day, maybe two.'

'And until then?' Gemma said.

'Patience.' Xavier nodded. 'Patience wins prizes.'

84

The conference started exactly at eight-thirty. People stood up, identified themselves and their role. Name tags gleamed. The programme was reviewed, tweaked and quickly agreed.

The event set-up was excellent. The meeting room had high ceilings and good air-conditioning. The walls were covered in large paper sheets for listing and discussion. Two note-takers worked on keyboards. The video and audio recording lights came on during sessions. A range of snacks and drinks covered several tables along the far wall, always on hand. Big screens were available for presentations and video replay.

They kicked off at pace. Fogarty took the role of facilitator, he called shots and raised issues. Key players presented an outline summary of their story, using standard outlining and presentation software. This formed the basis for interrogation by colleagues and the later integration of data.

Threads started to emerge. Within a couple of hours work was going nicely. Eilidh fitted in with an ease she attributed to the grillings Jamie, her editor, had given her as she developed her story. She began to understand how professional his approach had been.

Until now much of the intel had relied on inference and intercepted information. They turned to Eilidh.

* * *

Her story began with her arrival in London, and coincided with the paper's decision to have her coached by a seasoned reporter, Wally Hackman. They got on well.

He provided her with stories of corruption and misdeeds. Some he could prove, but couldn't proceed with for legal reasons, or to avoid exposing sources. Gradually, under his guidance, with her fresh eyes, she pieced together coincidences, interconnecting events, little snippets of information related to them, and the names of people involved.

Next, she made calls with the help of her friend and mentor. She started to build a list of contacts who were concerned enough to talk. She went to meetings, informative emails appeared and notes arrived.

By the time she had been plugging away for eighteen months, the story was tangible and taking on a life of its own. Then her coach took early retirement. His smoking and drinking had taken a heavy toll. He kept in touch, remained helpful and full of commitment. She had seen him two days before she disappeared.

'We need to stop you for a second, Eilidh,' Fogarty said. 'This old hack, is he still alive?'

'Yes, as far as I know.'

'Chief Inspector Martin, can you arrange protection?'

'Of course, Mr Fogarty. Give me a moment.' He rose, went over to Eilidh, took contact details, left the room and returned in moments. The buzz of conversation stopped as Cal looked over to Fogarty. 'Already done, he's been in protective custody for several weeks.'

'Efficient, Chief Inspector, efficient. Let's get back to it.

* * *

They valued Eilidh's contribution. It added a sense of qualitative texture, supported by detail, facts and time lines. She became a frequent focus. Her evidence about the civil servant who audited the letting of contracts brought the room to complete silence.

'What did you think you were finding, Eilidh?'

'Proof that many suspicious contracts bumping along at the very top of acceptable pricing are not only questionable, but almost certainly corrupt and fraudulent.' The interrogation continued.

'Drug smuggling, as well?'

'Yes.' She told them of the ports where large loads of drugs were being let through. 'Some contacts were scared—one in particular—he and his family were killed in a ...' Her face twitched, her mouth pinched and her eyebrows pulled together, 'car crash last week.' She lurched backwards, shaking, and wept, wiping tears with jerky hands.

'Get her out of here,' Fogarty said. Cal walked over and led her out. She turned a tear-streaked face to "Calum".

'I'll be out in a few minutes.'

The door closed silently behind them.

'May I speak?'

Fogarty nodded. 'Calum.'

'I'm involved in Eilidh's protection. She was taken by some nasty people less than two months ago. They drugged and abused her,' he shook his head, 'but made the mistake of not killing her. She was rescued in a fire-fight by her brother who was in the service. He was killed recently. She's recovering from a nightmare few of us could handle. The last question pushed a painful button. I'm sure she'll be fine. She needs a short break from this intensity.'

Fogarty called time. Conversation started straight away as people rose, talked, went to the bathroom, topped up coffees and made new acquaintances. The buzz was business-like, without much laughter. After some networking, transport came and people melted away.

They returned to the house in Arbor Heights.

* * *

The psychiatric nurse from Arran was in a downtown hotel in case Eilidh had problems. A car left to collect her. Eilidh was already pretty well back together and nearing the end of a chat with Sam.

'Sometimes I have a flashback, and then I'm in two realities. It's so scary thinking this might be the dream and not the other. There's the cat, Ned and a weird woman. Mostly I get an early warning and can stand up, move around … anything. I was concentrating so hard in the meeting and trying not to remember John, the Customs guy. He and his family were killed a week ago, just as he feared, in a suspicious car accident. He was so scared. Then I slipped sideways, and Ned was feeling my boobs.'

'Ned won't trouble you again, Eilidh,' Sam said.

She looked at him. 'How do you know?'

'He confessed to imprisoning you and molesting you. Someone put the frighteners on him. He's going to do time.'

'You?'

'Couldn't possibly comment. I told you to talk to Cal.'

She smiled and nodded. *Some big brother.*

The phone rang. Sam picked up. 'The nurse is here. I'm off until she goes.'

Eilidh nodded. 'See you.'

85

Shirl, Eilidh's flatmate, arrived home, late as usual.

Because of the age of the building, dim lighting illuminated the stairs to the flat. The working hours in Accident and Emergency, as a lowest of the low doctor, took its toll. She shuffled up two flights with a soothing bath in mind. Shopping hung from both arms. Her pack weighed a ton.

Key in the lock she pushed into the apartment, put on the light, turned into the hall and met a man with a small crowbar in his rubber-gloved hand. She screamed. Arms full she couldn't even lift her hands to protect herself. He struck her in the area of the temple, about level with her left eye. She collapsed like a sack of potatoes, a spurt of blood splatting on the skirting board, and moved like someone trying to pedal a bike in an uncoordinated way. Dimly aware, she sensed another blow coming.

'Don't hit her again.' A loud whisper stopped the movement. 'One more'll kill her.'

'She's not supposed to be here. Where was the warning?' He checked his phone. 'No bleedin' signal.'

A puddle of blood started to form under Shirl's head. She moaned.

'What a clatter when she went down. We better leg it.'

The two men ran into the hall and knocked an elderly neighbour straight back on to her bottom, as she came to investigate. Shaken, she pulled herself to her feet in painful increments and slid along the wall, hands skimming behind her. Reaching the door she found Shirl and cried out, first in distress and next for help. Shirl bled on to the parquet flooring, jerking and unconscious. The old woman found a towel and supported the young doctor's head. Blood spurted to her heart's rhythm from the wound. She pressed the towel against the flow. Another resident arrived, called an ambulance and police, and applied a compress to the injury. Her ancient neighbour sat down in a chair by the phone table.

Shirl's prompt arrival at the hospital she'd left barely an hour before saved her life. Shocked colleagues, who she'd left barely an hour before, began the fight for her life.

Within twenty minutes a neurosurgeon was operating. Three hours later, she was in the High Dependency Unit.

86

Eilidh sat in a corner of the lounge sipping a green tea, her mules parked at the side of the chair, feet tucked beneath her. A dark skirt and a bright floral blouse matched her new skin and hair colour. The shortness of the cut showed her pixie ears and the artistic shape of her head. The false amber of her eyes gleamed bright in her angelic face. Some of men, and one of the women, were taking a serious interest in her. Being fancied raised her spirits. They had fifteen minutes to go before the final session started on the second day.

"Calum" walked in, checked out the crowd and came over, a large mug of tea in hand. His jeans, white tee under a blue striped casual shirt, gun in pancake holster and the trainers made him appear American, but he didn't sound like one. His beard actually suited him, she thought, and the solid muscular power of his physique was evident as he moved towards her. He sat down in an easy chair close by, elbows on knees, beaker in his right hand. He gazed at her and nodded, but no smile. A butterfly fluttered in her stomach. She paled.

'Some bad news I'm afraid, Eilidh,' he said. 'Shirl was attacked at your flat about four hours ago. She's out of the operating theatre and the prognosis is good. DCI Swindon thinks she walked in on a search for something. No niceties: just tore into everything and ferreted about. Your room is a war zone. The rest of the place is trashed.'

'At least Shirl sounds okay.'

'You have an elderly neighbour.'

'Ida.' Eilidh wobbled in her seat and went even paler. Her eyes moistened, she blinked. Her lips twitched.

'She got knocked over by the burglars when she responded to Shirl's scream. She called for help, made Shirl comfortable, sat down and had a heart attack.' He sounded calm, composed and gentle in his sympathy.

'She's dead?'

'No. When they spoke to her, after the ambulance men arrived, they twigged she was having a coronary. She's in intensive care I'm afraid, it's touch and go.'

Eilidh sat upright as tears of relief and anger splashed down her face. Sam gestured, offering a hug. She held up her hand to hold him off. 'Lovely old Ida. We visit, twenty minutes now and then, a cup of tea. She bakes biscuits and cakes for us. Every couple of weeks we have a girls' Sunday lunch: a couple of sherries each and a bottle of wine.' She pulled a tissue from her pack and dried her eyes, her gaze became resolute. 'We've a job to do. I could do with that hug now.' Sam could feel her drawing strength from him. 'At least some people are surviving the battle.'

'Persistent bastards.'

'Aren't we?' She giggled.

87

The background work proved useful. Molloy was relentless in his questioning of Jamie Carron, Eilidh's editor from London.

Despite Carron's protestations about sources and such, Molloy wore him down. They even talked about the last meeting between Eilidh and Carron before she was taken.

'Excellent stuff, Mr Molloy, she's a great investigator and thorough thinker,' Carron said. 'She put a great story together and backed it up.'

At last Molloy believed he had pieced together as much as he thought he could without damaging Carron. To go further he needed the main resources from Eilidh's cache of information.

He emailed a brief headline report to Charlton. Twenty minutes later he received a call.

'Ben Charlton here, Mr Molloy. Thanks for your report, excellent stuff. It's supporting some other work we're involved in.'

'Thanks, Mr Charlton.'

'I'm going to pop over tomorrow and meet you. I'll confirm the time later. Thanks again.' The call ended as abruptly as it began.

88

When Eilidh entered, the group stood and applauded her. She gave a shy appreciative smile, nodded her thanks. Everyone took their places, knowing something had happened, buzzing with expectancy.

Fogarty walked over. 'You've had tough news, Eilidh.' Her face twitched but she kept control and nodded. 'Please share it, if you can.' He turned to the group, 'Say folks, give me your attention.' A hush settled on the company. 'I want you to understand what we're up against.' The pause was theatrical. 'Eilidh's had some bad news. I've asked her to tell us, so bear with her.'

Sam understood Fogarty's aim, understood and wasn't too comfortable as he watched Eilidh get it together. 'My flat … my apartment was raided around the time we finished yesterday. My flatmate, a young doctor, is just out of emergency surgery for a severe head injury. They think she walked in on the … ah … perps. Our dear friend, an eighty-four year old neighbour, went to her, got knocked over, still managed to save my friend's life and then had a heart attack.'

She paused, face pinched with anger. 'Two people I love …' blowing her nose helped, 'fighting for their lives because of what we are finding out, and the evil bastards who want to stop us.' Her rage added an electric surge to her last few words. 'I'll find and deliver the missing intel. I'll help get more. I will be a resource for uncovering and exposing these evil swine. I want to solve this for Shirl. God I hope she's okay and Ida, God bless her, the sweetest, most gentle person I ever met.' She dabbed her eyes. The audience sat quiet. 'Now let's get going.'

'You heard the lady,' Fogarty said.

They returned to business with ever more coherence

emerging. They examined the past for hints and connections. The value of her cache of evidence created excitement. The timeline and records had massive importance. Events and content were structured, as the data gurus pieced together her living jigsaw, and continued to interconnect other corroboration and occurrences. After four hours the pace started to flag.

'Okay people, take a break. See you in the morning,' Fogarty said. After a collective yawn and stretch, the buzz started as people drifted away.

* * *

Far from suffering nightmares and more flashbacks, Eilidh responded to the process with greater clarity and a gradual sense of healing.

89

In Brussels a secure communication provided partial information about the meeting. Names were not available yet, apart from intel pointing at a high-powered group involving serious players. In a classy office a pair of wet Cupid's bow lips became a straight hard line. Xavier picked up a secure phone.

'It's too slow. Why can't we get more information? What do you mean too risky? We have to know more so we can do some weeding over here.'

'I'm sorry. A leak from here, just now, is far too likely to be intercepted or traced back or both. Be patient.' His American contact said.

Xavier bridled but said nothing. *Bloody Yank!* They talked and made plans. 'Fast as you can then. Tomorrow at the latest, when the conference ends.'

'And the Brits?'

'Leave them to me.'

90

Next morning, the final few hours of Eilidh's story unfolded. In the flow of facts, patterns emerged, and with them, corroboration from unconnected sources. Eilidh was central to much of the discussion. Her confidence grew and, with the sharing, her memory, as she spoke and responded to questioning.

'How did you find out about the connection to the contractual issues in the USA?' an intense man asked.

'I received information from a contact in Internal Audit in a UK Government department, which handles a lot of procurement. My source developed a list of "usual suspects" as part of routine checks. She logged them for over a year and concluded no one was really interested, and was thinking about stopping right around the time I met her.'

'Why no interest?'

'Probably culture as much as anything. The job is to collect the information, not necessarily use it.'

'How did she find you?'

'We were put together by an unknown person who left my contact details with her.'

'An unknown person?'

'Yes. I had half a dozen or more similar events, plus the networking effect of being given names and phone numbers, and so on.'

'How many people would you say are in your network?'

'Around fifteen directly communicating, and about the same remaining anonymous. Some came and went, others provided leaks in the form of copy documents, reference lists and even URLs of files that are, or were, publicly available,' Eilidh said.

'Any log-ins?'

'Log-ins?'

'Secure links to Intranets, and that sort of thing.'

'Might have been, I don't recall.'

'We're digressing, Ms Duncan. You were asked about the links to the USA. Could you go back to that please?'

'The connection came through my contact producing a list of suspicious contracts.'

'How many?'

'150–200.'

'In how long?'

'Twelve to fifteen months.'

'What else?' Fogarty pressed hard.

'Contracts, contractors, consultants, suppliers, budgets, budget comparison.'

'Just the suspicious contracts?'

'No, Foggy.' The people laughed. In that moment, Eilidh blushed and gave a little girl smile. 'Mr Fogarty, sorry. I received a full comparative analysis.'

'Tell me more.' Fogarty stayed with the focus.

'Contracts are categorized. For example, type, code, cost, timescale, etcetera. These are then subcategorized into other relevant headings, with an eye to comparison and audit.'

'Useful?'

'My contacts thought so.'

'More than one contact?' Fogarty asked.

She paused and looked upwards, thinking 'Seven, now you mention it, all using similar software in different settings.'

'Did they know each other?'

'Not to my knowledge.' Eilidh's eyes flashed. 'You're aware of the journalistic code, Mr Fogarty. Never reveal sources.'

'Yes, I am.' He paused. 'So, you're saying the information was similar but from independent sources.'

'Correct.'

'What were they doing with the information?'

'They call it "cross-correlation". Any category can be used as a criterion for a data query. New queries can be designed and used to examine the data.'

'Please give an example.'

'Okay. One audit started to show a complex connection between some contracts. One I recall was the supply of specialist equipment to around forty major projects. Under detailed scrutiny they learned that two or three supplier firms charged triple the days of consultancy for the same type of contract. Raw materials were supplied at roughly five per cent over the norm. Other costs and figures proved the excess was running at between eight and ten per cent over a typical value.'

'About how much was the worth of the contracts your sources were talking about?'

'I think about £4 billion.'

'Mmm, around 300 to 400 million pounds sterling, being misappropriated, would you say?'

'Yes, averaging over four years, and on a small percentage of contracts, more as the business grows.'

'Were any names mentioned outside of your informant confidentiality?'

'One springs to mind because he was talked of as a sort of hero by at least two of the people, and I heard him mentioned in other situations. I'll mention the person privately to the Agency. They can decide how to proceed.'

'Thanks.'

91

'Our usual man Quentin has disappeared on family business. That's why you'll have to make do with me for an introductory chat.' Charlton said. *Chat?* Molloy found the interview with Charlton as hard as any he'd ever had. Charlton left promising to sort out a place for Molloy at Westferry Road.

* * *

'He shared names, places and events with pretty decent recall, Indira.' I've emailed you a note on the information.'

'Thanks Mr Charlton.'

'You can call me Ben, you know.'

'I can't, sir, it's a culture thing.' Indira said.

'Very well. I'll talk you through a summary.'

'Thank you, sir.'

'Our friend Pete Molloy became suspicious of certain events in Belfast. That Jim Thomas fellow was involved,' Charlton said.

'Part of the plot started in Northern Ireland?' Indira said.

'Perhaps. Molloy uncovered grounds for a more pointed investigation, and Sergeant Molloy, as he was at the time, was given permission to arrange a covert operation using a small team. Sam Duncan was involved as a link to military intelligence. The set-up was informal and quite secret. Duncan met the people a few times but, as they were out gathering information, the intensity of contact was low.'

'So, Molloy was suspicious, running a discreet operation to gather facts, and someone had allowed Sam to get involved.'

'Yes. At that stage, Sam hadn't met Molloy, due to illness on Molloy's part.'

'Right, sir, where is this leading?'

'The police team was assassinated.'

'But not Molloy.'

'No, he ended up in a stand-off with shady people, as we discovered recently. He was warned off, protected and let it pass. And by the sound of things, didn't forgive himself, either.'

'And Sam?'

'He got the jump on a man sent to kill him. Molloy followed Sam to try, at least, to protect him. He saw the assassin make his move but was too far away to intervene. He watched our man's moves. He has a powerful respect for Sam.'

'Bottom line?'

'A strand of this conspiracy and corruption is rooted firmly in the Troubles. There are people and factions amongst our Celtic cousins who are complicit in this situation.'

92

Bob Fogarty facilitated with an interrogator's awareness and pointed focus. The grilling went on. The avoidance of Customs raised eyebrows. Between contracts and contraband, the scale of the money involved was so large as to be almost inconceivable. The idea of the Bizz concept as a growing international organization astonished people.

Links and interconnections emerged and were pulled together. Sam watched with quiet consternation as a picture became clearer in mind maps, lists and graphs on large screens, covering different aspects. The eight 'focus' screens surrounding a summary on a big central display were filling up. It made sense with terrifying clarity.

'You're looking thoughtful, Calum. Get the picture?' Fogarty dragged him in.

'Only too well. Huge resources, vast growth potential and zero public awareness,' Sam said.

'So how do we break in?'

'I bet you experts have ideas.' People nodded, some pursed their lips, as they thought about the information they had heard and seen. 'Imagine, an invisible coup d'état by simply transferring all our money to the banks, corporations and politicians. Just like we're doing already, come to think of it. They're stealing our souls.'

'Bad people.' Fogarty nodded.

'These are vicious, corrupt, killers. My take is they're learning their craft. If we don't interdict them within the next few months, they'll be bloody hard to find, and even harder to stop.'

'Your Prime Minister, our President, the Chancellor of Germany, the presidents of France and the Netherlands and other major European countries want this fixed. We will fix it,' Fogarty said. He looked at the group. 'You got half an hour to eat and get back here.'

The session broke up.

They stopped for the day after another eight hours. The data people kept working, geared to continue overnight if necessary. The next morning would see the plenary session and the conference concluded by lunch time.

* * *

In London, Indira worked with the data and time frames as they arrived from Seattle. She linked these with Jamie Carron's evidence and parts of Charlton's subsequent interrogation of Molloy. She cat-napped, when she had to.

Archives and intelligence produced ever more supporting information and links into the British Establishment. Key trusted operatives and officials were questioned by members of the team, with further connections established.

Names were attached to events and a handful of very senior people had question marks placed over them. A data extract was transmitted to the USA where crunching continued. The data work would carry on after 'the Seattle Summit', as the participants called it, ended.

93

Sam, Eilidh, and Fogarty arrived back in the lounge at Arbor Heights. Cal said goodbye an hour earlier, as they left the conference building. He flew to London via Chicago.

Everyone seemed happy. Eilidh received over thirty business cards and was assigned an American guardian as far as the airport. Sam remained 'Calum Smart' to the group. Fogarty thought the handle was witty and kept saying: no such thing as a smart Calum.

Sam, Eilidh and Fogarty eased into confortable chairs in a corner of the lounge. The buzz of other residents was more or less gone. 'Okay folks, the conference is over.' Fogarty said. 'You have one more day here, and then you go home. The delay avoids any association with the people who stayed here for the summit.'

'We're to fly back through Dublin via Paris. Charlton decided the risk is not severe, and we needn't have the expense of military flights. We'll have your man Harpur with us as far as SeaTac.' Sam said.

'He trained as a SEAL,' Eilidh said, 'he fancies me and I'm warming to him.'

'I'm supposed to be impressed?' Sam said. 'It's the jewel of Scotland we're talking about here. The man isn't good enough for you.'

'Stop it, you big lug. No man will ever be good enough for me.'

'Dead right, lassie. These Yanks think they know a thing or two, but they bear watching. We need to be sure you don't end up being the protector.'

'Fuck off, Calum!' Fogarty chuckled.

'All this talking has made me hungry,' Eilidh said.

'Go find your walrus, young lady, and we'll head down to the diner at the bottom of the hill. Their grub is good, the beer is cold and the waitresses are passing fair.' They grinned at Sam. 'And Tonka makes people vanish in the restroom.'

Tonka walked in and stood near the archway, face impassive.

'Let's go somewhere we aren't known. We became memorable last time.' Sam said.

'Right, there's a Mexican down there too,' Fogarty said.

Sam looked at Tonka. 'Excuse me, my man wants a word.'

94

'Got the twitch, Tonks?' They were in the kitchen.

'Too right. All the key players are gone except for a girl who has a lot more information to share on the links to a major criminal network, politicians and corrupt businesses. Something's wrong. I smell it, mate.'

'Okay, I hear you.'

'The police are down to a couple of patrol cars. The layout of this place makes it almost indefensible without several teams of sound people.' Tonka said.

'We're exposed.'

'More, as time passes,' Tonka said. 'Are you sure about Fogarty?'

'We've spent hard time together. Iraq and other stuff in the Far East and Europe. I've got him out of the mire a couple of times, he saved my neck one time.'

'And if I take him out?'

'Big call, Tonks. Gimme your logic.'

'I've been walk about. The security is all but gone. There are two big SUVs left with around six people. The snipers left about twenty minutes ago.'

'So, we've two options, go for a meal and take our chances; stay here and almost certainly have a firefight.' Sam said.

'That's my assessment. Of course I could be wrong, in which case we'll look bloody stupid.'

'And Fogarty?'

'It has to be your call, Sam.'

'Usual signal.'

'Tough one mate.'

'Let's see what he says. If it gets to shove, protect Eilidh at all costs.'

Tonka nodded.

95

'What's happening?' Eilidh said.

'Concerns about security and eating out. Tonka's a bit wary,' Sam turned, 'Foggy?'

'As long as we stay in Arbor Heights, Sam, we're covered.'

'Even now?' Sam said.

'Especially now. The cover is intense, a local blanket. Want to stay here and order in some pizzas or a Chinese?'

'Not celebratory enough, I'm for a restaurant.' Sam said.

'Me too,' Eilidh said.

'Waberthwaite see the shift handover? It maybe concerned him unnecessarily,' Fogarty said, 'let me have a word with him. Where is he?'

'The kitchen.'

Fogarty left the room.

'What do you think, Sam?'

'Trust Tonka, Eilidh.'

'Fogarty?'

'Tonka calls it for me.'

Fogarty returned. 'We're okay. We're agreed. Dinner at the Mexican, it's still in Arbor Heights. He's checking a few things.'

'I don't know what you said to him, Fogarty, but he looks comfortable enough.' Sam said.

'We've got a car load of guys coming down the road behind us.'

'Many of the people going, with their guards and support, are bound to raise antennae. He's a sound professional doing his job.'

'You're right.'

They schmoozed for a while until Tonka returned.

'Happy then, Tonka?' Sam said.

Tonka nodded his head, 'The cover's fine, I've been worrying about nothing.' He smiled. Sam's heart sank.

'There you go,' Sam said. 'You were right, Foggy, as usual. I'll just pop out and splash my boots, then we can get some eats.' He stepped out rubbing his hands together.

'You safety conscious men,' Eilidh said. 'I'm so safe. You've got a nice smile, Tonka, you should use it more often.'

96

'That's one mother of a hot chilli, it's making my nose run.' Fogarty said.

'Hot food and cold beer, a hell of a mixture.' Sam said. They were at a large round six-seater table.

Tonka's coat lay on a chair. He ate, eyes roving, as he made brief but pleasant conversation.

Eilidh yawned. 'Well big man,' she turned to Sam, 'this trip's been worthwhile, I'm much better, especially with Shirl out of danger.'

'You're looking good too.

'Thanks.'

'So Brad, whatever his name is, the walrus, fancies you.'

'Navy SEAL.'

'Wimps compared to Tonka.'

'Oh stop it, you big so and so. He gave me a business card and wants me to keep in touch.'

'I thought you weren't doing that with anyone while we were here,' Sam said.

'So did I, but I fancy him back.' Her eyes sparkled. 'What's a girl to do?'

'Keep a low profile for now.'

'Why? He's inside the tent,' Eilidh said.

'Who says he can pee straight?'

She giggled and leaned back in her chair with a pout. 'Trust you, Sam.'

'Also, where do people peeing out of a tent pass wind? I should know, I've been a victim of that many times. Two of the culprits are with us right now.' She giggled some more.

* * *

Tonka left the table to find the restroom. He carried his coat.

Fogarty joined in the banter. Soon they were all laughing.

'Where's that dour minder of yours?' Fogarty glanced at Sam.

'Washing his hands.'

'I'll go find him.'

'No. Don't do that, Foggy,' Sam said.

'What's up?'

'We're not comfortable.' Sam's eyes were cool. 'Stay put. Hands on the table.'

'Calum?' Fogarty did a fine display of puzzlement.

Eilidh glanced nervously at each in turn.

'Sorry, my man smells something, and he has a good nose.'

'Where is he?'

'Walkabout.'

* * *

Tonka returned from the washroom area. 'What news?' Sam said.

'No protectors. We're alone.'

Fogarty paled. 'God. Jesussss!'

'They were there when I popped out. Then the large blond guy, one of your team Fogarty, the one with the twisted nose ...'

'Augie. The bastard.'

'He drove up in a blue ford and spoke to them. Our guys questioned him, but he was persuasive. They left.'

'So, no car, no cover, and a big hill to climb,' Sam said. 'Nothing like a spot of exposure to get the juices flowing.'

'We can't go back,' Fogarty said. 'It's probable they've stood the whole security team down, told 'em we've left town, and are waiting to kill us. Augie, for Christ's sake!'

'Betrayal hurts,' Sam said. His eyes were hard.

'Like a wasp sting.' Fogarty sat silent for a moment.

'What about our stuff?' Eilidh said.

'We've got what we stand up in,' Sam said 'You armed Fogarty?' A nod. 'Got the wee warrior, Tonks?' Tonka nodded.

'And a Sig,' Tonka added.

'I'm packing. How about money?'

'Three hundred,' Fogarty said.

'Fifteen hundred.' The corners of Tonka's mouth lifted in a quick movement. 'Emergencies come, and you never know.'

'Twenty-five,' Eilidh said. 'Girls expect the old men to pay.'

'Around four-fifty for me,' Sam said. 'So we've cash to get moving.'

'There's holes-in-the-wall all over the place.'

'Right, Eilidh, and each one is a tattle-tale. Every time we use one they'll be on to us,' Fogarty said.

Eilidh got up and went to the bar, spoke briefly and came back.

'Whose card will they be tuned in to?'

'Mine for sure,' Fogarty said.

'Mine, too, and yours is likely, Eilidh.'

'What I'm thinking is this,' Eilidh said, 'the people who are after us know we are here. You say we have half an hour or so before they expect us to leave.' The men nodded.

'What's on your mind?' Sam said.

'This building is a saw-tooth design, with a cash machine at the end of the first tooth. I noticed it when we came in, because I've been getting low. It's almost hidden from the road.'

'Okay and ...?'

'My daily limit is five hundred. Yours may be more. Let's get cash while we're known to be here.'

'Good idea, but if we all do it, we'll tip them off.'

'I have a company card,' Tonka said. 'It shouldn't be traceable outside our own people. It makes sense here. I should be able to get another five grand, if there's enough cash in the machine.' He stood and went to the front door. He was back in five minutes. 'Another five grand.'

'Good thinking, Eilidh.' Sam said.

'There's a watcher up the car park. Give me a couple of minutes.' He left.

Fogarty, Eilidh and Sam glanced at each other, as Tonka went back to the restroom. A waitress came over. 'Is everything okay, sir?' She looked at Fogarty.

'Absolutely fine, miss. Our friend is having a touch of digestive trouble. He had to go again. He'll be back soon. Thanks for your concern. Could we see the dessert menu, please?'

The server went off to get the menus.

* * *

Tonka returned and nodded.

Sam raised an eyebrow. 'Sorted.' Tonka said. 'We have an HK 416 ten inch at the door. There are two cars in the car park. The Acura is started and ready to go. We must leave now.'

'No time for coffee?' Sam said.

'What's an HK, Sam?' Eilidh said.

'A Heckler and Koch submachine gun.' She glanced at him, awareness growing. 'The watcher,' Sam nodded.

Tonka shook his head. 'Pay and move,' He went back towards the restrooms.

'I'll settle up.' Sam said and signalled the waitress. She came over.

'Your poor friend.'

'He's not getting better,' Sam said, 'We're parked in the parking area out back. Can we go out the exit? He needs to sit quickly, if you get my drift.'

'Poor man. Of course, sir. Use the fire exit. Just push the bar.'

'Thanks. My friends will go get him and we'll be off. I'll come with you and pay.'

The others made for the back exit. Sam walked over to the counter and paid $180 for the food, with a $30 tip in cash.

'Thank you so much, sir.'

'Thanks for a great meal. I'm sorry we have to go like this,' Sam said.

'I hope we'll see you again soon.'

'We're staying up near 100th Street, and I'm sure we'll be back. Thanks very much.' A 100-watt smile and he left. 'Good night.' On the way out he picked up the HK, checked the magazine, safety and rounded the corner ready to go.

The car came up lights off: an estate. Tonka got out of the driver's side. 'You drive, Fogarty. I'll take the back seat. Eilidh, in the back, lie flat and stay down. We may have to shoot over you. Fogarty, open the windows.'

97

Sam sat in the front, 'let's go.'

'Roger.' Tonka's voice, calm as ever.

'We're off. Fogarty, you know the terrain. Where should we go?'

'Out of the parking lot and turn right. The faster we can get across the city the better.'

Two muzzle flashes flared as they pulled out, the bullets missed. A man with a pistol stood in a braced position on the opposite pavement. The blast of Tonka's mini-assault rifle in the car hurt their ears. The shooter bounced backwards, fell half over the front of his car and rolled on to the road. Apart from a briefly arched back, he didn't move.

'So far, so good. We need to get rid of this car, soon.' Fogarty said.

'Where now?' Sam said.

'First right ...' They drove at the legal limit, following the road round and taking a right again. 'That takes us back in the direction of the restaurant, but higher up. When we get to California Street we'll hang a slight left and then second left.'

'Good you know the area.' Sam said.

'We want to lose ourselves in the smaller streets.'

They moved steadily, but not too quickly.

'How long before they have an APB on us?' Sam said.

'Depends on how fast they react to gunfire. Maybe the owner won't miss this auto, so the number may not get out for a while. I think we should assume no more than fifteen minutes before we change.' They turned on to a curving street. 'I've got a route in mind. We'll straighten up soon. Stay on this road and we'll come to a mall in about three-quarters of a mile.' They passed two police cars rushing in the opposite direction, lights flashing. They continued without hurry or attracting attention.

'That was quick.' Sam said.

'May not be us,' Fogarty said. 'The road twists because of the hills around here.' Fogarty said. 'When we get to the mall, we can find a quiet place to park, dump the car and grab a coffee.'

'Fine time to be thinking about coffee, Foggy.' Sam said.

'There's a book store where we're going, we can wait there while action man,' Fogarty jerked his thumb at Tonka, 'finds a car to take us the next few miles.' They drove into the Mall car park.

'One of you needs to get into that leisure store,' Tonka said, 'and buy a couple of matt-surfaced, dark sports bags, different brands.'

Eilidh asked Sam for some money, jumped out of the car and headed for the shop. Sam put the HK behind his seat and followed her about ten paces back, entering the store behind her. They were back in five minutes.

'What are you going to do?' Fogarty said.

'Explore and find a quiet way out of here,' Tonka said. 'While I'm doing that you people can come up with a plan. The bookshop will have maps and things. Use 'em. I'll dump the car away from here and wander back. I'll meet you in twenty minutes at the bookshop. He put his weapons on the seat, took off his coat and jacket, rolled up his shirt sleeves. 'Take the kit with you. Everything's light weight and should fold down small.'

Fogarty got out of the vehicle with one of the bags, his jacket on top of the HK. Eilidh carried the other, a dark blue bag, with Tonka's kit aboard. She stayed with Fogarty. Sam walked behind them into the shop. Fogarty went into the café area, ordered coffees and stayed with Eilidh, backs to the wall. Sam bought a map and a guidebook. In five minutes they were huddled around the table, Sam watching people as they came and went, holding his pistol out of sight.

98

‘Enjoy your jolly?’ Mike said. His smile belied the words. They were in a meeting room, swigging coffee and munching large sausage rolls. The smell of stale grease, and fast food wrappers added an unsubtle odour to the place. The table surface had dull patches where fat and meat juices congealed.

‘Worth the trip, mate. We’re into something big,’ Cal said.

‘Like what?’

‘International dimension with loads of crooked politicians, bankers, civil servants, spooks … the whole caboodle.’

‘I could have told you that.’

‘We’ve got our share of crooks, but the scale is awesome: Europe, USA, world-wide … Anyway, what about the medic and the old dear?’

‘Both on the mend. She’s a sweet old thing and I’m invited for a meal. On top of that, injuring an innocent doctor makes people mad,’ Mike said.

‘What have we got?’

‘Three solid leads, forty-seven maybes, and the usual heap of crap.’

‘What’s new?’

‘A positive connection to Bill Jenkins. The people concerned are known associates and low level enforcers.’

‘You think he fixed it?’

‘Not his style. Maybe he was pushed.’

‘Next step?’

‘A spot of joined-up action to annoy the big bastards is in order. When’s Sam back?’

‘Supposed to be soon.’

‘Let’s build the intel and wait for him. He’ll want a crack at Jenkins after their last meeting.’

99

'We were close, but not close enough.' Xavier's quiet voice had them leaning forward. He wiped his mouth with a hanky. 'We know of three people with Eilidh Duncan at the conference. One is a seasoned operative, a Calum Smart. This is his picture. The Duncan woman changed her appearance, and we have this picture, taken at the airport on her way to the USA. She may change her looks again. There is Duncan's old protector, Waberthwaite, and a US operative we know is assigned. There's limited data on them for now, but we have associates on it.

'Why not wait until they're back?'

'Nice idea Jack, but the security around the British team in London is too tight. They're exposed where they are, and we must get to them.'

'And London? Their influence is growing in the bigger picture.'

'You're right, Jack. We have to find a way to eliminate the problem but brutality isn't going to work.'

Xavier's phone rang. He spoke in a murmur no one could hear. Gemma stared at the table top. When Jack's foot caressed her ankle, she glanced at him without changing her expression and applied gentle pressure back. He was an excellent and inventive lover. Some of his desires had hurt at first, but she enjoyed the experience. A little torment added spice to their encounters. He liked her to give him a little hurt in return. She enjoyed the thoughts.

'Gemma, Gemma! Planet Earth calling.' Xavier almost whispered, cold as ever, eyes glinting. 'Things are a bit excitable over in Seattle. Our people managed to separate the Duncan girl, the Fogarty man and their protectors. Then it went …' he paused and his mouth twitched into a scowl, 'wrong!' The wet pout as he formed the 'W' made Gemma think of a lamprey. She shuddered.

'They got away?' The flat lack of emotion in Jack's voice added to the chill.

'Yes. Killed a couple of our operatives. Not USA security types, you understand. The police are treating the action as gangland related.'

'How long before the UK people realize the Duncan girl is at risk?' Smythsone said.

'Not too sure. Some Secret Service officials are on the case and getting nowhere, we own two people on the inside. Other assets are in play. We are controlling the communication flow short term and have advantages that I won't bore you with. Need to know, as they say.' *Arrogant shit!* Smythsone thought.

'How long have we got to find them?' Jack said.

'We have the lid on tight and will disrupt most real communication for another twelve to eighteen hours. Let's say we have twenty four hours to trace and kill them.'

'Surely they'll check in with base?'

'No matter. They're expected to be in the locale for nearly two more days. No one is looking for them but us and the Secret Service apparatchiks. They're ahead of us and avoiding contact. Give us a few hours to latch on to them. They don't know who their friends are. Can they risk giving their position away? I don't think so. We need only get on their tail, and I'm sure we can do that.'

'So, Xavier, what's the plan?'

Xavier laughed. 'Extreme prejudice on sight.'

100

'We need to factor some reality into our plans,' Fogarty said. 'The first is, outside of maybe three or four people who were at the conference, we can't trust anyone in the USA. We must get away from Seattle. We're in extreme danger if we hang around. I mean extreme, as in we're going to wind up dead should we stay here.'

'Name your top three people we can count on,' Sam said.

'Bill Sanchez, Martha Vinetti, Saul Gould,' Fogarty spoke without hesitation.

'There'll be others.'

'Sure, but those three are *go-to*.'

'Now, Foggy, of those three, who is least likely to be compromized, or risk their comms set-up being open to external interference?'

'Martha.'

'That was quick.' Sam appraised Fogarty.

'We enjoyed wedded bliss for five years.' Fogarty, half smiled and nodded. 'I wanted a family, and she didn't. We're still close. She's in covert stuff, up to her eyes.'

'Why would she be a go-to person?'

'She's connected to the organized crime and terrorism agency, OCATA.'

'Hmm. So how do we get word to Martha?'

'We don't, not here. We gotta move.'

'Tonka is hovering around the front. I'll have a word with him.' Sam rose and went out. At the door he paused, looked around and walked over to Tonka.

'We need to move, Sam,' Tonka said. 'I'm not sure about the four of us going together.'

'Bad idea. Probably best in twos, usual contacts but only if we must.' They had three pre-registered email accounts each, which Indira, back at Westferry Road, kept running with inane conversation.

'I've got three pay-as-you-gos for you and me.' Tonka said. 'Bought separately over the last couple of days at different locations.'

'Sound.' Sam said.

'Usual identifiers, reminders and kill-off rules.'

'Okay.'

'Let's ID where we're heading and get moving.' They returned to the coffee area together. Tonka joined the others at the table, while Sam bought him a coffee.

Tonka had briefed them when Sam returned.

'Right, Tonks. Let's split into twos. Eilidh and you. Fogarty and me. Now, Foggy, where's our first meet?'

'Alger.'

'Alger?'

'A small place just off the I5, twenty-five miles south of the Canadian border. There's a motel, somewhere to eat, and it's quiet.'

'How soon?'

'Twelve hours. Notify, if later.'

'Let's move.'

Eilidh came over, pale beneath the fake tan. Sam gazed at her and shook his head. 'Tonka's the option for you. He'll get you out safely. He's best of the best. Do what he tells you. You'll learn a lot, and we'll meet again tomorrow morning.'

'I'm scared.' Bright eyes studied Sam.

'You're not alone.' He chuckled. 'We're all petrified.'

Eilidh snorted through her nose. 'Maybe I'm more excited.'

'Beats the boredom on Arran.'

'Yep!' She hugged him. Some of her sweat dried, cool, on his cheek. He rubbed it and admired her courage.

'Do what he tells you.'

101

They split up in the shop and left separately. Sam and Fogarty walked across to the Transit stop and caught the 125 bus for downtown Seattle. They watched Tonka and Eilidh get in a car and drive off. Forty-five minutes later they were walking northwards along Spring Street.

'Let's have a coffee.' Fogarty spoke quietly.

'This place is loaded with Starbucks.'

'Nah, there's a small Japanese place up the street. We'll walk it in ten minutes.'

'Aren't you worried about us being spotted?'

'Not yet. It's night-time and only two of us now.'

'And getting out of here?'

'Trust me, Sam. We'll be safe.' They walked on.

An older Japanese American prepared the coffee with lavish attention and care.

'You want three or four shots?'

'Three will do for me,' Sam said.

'You, sir?'

'Same, thank you.'

Sam and Fogarty sat near the window, hidden behind plants and flowers. The proprietor delivered their coffees, went over and locked the door. Sam put the coffee to his lips and closed his eyes at the silky flavour of a magnificent mocha. They opened again at the cold touch of a pistol on the back of his neck. He glanced up at Fogarty who gazed at him, calm-eyed.

102

'Wonderful to have a Colt .45 on the nape of your neck.'

'Nothing personal.' Kenzo smiled. He listened professionally to their story, withdrawing the automatic after a minute. 'You always get crooks when you put money, people and politicians together. They steal our wealth and damage society's integrity.'

'Kenzo and I worked on a couple big deals on the international scene,' Fogarty said. 'How long's it been bud?'

'A while,' Kenzo said.

Fogarty nodded. 'There are people who don't like the idea of us staying in touch. Some of our work cut close to home, and not all the bad guys were buried.'

'What can you do to help us get away, Kenzo?' Sam said.

'I have a ten-year-old Forrester in the parking garage. I don't use it. The car's insured. Help yourself. It won't trace back to me.

'Who does it trace to?'

'A dead man.'

'Thanks, buddy.' Fogarty patted his back and received the keys.

'So now you have my ace in the hole. However will you repay me?' Kenzo said.

'Free haggis for life. What more could a man want?' Sam said.

'It is true what they say about Scottish people, then. No sense of taste and a severe shortage of wit.' The Asiatic face creased in a smile.

'Duhhh!' Sam shook his hand. 'Racist!'

* * *

Fifteen minutes later, Fogarty and Sam were on the Evergreen

Point Bridge, and half an hour after that they were on the 203 heading north.

'We can do this trip in a couple of hours,' Sam said.

'Sure, but we'll pull off the road in a while and spend the night in the trees and out of sight.'

'Is Kenzo in danger?'

'Probably. He can hold his own. This thing's low on gas, best fill her up.' They drew into a small petrol station on Fall City Duvall Road.

'Crazy, isn't it?' Sam said, 'It's only two and a bit hours since we left the restaurant.'

'Yeah, this place is open until eleven, I'll gas up. Go in the store and grab some food, drink, tissues, wipes and such. Plenty of those fuckin' E numbers you Brits like so much.'

'Doing the all-American thing, Foggy?'

'Try me.'

Sam spoke with the fake enthusiasm of a commercial voice over: 'Remember kids, as Uncle Foggy says, eat shite ... five hundred trillion flies just can't be wrong.'

'Go fuck yourself, and get that shopping.'

'Delighted.' Sam left the car smiling, his mouth partly open, his top teeth showing and his tongue touching his lower lip. Thoughtful. He pulled on a baseball cap and eased it low on his forehead, entered the shop and located the cameras, the peak of the hat covering his face.

The store was shelved floor to ceiling. The assistant welcomed Sam with a bright 'good evening, sir.' He took a small trolley and gathered supplies. In ten minutes he was at the counter. The woman was efficient as she scanned and bagged the goods into three brown bags.

'Before you finish, ma'am, have you any Scotch?'

'That aisle.' She pointed towards the back of the store. He selected a bottle from the range. They wouldn't be getting ratted, but the availability of a dram was a good option. He returned to the checkout, asked for two coffees to go, and paid.

Sam arrived at the car, opened the rear hatch and laid the

groceries on the platform. Fogarty looked anxious. 'Let's get out of here.'

'Here's a coffee.' Sam handed the container over. 'Cream and two sugars.'

'Thanks.' Fogarty pressed the cup into the holder, put the car in gear and started moving. 'We'll be rural soon and I'll be much happier.'

'Fine.'

'I'm going to take a little trip on to a trail down on the left in a few miles. We'll be out of sight.' He turned at a crossroads and right along the track, moving more slowly. He switched off the lights. There was enough brightness in the sky to move along at fifteen miles an hour. Sam studied his friend. Fogarty's eyes gleamed in the dim light. He was crying. Sam stayed quiet. They drove for five minutes.

'What's up, Foggy?'

'Kenzo dies if I don't betray you. They know about a car, not the specifics of this one. He can't have talked, they called me and know where we are.'

'Tracked your phone. Throw it out the window.'

'There's an ambush in a couple of miles.'

103

Two large men sat in a quiet corner at the back of the coffee bar, heads together. Ten feet away a buzz of humanity flowed in and out, picking up lunch at the bright troughs of refrigerated units. Sandwiches, wraps and cake slices chilled to perfection, raw and sliced fruit, sushi and salads, enticing and in their clear plastic containers. Small, expensive, bottles of pure juice and large cheaper containers of sugary drinks, stood to attention awaiting a buyer.

At the counter, baristas made fine coffee with the clatter and clink of trained expertise. Two people worked the tills at the end of a production line of high-speed friendliness and respect, processing time-poor customers with panache.

'He wasn't properly cautioned and the video evidence is missing,' Mike said.

'Pull the other one.' Cal shook his head.

'He walked yesterday.'

'He's a criminal, Mike, a psychopath. You know what he tried to do to Sam,' Cal said.

'And he's going to be reinstated.' He gazed up as a man in a hooded training top walked past, bacon roll in one hand and a coffee in the other.

'So an evil, corrupt man gets right back into the centre of things.' The sigh was long and drawn out. 'How can it be?' Cal shook his head again and sniffed the air. 'And how can anyone resist a bacon butty?'

'Search me.'

'Want one?'

'Yeah, why not.' Mike smiled, the scar on top lip twisting up.

'Another decaf soya mocha?'

'Lovely.'

Mike watched Cal walk to the counter, place an order and pay. The big man came back with agile athleticism. He sat down at the plastic veneer table. 'They'll bring the stuff over.'

'Thanks. The Crown Prosecutor says no merit in appealing the case.' Mike said.

'And the video?'

'Mislaid. Erased. Nowhere to be found.'

'You know what you're saying, Mike?'

'Sure. Shameless people do shameful things. Technically, he's pure as the driven snow, barring a few motoring offences.'

'Of course he is. Light as a cream puff. But that's not what I'm talking about.' Cal said. 'Who had the video?'

'We did.' Mike shook his head.

'It's one of our Agency mob who nixed the video. We have a major security breach.'

'This is a horror story, Cal. We've got kidnapping, dead bodies all over the place, a water-boarding and a mandarin, from the bleeding security services, no less, orchestrating the killing.

'The system supports crooks and killers.'

'That's as may be, Mike. I'm interested in the hows and whos. How was this done? Who made it happen? This has been organized, planned and implemented in our backyard. Someone we trust is screwing us.'

'Sam's word against his, and he's dead.' Mike said. 'Wardle says he was kidnapped and wounded by evil people. James Thomas esquire, a paragon of covert excellence, backs him up.'

'They're all the same.'

Mike shook his head, 'I'll say, Wardle came up to me after the court session and, in front of the press, thanked me for my timely arrival and rescue.'

'Maybe you'll get a medal.'

'I wanted to throw up on his shoes. He told me he was 'distraught Duncan had been killed'. I wouldn't mind, him sounding so posh and all, but he's a fuckin' street kid from Manchester. Fancy-talking bastard.'

Cal smiled. 'You gotta come from somewhere.' His over-emphasized West Indies accent brightened Mike's eyes.

'None of the survivors are talking either.'

104

'Why? Tell me.'

'I can't do it, Sam. I can't.'

'Kenzo is going to die if he's not already dead. We both know that. Maybe they don't have him. What do they believe about me?'

'You're a Limey low-life operative. And they think Eilidh and Tonka are with us.'

'What did they tell you to do?'

'Get on this trail, drive straight at the traffic circle and left at a crossroads about a half mile beyond that.'

'They'll have a field of fire set up before then. Somewhere past the junction? We'll never reach the crossroads.' Sam looked straight ahead. 'Will they know we're on the trail?'

'It's normal to use a spotter, but I haven't seen a car.'

'I hope Kenzo makes it.' He put his hand on Fogarty's shoulder. 'Pull over.' Sam got out and climbed in the rear. He pulled the HK from the bag, checked it, and tucked a spare magazine under his belt. 'Okay. Let's get back on the main road and head north.' They found a side track up to the right and soon swung on to a four lane stretch of highway. 'Cruise in the outside lane,' Sam said, 'Keep 'em driver side to us if you can. Cramps their style.' He remembered the harsh lesson when he and Tonka rescued Eilidh.

Two headlights jerked out from a dirt road a quarter of a mile behind them. 'Here they come.' Sam opened both windows and crouched.

'Moving up fast.' Fogarty's bellow came over the wind roar, flat, clear, professional. Sam nodded to himself. 'About 100 yards away and closing.'

'Let them.'

'You sure?'

'Yup,' Sam shouted, 'Karen's rules of engagement. *Do unto others before they do unto you.*' Fogarty laughed. 'Stop and go back as soon as we know we've got them. If we aren't sure, pedal to the metal.'

Sam braced his feet on either side of the transmission tunnel and twisted to the right. Resting his elbow flat on the seat-back, between the armrest and the door, he turned further at the waist and leaned the barrel on the rear corner of the window. His left side now pressed against the front seat, he locked his body and arms to create a solid firing platform.

'They got to make a move,' Fogarty said, 'we're close to a town. Christ! Here they come!'

The car, a dark Suburban, loomed in the open window. A seventy mile an hour slipstream roared. The large black bonnet passed Sam, the side mirror slid into view barely five feet away.

'You better get this fuckin' right!' Fogarty bellowed above the wind noise. 'There's an assault rifle sticking out the back of their car.'

The chrome corner of a window frame arrived opposite Sam. The driver came abreast: mid-twenties, pretty, in a hard-faced way. She glanced at Sam and glimpsed eternity. Her mouth opened to scream. The muzzle flash reached out to steal her soul. Her face disappeared in a welter of shattering glass. The Suburban jerked right, hit a tree and slewed out sideways, lurched on to the driver's side and ground up the road, sparks flying. A car coming towards them, braked hard, reversed, swerved round and shot away.

The hard braking thrust Sam against the front seat. They did a U-turn and were back at the big vehicle in moments. The driver's body dangled from the seatbelt. Her face pressed against the windscreen, bloodied and distorted by from punched holes where her nose had been, with three more in a jagged line from left cheek to forehead. A sightless brown eye glared angrily at her killer, the other, submerged in blood, an open eyelid visible under a, still running, wash of red.

The man in the front whimpered, semi-conscious. One bullet had smashed his jaw and another, his shoulder. The rear passenger struggled to release himself, stopping when the barrel of the HK poked his neck. 'Don't unclip yourself. Hand me the Armalite and that bag. Now give me the contents of your pockets.' He received a mobile and wallet.

'Please don't kill me.'

'Okay.' Sam said and knocked him cold with the rifle butt.

Fogarty had the woman's handbag, briefcase and a pistol. He took the injured man's wallet and phone. 'Let's go, partner.' Sam nodded and fired a burst into the communications equipment. The injured passenger screamed.

'Back to the roundabout.' They returned the way they came. Sam studied the map. 'Hang a right and right again on the next main road. I'm hoping the killers will be at sixes and sevens. We risk getting into police traffic if we stay on the 203 and this side of the river. I'd rather not harm any officers tonight.'

'Here's the turn.'

Two large cars passed in the opposite direction, moving fast. Fogarty kept to a sensible pace. They drove up the 405, moving westwards, before taking route 9. They decided to go east of Lake Stevens.

Sam stayed alert and quiet. 'Sometimes you have to kill,' Fogarty said.

'I know. Not often you see the whites of their eyes.'

'No.'

'Our lives depended on stopping them,' Sam said. His sigh came from the depths of his being. 'The light dawned in the woman's eyes, as I pulled the trigger.'

'You okay?'

'Yes.' Sam looked sideways at his friend and raised an eyebrow. 'She meant to kill us. She failed. We're alive. I'd better text Tonka.'

105

Twenty miles away Tonka and Eilidh were in the rear of a diner. The pay-as-you-go pinged. Tonka read the message with thoughtful expression. 'The lads had a little rumble, Eilidh. No injuries. We'll change our route to avoid the area.'

'You sure they're okay?'

'Absolutely. I wouldn't want to be the other guys.'

Eilidh nodded.'Can we get a message to London?'

'Not just now, there may be a leak.'

'I remember where one of my backups is.'

'Let's email later.'

'I want guarantees from Charlton about the security and sanctity of the sources.'

'That'll take a bit of composing.' He gazed at her, tilting his head sideways. 'No rush.'

'You angry with me?'

A tiny smile lit the craggy face. 'No, love. This is what I fight for: freedom, safety and respect for others. Corny to some; motivates me.' Eilidh took his hand and squeezed. She caught his eye; they nodded to each other. 'I've never told Sam.'

'I'll not tell on you.' Her laugh tinkled just loud enough to be heard over the country music. They ate some more.

Tonka eyed everyone who came and went. Guard up, focused. He made his decision.

'I'm off to get a car. You stay put. Eat a dessert and a coffee.' He rose and left the restaurant.

The server came over and took an order for a hot fudge sundae and a tea to follow. Eilidh explained that her uncle liked a walk after eating, for his digestion's sake.

* * *

Ten minutes later Tonka returned to the diner. The table lay empty, but for a cooling cup. Eilidh was gone.

106

'Quentin?'

'Just been told our people are isolated and on the run. Elements of the Anti-Christ are in pursuit. Two contacts so far. They may have separated.'

'High stakes stuff. What do you think?' Charlton said.

'Who can we trust?'

'I don't know.'

'Where are they?'

'No idea. Presumably still in the Pacific Northwest.'

'How about Fogarty's boss? She must be aware he's missing by now. She hasn't called.' Quentin said.

'Mobilize two teams to deploy to Canada, Vancouver.' Charlton leaned over. 'Indira, get me Johnny Bertram. Sorry, General Bertram on the phone.'

'Anything else, sir?'

'Tell 'em to be ready for bear. We need more information before we commit.'

107

'Got a shot on their internet. Kind people here.'

'Who were you in touch with?' Tonka said.

'I just left a message for Shirl.'

'On her email?

'Of course. They'll not connect it with me.' She stared at Tonka's face 'Will they?'

'Don't be too sure. They can track anything.' He shook his head slightly. 'We must assume they'll be here in ten minutes.'

'Sorry.'

He regarded her with strong grey eyes. 'Please talk to me, love. No surprises. I don't like killing people. Decent folk shouldn't die because of a slip-up.' She flushed. 'Let's pay and go.'

They walked to the counter, paid the server and strolled through an untidy car park.

Face impassive, he checked around and nodded to the right, 'We're in that truck.'

They moved off immediately. He sighed.

'You're angry with me now.'

'No. I'm annoyed at myself for not briefing you properly.' A large black car hurtled into the parking lot as they exited. Tonka drove at the speed limit and turned left. 'That was quick, bloody quick.'

'Them?'

'We must assume so.'

'And, if not?'

'No matter. Always think the worst; minimizes surprise.'

They came to a junction. He turned off, found cover, drove down a trail, switched the lights off and got out of the SUV. 'We'll stop here and do some thinking.' He turned to her. 'One more thing. No more emails or anything until we get to safety.'

'I promise … Why not keep going?'

'Imagine they made us at that place. They'll have a pretty good idea of our time to get anywhere, and will use that to model a time and distance profile. When resources are limited, you apply them in a focused way. We'll be inside their loop for a while. They may not search in the right places.'

'How long until the owner misses this car?'

'Couple of hours; more, if they have something to eat after the movie. Let's get away from the car. Grab your gear.' They moved in silence towards the sound of a river. In the moonlight water flowed unhurriedly. 'Right, Eilidh. We want to go through our stuff and check for any type of tracker device.'

'Okay, where do we start?' Have you been given anything, any presents, money basically anything at all?'

'Only a couple of business cards.'

'Let me look.'

'Bradley Harpur.' He rubbed the card between his fingers. 'Here we are. There's a small GPS device in this. He folded the board back and forward until a split cracked the surface. This is why they're so close behind.' He reached into his coat and pulled out a tough, sealable plastic bag that he handed to her. 'Get the stuff you must take with you into this: money, toiletries, anything you want.' She started to pack the bag, no questions. 'Give me a sec,' he said, 'I'm going to backtrack.' He disappeared without a sound, his shape becoming indistinct, as he vanished like a ghost.

She pulled her arms round herself muttering angry words. She shook her head, indignant as the betrayal sunk in. For a short while the humiliation and hurt basted her in resentment.

She calmed and regained focus. She took cash, coins, the pay-as-you-go phone, toiletries and sealed them in the bag. She noticed a strap she could use to attach it to her body. She experimented until, at last, she decided to fit the pouch around her waist and into the small of her back. Work done, she sat on the rock, ears pricking at every sound.

She imagined bears, wolves and evil men. Even with the river burbling, almost silent, her edginess grew with every breath. How long had Tonka been gone? What if he never came back? She needed a plan.

108

'It'll be dawn in a three, there-and-a-half hours, Foggy.' Sam woke up, stepped out of the car and peed beside a tree. They were parked in the brush off a road north of Sedro Wooley. He climbed back in.

'I'll take some shut-eye. I've checked out the AR15. It's in good order. There's five mags in the bag.'

'Before you rest, I want to talk.'

'Something on your mind, Sammy?'

'You.'

'Me?'

'You sold us out, Foggy. Give me the details.'

There were tense moments of silence. Fogarty noticed the Browning in Sam's hand. He screwed up his face. 'Thirty pieces of silver, pure and simple.'

'The team who hit us in Scotland? The firefight?'

'Not mine, I was a link.'

'The set-up came through the US Embassy in London. Who triggered the attack?'

'Wardle.'

'Right. Don't move like that.'

'Sorry.' Fogarty's hands wavered in placation.

'France?'

'Innocent.'

'Last night? You had me dead bang, then Kenzo helped out.'

'I couldn't.'

'Keep talking.' Sam's face was stone. 'Everything.'

'The UK stuff ... I didn't know they'd targeted you until afterwards. Wardle told me later, when the hunt was on. That psychopathic piece of shit described you as a poxy, bloody jumped-up squaddie. He likes hurting people.'

'I know.'

'Next, you're alive and in Seattle, with Eilidh following. The pain of knowing, of being trusted. Once State-Side you guys were in grave danger.'

'Did you report my survival?'

'If they do know, I didn't pass it on.'

'Tell me about the restaurant.'

'I had to commit. The protection unit went away. Anything else was going to result in good men dying. The story was, we had secret people coming and cover arranged, that's why those two guys were outside: evidence of cover that didn't exist. A hit team was heading in. Waberthwaite pre-empted action.'

'He's good.'

'Yeah, cool, tough and a wonderful pace. When did you make me?'

'We were uneasy before dinner.'

'You didn't take me out.'

'No. You and I have been in too many dark places for me to choose murder as an easy option.'

'For me, the clincher was Eilidh.'

'How so?'

'She's brave, feisty and mentally tough. What she's just been through, her stunning performance … Man, she's a piece of work.'

'And?'

'At the wire, I'm not a betrayer of people. I'm a betrayer of governments and agencies.'

'How did they catch you?'

'A honey trap and money, or you could say, I was lonely and broke. Sounds simple at first: nobody gets hurt, cash flows in, bills get paid, no need to damage the good guys, until a conversation with your Wardle.'

'Nasty man.' Sam said.

'Too true. You don't ask for details or questions, it's like regular business. You're asked, you deliver, you're respected. Like operations, exactly the same. Once you're in, you forget you're tainted. Corrupt.'

'Seasoned pros armed to the teeth on a Scottish country road.'

Fogarty snorted. 'Wardle called it, set it up pretty well and screwed up on the detail. The mercs thought they were up against civilians.'

'No questions about killing ordinary citizens?'

Fogarty's eyes glistened. 'I gave him contacts, *mention my name*, that's all. When he told me his intentions, I didn't get it at first. The guy is amoral. Later, the sleepless nights started. You guys show up, full of trust.' Thunder rumbled in the distance. A spatter of raindrops slapped the world, but the sky remained clear. 'I think you head to a tipping point where you either embrace the darkness, or you don't.'

'And now we're both alive, here, in a forest clearing. There's a decision to be made. Why did you return to the side of the angels?'

'Conscience. Pain. Redemption.'

'If you don't mind me saying, you sound like a movie cliché. So you're guilt-ridden and wanting to be reinstated? Get on with it.' Sam gave a come-ahead gesture with his left hand, fingers rocking vertically. Moonlight glinted in Sam's eyes, feral, dangerous.'

'As I say, Eilidh was the clincher. All the way through the debrief, as she hurt and fought and shared, she won my respect and admiration.'

'You threw in with us?'

'No, the pull was hard, the easy life. I decided when I was certain you were going to die.'

'When?'

'At the restaurant. When Eilidh chatted with me after our meal.' He paused and looked at Sam in the moonlight. 'You look thoughtful.'

'You have no idea, Bob. We decided it had to be you.'

'Not me, Sam, the big blond-haired guy, Augie. The man who took the protection away. Decision time, and now we're here.'

'You're alive because I couldn't forget the desert and that drug thing: the debts we owe each other.'

'You trusted me, even though you knew the danger.'

'Tonka and I talked it over a few times. Security was weak when we showed up, strong as the delegates arrived, and catastrophic after they left.'

'Why did he agree with me about the Mexican meal?

'He didn't. We decided we had to escape and went along with it. It took us away from the centre which we decided was more dangerous.'

Fogarty grinned, 'Augie fell in with your plans.'

'Appears so.' An owl flew silently near them, wings flaring for a second.

'And you didn't kill me.'

'No. We were ready to. When he returned to the restaurant he needed a signal from me and he'd have killed you. My gut said you were with us. I saw your reaction to the watchers leaving and decided to believe. Any wrong move and you were dead.'

'I want her to live, Sam. She deserves to.'

'Right, and she's not safe by any means. She may already be dead.'

'You going to do me now?'

Sam gazed at him hard, implacable. Fogarty stared back. Sam holstered the Browning, stood and picked up the AR15, checked it and started to move away.

'Take a snooze. I'll handle the rest of the watch.'

'You gotta damned Rolex with you?'

'Watching for evil people stupid. I'll do my sentry bit in the open not in a car seat like you did. Get that ugly head of yours down.'

Fogarty closed his eyes and slept, a half-smile on his face.

109

Tonka returned, materializing, ghost-like, without a sound. 'They'll find that little GPS bugger 400 metres of rough terrain in the wrong direction,' he said. 'We're a hummock away from the road. No night-vision stuff can spot us unless it's airborne. Let's get organized before we head off.' He pulled out a map.

Eilidh glanced at him, angry. 'He convinced me he wants to spend time with me. Mealy-mouthed swine.'

'Okay, love, he put a bug on you. He broke your trust. That hurts.'

'Yes ... bloody does.' Her eyes glinted with anger in her moonlit face. 'I'll get over it.'

'We all do. Focus. Save the pain for later. We've got surviving to do, and a plan to get out of this.'

'I don't know about that stuff.'

'You're going to learn. Plans are useful.' He moved beside her and laid the map on a rock. They hunkered down together. He lit the page with his mobile screen. 'We're meeting in Alger, there. We're about here.' They talked for five minutes and were ready to move off when they heard the crunch of car wheels on the rough track over the mound. Tonka pulled out his mini-assault rifle, and released the safety. The sound of the vehicles disappeared down the track. He beckoned Eilidh and put his mouth to her ear. 'Swim time.'

'Swim?'

'Swim. We're about twenty miles from Alger and it'll help us get away from the searchers. They have resources and manpower. All we have is a river to slip into. We're on the south bank and will gradually work over to the north. This one seems to flow pretty well. Should take less than an hour. We're two miles from an exit point on the other side. We have nearly three hours of darkness. I think we can make it.'

'It'll be cold.'

'Yes, but we'll be working hard.'

'So we just jump in?'

'Did you get your stuff together?'

'Yes.'

He gave her three energy bars. 'Eat them.' They chewed quickly. 'Right, strip as far as you're comfortable, starkers, if you can manage it. We'll need dry clothes when we're over.' He produced two heavy-duty black plastic bags from the sports bag. 'I bought these in the store on my way back to the bookshop. They're the sort of thing sailors use to keep their stuff dry. Handy if it get's wet, especially if you have to swim for it.' He handed her one and stripped off completely.

'No time for modesty.' She paused at her bra and pants.

'You choose. You've got the information.'

She removed her underwear. 'I guess I am that sort of girl.' She giggled.

Tonka didn't smile. 'I'll show you how to seal up when you're ready.' Tonka, placed his stuff tidily in the sack, weapons on top. Eilidh copied him. 'Take the thing off your waist, Eilidh, and put it in the big bag. You might snag on something.' Tonka took the remaining gear and hid it in some bushes.

Holdalls sealed, they made for the water. Tonka attached a strong cord between the sacks. 'We must keep contact. If the rope snags, hold on to the bag as best you can. Any difficulties, I'll be with you.'

'This is cold.' She spoke in a high-pitched whisper, whilst inhaling.

'What do you expect? It's coming down from icy mountains, but not life-threatening. We've got to work hard and keep working, that keeps us alive. Stick together and use your bag for floating. If they catch up, we'll figure out what to do.'

'Okay.'

'If you're not kicking and working, try to keep your feet out in front, to ward off rocks.'

They moved further into the water, slipping on stones. They both skidded a couple of times, picking up bruises and grazes, hurting unprotected naked flesh and bone. Out in the current, Eilidh struggled to hold the bag and stay upright. She swallowed some water and coughed. Tonka steadied her.

'This is no fun,' she said.

'I know, love. You want to relax a bit more and let some of the movements happen. You'll soon learn.' Gradually, she righted and adjusted herself in the flow. 'We're out of their sight now. I don't think they'll look to the river first. They might if they find our spare stuff, but it's well hidden.'

Soon the river moved them along at a surprising pace. Once or twice they grounded. They became effective at working together. The water propelled them with power. After thirty minutes, they passed houses on their right.

'We're getting near where we want to get out. Let's crab across the current, that way.' Both of them felt the uplift of a journey well made.

Something large and hard grabbed Eilidh.

A floating tree pressed over her head and drove her downwards. Then her knees were on rough gravel, the remorseless power pressed her down. The riverbed rose to meet her, visible in the moonlight. She struggled, near to panic, caught in the thrust of the water and the tangle of the wood. The exertion tired her and branches held her fast. Soon her elbows dragged on pebbles. Her face neared the river bottom.

She fought to calm herself, hold her breath and figure out how to break free. The strain of not gasping grew hard. She started to accept the inevitable and, as her mind let go, Ned was groping her, the swine! Her rage brought focus and a few more seconds.

A strong hand grabbed her. Tonka pulled her sideways, pressed his feet on the gravel and she started to come free. The cold numbed her as branches clutched like dead fingers, scraping away at her skin. They surfaced and sucked in great gulping breaths, their bags floated alongside.

'Head for the shore, Eilidh. Not far now.' A beach lay ahead. She heard the gurgle of water on rocks and stubbed a big toe on a rock.

'I can feel the bottom. We're okay.' She pulled her bag on to a flat rock, grabbed Tonka's and heaved it up too.

'Well done, love.' She saw Tonka's teeth gleam, maybe he smiled, she couldn't tell. The tree rolled and a branch hit him hard on the side of his head. The blow knocked him forward and parallel to the shore. She realized he was unconscious as he flopped into a faster rip of current and slipped away.

110

A spit of sand ran the length of the rapid which gurgled and slurped in timeless movement. Eilidh sprinted along the beach, her breasts rising and falling in her rush. A brief gleam of Tonka's white body flashed like a fish belly, and pinpointed him as he drifted into a pool.

She raced to the edge without stopping. Her feet lost traction on the sand and pebbles as she dived. The bellyflop stung. In moments she had him by an arm and pulled him to her. His chin hooked by her elbow, she brought his face out of the water.

She scissor-kicked until her feet found purchase on shingle. Gripping his armpits tight, she struggled to the shore and dragged him from the shallows. They were only forty yards from their bags, yet the dash had seemed like miles. Tonka's scalp wound stopped bleeding; almost invisible under his short hair. She rubbed him to get the circulation going and, leaning back to rest, noticed his eyes were open, regarding her.

'Brave girl. I was out for a moment and you got me. Thanks.'

'You're worth the effort. I seem to remember you saved me a few minutes back. Honour's even, mate.' She did a passable attempt at a West Midlands accent.

He smiled, an unusual occurrence. 'You're brave and resourceful. I'm trained for this, you aren't. The medal's yours, love.' His eyes offered the regard and respect of a tough warrior. 'You're special.' She smiled as if her heart would burst and said nothing. 'We'd best get off the beach and dress.'

In the shelter of nearby bushes the air felt impossibly warm. Tonka rummaged in his bag and came up with paper towels. 'What else have you got in there?'

'Bare essentials. Dry yourself briskly and get clothes on. No, don't rush. Brisk means thorough and quick. Dry yourself thoroughly. The less damp on your body, the better your warming-up will be.'

'You're bossy.'

'Heroes aren't perfect.' He delved in again and produced more energy bars and a bottle of energy drink. 'Get this down you.'

They scoffed the food and liquid. She laughed, a quiet tinkle against the bustle of the river. 'All that water, and now I've got to pee.'

'Don't go far.'

She went into some bushes and squatted. She sighed with relief; a deep grunt beside her made her finish extra quick. A large hairy shape brushed against her. The growl, at such close range was bad enough, and the breath horrific. Her face squirmed in distaste. The creature moved. She stared at a full-grown black bear. Her hair stood up and she screamed. The beast jerked away then stopped, eyeing her. Move? Don't move? She tried to remember the advice. Eye contact? No eye contact? The fear tore at her yet she stood her ground and stared the bear in the eye. The beast growled, showing large canines under stretched writhing lips.

A loud thwack made her jump. Tonka hit the beast across the backside with a branch. 'Boo!' he yelled and whacked once more. The beast wheeled and ran off, crashing into the undergrowth. 'You bring a whole new sense of perspective to bear naked, Eilidh. You can't run very fast with your trousers round your ankles, as we men discovered years ago.' She blushed and pulled her pants up.

'I need to go again.'

'Not surprised; I needed to go, too, and I didn't pee on a bear.'

'I didn't pee on the bear.' She giggled. 'I peed beside him.'

'Poor bear.'

'Poor Eilidh.'

'Finish peeing and get your jacket on. All this excitement

cools you down.' She gave him the finger, returned to the same bush, finished her business, stomped to her bag and yanked her jacket on.

After more fluid and another energy bar, they studied the map and planned their next move. Eilidh put ointment on Tonka's injury.

'The cut looks clean.'

'Doesn't feel too bad. I'll live, thanks.'

A voice boomed out. 'Keep your hands where I can see them.'

* * *

'Brave call not to kill me, Sammy.' They were parked near the crossroads at Alger.

'We've broken our share of rules. Kenzo not killing me and the firefight clinched it.'

'So honour's even?'

'No. Given time, and a successful escape from here, we'll be well on the way.'

'I wonder how the others are doing.'

'Tonka aimed to text at sun-up.'

'The sun is up.'

'He'll communicate when he can.'

'Let's get some breakfast.' They drove to the I5 and turned south. 'There are a couple of places a few miles down the road.

The text was a long time coming.

111

A policeman walked out of the woods gun raised. 'That bear nearly killed me in his rush. Made me suspicious and, lo and behold, I find two vagrants.'

'We're not vagrants. We're lovers,' Eilidh said.

'So, where's your car?'

'Up the river a bit. We've been swimming.'

'I'll drive you to your vehicle and check your credentials.'

'Thank you,' Eilidh said.

'Both of you assume the position.'

'What's that? We're foreigners.'

'Makes no difference, ma'am. Lean against the rock, and I'll pat you down for guns and stuff. Take the coat off, mister.'

'Can't you just let us get on with our visit down here? We're doing no harm.' Eilidh said.

'No ma'am. Can't do that.' He closed with Tonka. 'I told you to assume the position.' He barely got the words out before he was disarmed and made to sit down. Tonka looked at his gun.

'We won't harm you,' Tonka said. 'Give me your handcuffs.' He secured the officer's left hand. 'Now, you're going to do some tree-hugging.' He walked the man over to a twelve inch diameter tree. 'Hug the tree.'

'The bear might come back.'

'You've got a point. I'll secure you safely.' Eilidh watched, bemused. Tonka took the cop's keys and communicator. 'Sit down here. I'm going to tighten your boots.' Tonka double knotted the laces. 'Now, put your feet round the tree.' He indicated a birch about twelve inches in circumference. He threaded the handcuffs through the lace loops. 'Where's your car?' The answer included threats of dire consequences.

Next, Tonka removed the magazine and disassembled the

automatic. He took the spare ammunition and put the pistol parts a good stretch from the officer. 'I don't think the bear will come back. Stretch round the tree, undo your boots, reassemble your Glock, load up and fire off a few shots, someone is bound to hear. Either that or walk out.'

'We're sorry for the inconvenience,' Eilidh said.

They walked away. The vehicle was where they expected. 'He says he was having a pee too. He probably didn't call us in. But they'll have this car on GPS. He should get himself free in twenty minutes or so. The thickness of his waist will slow him down.'

'What excitement: cross a river at night, avoid getting eaten by a bear, tie a policeman up, and now we're stealing a squad car,' Eilidh said.

Tonka glanced at her. 'All in a day's work. Let's go up the road and call Sam.' They entered the vehicle. The policeman's hat still rested on the dashboard, Tonka put it on. He checked the map, turned the automobile around and after half a mile took a left by a farmhouse. With a highway in view they pulled over. Tonka took the fuses out of the computer and GPS system. He checked a map and planned a route to a convenient meeting place near Interstate 5 avoiding Sedro Woolley and Burlington.

They left the police car behind some trees at an agricultural equipment yard, communicator on the drivers seat, walked across the railroad track and a quarter of a mile to a retail area.

'How are you feeling?'

'Piece of piss, Tonka, a piece of piss.' Her smile was wide, bright and tired at the edges.

'It ain't over until it's over. But you've done well, Eilidh.' His impassive face stayed alert. Eyes ranging, seeking, watching.

Eilidh's heart soared with pride as Tonka texted Sam.

112

'Truck stop off Interstate 5, at Cook Road.'

'Got you.' Sam said.

'Car park at the Shell station, there's a diner on the right.'

'There in ten.'

'Roger.' Tonka broke the connection.

Moments later, Sam and Fogarty took the ramp for Sedro Woolley, turned left across the I5 and left after the north ramp. Tonka and Eilidh appeared in the car park. Fogarty stopped the vehicle. Sam stepped out, opened the back, packed their kit in the boot, as they climbed into the rear. He closed the boot and returned to the front. They were moving before he had his seatbelt fastened.

Fogarty turned north in line with the I5. 'We'll head back through the country; a tad longer but not too far. We can relax on the way to the motel at Alger. Next, we'll have a bite at the local Bar and Grill. It's an okay little place and should be open when we get there. I hear they do the best fried chicken in the county, and I might just have that for breakfast.' They followed the next right turn.

'Got a bash on your head Tonka?' Sam said.

'Whacked on the head by an angry tree. Eilidh saved me.'

'Looks sore.'

'I'll get it seen to when we're out of this mess.'

* * *

The drive took them up and down hills. At places, they were on roads with surfaces as rough as sandpaper. Spectacular views of mountains and lakes hid round corners, the trees standing tall, and opening on to vistas like curtains. The peace and tranquillity of the drive interested and eased tension, as nature's beauty unfolded and presented timeless loveliness.

'Gotta do the bathroom.' Fogarty parked in a clearing at the roadside.

'Me too,' Sam said.

'Is there scope for bear-free privacy?' Eilidh said.

The four of them got out. Tonka followed Eilidh. 'I'll stand guard.'

Sam and Fogarty stepped into the wood. The sound of water falling soothed Sam, as he stared at a patch of moss. A sudden movement caught his eye.

A squirrel pushed its head round a branch and studied him. He nodded to the little face and half-smiled; no worries in your life, wee man. He zipped up and returned to the car. Moving once more at a leisurely pace, they eased along towards Alger.

* * *

Forty minutes later they parked at the motel. 'Fogarty's taken three rooms to give Eilidh privacy. Let's get food and some shut-eye,' Sam said.

'I'll eat last,' Tonka said, 'and keep watch while you lot stuff your faces.' He headed for the undergrowth opposite the diner.

'No you don't, Tonka.' Eilidh sounded assertive. 'I'm bringing you some food. What do you want?'

'Burger and fries.'

'Coming up.'

'Where will you be?'

'Just wander into the trees. I'll find you.'

They walked up the ramp into the diner, past a large window that overlooked the parking area. Inside, they stood at a small wait-to-be-seated counter attached to the bar, with racks for menus and a Wi-Fi credit card reader nearby.

The three of them ordered fried chicken from an amiable, maternal woman who was wearing jeans, a check shirt and a blue and white striped apron. She took them to a booth to the left of the window, which gave a good view of the entrance and road. Eilidh ordered for Tonka.

'He's tough, Sam. How do you neutralize a guy like that?'

Fogarty said.

'With difficulty. He's a hard man to beat. Surrender, is the best answer. Don't try, especially not in cover. In give or take action, he's deadly.' Sam gave Fogarty a thoughtful glance, making eye contact a little longer than usual.

'He's relentless and ahead of the game,' Eilidh cut in. 'He's almost gentle in the way he shepherds you through a hard situation, like a ghost. When those guys were after us he spirited me away. He's so aware. You know he's keeping you safe.' Fogarty nodded.

The burger arrived in a paper container along with a large root beer with a plastic lid and a straw standing to attention. Eilidh thanked the server, who smiled and went off. 'I'll take this over.' She was up, out and walked across the road, not a car in sight.

The trees stood quiet; no sign of Tonka. She spotted a foot, motionless, lying lazily with the side of the sole nearly touching the pine needles. She went close enough to recognize Tonka, white-faced and unconscious. Instinct made her turn, as a man grabbed for her.

113

‘We have an operative with them.’ Xavier’s voice was little more than a whisper, yet somehow, poisonous and corrupting. His in and out breaths hissed like a sucking wound.

‘The Duncan woman has a story to tell,’ Samson said. Smythsone kept quiet.

‘Yes, and her files are missing,’ Xavier spoke. Smythsone expected to see a forked tongue flicker between his lips. ‘And she mustn’t get anywhere near them.’

The clock showed 23.13 on the meeting room wall.

‘What steps have been taken to secure the situation?’

‘We think we know where she is.’

‘And action?’ Samson didn’t like vagueness. ‘What have you arranged?’

‘You know how I hate violence, Jack.’ Xavier said. ‘We shouldn’t draw attention to ourselves.’

‘Stop playing, and get to the point.’

Xavier’s chubby face remained impassive. He paused. Smythsone watched the tension rising as Samson’s jaw muscles rippled. Xavier nodded. ‘Sorry Jack, I’m annoying you and I apologize. My instructions are extreme prejudice.’

‘Eilidh Duncan?’ Gemma said.

‘We’d like to …’ the pause was filled with a louder, wetter inhalation, ‘interrogate her, if we can.’

‘And?’

‘Oh, Gemma, you seem to be finding your feet. You aren’t getting angry with me are you?’

‘You are dragging this out a bit.’

‘Should luck favour us, we’ll grab her. If there’s no luck, she will die along with the rest of them.’

‘And her information?’

He gazed at Smythsone, a toad awaiting a chance to shoot its tongue at a fly, and shrugged.

'How soon do we act?' Samson said.

'Very,' Xavier smiled gazing at both of them in turn, 'very soon.'

114

A hard hand covered Eilidh's mouth. The jolt of adrenalin gave her strength. She dropped the food and flailed away at her assailant, impossible to restrain. The fears of her captivity leapt back from the recesses of her mind. Her power grew.

She raised her arms and dropped down. Her clothing slipped from the grasp of her attacker and, as he struggled, the grip on her face loosened. A finger came her way and she bit hard. Her attacker grunted with pain. She screamed for Sam.

115

'Hey Mike, this lead may have legs.' Cal said.

'Why?'

'The source: Stanley Parker, legal eagle and friend to the down-and-outs.'

'You mean the whisky drinker's friend?' Mike said.

'The same. Someone in his parish doesn't approve of flattening old ladies and savaging young doctors.'

'Got enough for an arrest.'

'Yeah, or at least for a little help with our enquiries. Show some of the gruesome photos of the silenced ones. Let's sweat 'em.'

'Right, who have we got to display and create fear?'

'The Spanish concrete swimmers for a start. Then we've Jackie Steele ...'

'Nah, Fuss may have to do his act again at some point.'

'Okay, we've Romeo, Tommy Bain, Devlin Forsyth and Maybelle Jones.'

'Well she's not dead yet. Still fancy giving her one?' Mike said.

'Takes all types mate. You can admire skinny women with power bras making the best of their limitations, or take up with a sleeker, more rounded option. Like my ancestors, I have no problem with a bedspring-stretching partnership or, come to think of it, any shape, size or physique.'

'You and her?' The laugh burst out. 'A bedspring-bursting partnership.'

'You saying I'm fat, Mr Swindon?'

'Not for a minute, apart from the blister hanging over your trousers.'

'Racist!'

'How can you say such a thing? I'm only suggesting you're a touch overweight.'

'You're a racist.'

'How so?'

'Seeing as I feel insulted, and I'm an African Brit, if you offend me, you're being racist, you pox-ridden, Anglo Saxon pervert.' Mike laughed.

'Let's put 'em under surveillance for a few days. See who they see and lift 'em when we're ready.'

'It's a plan.'

116

'Eilidh.' Sam stood, turned and stared across the road. He reached under his jacket for the Browning. The sharp pain of a needle in his shoulder hurt then numbness, he stumbled, the hand he put out didn't support him, he fell on to the table knocking food and drinks to the side as it overbalanced and tipped him to the floor

'Sorry, Sam.' Fogarty watched Sam drop, paralysed. He picked up the automatic. The server and her colleague watched, transfixed.

Fogarty pulled out his credentials. 'Secret Service, ladies. Please go into the kitchen and stay there. Lie on the floor. *You will be safe.*'

With an awful sense of failure and dread Sam lapsed into unconsciousness.

117

Recognition flared. 'Brad Harpur, *you bastard!*' Rage clothed her in a battledress of anger and pain.

Eilidh broke free of his grip. She screamed as she attacked him, eyes wild. She moved forward and lashed him with kicks and blows. The hurt and fear of the past weeks fuelled her assault. Harpur winced and gasped at some strikes.

He caught her, and, strong as he was, found her hard to control as she writhed, kicked, scratched and bit. He held her shoulders and avoided her head as she lunged backwards towards his face and hammered away at his shins with her heels.

'Eilidh, Eilidh, calm down, calm down! I'm not here to harm you.' She continued to scream and flail at him. 'We've come to take you to safety.' Her wildness subsided gradually. She looked at him, eyes still flashing, chest heaving. It wouldn't take much to set her off again.

'On the side of the angels are you?' The last part of the statement was close to a scream.

'We were concerned you all were in danger. The set-up at the Mexican place happened too fast for us. The guys Augie sent away came back and we rushed down, but you were already gone and two criminals were dead. You people know your stuff.'

'How did you get past him?'

'I didn't. He was lying unconscious when I came by.'

'He wouldn't just go to sleep.'

'I guess not. I checked him over. He's had a nasty blow to his head.'

Eilidh puffed out her face as she exhaled. 'He took a knock from a tree in the river.'

'A good escape plan,' he nodded admiration, 'he's got a serious head injury .His pupils are different sizes.'

'What about Sam?'

'Fogarty's taken care of him.'

Eilidh looked across at the diner as two men carried Sam out of the door. She ran over the road. His eyes were part open but he wasn't seeing much. 'What have you done?' Rage and fear distorted her face.

'Drugged him. He'll be okay in five minutes,' Fogarty said.

'Why?'

'He's a lethal man, Eilidh, with you in jeopardy he'd shoot first and ask questions later. I had to subdue him until he knows things are okay.'

'How did these people know we were here?' She paused and stared at him as the light dawned. 'The pee … when we stopped for a pee.'

'Right, I sent a signal. I know who some of the good guys are …' She eyed him up and down. He dropped his eyes for a moment and spoke in a low voice, '… owing to the fact I've been one of the bad guys.' He lifted his hands with a small shrug.

'You were so competent and clear at the debriefing.'

'Sure, I'm a pro. I was getting your story. The minutes, data and interpretation are documented. One or two of the people present are on the dark-side. The Intel is compromised, but they don't have your files.'

'So why are you here now?'

'Sam and Tonka made me at the Mexican restaurant. I'm alive because of Sam. He chose to trust me. We've been in awful places together. Bottom line, I couldn't kill you or him. The rest of the story will work out one way or another.' He paused, lifted a finger and gazed into her eyes. 'I drugged Sam because he'd have killed me if things kicked-off with Tonka. Where's Tonka?'

'Unconscious in the trees. Harpur thinks it's the bash on the head.'

'Right, we better get out of here. We're rendezvousing with a chopper a few miles up the road in ten or fifteen minutes.'

Sam placed an unsteady hand on Fogarty's shoulder. 'I

heard that. Let's move. If your guys can find us, so will the evil empire.'

118

Late afternoon sun breached the clouds and poured bright golden light on to the road where contrasting tree shadows made dark inky puddles of blackness.

The Subaru became part of a convoy of large four-wheel drives. They were in a Humvee for space. In the back, Tonka drifted in and out of consciousness wedged between Eilidh and Sam. Tonka alternated sweat, his face was chalky with a blue tinge around his lips. Eilidh talked to him and squeezed his hands as she worked to keep him conscious.

'He needs hospital, fast.'

'I don't need it,' Tonka said, his voice slurred.

'Don't argue,' Eilidh said. 'You're going, and that's that.'

'What did you give me, Foggy?' Sam said.

Fogarty spoke over his shoulder, hands gripping the wheel. 'A new stun drug: drops people instantly, and they come back just as quick, if we let 'em.'

'I feel okay.'

'That's what they all say. In fact, most people feel a rush of energy from the antidote. ' He half-smiled to Eilidh. 'You gave Brad a rough ride, young lady.'

'He's lucky I didn't get mad. Next time, he'd better level with me.' The flash in her eyes made Fogarty grin. Harpur's neck reddened in the front seat. 'What have you got to smile about, Foggy?' Her appraisal was hard. 'Don't you dare drug my brother again.' A small upturn appeared on the corner of her mouth.

'Sorry, Eilidh. I promise to be good,' Fogarty said.

Sam said, 'Move fast boys.' Sam gripped Tonka's shoulder, 'how're you feeling, matey?'

'Weird, drugged.' Tonka nodded forward with a temporary

loss of consciousness.

Eilidh and Sam eyed him with concern and exchanged glances.

'At least we've more space in this car than the Subaru,' Eilidh said. 'Are you comfy Tonka?'

'As can be, young lady.' He blacked out again and fell back against her, mouth open. Almost at once his eyes opened. He paddled slightly.

Eilidh gripped his hand. 'Easy, Tonka. Just relax and stop fighting it.'

'Can't. If I quit I'll die.'

'We'll get him to hospital.' Fogarty said.

'I think he's suffering from intracranial pressure.' Harpur said. 'He's partially conscious and needs medical help, pronto.'

* * *

Two rockets flashed down like demented fireflies on crack. They destroyed the Subaru in front of them and the driver with it. Another two missiles detonated in the wreck. Fogarty spun the wheel and turned towards a clump of trees.

Another Humvee was straddled by two rockets, which blew a wheel off with a bang, followed by a screeching of metal as an axle stub and body panel scraped along the road. Harpur began a communication with his base as stones and debris rained on the vehicle.

'Looks like a Hellfire strike.' Harpur said while Fogarty wrestled with the steering. A tyre bounced towards them and hit the front bumper with a deep bass thump and enough force to shake everything. 'Roger. Chopper inbound, guys.' Tension and helplessness, harsh reminders of high-tech warfare. 'The injured person is serious and deteriorating. We need urgent medical assistance.'

Fogarty said. 'There's a doctor in the Blackhawk.'

Another rocket lashed through the trees and blew the rear door off a vehicle nearby. Pieces of glass tinkled as bits of tree and clumps of earth bumped on the car roof and bonnet. 'There's got to be something firing them.' Harpur said. 'What about a

Predator?' Two more rockets lashed at vehicles nearby. The big vehicle rocked.

'Predator?' Eilidh said.

'A drone, like they use for chasing terrorists, invisible from the ground.' Harpur put his hand on his ear. 'Roger.' He turned. 'We're being attacked by a robot.'

'Get 'em to trace the control.' Fogarty said. Harpur relayed the message.

Harpur listened. 'The Air Force is moving. The drone was detected and two fast jets scrambled a short while ago. Any time now.' Two more missiles hurtled into the trees. Earth, rocks and debris rained down.

A distant bang. Harpur talked, head lowered. 'Roger. One less drone guys. The air force will cover us to the RV.'

They drove out of the trees and turned left on to the road.

'How far, Harpur?' Sam said.

'A couple of miles to a big clearing at Lake Louise.' Fogarty drove forward as fast as he dared on the winding road.

'Tonka's out, Sam,' Eilidh said, the quaver in her voice disappeared into silence.

'He'll be okay, Eilidh. He will,' Sam said.

Driving round an 'S' bend at pace they confronted an Apache gunship hovering forty feet up. Its M230 Cannon turned towards them. It opened fire ripping away like a buzz-saw.

119

'What did you do?' Smythsone said.

'Simple actually.' Xavier milked the moment. 'We have people over there and on side. All we need is a drone, one of those Predator things, and a few nasty men in ugly vehicles.'

'Rockets, red glare kind of thing?' Samson said.

'Precisely, and we know their location. I'm afraid Miss Duncan won't live to tell her tale.' He giggled, a shrill, effeminate sound. 'Now then, Gemma. Some of your London policemen are becoming too annoying for words. Can you please pop across the Channel and make something happen? Talk to Wardle. He responds to a little *tête à l'aine*, doesn't he?' His juicy snigger hurt.

'What's the problem, Xavier?' Smythsone said.

'They are following through rather too effectively on the recent killings of your colleagues. The assassination of Duncan is irritating people. We need to pull a few more threads … er … strings.'

'We can't simply kill them off, you know how the press and public react to murders.'

'I'm not talking about murder, Gemma,' his tone was like a slap in the face, 'just do something creative and slow them down, or lead them astray. You can even fuck them if you want.'

'Easy, Xavier. She's one of us. Don't talk to her like that.' Samson's eyes flashed.

'I am responsible for a large part of the European operation.' Xavier's face twitched with emotion. 'You … in this team, you work for me. I don't have time for incompetence.' His voice squeaked as he raged. Spittle sprayed the table. His countenance paled to a chalky white. His eyes bulged. His breathy bellow still didn't achieve loudness.

'Fix it! Fix it like I'm fixing the Duncan woman … permanently! Kill them, beat them, transfer them, break them, bribe them! Have I gotta do every bloody thing myself?' His ragged in-breath was the only sound in a sudden, total silence. 'Stop them getting in the way. *Stop them.*' He gasped in a deep whistling breath and changed personality as control returned. In moments, his calm astonished them, as if nothing had happened.

'I'll catch the next plane,' Smythsone stood up, pale, her mouth a straight line. A blush settled like an unhealthy stain on her neck, and half-way up her throat. She made for the door, walking stiffly.

'Do that.' Xavier leaned back in his chair. 'Don't come back without a result. The London debacle is annoying our leadership.'

'I'd like a few words with you,' Samson said.

'The operative word is "few", Jack, I'm a busy man.'

'You are a capable guy, Xavier, and you're out of line. That woman who just left enjoys strong approval from the top.'

'You're right, Jack.' Xavier leaned back, half-smiled and tented his fingers in front of his face. 'But which top would that be?' Eyes glassy, he smiled like a ventriloquist's dummy. Samson broke eye contact first. Thin-lipped he stalked from the room. Behind him, Xavier giggled.

120

Sam watched the swirling gout of flame burst from the cannon in a lethal hail of anger and braced himself for death. The projectiles darted over their vehicle. Behind them a shrieking sound echoed, as myriad shells ripped into their target. Sam turned in time to see a large dark vehicle shredded.

'Bad guys,' Harpur said.

'You sure?' Sam said.

'Absolutely. Our team uses transponders. We do try to avoid blue on blue, you know.'

'No one will come out of that alive.'

'But we will.' Harpur nodded, eyes crinkled with seriousness.

'Come on you guys,' Eilidh said, 'Tonka needs to get to hospital.'

They accelerated, and in less than three minutes they were at the open space at Lake Louise. A Blackhawk, rotors turning slowly, waited. They parked clear of the blades. Two stretcher-bearers came out and lifted Tonka. A woman in military fatigues identified herself as a doctor. She gave Tonka a quick assessment. 'We're running this close. I'm going to drain off fluid before we fly, or he'll die.' On board the helicopter she started the procedure. She shaved hair on the side of his cranium.

'Help me.' She handed Sam gloves. 'Hold his head steady.' She pointed at Eilidh. 'Do you get squeamish?'

'Not particularly.' The doctor gave her gloves.

'I'm going to open his scalp and put a drain in. Keep me supplied with dressings and do what I tell you.' Eilidh put her gloves on.

The doctor cut through the skin and quickly exposed Tonka's skull. The bleeding was heavy, she controlled it. She went to work with a shunt which had a self-tapping element. 'Nearly through.' Blood squirted from the hole with clear fluid. 'That should do it.' She sealed off the drip and taped the drain in place. 'We're good to go.' She fixed a line to his arm.

Suddenly, Tonka tried to sit up. 'Easy, Tonka,' Eilidh soothed him.

'What's happened?' His voice was thick, dry mouthed.

'Nothing much, Tonks,' Sam said. 'A hasty escape, a rocket attack, a run-in with an Apache gunship, and you slept through it all.' Tonka's eyes glistened with pleasure. His face changed.

'Head hurts.'

'Of course it does, you ageing war-hound,' Sam said.

'What's happened, Sam?'

'You've had a tap in the head.'

Tonka's eyes closed and he fell asleep.

'He's sedated,' the doctor said, 'and looking good.' She spoke to the pilot and the engine note started to change. 'We'll have him in an excellent hospital in fifteen minutes.'

'Great.' Sam smiled. Eilidh sat beside Sam and held Tonka's hand. Fogarty and Harpur sat opposite.

'They're still after us, Sammy,' Eilidh said.

'Just as well I'm a dead man.'

121

'How did they escape again?' Xavier's skin was mottled pink and white with anger. Spittle frothed at the corner of his mouth.

In the United States, a person with significant covert experience knew the best course of action: blame someone. 'Bob Fogarty turned away from us.'

'Turned? Turned?' Xavier's volume shared his anger. 'Then kill him.'

'We don't know where he is.'

'Why, pray tell?'

'He disappeared when the shooting started.' The contact said.

'Doubtless you can manage some lethal force.'

'He *is* targeted.'

'How many people were lost?'

'Seven in Seattle.'

'It's not in the news?' Xavier said.

'Mostly, their affiliations are to organized crime and mercenary outfits. We lost a covert asset in the Secret Service. She was driving and not expected to engage when Fogarty went AWOL.'

'What is the US Government doing about this?'

'Nothing much. The President called for action against us, and people are working on it. But, if you build a top secret group, you disenfranchise the people involved to an extent, because of the secrecy. No matter how well-meaning, their flexibility for action weakens.

'Try telling that to men blown away by an Apache.' Xavier's anger blurted from the phone.

'Sometimes, things go wrong. That was Fogarty, as a matter of fact. His status is high enough to make things move, and he did. We'll get him.'

'Do they know who you are, and where you are?

'No, we don't think so. They're aware of us, but not who we are. Senior people like Fogarty can access specific assets at short notice in an emergency. Most of the time the bureaucracy means they're forced to go through channels to make serious things happen quickly, especially abroad, and leaks happen. The same rule applies in Europe pretty much, with a few deviations. One exception is the Agency in London, the one Duncan belonged to; its responses are quick and professional.'

'We use government assets without all of them being engaged in our corporation.'

'How do you feel we should tackle our problems?'

'Bribery, murder, blackmail or, ideally, ongoing corruption. We'd best shut this Agency down.'

122

The twin engines roared as the Black Hawk thundered along at maximum speed.

The doctor's calm voice came through the headset. 'We should be at the University of Washington Neurological Unit in ten minutes.'

'How is he?'

'Not good, I thought he was fine when we relieved the pressure. The fact he managed to keep going for hours after his injury says a lot for his strength and fitness. His head is bleeding on the inside. He needs immediate surgery. His blood pressure is falling.'

Sam looked at his friend's face, slack and unconscious. 'At least he's in good shape. He's got a chance.'

'Every minute is important.'

Eilidh watched the conversation, face rigid, holding Tonka's hand, and clenching the other in front of her. Fogarty sat silent. Sam watched with a feeling of helplessness. The doctor attended to her patient.

They were five minutes out when Tonka convulsed. The doctor talked into her headset. She turned to Sam. 'We have good guys on the ground waiting for us. John Walstock, one of the best neurosurgeons on the West Coast, is standing by.'

Next, Tonka struggled but with surprising energy. The doctor tried to soothe him. Sam unclipped his belt and moved her back. 'He could kill you.'

'Sam, Sam is that you?'

'It's me, Tonks.'

'What's happening?'

'You've had a bad head injury, and we're heading for hospital.'

'Medevac.'

'Yes, Medevac.'

'Did we get those Irish bastards?'

'Every one.'

'Blood on your hands. Are you hurt?' Eilidh noticed Tonka's eyes were closed.

'No, I'm fine.'

The doctor's voice was in Sam's headset. 'Keep him talking. Stay on topic, don't confuse or upset him. I can't administer more sedative.

'Got the watcher?'

'Yes.'

'Armed?'

'Armalite.'

'No shots, Sambo.'

'No.'

'Used the knife, did we?'

'Had to.'

'Not a sound, Sam. You're so fuckin' quiet.'

'Had to be.'

'Saved our lives, big man.' Tonka laughed and started to cough. He convulsed again and talked some more. 'The covering fire was a fuck-up. That idiot Major screwed it up. Wouldn't listen.'

'Where are you thinking of?'

Tonka didn't hear Sam. 'They bayoneted the Duncan lad, sir. Fuckin' stuck him. He's on a chopper with the Argie bastard who did it. Yeah, I saw him. He's a bit of a mess.' He convulsed once more and fell back, unconscious.

* * *

The helicopter whirled round the medical centre and landed on the helipad. Sam and Fogarty helped lift Tonka out. The Emergency services took over and moved him away quickly. The doctor rushed off with them to make her report.

Eilidh glanced at Sam as they walked across to a waiting area. Harpur and four other men provided a ring of armed protection. Sam could tell she was straining to take in what she'd heard.

* * *

When they were sitting in a private meeting room with only Fogarty for company, Eilidh stared at Sam, eyes locked to his. Once or twice she seemed close to speaking then stopped, and maintained a thoughtful silence. She sat quietly for a few more moments. 'These pros are truly respectful of you, Sam. Aware of what you might do.'

'It seems so.'

'Did you kill a man with a knife?'

'Yes.'

'Tell me.'

'We'd had intelligence about be a bank raid in a town in Northern Ireland. Eight of us went in to stop the action. I took point.' He paused.

'Go on.'

'Are you sure you want to hear this?'

'Please, I want to understand.'

'I was following a contour and saw movement. I got there as the guy was putting an Armalite to his shoulder, about to fire. I couldn't risk any noise. I took the gun off him and killed him.'

'With a knife?'

'Yes.'

'How?'

'Sorry, love. I'm not going there. Took me a while to get over that one.'

Eilidh paused, then stood up and walked over to him. She grasped him in a fierce hug. 'You're solid and brave. Thanks for being here for me.'

Fogarty said, 'Eilidh, if I may intrude,' she nodded. 'that big brother of yours saved my life on two occasions. He has undertaken some of the tough and dirty work that needs to be done to protect our people. He is a decent man, more decent than I have any right to expect. You're a lucky girl.'

'Yes, Fogarty, I am a lucky girl.' She turned and hugged

Sam again. 'With a hairy-arsed killer like you around I'll never be scared again.' The three of them laughed, eyes moist with emotion and the release of being safe.

* * *

The doctor came back half an hour later.

'Sir, your colleague is in theatre and he'll be a few hours yet. He'll be stable now he's properly in care. You can't do any more. I'm heading back and someone is waiting outside to speak to you. Good luck with the mission sir.'

'Thank you, doctor. What you heard on the way in ...'

'I don't know what you're talking about.' They nodded and shook hands, the medic left.

123

'I'm going to straighten out some things here before I head for Europe,' Fogarty said. They had been flown to Boise, Idaho, by the military, with arrangements for onward travel made by the Agency. The food court was busy, the tacos were good, and they were loosening up.

'What's your plan?' Sam said.

'My people knew I was being turned by the Bizz guys. We agreed I should play ball and find out what I could. I went a tad farther than envisaged, I'm tainted. The only way forward is a clean breast and forgiveness.'

'Good luck with that.'

'If it works out, I'll be close behind you.'

'I hope it does. We're routing through San Francisco and up to Vancouver for a debrief and medical check. We'll head over the pond from Canada.'

'Right, I'm for DC. My plane's been called. Safe journey,' Fogarty said.

Eilidh considered him. 'Goodbye, Mr Fogarty.' She shook his hand and looked away.

Sam walked with Fogarty part of the way to the gates. 'She's not sure about you, Foggy.'

'Not a surprise, I'm sad to say.'

'She's fair-minded. You'll win her confidence back,' Sam said. 'Mine, too.'

'Sorry, I've hurt you guys.'

'I hear you. Take care.' They shook hands, turned their backs on each other and walked away.

* * *

Two hours later Sam and Eilidh were on a flight to San Francisco. They arrived in a secure house at Port Moody near

Vancouver early that evening. A local hospital provided facilities for a full medical check. The doctors were British military.

* * *

After a day's intelligence debriefing Sam and Eilidh were taken to Vancouver International Airport. They waited for their flight: Air Canada to Paris via Montreal. They sat in the Aquarium and Creek area. The totem face and the fish tank held their interest for a few minutes, until a table came free near the creek. Sam bought some coffee and biscuits.

'Bloody Paris, Sam. I'm tired of all this charging about.' She sipped her mocha and looked at him with a chocolate upper lip.

'Boring, old spooky stuff.' He leaned back in the curved seat, hunched and stretched his shoulders a couple of times. The girder ceiling was bright, and the bluish carpet soothed him. The people in the food area across the way seemed fenced in.

Eilidh's sigh was long and weary. 'I'm not sleeping. All those questions make my brain ache. I can't stop thinking.'

'So you beat up on your big brother to get even?'

'I'm sorry. What's this about going back via Dublin?'

'Convolution.'

'What's that supposed to mean?'

'It makes us hard to track.'

'Big silly words.'

'That one's on me.' Sam grinned and received a scowl in return. 'The Agency let me organize the travel. We're getting Business Class from Montreal.'

'Sorry, I'm just pissed-off.'

'You can sleep on the plane.'

'How do you always manage to nod off?'

'Training and savvy.'

'What's the trick?'

'Think of a fantastic, pleasant experience. Immerse yourself in it and drift off.'

'And if you can't think of any?'

'Make one up and enjoy it.' Sam reached across and

squeezed her shoulder. 'We're alive. We're heading home. The bad guys are still after us, but we're here and safe for the moment.'

'Why are we flying scheduled?'

He held up two Canadian passports. 'We're off the radar.'

'And in Paris?'

'We're being met by a wonderful friend.'

She smiled. 'If he's who I think he is, I'll be pleased to see him.'

'Me, too.'

Sam didn't share his concerns with her.

124

'Remember me?'

'Fog man.' An earthy contralto voice warmed him. 'You've been raising eyebrows.'

'Just running around the woods with a wild man.'

'So I hear.'

'How safe is it to see you?'

'Not very, we have some leaky places; this line is secure.'

'I'll be in town in around five hours.'

'What do you need, partner?'

'Redemption and a bed for the night.'

'Meet me in the usual place.'

'And the bed?'

'My place, for sure. You'll need to be mighty convincing if you're going to get more than food and a place to rest that craggy head of yours.'

Fogarty cackled. 'I've a story to tell.'

'I've heard some of those before, Fogarty, remember the word: convincing.'

'I won't forget. Are you protected?'

'Yes. You'll need me to get close to salvation.'

'Yes. There's work to be done in Europe.'

'There's work to be done over here. See you, Fog man.' She hung up.

Fogarty sat back and grinned.

125

The 777 landed with a bang at Paris Charles de Gaulle Airport. Sam, face resting against the window, yawned, and was wide awake as the engines roared into reverse thrust. He sighed and stretched as best he could in the confines of the seat. He checked his watch and then Eilidh, who dozed in the seat beside him.

'We're here, Eilidh.' Sam said, his voice almost a whisper.

'Oh, Sam, wha—? Where are we?'

'Paris.'

'Give me a moment.' Her eyes closed again, and she took a couple of deep breaths.

'Time to head for the gate.'

'Mo's coming?'

'Yes, he'll meet us at Customs.'

'And we're on a devious route to avoid killers?'

'Anyone who swims rivers at night and goes to the bathroom with bears is well into defensive routing.'

'Oh pu-leeeze. I don't need new descriptions for travelling without being seen. I need rest.'

'So doze. We'll get back okay. We're going to take a little longer, that's all. As a bonus, we get to see Mo.'

'Lovely man.'

'And, you're the one we're protecting, I'm just a petty official as far as the world is concerned. You, my girl, are the icing on the cake.'

'I thought Mo would play dead, like you.'

'He couldn't. Too many people clapped eyes on him after the event, what with his men being killed and all. They came out with a story about me going ahead in a separate car for security reasons, and being blown up on my own.'

The flight attendant came by and welcomed them to Paris.

In minutes they were walking towards passport control.

Sam remembered his arrival in Nice a few weeks before. The process was almost identical. Mo awaited.

'Hello, my cask-strength hero.' He gave Sam a hug and turned to Eilidh and, picking her hand up, gave it a gentle kiss, while rolling his eyes up to meet hers. He smiled. 'Give me your baggage tags and I'll get your stuff picked up.' Mo eyed Eilidh up and down. 'It is beyond comprehension how someone so beautiful could share parentage with such a Neanderthal beast of a man.'

'He may be ugly, but he's all heart.' Eilidh said.

Mo shrugged and waved them forward. 'Follow me.' They strode through a maze of corridors to a helicopter, had a seat while their baggage was reclaimed, and arrived at a military establishment somewhere to the north of the city forty minutes later.

* * *

'The long way round,' Sam said, 'but we get into the UK with minimum fuss. We'll fly to Dublin tomorrow, take a drive into the North, and a chopper will drop us off in the UK.'

'And, in the meantime, I'll be delighted to entertain you in the Officers' Club.' Cassanet took Eilidh's hand, 'You know, even somewhat battered and worldly-wise men make excellent lovers.'

'You look too young and handsome to be worldly-wise, monsieur.'

Mo nodded his head accepting the compliment. 'Of course, it's to do with clean living. So much better than that desperado you call a brother.'

'I wish I could make wild music with you, *Directeur*, but my heart is elsewhere.'

'Surely not a Yankee … eh … a call-himself-a-soldier?'

'A secret.'

'Pah! I will never sleep again, tormented by my love for you.'

'Keep talking, you French reprobate, and I'll arrange a

permanent lights out,' Sam said.

'You, you ... sheep-shagger.' Eilidh snorted in the background. 'You have no sympathy for a man with a broken heart.'

'None.'

Cassanet waved his hands in the air shrugged and gave a quizzical smile. 'Oh well my friends, we better get down to business.' He looked at Sam, dead serious. 'Eilidh, too.'

* * *

'The car my men died in was rocketed by an attack helicopter. We followed through on intelligence and found a rough trail that takes us into Italy. We can't say exactly where because, as usual, the administration and military are lost in a mire of bureaucratic confusion, then throw in the Italians ... pouf!'

'Powerful people,' Sam said. Eilidh perched on her seat leaning forward, listening hard.

'Oh yes, power; power and the ability to project it.'

'You've got something?'

'Of course. We followed leads and started to dig in the Italian area. Whatever we say, the Italians aren't all stupid, and many of them really care about stopping corruption and the evils of humankind.'

'You're on a trail?'

'Yes, back to the European Parliament and beyond.'

'Any names?'

'The Smythsone woman comes up.'

'An ice maiden, that one.'

'Yes, lawyer, capable and with good reasons to visit her clients.'

'Visit who?'

'We are having trouble getting precise information. We know where she goes, but we must manage our visibility with care.'

'Surely her presence is a matter of record?'

'Of course, but there are records, and there are records.'

'No help anywhere?'

'We face a strong overseeing intelligence presence, and it hates enquiring French people.'

'Okay, we know she visits. Where does she stay?' Sam said.

'Hotel de Ville, Strasbourg, and the Hotel Metropole in Bruxelles. These are full of people who may or may not be problematic.'

'Any repeaters?'

'An American billionaire, and a woman, who is senior in the IMF.'

'How might we help?'

'Pass the word and get some Brit assets engaged.' Cassanet said.

'I'll talk to Charlton.'

'Thanks, mon ami. I will give you a dossier before you leave,'

'Anything occur to you, Eilidh?' Sam said.

'No. Just how tangled all this is.'

'It'll stay tangled until we get much closer to the top,' Sam said. 'Mo, it sounds like Smythsone is a useful link. She's the main connection to the London cabal ...'

'And she's visiting Europe quite a lot and, more recently, Singapore and Hanoi. We need to think about this. Let's eat some lunch and get you refreshed and relaxed for the next leg of your journey.'

'Sounds good.' Eilidh smiled.

'Some new passports and so on will be arranged.'

'When are you supposed to travel?'

'There's a flight around eight.'

126

The phone on Mike's desk rang. He listened and hung up.

'Tweedledum is locked up. Maybe you should pay him a visit.'

'Too easy?'

'Who knows? Talk to him.'

'Okay. Racist.'

'Fuck off!'

'Told you.' Cal left the room, smile a mile-wide.

* * *

'Barney, my boy, we're getting nowhere with you.' Cal sat opposite a thug; the only word he could think of to describe him.

'I'm saying nothing, and you can't make me.'

'You're right.' He turned towards the DC. 'DC Binstead, what grounds can you offer for detaining Mr Rubble? *Apologies*, Mr Roundel?'

'None, sir.'

'Then we'll just have to let him go.' Cal turned to the prisoner. 'We think you're heavily implicated in the injury of a little old lady, and a serious assault on a doctor. But we don't have the evidence, or time, to attempt to sweat information out of you. Therefore, you are free to go.'

'Go?' The surprise echoed in from the walls.

'Go. You refused to cooperate, as is your right, and we accept that. We have suspicions, but not enough evidence to bring a prosecution. What can we say but goodbye?' He leaned towards the recorder and noted the time as 18.57 when the interview ended.

'I'll leave DC Binstead to handle the niceties, give you your money and other stuff back. Goodnight, Barney.'

Binstead took Roundel through to the desk where the

Sergeant duly released him with prompt, impersonal informality.

Flo' Binstead put on her coat and went out to the pool car from Westferry Road. Cal drove off as soon as she had her seatbelt on.

'I hope he only gets a hiding, sir.'

'Me, too. Maybe nothing will happen. A good bashing might loosen Roundel's tongue. If he gets duffed-up we might get more … or less. Whatever, we did our duty, and events will take their course.'

They stopped at a red light. 'Do you care if he gets a rough time?'

Cal turned towards her. 'Frankly my dear, I couldn't give a damn.'

They both laughed. The lights turned green.

'Sounds like a good one, you two.'

Flo' started and looked round. 'I forgot you were there, sir.'

'No matter, ma'am. I'm only an American observer.'

'Of course, sir.'

'Roundel has been released as bait,' Cal said. 'Flo', Mr Fogarty, worked with Eilidh Duncan in the States, with connections to their government.'

'We miss the Colonel, sir.'

'We all do.' They drove on in silence.

* * *

A few hours later, Barney Roundel was fighting for his life.

127

Smythsone was looking forward to a night in on her own. A hot bath was running. She was nonplussed by Xavier's behaviour and obvious power. Not many people scared her, but he managed. Her phone rang.

'Hello Gemma.' The slight oriental intonation gave the show away.

'Kenneth, wonderful to hear from you.'

'I know this is short notice, but I wonder if you could manage to join me and a couple of colleagues for a meal.'

She sighed. 'It sounds urgent.'

'I'd rather say important and opportune.'

'Of course. I'd be delighted to come.'

'Excellent, I'll send a car for you. Say an hour?'

'That'll be fine.'

'See you shortly.'

After half an hour, the heat of the tub had done its work, and she started to relax. Then a thought about the trap Jim Thomas had laid for Maybelle insinuated itself and demanded attention. The similarities began to scare her: a call from a trusted senior person; an assassin waiting in the wings.

She dressed on autopilot: simple, high-quality clothing that matched her skin tone and displayed her figure. All the while her mind played and replayed her fears. In the end, she could think of no justification for being fearful and, if there was she'd be sure to die anyway. With her fears suppressed she put on a stunning silk stole.

The concierge rang to tell her the car had arrived.

Smythsone walked with a confidence she needed to show. Inside, she trembled just a little. In her mind, she knew she was doing well, and earning a powerful place. Yet, in five minutes she might be dead. She strode on.

* * *

'Gemma, my dear, you are radiant.' Kenneth Chen walked across and they performed the two-cheek pouting, as would most people with their social standing. He took her over to a booth where Jack and Justine were sitting. The restaurant was a Michelin three-star, with unobtrusive service to match. The booth was private in its quilted burgundy leather upholstery. The tablecloth was almost impossibly white and smooth. The glassware and cutlery gleamed. Three perfect roses in an elegant, slender crystal vase stood in beautiful simplicity at the centre of the table.

'No Xavier tonight?' Smythsone said.

'No, he isn't focused on London at the moment. The failures in the USA are taking up his time,' Chen said.

'His ass is hurting, and we wanted to make sure your feathers weren't too ruffled by recent meetings with our European Executive,' Jack said.

'Yes, my dear,' Justine smiled and patted the seat beside her. 'You've had a rather tough introduction to our cabal, and we want to push beyond that.' Her French accent was enticing as ever, and her eyes betrayed interest beyond business.

'You didn't invite me here to soothe me,' Smythsone said.

'No, Gemma, not only that. But we are concerned, believe me,' Chen said. 'We have other key groups and we'd like to have you on one of the Boards.'

'Interesting.'

'Good. The area is South-East Asia.' We have a team covering Vietnam, Laos, Thailand, Cambodia, Singapore, and an emerging opportunity in Burma. Keep excitable people in line, and us in touch with events.'

'I have legal commitments in the City.'

'Key accounts. Of course, influence has its own rewards. We want you to become a powerful, discreet player.'

'Okay.' She didn't sound too sure.

'The money will be breathtaking. We'll find a way to ensure

your success at the highest level. Yet we mustn't put noses out of joint or create suspicion.' Chen was a persuader.

She paused and smiled. 'I can't wait.'

'Excellent.'

'What about that dangerous Duncan woman?' Smythsone said.

'We've developed a central contact,' Chen said, 'and arranged a suitable end for her in Dublin. She is travelling under an assumed name with a guardian who might as well disappear at the same time.'

'Her plans are that clear?'

'To us, now, yes. They will use a familiar route. Remember the vanished policeman? We think they're using a similar route. They are heading for Belfast International via Dublin. We'll waylay them when they get their rental car. All the assumed benefits of entering through Ireland are gone.'

'Who fixed it?'

'Never mind. Suffice to say we have friends in low places.'

The conversation went on for two hours over dinner and drinks. Samson suggested they share a taxi and went home with her. She knew she had him, and, as it always did, she loved the electricity of true power surging into her. They enjoyed a night of passionate sex, with both of them exhausted in the morning. Neither of them loved the other except as a means to an end, but liking and lust made enjoyable bed fellows.

Samson left before breakfast and Smythsone enjoyed a lingering shower. Next she went to her office and started to reduce her commitments: assigning partners and associates to all but her most prestigious cases and clients. By the afternoon she had managed to get rid of the 'dross' accounts.

She flew overnight to Singapore for a key meeting. She didn't know she was the subject of a conversation 6,000 miles away.

128

The phone rang three times. Strangford paused and picked it up with a sigh. He gazed at the Dublin rain slapping his window.

'Mr Strangford.' The East End accent was in his face, both friendly and strong, king to king.

'Mr Jenkins, a pleasant surprise.'

'I hope the line is secure.'

'According to my technical people, it's guaranteed.'

'Excellent.' After a pause, he heard an intake of breath in London. 'Do you miss Denny?'

'Every day, as God is my judge.' Strangford smiled. 'A day without Denny lacks excitement.'

'Amazing he should disappear as he did.'

'Hard to fathom.' The educated Irish brogue sounded warm and buttery.

'Can you do me a favour?'

'For you, Bill, anything.'

'I need two annoying persons to disappear as thoroughly as Denny. They're due in to Dublin on a flight from Paris, and heading for Belfast in a hire car.'

'This is a short-order call, Bill.'

'I know, but blessings will flow from it.'

'Anyone I know?'

'No. A tall dark skinned man and a lean, pretty young woman. It's an urgent job for a customer. They'll be travelling on French passports.'

'A double murder? Nothing to it.' Strangford looked at the wall opposite and thought of Denny's body flopping on to the plastic sheeting.

'It keeps the wheels of business grinding on: a favour here, a favour there. This is a big personal favour for me, Mr

Strangford.'

'How can I refuse?'

'I won't forget this.'

'What particulars do you need?'

'Photographs of him and her, obviously dead.'

'How does that work?'

'Heads separated from bodies always makes the viewers feel confident.'

'What's in it for me?'

'A get-out-of-jail free card, and a quarter of a million euros.'

'God, he must be stirring that hornets' nest pretty hard, the wild man.'

'The wild man's dead, it's his sister they want. The hornets are restless and raging.'

'I'll get on it, but I don't want to be involved other than as a contractor on this.'

'Me neither. We got the assignment from some very dangerous people. I was only brought in fifteen minutes ago from a rather, shall we say, top level source.'

'Just as well I said yes to an offer I can't refuse, eh Bill?'

'Exactly.'

'Send me the flight information. We'll sort it.'

'Call me when it's done, and send me the photos.'

'Okay. Speak afterwards.'

'Good man. Bye.'

The phone clicked, Strangford hung up and sat back. The feeling was bad, but no option. *Fuckin' Brits.*

129

The men stood in an abattoir twenty miles north of Dublin. The place was closed for the night. The shine of stainless steel reflected light all around. Strangford, tall and solid, his sandy hair hidden under a balaclava, rocked restless and edgy.

'Dirty work,' one of the men said.

'Yeah, but sometimes ugly stuff must be done to grease the wheels of business,' Strangford said.

A mobile sounded. 'We'll have them here in ten minutes,' Declan said.

'Right. We do the job quick. Once more from the top: Declan, you're the butcher. Stick 'em after Bingo gives 'em the shock. No damage to the head and try not to splash the blood around too much. Fast as you like, lop their heads off with that chainsaw, and put 'em on the spikes over there. '

'Right. Where they do the pigs heads for snouts and pituitaries.'

'Right, Declan,' Strangford said. 'You okay about this?'

'Gotta be done, as you say. A feckin' job.'

'You two, ready with the body bags?' Two men nodded.

'Shouldn't be too much blood. I'll drain 'em well.' Declan said. 'Someone remind me not to gut 'em. Don't want to be on autopilot.' He laughed.

'I'll feckin' remind you, Declan,' Strangford said. 'Things are fixed at the crematorium for an early burn, and they'll be gone.'

'This is awful work, Mr Strangford.' One of the men spoke up.

'Sure an' it is. We'll have a drop or two when we're done and everything's cleaned up.' Strangford stared at the pulleys, chains and electric tongs: for stunning pigs, not people. A ghastly task. He'd killed a few in his time, but this was the coldest execution he'd ever heard of.

* * *

Next, the sounds of hooded, gagged and frightened people, accompanied by loud swearing from a couple of his men. The victims were coming for the killing.

Declan, switched on the tongs and fiddled nervously with the controls. The saw hung from its cable near the bleeding area. He wore a maroon rubber apron and large yellow gloves. In his hand, a thin-bladed knife. His assistant, dressed the same, shook nearby. 'Remember, squeeze their ears with the tongs and press the button.'

'So I just push the button?' His number two twitched with nerves. He looked at the spikes and back at the door the victims were about to come through.

'Easy as puttin' a kettle on.'

'Will they struggle?

'Up to them. They might pray or somethin'. The electricity will soon quiet 'em down.'

'Stun 'em?'

'Right. They'll jerk a bit. Put the hook through the rope on their ankles and I'll lift 'em up with the hoist. Make sure their faces don't get bashed when we lift 'em.'

'You mean grab 'em?'

'What do you feckin' think? Once they're up, push 'em towards me on the rail and I'll stick 'em. They'll feel nothin'. The blood goes down the hole there, unless you want black pudding.'

'Stop it.'

'Get the job done. I'll take their heads and you spike the first one. I'll bring the other over.'

A large swallow. 'How do I do spike 'em?'

'Hold 'em by the ears and bang 'em on the spike. Throat side down, you feckin' twat.'

* * *

Two people were hauled into the killing area: a male and a

female. They were taken to the tongs.

'When you stun 'em, be sure not to touch 'em, unless you want a big shock.' The assistant's face turned light grey as he wrestled with the tongs. 'Stand still. You'll not feel a thing.' He opened the scissor-like electrodes and stepped towards the whimpering woman.

130

‘It’s gonna kick off.’ Mike’s voice burst from the radio. The surveillance had been tight and unnoticed.

‘With you.’ Cal, Fogarty and Binstead left the car and walked briskly down the road. They paused at the corner and checked the rear door of a pub.

‘They’ll be out anytime now.’

‘Weapons?’

‘Expect knives, possibly firearms.’ The three of them were wearing vests.

‘Don’t engage, Mr Fogarty,’ Cal said. ‘Stay here.’

‘Roger that.’

A fine, misty drizzle added gleaming crystals to the air. The light at the exit shone on an area roughly four metres by four metres, with the fire escape door in the middle. On the right side as Cal and Flo’ faced it there were two large, wheeled dumpsters of different colours, which appeared as a pale or a dark grey in the sodium yellow of the light.

Cal went up between the two skips. Flo’ hid at the left-hand corner of the wall where she was joined by uniformed constables.

The fire door burst open and five people came out, one being dragged, struggling, by two large men, one black and one Asian. The other three were almost dancing with excitement. The leader, an arrogant hard man with a severe face and flinty eyes, slapped the prisoner lightly on the face, sneering and coming close until they were nose-to-nose. Next, he pinched the captive’s cheeks together hard, squeezing them together over the man’s mouth so his lips made an ‘ooo’ shape and started to bleed. Roundel’s pallor was greyish green in the lighting.

‘We’re going to have a little talk, you and me, Rounders.’

'What's the problem?'

'Screw-ups, sonny, screw-ups.'

'She walked in on us. The watchman never called.'

'Says he did. Phone shows he texted you.'

'No signal. Text came in after we left. I didn't mean to screw up.'

'Too bad. What have you done, you stupid fuck? A doctor critically injured and an old lady with a coronary? We can't have that. The old man don't like screw-ups. His boy, he tapped his chest, don't like screw-ups, and you're a stupid piece of shit.' The main man pulled out a carpet knife and pressed it into Barney Roundel's cheek. Blood squirted from under the point. 'You're getting a written warning tonight, all over your fuckin' face.' He started to carve slowly. Roundel screamed a hollow, vomiting sound, projecting a mixture of pain, fear and horror.

'*Police!* Drop your weapons. Stand still.' Cal's voice roared like an express train bursting from a tunnel. The criminal group froze, confused at first.

Like a starburst, the five men round the victim tried to run off. One, an African Brit, grabbed for the fire door and found himself gripped by Mike Swindon, who turned him and threw him into the arms of two waiting constables, who dragged him to the floor and cuffed him.

Binstead grabbed the first man who came her way, and received a hard elbow in the eye for her trouble. She hung on, and a colleague dragged him off her and punched him hard in the kidneys. Two others ran past them, into a waiting group of officers.

The man wielding the blade came at Cal with a vicious slash. Cal blocked the blow with his left forearm and took a cut through the jacket sleeve, a couple of inches above his watch. He slammed his fist into the man's jaw, which started his assailant's knees buckling, but didn't stop his aggression. Cal leaned backwards, tucked his chin in and swayed back to avoid a wild backhand slash at his face.

He stepped in behind the swipe, as the man lost his balance, then followed under the assaulter's arm and grabbed his wrist. He held the limb away from his body and punched the man hard under the Adam's-apple. The bad guy started to gurgle. Cal's next punch smashed his nose. The aggressor lurched back and struggled to free his hand and blade. Cal twisted the man's wrist locked out the arm and leverage pressure on his elbow. His assailant dropped the blade with a satisfying squeal. He arrested and cautioned the criminal before handcuffing and passing him to a constable for medical attention and removal.

Mike came over. 'You're bleeding, mate.'

'Shit!'

'So's he.'

'Good.'

'That's a wicked right hand.'

'Not fast enough the first time.'

'It's fast enough, believe me.'

'And HIV tests galore. Bastard.' Cal shrugged. 'Our man might do some singing now.'

'I can hear him practising his scales already.' Mike patted Cal's shoulder. 'Off you go and see the paramedic.'

* * *

Cal walked over to an ambulance, one of two which had arrived. 'Can you fix this?'

The paramedic, a trim pretty brunette, said: 'Let me have a look.' She asked him to take off the jacket and his shirt, now soaked with blood on the left forearm. 'You'll need a couple of stitches. Best go A&E.' She wiped the wound and applied a bandage, appraising his powerful frame. 'You hooked up?'

'Not at the moment.'

'Fancy a beer sometime?' He gazed at her and then gave her his 2,000-watt grin.

'Here's my number.' She wrote her mobile down and handed it to him.

'Here's my card.' He offered his hand 'Cal.'

'Ginny.'

'Pleased to meet you, Ginny. See you soon.'

'I'll call you later,'

'Can't wait.'

Cal headed for the car, and Fogarty walked over. 'Tough night, Chief Inspector.'

'Not bad.' Cal paused. 'In fact, pretty good. A fight, an attractive woman in prospect. Now all that's left is eating and drinking, and I've cracked it.' He waved Mike over.

'Can you involve Mr Fogarty in the questioning?' Cal said.

'Yeah. How's the arm?' Mike said.

'Got to go for some embroidery.'

'Nice looking woman there.'

'Yeah.'

'Thought you liked big sistas.'

'Racist.'

'Ha!' Mike laughed. 'Lucky bugger.'

'I can't help being good looking.'

'Let's go, Mr Fogarty. DCI Martin is in need of treatment for a number of conditions.' Mike and Fogarty walked away.

Binstead came over. 'You're nuts, boss.'

'Coming from you, Flo', that's praise indeed. Your eye looks sore.'

'I'm going to have a shiner tomorrow.'

'Hard woman. The odd ding and bump makes people more interesting, don't you think?'

'Mike wants the car. Keys please.' She held out her hand and waved her fingers in a give-them-to-me gesture. He handed them over.

Two hours later, he was stitched up, Ginny dropped by as he waited for a dressing. When she came off shift, they went out for a late supper. Goodnight was a pleasant kiss. They agreed to meet again, and soon.

In bed, Cal read a text from Ginny in his phone a couple of times. He fell asleep thinking life was good, *ace*. And as for Ginny: *ace plus!*

131

'Stop!' Strangford's volume made everyone freeze, except for the butcher's assistant who was concentrating on the tool for the killing. The apparatus neared the woman's head. 'Declan! For fucks sake, make him listen.'

Declan dropped his knife, waddled over and switched the power off, took the tongs and smacked his helper on the head. 'Listen to the man!'

'This isn't right,' Strangford said

'No, it's feckin' wrong.'

'Shut up! The man's too short and the woman's too fat.' Strangford's voice came out muffled from the balaclava. 'Let's have a look at him. Undo his mouth.'

'What's your name?'

The man blinked in the light. 'Yves Dortan.'

'Why are you here, Mr Dortan?'

'Business trip. Are you going to kill us?'

'No.' Strangford turned to the men who had brought them in. 'Show me their papers.' They were handed over. 'He doesn't look like a tough guy to me, and as for the woman, she's big, fortyish and has a hairy lip. Nothing like the target.' He shook his head. 'You two, take them to the middle of town and let them go. Blindfold him again. Mr Dortan, say nothing, don't make a noise, and you'll get out of this alive. Tell your partner.' There was a burst of rapid-fire French.

The captives were led away. The men stood, relief stark in their posture.

'Thank God for that,' Declan said.

'Yeah. Now, as for that drink we were talkin' about … give me five minutes after we get back to base, then let's murder a curry and a few pints. First, I have a wee call to make to a chubby, evil, English bastard.'

132

'I shall miss you and your enticing beauty,' Mo said.

'That's the nicest compliment I've had for a long time,' Sam said and fluttered his eye lids.

'Not you, you dilapidated excuse for a real man. I mean this delightful young woman, who has captured my romantic French heart.'

'You say the most wonderful things, Mo,' Eilidh said. 'At least we had time for a lazy meal before our departure.'

The big man sighed and then straightened his face. 'Sorry we're so early, but the best way for you is Amsterdam by train and fly from Schipol. The route changes combined with the *hélicoptère* from yesterday, make you hard to trace.'

'Are all the arrangements made?'

'Yes. You will be met at Lille and have cosmetic adjustments. Our Dutchman will take care of you at Schipol. Enjoy your journey.' Mo reached inside his long tweed coat for a rolled A4 envelope. 'Nearly forgot. Here's the dossier I promised, Colonel. You must read and digest.' He turned to Eilidh. 'Make sure he chews it well and drinks plenty of water when the time comes.' He smiled, winked at Eilidh and walked away.

An operative signalled them to a car. Twenty minutes later they boarded an early train.

* * *

'Rouen to Lille and we'll be in Schipol for a mid-afternoon flight.'

'Why?'

'Take an unexpected route. A Dutch contact is sorting our travel. He'll put us on the plane and no hassle. Lille first for a change of appearance, and French passports, as Mo said.'

'Any word on Tonka?'

'Yes. I spoke to him last night. He sends his love. He's largely fixed, but they want more healing time for his head. He'll be back in a couple of weeks.' The train entered a pretty station, people got on and off. No one paid them attention, lost in their early morning trips to work or school.

'I never thought of a commute as enjoyable.'

'Wonderful,' Sam said. 'Don't let your guard down. Anyone, here or anywhere else may be after us.'

'Thanks a bunch. Normality just evaporated.' Eilidh's wistful frown spoke volumes.

'I think we should be okay, but don't stop being aware. You'll learn.'

* * *

The stop in Lille was uneventful and brisk. They arrived at 08.40 and were on the 10.30 TGV via Brussels, with a connecting train, due at Schipol Airport just after 14.30. The big train whispered along at immense speed. They were soon caught in the rhythm and pace of the journey.

'You look thoughtful,' Sam said.

'You look like a Latin Lothario,' Eilidh said.

'Brown lenses and black hair do that to a man. Makes me sexy, right?' The landscape outside the window hurtled past as the train raced through Belgium.

'To be honest, you're the wrong shape. Lotharios are cool, slim and hugely attractive to women.'

'Now wait a minute …' Sam smiled, his eyes crinkled. 'Look at you … a platinum-blonde scrubber.'

'Scrubber! How dare you?'

'Spiky hair, spiky by nature, I always say.'

'I didn't choose the outfit.'

'I'm surprised you can breathe, those pants are so tight.'

'Stop being an old …'

'Lothario?'

'Brother!'

'Want a coffee?'

'Yes please.' Sam went to the buffet car. People sat on stools at the rounded tables. He picked up two coffees, two baguettes and some fruit. Back at the seat he placed the food in front of Eilidh and sympathized with the wistfulness etched on her face.

'Hiya, toots,' Sam said.

'I'm not going to rise to verbal abuse.' Eilidh rested her head on the window glass and watched some cars on the *Péage* being overhauled by the TGV as it sprinted along some hundred miles an hour faster.

'What's chewing you?'

'Shirl and Ida. Shirl's been an excellent flatmate, caring and fun. We're lifetime friends now. God, the pain she's had.'

'Yeah. She didn't deserve it, but she's okay.'

'What about Ida? Once or twice when I was down about the job and other stuff, she'd make me a cup of tea, sit beside me, hold my hand and rub the back of it with her thumb.'

'I know about loss, the emptiness when you go out and people you like and respect don't come back, an awful pain, jokes one minute and gone the next. Ida is recovering, it may take time, but she's still around.'

'Can I visit Shirl?'

'Are you prepared to put her in harm's way?'

'It's not fair.'

'Never is, especially if you're on the side of the angels. You can bet she's being watched. Shall I see if we can fix up a video link? The guys have some new software to allow highly secure contact between ordinary computers.'

'Why are they hunting us so hard?'

'Fear. They don't know what you know, and even with a listening ear at the debrief in the States, they *are* scared.'

'Amazing.'

'And human. They're evil, know what they are and don't want to be caught.'

'They want to catch me?'

'Only if they can do it safely. They want to kill you, and will the moment you're exposed, or after you tell all.'

'We're safe here on the train, right now, aren't we?'

'As best we can be. It'll be even better when we leave Schipol.'

'Still, no chance to relax.'

'Right. We must stay aware every sodding step of the trip.'

133

‘Hi, Martijn.’ The lean Dutchman met them as they entered the airport from the train.

‘You are French today, Monsieur Scot-Effrayant. We have you two well covered. Give me your stuff, and we’ll take it to the plane. Fantastic name.’ He signalled. Two people came over and took their luggage.

‘Th’auld alliance,’ Sam said.

‘Maurice is a piece of work.’

‘Isn’t he? And he calls me “Scary”.’ Sam said. He gestured to their host. ‘Eilidh, this is Martijn vanVenendaal, our protector until we’re airborne.

‘And Mademoiselle Scot-Effrayant, how are you?’

‘Tired and ready to fly, Martijn. I remember you from Seattle.’

He bowed slightly. ‘I’ll take you through security, and we can have a drink in the lounge. Your flight goes in an hour or so.’

They were soon on the vast concourse and entered a lounge where van Venendaal showed his papers. In minutes they were having a coffee and some biscuits. ‘Not long until the flight. We’ll put you on directly, no need for gates and such.’

‘Any news from the frontline?’

‘Mo’s people were grabbed in Dublin.’

‘Oh dear.’

‘They’re safe but a little shaken.’

‘It’s an amazingly long arm these people have.’

‘I don’t think they can have a line on where you are at the moment.’

Twenty minutes later, they boarded the plane and took seats at the emergency exits.

134

'That taxi driver was in a hurry.'

'We've two hours before the London sleeper leaves,' Sam said, 'Mo made the arrangements.'

'Sleeper?' Eilidh said. They were in a pub near Inverness station, just to the right of the car park. 'What's all this about?'

'We changed our arrangements yesterday because Westferry Road is porous.'

'You mean the Agency.'

'Yes. The route via Dublin and Belfast became too high a risk. That's why we're travelling as French citizens. I think we can get to London undetected. After that, it's in the lap of the gods.'

* * *

'The food wasn't bad.'

'Always steak pie for you, Sammy.'

'Yum.' Sam looked down the bar filled with optics and six mainstream beers on a large brass gantry. The dark wood and lighting was intimate and formulaic; six fifteen and the place buzzed. The booths round the walls were now half full. People were stoking up for the night ahead. He kept eyeing the crowd, aware.

'What about the Dublin arrangement?'

'Mo sent two people to fly as us from Paris to Dublin around teatime. He notified the Agency we were on our way, late, because you'd been a bit sick.'

'This is all kind of confusing, as well as exciting.'

'Us coming in undercover isn't in Charlton's script.'

'You trust Mo?'

'Completely.'

'Like Fogarty?'

'Ouch.' A one-armed bandit dropped a jackpot and the players cheered. 'The French are using mega resources to help us. Mo's family is in hiding. The opposition tried to kill us. Mo's kosher.

'Are we talking about a mole?' Eilidh was wide awake, asking, thinking, looking sharp.

'I hope there's only one, but whoever's doing the naughty, they're in the heart of things.'

'Who?'

'Charlton, Quentin, Indira; or all three.'

'Surely not.'

'I must find out.'

'And then what?'

'Sort it.'

'With a knife?'

'That's cruel.' Sam stopped speaking for a moment. His eyes sparkled and hardened. 'Not funny … but yes, if I have to.' He thought for a moment. 'You wanted to know, so I'll tell you, and I'll try to forgive you for pushing it.'

'I'm sorry, Sam. It just seems so unreal all this rushing about the Western world.'

Sam held up his hand. 'Shut it, Eilidh. Want to stay alive? Stick with the programme.'

'Is he bothering you?' A man stood at their table, legs apart and thumbs hooked round his trouser buckle. He swayed as he spoke in a pristine Inverness accent. He oozed confidence, eyes fired up for trouble.

'No thanks. We're fine.'

'He looks like a dago to me. He shouldn't be bothering a lovely girl like you.'

'He isn't bothering me.' Eilidh gave him a dismissive stare. Sam regretted they were in a booth at the rear of the pub.

'So fucking what, I don't like him.' He grabbed Sam's lapel and tugged at him, a bottle lashed towards Sam's head a split-second later. Sam blocked the blow; the bottle broke free of the man's grip and smashed on the wall scattering glass and beer on to people at a table nearby.

'Now see what you made me do?' The man's friends came over to cajole him away. He reacted with rage. 'Fuck off and leave me be. He's going to pay.'

The boss of the bar team came over. 'Hey, Jonesy. Stop this.' The man hit him in the face, and the barman sat down on the floor, blood on his lips.

Sam slid out from the table. 'What's with you? We don't want trouble, and we'll leave now.' He offered a hand and helped the barman get up. The man, Jonesy, moved forward, rage lighting his eyes.

Eilidh stepped in front of him. 'Leave us alone, you drunken idiot.'

'I thought he was annoying you.'

'You're annoying me.'

'Then fuck you, ya bitch.' He stood with his feet apart hands on his hips, cocky. His breath burst out of him as she slapped his face with an almighty thwack. He held his cheek. The place went silent. He screamed with fury and charged towards Eilidh. Sam's elbow strike to his head silenced him. He dropped like a guillotine blade to lie unconscious on the floor.

Sam turned to the bar manager. 'Are you okay?'

'Aye, I'll live. Shall I call the police?' The babble in the bar started up again. The man on the floor groaned.

'Up to you, chum.' Sam eyed the people round about. 'This is like the Wild West.'

'We don't need the hassle, if you're okay with that. Jonesy is an idiot.'

'We'll go. See that fierce pair eyeing me up and down. What's the chances they'll kick off?'

'Probable. Nasty pals of his lordship, on the floor.'

'Right.' Sam strode over. They scowled below a print of The Monarch of the Glen. If they expected words, they were mistaken. He closed with the first one and nutted him on the bridge of his nose. The man sank to the floor as he grabbed the bigger of the two by the throat, elbow bent, squeezing his

Adam's-apple hard. The man's face twisted, he gurgled and clutched at Sam's forearm. There was no give at all. Sam moved in close, picked the man up and ran with him to the wall, slamming him hard against the panelling. The fellow slid down groaning.

'Don't you or any of your mates come after us. Next time, it's hospital, understood?' The man didn't speak. Sam smacked his head. 'Got it?'

'Yes.' A weak whimpering voice said it all.

Sam turned back to the barman. 'That should settle things down.'

'Want a job?' A happy bar keeper looked at the three bullies.

'Not just now, but thanks for the offer.' Eilidh handed him his backpack and wheelie case. 'We're out of here.' He turned and a large man blocked his way. 'I'm not looking for trouble.'

'Too bad.'

'Leave them be, Dougie.' The barman came up beside Sam.

'Naw. I'm going to sort him.'

Sam waved his finger in the air. 'We're leaving. Please stand aside.' The big man grabbed for Sam, then started to scream. His broken knee wouldn't support him. He fell like a toppling tree on to a table. 'I tried to tell him, he must have wrenched his knee. He'll be fine in a couple of months. The faster you get him to the Raigmore, the better he'll be.'

The crowd parted for Sam and Eilidh like the Red Sea for Moses, clapping and whistling as they exited through the leaded glass doors.

Turning left for the station, Eilidh said, 'We weren't exactly looking for trouble.'

'Please, no jokes about covert movement and under the radar.' He glanced sideways at her. 'Let's board the train.'

* * *

Once they found their berths, Sam called Karen from a public phone using an interconnect number to hide their location. Afterwards, Eilidh and he schmoozed in the bar until the train neared Aviemore.

135

Gemma Smythsone closed her apartment door behind her. What a wonderful day: the tickets for Belgium were in her bag, she'd spent the last three hours shopping. A long soak in the tub beckoned. The people in Singapore were hugely deferential. She loved it and wanted more.

Kicking off a fabulous pair of high heels in the hall (wonderful things housekeepers) she loosened her blouse as she walked through to the bathroom. She turned the handle for a quick flow of hot water into the deep cast-iron tub.

She took off her blouse and reached for the zip on her dress as a strong arm grabbed her from behind. A gloved hand pressed on to her mouth.

'Good evening, Gemma. No need to shout. No one can hear you.' Her mouth was released. She felt an electric tension burst round her body.

'Please don't hurt me.'

'That depends.' The voice as quiet, American.

'Did Xavier send you?'

'Can't say.' His calm assurance terrified Smythsone. 'Question time.' A slight prick in her neck and she faded away.

She awoke in a tepid bath, shivering, and a man in a ski mask took her hair, not too roughly. 'I only ask questions once.' She felt even colder. The American accent was calm, business-like … assured.

136

'Top bunk or bottom.'

'Top. Don't want you landing on me during the night.'

In such a tiny space they agreed Eilidh should get ready first. Sam went into the corridor to use his pay-as-you-go mobile. Eilidh came out a few moments later, heading for the toilet.

Watching the toilet door, Sam made his call.

'Coalville Manor.' The ancient reedy voice greeted him.

'This is the Vicar, remember me?'

'Once seen and all that, sir.'

'Two rooms for tomorrow, please, adjoining.'

'Special requirements?'

'Discretion and my trunk.'

'No problem, sir.'

'See you then.'

'Yes sir. Good night.' The phone disconnected.

* * *

Sam waved Eilidh into the cabin. Told her to lock the door and only open it for him. When he returned from the lavatory he stripped to tee shirt and shorts, and slid into his bunk. The train moved with a gentle rhythm. With the door locked they lay in their bunks and chatted.

'You wanted to know about the knife,' Sam said.

'You don't have to tell me.'

'I will. You keep mentioning it so I'm going to tell you. You too mustn't forget, ever, that people have died, and will die, for you.' Her eyes brightened, and tears welled invisible in the top bunk. 'My skill and the skills of people like me keep you alive right now. Frankly, I could do with a wee bit less of your mouthiness when you're reminding me of tough times.'

'I'm sorry. I don't think.'

'Yeah.' She lay chastened, listening. She heard Sam swallow. 'I used a fighting knife on a seventeen year old.' He hefted his Gerber folding knife, flicked out the blade, got out of the bunk and held the blade up for inspection. 'This is the knife. He was armed with an assault rifle. We were on a mission during the Troubles. No time for thought, it was him or my mates. I knocked the gun down, grabbed him, lifted his chin and stuck this in under his ear sawing around to chew up his brain stem and general wiring. He jerked a couple of times and dropped like a sack of potatoes. It was his blood Tonka was talking about the other day.'

Eilidh sobbed and looked at Sam with an unaccustomed intensity. 'But you care.'

'Yes. I stopped the spook business years ago because I care, and the tough stuff was changing me, stealing my soul.'

'You went back into the life for me.'

'Yes, and there's a price to pay. For both of us to pay.'

'Is there a higher good?' The train rumbled on.

'I believe so,' Sam said.

'Me, too. What are we going to do?'

'See it through, pay the price, protect our folk. Stop the evil.'

'Bob Fogarty was scared of you when I called for help the other day.' Eilidh's statement asked a question.

'Yes.'

'What scares him, Sam?'

'What did he say?' The train started to slow for some reason.

'He said just that you might kill him. He looked sad and scared.'

'Yup. We best get some sleep.'

'He thinks you're very dangerous.'

'He's right. If you aren't safe I'll be just that.'

'Come here.' He leaned over, and she hugged him hard. 'I feel safe, big brother.'

'I suppose I feel better for sharing, being understood.' He

smiled in his gentle lopsided way. 'One more thing, young lady. If this gets sticky, do what I say: no discussion or dissent. I'm trying to get us home, safe, and make sure we're among friends. I can't guarantee anything.'

'You're still loveable, even for a hard-bitten killer.' He regarded her and nodded his head.

'Good night.' He slid back into his bunk. Being longer than the bed didn't matter. A tough day beckoned. He pulled out an unused pay-as-you-go mobile and texted Cal.

Wrinkly accommodation. 08.30 tomorrow.

That would get Cal thinking, and he'd figure it out.

* * *

He fell asleep smiling, and was ready and dressed when the breakfast trays arrived.

137

The train arrived in Euston Station, London, at 06.45. Eilidh and Sam were ready to leave and caught a taxi. They exited the taxi about fifty yards from the hotel. Eilidh led the way with Sam following her a few paces back. She sported a baseball cap. Sam wore a training top, hood up.

The old reception area remained unchanged and familiar. There was a door in the wall and window-like opening with a pull-down roller blind designed to slide down a shiny brass groove and lock on the counter. He'd never seen it closed.

'You've changed, sir.' The old man at reception was an hour away from finishing his stint as night porter.

'Yes, been travelling around. An old familiar face will be back soon.' Sam said.

'The lady is yours?'

'In a manner of speaking. My sister. She may stay while I do some business after breakfast.'

'Radar?' The wrinkled face gave a twitch of a smile.

'Switched on if you don't mind.'

'Of course. Eyes open?'

'Please. No one is expected apart from a breakfast guest.'

'We'll arrange a suitable booth, sir.' His smile moved his wrinkles into multiple grins.

Eilidh came to reception. 'Have I time to freshen up?'

'Yes, you've got half an hour.'

'Thank goodness for that.'

'Yup.'

'Cheeky!'

The old man bowed. 'Let me carry your bag, madam.' She gave it to him. 'Please follow me.' Sam crossed to an old brown leather Chesterfield and sat down with a sigh. In a few minutes, the night porter returned. 'You have something in storage,' he looked around, 'Colonel.'

'Yes.'

'It's waiting in your room.'

'Thank you. How close is my sister?' Sam said.

'Next door.'

'Excellent. A connecting door?'

'Naturally, as requested. We'll keep an eye on her.'

'Thanks.'

Sam went to his room. He knocked Eilidh's door and asked her to stay put until he rapped the door again.

In the room he found the large case under the bed. He pulled it out and removed a Harris Tweed jacket followed by a Colt .45 1911. He stripped, checked and oiled the gun and, satisfied, wiped it down. He took out a box of Federal Eagle 225 grain ammunition and loaded three clips, putting one in the gun and the others on the bed. Next, he removed his holster, a Kilpatrick HD 400, wiped it with a towel, put the clips in their holders and fitted the Colt.

He secured the case and slipped it under the bed. It would be removed once he left on business. After a shower, refreshed and dressed, he strapped on the holster, put on his jacket and checked his appearance in the mirror. The gun stayed invisible. The fighting knife nestled in his trouser pocket with his change.

He tapped on Eilidh's door.

'Ready for breakfast?'

'Can we avoid a punch up with wild men?'

'Maybe.'

She came out of her room and hugged him hard. 'I could eat a horse.' Her clear-eyed freshness comforted Sam.

'Can you make do with a full-cooked?'

'Only one?' Such a beautiful smile.

* * *

Cal sat in a curved booth in the downstairs restaurant. He did a double-take as they walked towards him.

'You're a bit more like a white man now,' Cal said.

'I'm not missing the beard,' Sam said.

'I do like the platinum-blonde style, you sexy thing.' Cal wiggled his eyebrows.

'Careful, big man. If you weren't an uncle to me I'd punch your lights out, and I punch my weight,' Eilidh said.

'So, I should be afraid of flea bites?'

'You're all mouth.' She stared at him.

'Racist.' They laughed.

The wrinkliest waiter in the world came over for the food order. 'Usual monstrous fry-up, sir?'

'Sounds good.'

'How many?' The waiter smiled, revealing loose-fitting dentures, then licked his pencil stub.

Sam looked round. 'Three and a big pot of tea.'

'Coming right up.' The ancient walked away with surprising agility.

'You guys are getting around.'

'Jet setters, dear boy. Is Fogarty with you now?' Sam said.

'He arrived, cursed you for keeping a man of his age busy. He took the night off and was in this morning, early doors. He is presently with Mike, interrogating some bad people we nicked late last night.'

'Is he secure, safe?'

'Yeah, in the nick.'

'Right, when we're done, I want you to take Eilidh, go to the nick and stay there until I call.'

'What's going down, mate?'

'I can't talk right now.'

'You've got your battle face on,' Cal said.

Eilidh watched the conversation like a game of tennis, turning her head one way and then the other.

'Get to the nick, stay off-line and make your presence clear.'

'What about HQ?' The knowing light gleamed.

'The nick; no contact. Keep Eilidh there.'

'Back-up?'

'Later.'

'Fuck it, Sam!'

'*Later*, Cal.' The sharp edge grated.

138

The meeting room in the police station wasn't the prettiest place on earth. A couple of worn noticeboards sported content: one covered in a hotchpotch of social information, offers and holiday postcards, the other an organized space for official documents and directives. The wall was ancient magnolia.

A clock on the wall clunked off the seconds with eternal patience. Down the corridor an aged vending machine threatened to squirt out a range of sludge. Cal reckoned every drink tasted the same: tea, coffee or chocolate. The only alternative was the soup, and the less said about that the better. Cal and Eilidh sat at a well-used table with two pairs of empty plastic cups in front of them. They had finished on the family catch-up and were down to business.

'Sam's off to rattle cages,' Eilidh said.

'That's why we're here,' Cal said. 'Safe in this concrete pillbox.'

'He worries too much.'

'He didn't tell you the full story about Dublin, then.'

'What's to tell?'

'Two French people took your place. They were taken to an abattoir instead of you. The deal was your heads were to go on spikes with your bodies displayed.' He paused. Eilidh stayed silent, shut her eyes and shook her head. 'Fortunately, one of the Irish gangsters figured it wasn't you two, and released them.'

She pressed her hand on to her forehead and pushed her hair back. 'As I said, he doesn't worry enough.' Her version of Sam's lopsided smile drew a laugh from Cal.

'These are terrifying people,' Cal said.

'Tell me.'

'And why is that?'

'They want to know what we know, and get their hands on my notes and documentation.'

'Right, it's what the bad people fear is in your information that's driving them wild.'

'Of course. I have evidence.'

'What a journalist calls evidence and a policeman calls evidence are two different things.'

'Our legal guys sounded positive,' Eilidh said.

Cal smiled. 'Of course they did. The evidence rule still applies—one for public consumption and another for prosecution.'

'What are you driving at?'

'As long as the opposition believes you have something big, it feeds their fear, their paranoia.'

'And if they can get their hands on the stuff?'

'They find out who helped you and what you know. With that information they can destroy both the paperwork and eliminate any human elements that endanger them.' He stopped and gazed at her.

'Go on.'

'If your stuff get into the hands of proper investigators, like me and Mike, we could organize a thorough investigation and chase down a lot of these bastards.'

'Proper investigators?'

'I mean professional criminologists.'

Attractive eyes narrowed. 'Liar. You mean I'm a hack and hacks aren't criminologists.'

'Yeah.' The million-watt smile made argument impossible.

'What about the eyes and ears scattered around? The vested interests?'

'Not everyone is evil or corrupt. There are decent people caught up in this who will come forward. Think of the risks people took to help you.'

'I want to be acknowledged as an investigative journalist.'

'You've got a dilemma. You'll have to decide: do the right thing or go for glory.'

'Why not both?' Eilidh said.

'Don't hold your breath.' They sighed. Cal looked at the coffee machine, 'any particular flavour of crud take your fancy?'

139

'Vicar, I heard you were dead.'

'I'm in the resurrection business, Bill. Can you spare me a few minutes?'

'Where are you?'

'Ten minutes away.'

'All right, if you must.'

The receptionist was charming as ever. She had the security badge made out when he arrived. On the wall was a picture of Bill shaking hands with a minor member of the Royal Family, with a shiny suit, shiny face and shiny tied-back hair furthering the corporate illusion.

'Do you mind looking after my bag?' Sam asked.

'Not at all.'

'Thanks.' She put it under the counter.

She led him to the lift with a pleasing wiggle of taut buttocks, and accompanied him to the Executive Suite.

The doors opened, and a large muscular man met him. The receptionist returned with the lift. A few words, a swish of the detector wand and Sam was ushered into Bill's office, opulent in black and chrome; the aircraft-carrier-sized desk impressive as ever. Bill had his hand behind his head pulling his pig tail.

'What can I do for you, old son?'

Sam walked towards the desk noting the man seated at the end of the desk. The tight platinum-blond of Charlie's hair was stark as ever. He looked in surprisingly good shape for a man alleged to be at death's door bare weeks before.

'Hello, Charlie.' Sam raised his hand and smiled. 'I'm not looking for trouble.' Sam walked over and offered his hand. It wasn't taken. The wary hostility in the dark, ball-bearing eyes said enough. *Once bitten.*

There wasn't a seat for Sam. He heard the office door click shut. Nothing like having a muscle-bound goon behind you.

'Cut to the chase Vicar. We haven't much time, Charlie's heading off shortly.'

'I'd like a quiet word.'

'No. There's nothing you can say that he can't hear.' Bill Jenkins said.

'Okay. I'm here to find out if you were linked to a plan to kill Eilidh Duncan and her minder in Dublin yesterday.'

'What makes you think I am?'

'The Dublin team were called in. You've done it before, the time when Jason got hurt. I thought we had an understanding.'

'You thought wrong.' Bill looked to Sam's right. 'Billy, don't come any closer, you're making The Vicar jumpy. He can be a bit vicious when roused, right Charlie.' Charlie glowered and stroked the bridge of his nose unconsciously.

'Thanks Bill.' Sam said. The disrespect sent a message. The show went on.

'What if I did send a signal? Your poxy little sister means nothing to me, not a fucking thing.'

'Come on, Bill. We talked about this.'

'That was then, and this is now. I mean, coming here alone, without your hard men, what do you expect?'

'Yeah, what?' Charlie said, sneering in accompaniment in his affected cockney accent.

'Courtesy. Professional respect.'

'Pull the other one,' Bill said.

'It's got bells on,' Charlie said. 'There's a spike for your sister's head, your wife's head, your kids' heads, even your big, ugly head, as well.' Charlie laughed, bunched cheeks half hiding his eyes, as his thin-lipped mouth cracked open like the Alien's egg, emitting a breathless jagged sound as it displayed his inward-facing jagged white teeth.

Bill shrugged. 'There you go, Vicar. We have spoken.'

'I've listened. Not much point in staying.'

'Nah, fuck off!' Charlie said.

'Lovely to meet you again,' Sam said. He strode to the door which clicked open as he reached it. The tough guy, nodded his head sideways in invitation to leave, closed the door and walked him to the lift.

'See yourself out, sunshine. Wish they'd let me give you a tune up.'

Sam pushed the button and turned in a rapid movement, straight into the villain's space. The man jumped back into a fighting crouch.

'Awesome. Fearsome. For a man with terminal halitosis you're quite something.' He stepped into the lift. On his way out Sam said a pleasant goodbye to the receptionist who gave him his bag. He could tell she liked him. One out of four wasn't bad. He caught a cab and headed for Westferry Road, a thoughtful man. What an awful bunch! How did they know he wasn't backed up?

Two minutes later, he rolled his eyes. *Fuck it! Enough is enough.* He asked the driver to stop, got out of the cab, sent a text and walked back.

140

Cal fetched a drink for Eilidh and went out for some sandwiches. She made notes in a small wire-bound A6 notepad with separators. When he returned after fifteen minutes, she lay back in her chair, face drawn, pale. He sensed discomfort.

'However I think about it, Cal, I'm under the cosh. The notes are key for my paper, the opposition and the cops.'

'Yes.' The silence stretched out, their heads lifted and eyes locked. 'So where are they?'

'The main lot were hidden by Shirl.'

'Something clicked?' Cal said.

'Yes. I was thinking of her this morning, and there it was. I'd just got back from the last meeting with Jamie, my editor, the night I was taken.'

Cal leaned forward, experienced antennae abuzz. 'So, Shirl knows. Last meeting?'

'Yes. I came in and was running a bit late, Shirl wanted to chat. I said I needed a shower and had to put my papers somewhere safe. She offered to sort it.'

'So, Shirl hid your papers?'

'Right, about nearly 1,000 pages of printout and notes, a 16GB pen drive with copies of documents, flip-chart pictures, photos, URLs, interview transcripts, and wider background detail than the hard copies, and four DVDs of voice recordings.'

'What are we looking for? A shoebox? A carrier bag?'

'A pilot's case.'

'Why Shirl? Why right then?' Cal had his questioning face on, firm-eyed and serious.

'I normally kept them at my bank. It was shut when I got out of the meeting with the editor, and I wanted to keep them safe until I could move them back.'

'So we only need the pen drive?'

'No, the papers are important. There are other notes and developed thinking scribbled all over the place on printouts during chats with my editor and sessions with my mentor.'

'The old hack you mentioned in Seattle?'

'Yes, that's him.'

'Why is the paper so important?'

'I spent days with Wally going through everything. Some stuff I captured in an outliner, but, when things start to go fast, paper works best for me.'

'So you leave it on paper?'

'No, you big, ugly interrogator. I transferred chunks, but not everything.'

'You being racist?'

'How is "interrogator" a racist word?'

'Anything that makes me feel bad is racist, whitey.'

Eilidh shook her head and got some change out of her purse.

'Another sludge?'

'Trust you to change the subject.' They eyed each other and smirked.

'There's a day's work to go into capturing and organizing the ideas, that's all. I'd have done it by a couple of days later. Those days never came.'

'So now what?'

'Let's visit Shirl and find out what she did with the stuff.'

'We're supposed to stay here.'

'I'm going. You can't make me stay here.'

'Sam'll have given Bill Jenkins the good news by now.'

'Good news?' Eilidh said.

'He's following up on that plan to get you two in Dublin yesterday. He's asking Bill a few questions.'

'You think Bill will talk?'

'Nah, but worth a try. They'll probably throw Sam out on his ear.'

'He won't like that.' She stood up. 'Are you going to look after me or not?'

141

The powered doors slid open once more with the same gentle rattle on their runners. The cluster of yuccas and rubber plants were still on sentry in the stepped brick feature, beside the white marble-topped reception counter. The attractive woman in the high-necked royal blue blouse and red tartan skirt rose as he entered and gave him another warm smile.

'Hello again, Sally, isn't it?' The receptionist stared at Sam, hesitant for a moment.

'Yes, of course. You've popped back, Vicar.'

'Right.' Sam smiled with genuine warmth. 'Please ask Bill if I might have another quick word.'

'Of course, sir. If you were wanting Charlie, as well, I'm afraid he's gone for the day. Would you like me to look after your bag again?' Sam sat in the corner.

'You're thoughtful, thanks. It's lighter because I was able to post the parcel.'

She nodded, 'I'll take you up.'

'Excellent.' Sam rose and followed her into the lift.

* * *

With a ping the doors opened into the reception area near Bill's office. The large man's prominent muscles strained at the material, hot dogs under a melted cheese slices. He stood in his neat dark suit, hands clasped about belly level. 'Thanks, Sal. I'll take care of The Vicar.' Sam noticed the glint in her eye as she turned away. The woman doesn't like you, boyo.

'See you on the way out.' He nodded to her, smiling. He heard the doors close.

When Sam turned the man was very close with the metal detecting wand in his hand, cocky. 'The usual formality, Vicar. I hope he'll want me to throw you out this time.'

Sam spread his arms and, as the wand came round to his right hand, he jabbed the small needle into the minder's forearm. The man's eye's bugged in his steroid acned face and his lips slackened. Sam gave him a bye-bye wave as he collapsed, unconscious, to the floor. *Thanks, Foggy*. He reached round the pillar to the electric button, clicked Bill's door open, grabbed the man by his collar and dragged him into the suite.

Bill rushed round his desk protesting. Sam dumped the gorilla in an untidy heap beside the door, thumbed the lock shut and turned to the angry crime boss.

'Time for a proper chat I think. Be a good lad and press the "don't disturb" button. I'd leave the panic button alone. Play your cards right, and you'll get out of this alive.'

'Who the fuck do you think you are?'

'A hurt and angry man.' Sam produced the .45 and levelled it. 'No fancy moves, or you'll be roasting down below, and someone you love will be dead very soon.'

'I've got rights.'

'Not today, sunshine.'

'You can't do this.'

'No need for clichés, Bill. We know each other better than that.' Bill glared hard at Sam. 'I thought we had an understanding ...'

'About what?' Bill turned a queasy colour.

'Family. Not harming them. My sister's head should've been on a spike in Dublin last night. Your brother Charlie told me, barely an hour ago, about getting my wife, kids, and even *my* head on spikes.'

'He was joking.'

'Eilidh should have died yesterday, and you set it up.'

'It didn't happen. She didn't show.' Bill paused and looked at the floor.

'Hmm, you know about it, and I'm glad you saved me the hassle of more small talk. There isn't much time.'

'What are you talking about?' Bill was changing from pink to grey-white, like a chubby chameleon.

'Remember when we discussed endangering our families? You know after your boy ...?'

'Jason.'

'That's him, Jason, the hard man who got injured in Ireland a wee while back.' Sam's eyes were direct and cold. He leaned back on the table beside Bill's desk and stuck the letter-opener through an orange in the fruit bowl. 'Not much time, as I say, Bill.' He pulled the blade out of the orange, splattering juice across the blotter and stabbed an apple.

'Out with it, you fuckin' swine. I won't forget this. I fuckin' won't.' Bill's body wobbled in its cocoon of pristine pinstripe, his yellow silk shirt-front quivered like a waterbed mattress. His eyes bulged, and his face turned from pale to puce.

Sam took his time before speaking. 'If you survive, I don't want you to forget this, not ever. You have a chance to be cooperative, and so far you've blown it. I haven't decided if I'm going to let you live or not. One thing's for certain, you don't ever want me to have to come back and talk to you like this again.'

'What do you want, for God's sake?'

'Names. The insider in our team and people you know in what we'll call the Corporation.'

'No chance. You'll get nothing out of me, you Scottish bastard.'

'I think in different circumstances you'd be right.' Sam nodded. 'I'd respect you for it, too. I'm not going torture you. I might kill you but it'll just be a quick bullet or slice with a knife.'

'I-do-not-grass.'

'Sad that, time being so short and all.' Sam reached in his jacket, pulled a mobile phone out and laid it on the expensive black wood.

'Who for?'

'Jason.'

Bill's demeanour changed. 'You can't touch him. He's in the nick.' He laughed.

'Aye, for maybe the next ten minutes or so, as your brief does his bit and springs him. I hear he took a swing at a policeman last night, silly boy. Why take on a regimental heavyweight boxing champion? So stupid. Cracked jaw and squashed nose. He'll be catching up to his uncle in the ugliness stakes.'

'Cut the crap. What are you telling me?' Bill's stare was intense.

'See that mobile?' Sam waved at the phone. 'It's got a text to transmit. It better be soon because some expert men are tasked to kill him when he leaves the police station.'

'I don't understand.'

'No signal from me, and he dies. If he comes out in thirty seconds, we're already too late. I think anything more than five minutes, and it'll be touch and go.'

'You won't.'

'After yesterday it was touch and go. After this morning's meeting he can die, guaranteed. And, don't tell me you don't grass. Write the names on a piece of paper now, and I'll send the signal.'

'And if I give you false information?'

'Jason's toast, you're toast and Charlie's toast. If I don't get back to confirm this, you're already targeted. I have a feeling Charlie will be toast one day, whatever happens.'

Bill's face rippled with rage and fear. He glared at Sam, took a pad and wrote.

Sam picked up the paper and nodded. 'Thanks.'

'Fuck you!' Sam grasped the mobile.

'Is the signal always this bad?' Bill jumped to his feet, Sam thumped him in the chest with the .45. He bounced half onto his seat, then twisted as it slid out from under him. He fell, knocking the vertical blinds this way and that, grazing his forehead on the wall. He rolled on to his hands and knees.

'Just joking.' The phone pinged with an incoming message. 'Jason will live, Bill. But I'm leaving a sign. You need to understand how badly you let yourself down.' He waved an upright finger in the air.

Bill's face was moist with sweat and an unhealthy pinkish grey when he pulled himself up from the floor. He was nearly in tears, quivering with emotion, almost a blur. He didn't speak. His breath jerked like a whooping cough victim.

'Only one thing to decide now, Bill. Do you live or die?' Sam put the .45 on the desk, pulled out his fighting knife and locked the blade. 'Sharp as a razor, this.' Bill tried to move away, and Sam caught him by his pigtail. He squealed with pain as he was dragged backwards between Sam's thighs.

Clenching Bill's hair in his left hand, Sam drew Bill's head back and gagged at the stench of loosening bowels. 'Last night, Jason stuck a Stanley knife in the face of a man he was chastising, to remind him of his sins.'

'Get on with it.'

Jenkins stared at the blade. 'OK.' He stuck the knife in Bill's right cheek and made an inch-long vertical cut. Bill struggled again. 'Remember the fear, Bill, the powerlessness.'

'Fuck you!' His voice lacked energy.

Sam jerked the pigtail hard and severed the braid at the base of the skull. Bill groaned. Sam put the hair in his jacket pocket and pushed Bill away without any force. Next he took Bill's belt off and lashed his elbows together. 'No more heads on spikes, got it?' He watched a broken man crumple to the floor, blood dripping from his face on to the shag pile. 'Stay down for ten minutes, old son, then call whoever you like. No communication with these names, ever, or I'll be back.' Sam found the private toilet and washed Bill's blood off his hands.

* * *

On the way out Sam gave a shot of the antidote to the big man on the floor after securing his wrists. The bouncer groaned and threw up.

In reception, he went to the counter and said a jovial goodbye to the receptionist who beamed a warm smile his way and handed him his bag. He walked out with an energetic, almost boisterous, step.

142

'She's not in the hospital.' Cal said.

'The flat?' Eilidh said.

'No.'

'Up north? Scotland?'

'What do you expect, the Isle of Man?' Cal grinned. 'Nice place, the Isle of Man.'

'How do you think we hooked up? I'm Scots ...' she emphasized her nationality by waving a thumb at her chest, 'you do a degree in Edinburgh and move to London. Who do you know best?'

'Scotch people.' The smile was as big as it was cheeky.

Beautiful eyes flashed. '*Scots* people. I see I've got to teach you more than your job, Chief Inspector.'

'Train or plane?'

'Let's do the train.'

'God forgive me if I'm making a bad move.'

'Bring your gun.'

Cal held his hand up for attention. 'You need to understand my skill set, my capability.' He opened his mouth to say more and stopped.

'What aren't you saying?'

He shrugged.

'*Cal?*'

He looked at her then put his elbow on the table and propped his head with his hand, temple on a large left thumb, fingers stroking his forehead. He gazed at the surface for some moments. 'I can do war, soldiering, police-work, but I'm not an operative. I can't do the dark side.'

'What do you mean ... dark side?'

'Handling myself as a spook, or doing Special Forces work.'

'Sam can?'

'He can, and he's bloody good at it. When it's down, dirty and in your face and you have to decide, to act, he delivers.'

'He's tough, I've seen him fight.' Eilidh said.

'Of course. But that's not all. He's a brilliant strategist and operative. Why do you think he's a Colonel?'

'It never occurred to me.'

'The Dark Art, you see? Foresight and courage. He killed two men getting you back.'

She glanced at him, shocked at first, head shaking side to side for a moment, a stalk of grain in a gentle breeze. She stilled. 'I never knew. I heard bangs and remember being dragged up a wet place. One of the few things I recall after the sedation, my clothes were stained with grass and mud. That explains it.'

'You were in a flat-out firefight.'

'And the big bang?'

'A grenade meant for you.' Cal said.

'No one told me.'

'You were a basket case.'

'Sam gave it all up. That's why he entered the Ministry.' Eilidh said.

'Then he left the preacher thing, couldn't hack the bureaucracy of God, so he says.'

'He made a good move,' Eilidh said, 'his new business works. He loves the locals, and the locals love him.'

'Doesn't change what he is, Eilidh.'

'What's that?'

'A tough, seasoned operative.' Cal's face became serious.

'A killer?'

'Yes, I'd say … of last resort.'

'I met a man back in the USA, who's truly seasoned and who's scared of Sam.'

'Let's stop this. What I'm saying is I'm not nearly as well-qualified as Sam to be babysitting you.'

'Okay. Enough said.'

'What's this I hear about … Dances with Wolves … eh no

… Pees with Bears?'

'Who told you that?' Eilidh said.

'A seasoned operative of my acquaintance.'

'You'll just have to up your game, tough guy.'

'TFR.'

'What's that mean?'

'Guess.'

'No, tell me.'

'*Too fuckin' right.*'

143

Jason Jenkins left the police station with his lawyer, a seasoned criminal defender. His face was bandaged and his next stop was at a private hospital to have his injuries from the night before fully assessed, and make a start on treatment.

The black Range Rover stopped in front of him. A goon got out and opened the door. Before he could step in, three sharp thuds rocked the vehicle and three columns of glass blew out of the windscreen. He had little time for shock, as three more thumps pummelled the car, raising jagged holes in the roof and punching through the rear seats.

People passing by barely heard the strikes, the traffic and street noise too loud, but Jason Jenkins did as he watched the jagged holes appear.

Jason's phone rang, a Scottish accented voice spoke. 'Enjoy your day. Better get back to the office and give the old man some TLC. He paid quite a price for your life.'

144

Sam entered Agency HQ at Westferry Road, using the underpass entrance.

'Morning, David.'

'Morning, Colonel.' The guard paused and did a double-take.

'The Lazarus effect,' Sam said. 'Gotta dash.'

He walked across the reception area, silent on the carpet tiles and stuck his head round Quentin's door. 'Where is he?' He smiled at Indira.

She gazed at him and blinked. 'With the boss, Sam.'

'Come and join us,' Sam said.

'Right. Do I need my pad?'

'Yes, bring that little recorder thing, a laptop … record and take notes from the get go.'

They went to Charlton's door, knocked and went in. Charlton glanced up, eyes narrowed at the interruption. They widened when he saw Sam. Quentin stood up in a rush. 'Sit down Q. Indira, over there.'

'The dead man rises and returns,' Charlton said. 'You have something on your mind.'

'Betrayal.' He stared at the intelligence man. 'Quentin sold out.'

Charlton rocked back and shook his head, 'You're sure?'

'Absolutely.' Quentin's face betrayed shock morphing into denial.

'I've confirmed it just now. Some moves were made over the last couple of days, assisted by a few connections via Fogarty and Cassanet. Both would dearly like to meet Quentin for a little chat.'

'Keep talking.'

'We've been under the cosh, Ben. High level leaks and aggressive situations since the Lawick woman was arrested. Mo and I decided to change my route. Mo called Quentin yesterday, early afternoon and told him Dublin was still on. You were held up in a long meeting with Parker yesterday afternoon and evening, covering intel from the banking network, and notified that I wasn't returning for another 48 hours. Cassanet notified Quentin—only Quentin—and told him the travel plans.'

'You tested me, too,' Charlton said.

Sam nodded. 'Quentin told Bill Jenkins, who arranged for our Dublin gangster friends to kill Eilidh and Calum—that's me—chop our heads off, and display them as proof for the big guys, wherever they are.'

'It's true. Cassanet called, but we didn't discuss Sam or anything like that.' Quentin had the pallor of a sick man.

'Bottom line … Quentin notified some nasty people who arranged for two French people to be jumped and executed in an abattoir twenty miles from Dublin. Mo risked two operatives and, thank God, common sense prevailed. The killings didn't take place.'

'I deny this, sir,' Quentin's formality was surprising. 'You're wrong, Colonel.'

'I'm stunned, Sam.' Charlton's face took a queasy pallor. 'What makes you so sure it's him?'

'A recording of his call with Cassanet.' Sam replayed a relevant extract through his smartphone.' Quentin's eyes widened and speeded up their nervous movement. 'Going to keep denying it, Q?'

'It must be a fake, I absolutely deny any such conversation took place, it's an unbelievable assertion.'

'Then there's the small matter of a meeting and conversation with Bill Jenkins.'

'Preposterous!' Quentin entered full spluttering and indignation mode. 'And when was this supposed to have happened?

'Day before yesterday, around midday.'

'I slipped out for an early lunch. Everyone knew that. Went over to Canary Wharf, did a bit of shopping, had a bite to eat and came back.'

Sam spoke directly to Charlton. 'The Yanks put a full court press on Quentin via Fogarty. He left the office and stopped by the Billet-Doux near the Tube. Here are surveillance photos of him going and returning.'

'That proves nothing, Sam. It's a set-up, Ben, a set-up.'

'Quentin and Bill Jenkins met in the back and had a coffee. Here's a snap from a video of that.' Sam held up his mobile, showed Charlton and then Quentin. 'Indira, put this URL in the laptop.' She typed in the link. 'Play it.' She clicked the link and turned the screen to them. Good quality video appeared. The sound clarity surprised them.

Quentin's voice: 'Flight Air France 1278, due to arrive at 16.45.'

Bill Jenkins' voice: 'Got it. Air France 1278, arrives 16.45.'

Quentin said, 'They want proof of death. Decapitation, then display the heads with the bodies.'

'I'll sort it.'

'Thanks Bill.'

'Permanent disposal to follow.'

'No problem. What's the pay?'

'Quarter of a million each. Make sure the contractor gets his money.'

'Pity.' They saw the exchange of smiles.

* * *

Quentin stood erect in best military fashion. 'I can't believe Jenkins talked.'

'He did.' Sam turned to Charlton. 'Get this miserable fucker out of here.'

Charlton froze for a long moment, staring at Quentin like a distraught mourner at a funeral. He sighed from the depths of his soul. 'Anything to say?'

'I needed the money for security in my old age.' Indira sobbed and kept writing. 'I'm sorry, Ben. Sorry.'

There was a knock at the door. Charlton's two minders came in. 'Take this man away and lock him up with a full suicide watch.' They secured Quentin and left. Charlton studied Sam's eyes. 'Heart breaking.'

'Yup.'

'What about Jenkins?'

'Rattled, soiled, tired and emotional, otherwise fine.' Sam paused. 'I arranged a wake-up call for him.' Charlton made eye contact with Sam for a moment. He didn't ask.

'What's your plan?'

'Strategize with you and take the battle to them,' Charlton smiled.

'Prisoners?'

'Depends on the end game. In principle, fine, but this is war.'

'Waiting for Waberthwaite?'

'Maybe. Let's see how the clay shapes. Fogarty is needed for sure, ideally both of them. They're a couple of great assets.'

'Eilidh?'

'Locking her in her flat isn't going to work.'

'Tell me more.' The screw turned. Five minutes later Charlton was making urgent calls.

145

Sam offered Quentin a seat at the meeting table, he preferred to stand. 'We need some answers, and doubtless Ben will assist you to provide them. I want one thing from you: info on the British and European operation of the Bizz empire.'

'What's in it for me?'

'Negotiate with Ben. Right now the best I'd offer would be a painless death after a full disclosure of your knowledge,' Sam said.

'Oh, sit down Quentin!' Charlton barked, unusually for him. The knock at the door was quiet by comparison. 'Indira, please bring some coffee in.' Charlton's men stood in the corridor. 'Give me your full story, Quentin, starting at the beginning: how you were approached, by whom, and how you benefit,' Charlton said, 'you know the drill.'

'Better than most.'

'Help us and we'll help you.'

'I must get on,' Sam said. 'Things to do, people to see.'

As he finished the information, Quentin said, 'May I say something, Sam?' Sam's eyes flicked to Charlton.

'Go for it.'

'I'm truly sorry.'

'For me, Quentin, I accept. As for Eilidh, knowing what she's been through and what was planned for Dublin, I haven't it in my heart to forgive.'

'What about your God stuff?'

'God forgive me,' Sam's eyes were like stone, 'Jenkins is an animal and behaving to type. You've seen us in battle and dark places, *Quentin*, struggling to cope and taking the pain for thirty years. You deserted us, took the bad guy's shilling. You put the crosshairs on Eilidh. You're a traitor of the worst sort.' Quentin bowed his head. 'Ben Charlton is where you need to place your hope.' Sam nodded to Charlton.

'Once you're in, you go operational. It isn't people any more. You know how it is.'

'Yes.'

'What about Fogarty?'

'Legitimate. Inside man.' Quentin jerked back.

'That surprise you?'

'Yes. I spoke to him when you were in Seattle.'

'At crunch time, he held his hand up.' Sam said. 'He saved our lives twice and may have sacrificed a friend. Anyone else in that position and we'd have been dead. You set Eilidh and me up for death, in an abattoir, *for fuck's sake*.'

146

A large man and a slender medium height woman with bright red hair talked in a relaxed, almost intimate way. The stainless steel seats at the head of the platforms in London Kings Cross Station weren't exactly the First Class lounge. Bored passengers sat in ones and twos. People walked past with an air of direction and purpose. The public address system echoed its barely intelligible messages to travellers.

'Let's just sit quietly at the back here, and watch the world go by.'

'I feel like a spy.'

'You don't look like one, not with the day-glow hair.' Cal kept his eyes on the crowd.

'Day-glow, indeed! It's shiny and incredibly fashionable. Besides, it's pure platinum under the wig.'

'What's the style called?'

'A bob.' Eilidh's mobile pinged. She fumbled a moment with her bag, got the phone out and read the text. 'Sam wants to meet us.'

'Where?'

'Use this exit from the station, straight on at the lights, you'll find a small shopping area on the left and a place called Madrigal, downstairs.'

'How soon?'

'Now. What can I get you? I'm taking orders.'

'Giving them more like,' Cal said, 'I'll have a large mocha and a chocolate chip cookie.' They stood up. Moments later, two compact, unremarkable men got to their feet and followed them out.

147

'How soon can you get here?' Cassanet's voice had an audible smile.

'Just a couple of things to do. I'll be over this evening. The time depends on flights.'

'Keep me posted. The briefing is in The North. We've action to plan. Can Fogarty come?'

'Sorry, Mo, he has places to go, people to see.'

'These Americans, always busy.'

'He has meetings scheduled.' Sam said.

'Of course he has, between a couple of calls and a power dinner.'

'They're tracing some tricky stuff in the States.'

'So they get the old trickster on it.' Mo said.

'Wouldn't you?'

'Maybe.' Sam imagined the shrug. 'I spoke to Charlton.'

'He's ... eh ... busy.'

'I let you go one night, and you irritate horrible, evil people.'

'He told you.'

'Enough.'

'My resurrection will get out soon.'

'Ah, my friend, that is bad news.'

'Yeah.'

'Try to be here tonight, we need the planning time for tomorrow's fun, and perhaps a glass or two.'

'Fast as I can.'

'Gird up your jockstrap and get moving. Delay costs lives.'

The phone disconnected.

148

The interior displayed rugged brickwork, wooden beams in a matte maroon, and a flooring of light tan stone tiles, with a diamond motif to match the woodwork on each corner. The seats were woven fabric. Just past the window seats, two wide flights of a descending staircase led to the lower level. They went down. Sam finished his call and put his phone down.

He was in a brick booth to the right of the foot of the stairs. He waved and gave a little smile. They joined him, one on either side.

'How'd the cage rattle go?' Cal said.

'As expected. He talked.'

'What's your plan, Sammy?' Eilidh said.

'Talk your trip through, provide support and wave you off.' Eilidh sat back. 'Not in the script, Eilidh?'

'I thought you'd be angry.'

'At one level I should be. At another I can't be.'

'Tell me.'

'You are diving headlong into a dangerous world after surviving a couple of near-death experiences. As a brother I want to protect you.'

'I'm a grown-up.'

'Right. Not a bad epitaph.'

'Now, Sam …' Cal quieted when Sam held his hand up.

'I'm here to let you go and support you in what you're about to do.' Silence came when a server arrived with coffees and biscuits.

Eilidh gazed at Sam with a mixture of emotions on her face. 'You're not going to stop me?'

'How could I? Cal briefed us in. You should go.'

'What about the danger?'

He poured two white packets of sugar into his cappuccino and watched them sink through the froth. 'A fact of life. Better to support the headstrong than fight them. Why not call her?'

'I did. She can't remember. We hope the memory will return when we're face to face'

He locked eyes with his friend. 'Cal will need looking after, too.'

'Watch your mouth, wild man.' Cal shared an edgy grin, highlighted by a small moustache from his latte.

'No, I'm going to make sure yours is watched.' Sam lifted his hand and waved. Two men waved back from a booth at the far wall. 'That's your cover. They are assigned to guard your backs.

'Travelling with us?' Eilidh said.

'Every inch of the way.'

'Guards,' Cal said.

'No, *protectors*. There's a difference,' Sam said. 'There's a team of four, two of the team will be on you at all times. The other two close by. These mobiles give you dedicated and secure contact.' Sam handed over two small handsets. 'There are some numbers in the address book. A and B are your minder pairs, C is Cal and E is Eilidh, I is Indira. If you need any comms support to me or anyone else use the I. Indira is living in for the next few days. She'll be available round the clock. These phones won't accept incoming calls except from the five letters. Bottom line, Indira is your link to the outside world.

'Q isn't there,' Cal said.

'No. Indira's enough. Any hassles can route through her.'

'There's more to it.' Sam glared at Cal who sat back, as if slapped.

'In what way, you big galoot?'

'Bloody men.' Eilidh's snort made Cal and Sam glance at each other. Sam smiled.

'Yup, bloody men,' Sam winked at Eilidh. 'Don't get off the train at Edinburgh, travel to Kirkcaldy. You'll be met.'

'We were going to Inverkeithing.'

'Sure, bought tickets to Edinburgh and planned to stay on the train. Take one more stop. You'll be collected and taken to a safe place.'

'What about Shirl?' Eilidh said.

'Tomorrow. You'll work out your own plans for approach and contact.'

They said their goodbyes fifteen minutes before the train departure. The minders followed.

Sam watched them go, called for the bill, paid upstairs and entered a waiting car through one of the rear exits of the mini mall.

149

The layout of the runways and the flower-like aprons caught Sam's eye. The BAE 125 landed with a gentle clunk at Évreux-Fauville air base in Normandy. The engines whistled with reverse thrust, and the brakes gripped. The medium-sized business jet taxied to some buildings off to the side of the taxi strip. Doors opened, steps dropped down and Sam set foot in France once more.

For a moment he thought of Prime Ministers and Presidents striding down stairs to applause, with teams of functionaries surrounding red carpets, and rows of soldiers awaiting inspection.

The idea tickled him, as he looked at his one-man welcoming committee standing like a Sasquatch a few yards away.

'Hello Sam, I knew they'd get you here *à toute vitesse*.'

'A fast flight from City Airport. Someone pulled strings.'

'You're most welcome, my dear friend.' As they moved away the jet swung around and started to taxi back towards the runway.

'How polite of you.' They hugged.

'The walls have ears. I must be totally polite to foreigners. PC – the new civilisation.'

'The nearest wall is fifty metres away.'

'We French have excellent ears.'

'Hmm,' Sam stood back and looked at Cassanet. 'You, De Gaulle, right enough, lugs a plenty.' Wind whipped across the apron. Cassanet waved his hand in the direction to walk. He led Sam to a tarmac strip bounded on the right side by a large oak tree in full vibrant leaf, bright as a green beacon in the early evening light, and entrancing against a bright blue sky.

'No passports here, Mo?'

'No need for formality with our military friends.'

'Right.'

'We're going in, and a strong political will is with us. A team is waiting to tackle the people who killed my men. The Italians are with us, and a our special forces are lined up.'

'And?'

'And, we are going north.' They approached a smart office building through a small car park. 'The Belgians are on board and offer full assistance from the DSU and their surveillance and intervention units.'

'Excellent, nothing like having the security people on side.' Sam said.

'Our American friends completed our intel about the team who seem to run a significant and corrupt European version of the conspiracy you uncovered in London.'

'I heard.'

'Sure. I know the man who did the digging,' Mo said. 'A lovely place to dig, beautiful and evil, such a dramatic combination.'

'We had some additional intel this morning. Still, no arrests, no convictions, only hearsay.'

'We must give them ... what's your Scottish word? A shoogle, that's it, a shoogle.'

'That's why I'm here.'

* * *

They came to a door mid-way along what Sam took to be the side wall. Cassanet inserted a card in the lock, entered a passcode and the door clicked. Cassanet grasped the long shank of the handle, pushed down and they entered the building. 'Of course, with one out of the five dead in the London operation and another in a coma, the toll adds up and must hurt them.'

'Yes, a big fear, so they kill their own.'

A shrug of anthropoid shoulders. 'The body count is not so high.'

They walked down a silent corridor with dark green floor

tiles, light green wall panels interspersed with frosted glass windows 'You've got to be kidding. There's been murder after murder.'

'Tell me more, I need to understand from your perspective.'

'Imagine a conspiratorial group of criminals, public servants, bankers and corporate apparatchiks busy ripping off the government. We call them Bizz, a name we got from one of their people when he was questioned.'

'Bizz? Excellent name,' Cassanet said. 'I've heard of *EuroBizz*, the Americans can have *YankeeBizz*, and you can call yours *AngloBizz.* And, this morning you managed some interrogation, too? *Bordel de merde*, is there no beginning to your talents?' Cassanet grinned.

'What are you like, Mo, I'm glad I'm on your side.'

They reached a door on the left before a double glass entry into a waiting room of some sort. Mo waved his pass at a sensor, and they entered the room. He waved Sam to a seat on one of the chairs spaced around a long coffee table. Mo picked up a flask and poured strong coffee, handed a cup to his guest and sat at ninety degrees to him, elbow on the arm rest and long legs spread out.

'Interrogation, you wild warrior. Formal or informal?'

'Informal.'

'Off-piste, an excellent way to do things.' Cassanet smiled. 'How informal?'

'Not an approach approved of by HMG.'

'You naughty boy.'

'Not me. I popped in, asked the questions, got the answers and walked out.'

'It's not exactly the way your boss puts it.'

'Okay, it was a tad off-piste.' Sam said.

'What about this man Wardle?'

'He's dangerous, connected and being promoted while an internal enquiry is carried out into our traitor.'

'Ah, the fabled British enquiry. So exciting. So slow.'

'Slow is good, Mo. Slow is excellent, as long as it works for us. Sad to say the networks keep communicating.'

'For Bizz the tough time must be recruiting, getting organized, establishing communication lines, structures and procedures.'

'Yes, they're creating an organization and people keep interrupting them. They can't get their act together.'

'Now add a beautiful and clever investigative journalist following her nose and putting things together …' Mo said.

'Makes 'em mad.'

'Of course, but the structure doesn't seem to exist to take a measured approach.'

'It's only a matter of time. In one way, Mo, you're right, but in another, their cell structure works well.

'At a basic level, they channel the money well.'

'Right, but the biggest people are invisible.' Sam said.

'Or maybe visible, but just not recognized for who they are.'

'Good point.'

Mo smiled. 'So, they are still going forward.'

'In their own way.'

'So what happened to blow things up?'

'Poor communication and inexperience.'

'They can buy experience.'

'They did, but there isn't much evidence of them paying attention.'

'So, tell me what you think happened.'

'Three or four factions started out solving problems in their own special ways.'

'How exciting for you. Enemies everywhere you look.'

'Spot on. The first killing was a young prostitute, beaten to death by some neo-Nazi thugs by, let's call them *Faction 1.* Next, the guy who kidnapped Eilidh had his throat cut, *Faction 2*. Then one of the thugs died as a side-effect of a punishment beating gone wrong *Faction 2 again.*'

'The evil men do, *mon ami*.'

'A close family friend was murdered in mistake for me call them *Faction 3*. An Irish criminal got blown away by some protectors when they tried to harm my family.'

'Never fuck with the Scots. That's why we French love you so much. Are you done?'

'No.'

'My bowels are agitated.'

'The people who drove the van used to kidnap Eilidh, and connected to the young pro, were given a concrete overcoat on the Costa Del Sol, *Faction 2*.'

'Now we are done?'

'No. Two key people in the London criminal world were assassinated: one to seal his lips *Faction 3*, and the other, as we later discovered, *neo-Nazi* revenge.'

'Finished?'

'Almost.'

'Almost? *Merde alors*. You mustn't forget the four mercs blown away when they tried to stop Tonka you and in Scotland.'

'You know the rest.'

'I'm out of fingers. You Deadly Dudley, you.'

'It is crazy and, because of the disconnects, the press haven't got a handle on it.'

'Lucky indeed. Then there are my dead people murdered by *Faction 4*, and more who died when you went on a rampage in the States, *Faction 5*.'

'Hardly a rampage, self-defence.'

'I'm too tired to argue. You brought a gun?'

'Yes, but where's my Browning?'

'In Nice.'

'What've you got with you?'

'Colt 1911.'

'A cannon. Let's kick ass!' He grinned at Sam.

'I've seen action today.'

'We French *take* action too, we don't *look* at it. Seriously, Sam, you've been winding some evil people tight, like springs. I think it's what your Prime Minister would call a *rollicking good show*. *Dangereux*, but stunning.'

'Yeah, the American side needs developing. They're good

investigators, but assets have slipped into corrupt ways. We have to be cautious.'

'We all have the same problem, people putting the money before the country. *Madam la Guillotine* is not such a bad idea for traitors.'

'It's only money.' Sam said.

'Don't forget the lives, like my boys splattered all over a cliff in the Alpes Maritimes.'

'Apologies. What do you want to do?'

'Take a few hours to plan and many more to eat, reflect and get ready for tomorrow.'

150

They met in an upmarket hotel in the maze of streets near the centre of town. The splendid cast-iron gates shielded an elegant entry, an exquisite glass conservatory filled with bright coloured plants and a brick walkway. The place crawled with liveried flunkeys. A small garden opened out at the side of the hotel. Samson and Smythsone, after an energetic night, enjoyed a swim and gentle stroll round the garden before breakfast. The meeting started on time.

'The profits continue to please our highest echelons.' Xavier slurped his words as usual. Heads nodded in approval. The atmosphere stayed tense. 'The failure to kill the girl in Dublin is a source of frustration and embarrassment to me and this team.'

'She wasn't there, Xavier. Everything was arranged, simply the wrong people.' Smythsone spoke in a quiet, assertive voice.

'We appear to be ineffective. We can't interdict a damned journalist? It's not acceptable. She must die.'

'What about her information?' an American voice cut in.

'Lost. Nobody knows where and the source needs to be eliminated. Simple as that. Now, Gemma, you were responsible for setting this up.' Xavier said.

'Yes. I used the intel supplied by an asset, to arrange the action. Our London crime lord followed through perfectly, as did his Dublin counterpart.' Smythsone said.

'The intel was wrong.' Xavier coloured up at first, and then developed pale spots on his cheeks and jawline. '*Wrong. Wrong. WRONG!*' His face jerked with rage. 'Have I got to do everything myself? Every time? Fix every little problem?'

'Calm down, Xavier. No one is trying to fail here. We get sound intel, we act correctly, set the job up and the victims don't show. Shit happens.'

'I don't care. You better fix this, or I'm going to do some,' he paused and gazed around holding Smythsone's eyes, 'reorganizing.' His cheeks were bright red. A coffee-stained dribble of saliva stained his white shirt front.

'Stop being such a wanker and bully,' Samson's voice managed to be strong and cold. 'The moment things go pear-shaped you start to rave and threaten. You're not the only one with strings higher up. Any more of this and I'll use my contacts.'

'How dare you call me names? I am the leader in Europe. I am … I am … He jerked. My apologies, colleagues. I am so upset. We face such a bright future, and some people are getting in the way.' The sibilant breathlessness made each chunk of Xavier's regret sound like it was being pulled out like a rotten tooth, and without anaesthetic. He focused on the table top eyes giving the lie to every word.

Silence settled on the room, the awkward quiet succumbing at last to business matters. The meeting gradually found an even keel and went on, becoming more productive as time elapsed. Xavier, withdrawn and thoughtful at first, regained effectiveness and contributed well, if a little subdued.

151

The Super Puma flew them to a helipad on the outskirts of Bruges. The view of the spires, narrow streets and canals reminded Sam of a break he and Karen had enjoyed five or six years before. The stay had been fantastic, beautiful buildings, loads of moules et frites and plenty of excellent beer to wash it all down. Karen loved the chocolate and holding hands as they cruised the canals, not to mention a few nights of child-free romance.

'Time you were present and in the moment.'

'Right. I was reliving a trip with my wife a few years back.'

'Always sex with you *Ecossais*, that's why you have the kilt, no?'

'You're right, Mo. We Jocks are more romantic than you Frogs.'

'What's that supposed to mean?'

'Up yours, *Monsieur Grenouille*.' Cassanet threw his head back and guffawed.

The large helicopter settled on the pad. They stepped out and were met by two Chief Inspectors with a car and driver each.

'We are agreed on action?'

'Yes. The intel better be good.'

'Perfect. Try not to kill anyone, mon ami. The Belgians like gentleness and sensitivity above all.'

'I'll do my best.'

'Pick up in two and a half hours in the car park under the square. You know the place.'

'Yup.'

152

Gemma Smythsone and Jack Samson enjoyed a drink at Ostend Bruges International Airport.

'The request from the Lazareau guy was genuine enough, honey.'

'How did they know where you were?'

'Same way they'd know where you are; our passports.'

'Of course.'

'If you fly private, you can make mistakes. My people didn't sort the paperwork properly. No big deal, I promised to arrange to straighten everything out when I get back to the hotel. My plane will drop you off at London City and pick me up in a couple of hours. Gotta get to a meeting in Boston.'

He ordered them each another Martini and arranged a date, day after next, in London. They said goodbye with a formal two-cheek kiss. He walked away, smart and strong. He never looked back.

Gemma sat, thoughtful, on the plane. As the Gulfstream V zipped down the runway she sat back wishing she could share about her interrogation with Jack, but not trusting their relationship enough. She'd work on that. As for Xavier, what a horror of a person, aggressive and lick-spittle. He made her skin crawl. Kurt would be above all that: snooty, bloody Nazi.

* * *

Xavier neared the trees. How he loved their slender beauty. Birds scampered about, and he admired them too; their ability to fly with such speed and agility.

When the arm cradled him, at first he felt soothed. Then they moved into the trees. He couldn't resist the strength.

'One word, Xavier, and it'll be your last.'

'Take my money.'

'I don't want it.' The accent was deep, maybe English. 'We want you to understand: we watch you; every day; all the time.' He heard a quiet click and his head was locked tight and face turned upwards by the force of a forearm under his chin. A fighting knife was held in front of his eyes. He started to squeal.

'Welcome to the real world.' Whimpering, he felt the blade against his throat and shuddered as the cold metal was drawn round his neck, ear to ear.

* * *

Jack wore his power like a bulletproof vest. He was affable, appeared kindly, but the clout always protected him. When he let himself back into his room to collect the remainder of his belongings, he was working at two levels: one on the deal he wanted to achieve in the States; the other, new ideas for sex with Gemma.

His preoccupied mind meant he was unprepared for the force of nature that slammed him onto his bed, and would give him whiplash twinges for the next couple of weeks. He tried to respond, but a man of awesome strength pinioned his elbows.

'I hear you like tying women up. I wonder how you like it.'

Jack didn't bluster. 'What'd you want?'

'Your attention, *mon ami*.' The balaclava and black outfit couldn't hide the size and power of the man.

'You gonna kill me?'

'Not unless you ask me nicely.'

'So what's your point, Frogman.'

'I've got my eye on you.'

'Watch I don't poke it out.' An arrogant sneer and contempt changed Samson's day.

'Oh, my darling, man. That's nice enough for me.' The big man straddled him, and large hairy wrists crossed over his throat in a classic judo stranglehold. The loss of the blood supply to his brain was almost pleasant.

His last conscious thought ... something new to try with Gemma.

After two minutes Samson came to. He was naked, his

clothes, briefcase and mobile were gone, his wallet empty. He lay on his face. Apart from his secured elbows, and being tied to his bed, he was unharmed.

* * *

Justine Corlay returned from a walk and let herself into her room. The draught from the window reached her. She didn't remember leaving it open. God, she loved this hotel.

She pulled the window shut and was about to turn back into the room when everything went dark. When she awoke, she was blindfolded.

'Hello, Mademoiselle Corlay, this is your conscience calling.' The French was controlled, slow-paced and not too heavily accented. 'We want you to know that you are under investigation for corruption, with particular emphasis on the meeting here today. Isn't your Monsieur La Salle a rude little fellow? You will find a new number in your mobile phone. Call us if you want to be allowed to atone for your sins.'

'Who are you?'

'A close friend of your worst nightmare.'

'Do you know who I am?'

'Of course. That's why I'm visiting you.'

'I am a senior official in the IMF.' The spluttering paused for a moment.

'Of course you are, *petite*, and as corrupt an old whore as one might ever meet.'

'Are you going to hurt me?'

'Of course not. Not even a little, much as I think you'd enjoy the experience.'

'So, why me?'

'Because we want you on our side. When the rest take the fall, we'll make you a heroine.'

'They'll kill me.'

'One way or another you may be right, but with us you might live and find a new life, maybe even a variety of lovers such as you enjoy.'

'And if I refuse?'

'Your esteemed CEO will get to view some exciting movies and hear a few tapes. I have confiscated your mobile, your papers, your laptop and a couple of minor bits and pieces.'

'What now?'

'Nothing. I've even given you a replacement phone. Free your hands, wriggle your fingers and give me a call. Oh, and one last thing, the phone number is a one-shot item. Do anything but call me and the number will disappear and, along with it, your chances of redemption. You have twenty-four hours.'

She started to cry. 'They'll kill me.'

'There, there, little one. In this case, it's better the devil you *don't* know. We have honour and, most of the time, we play to some sort of rules. I look forward to hearing from you. *À bientôt*.'

Corlay cried for a couple of minutes, freed her hands and checked her phone.

* * *

Two hours later, a nervous assistant hotel manager knocked on Samson's door. The hotel was horrified that he had been the subject of a vicious attack and robbed. They called a doctor and the police.

The doctor gave him a clean bill of health and suggested he relax for a couple of days. Clothes, a phone and all the equipment he needed were delivered by his people inside two hours. Now and then he couldn't help himself thinking about the big man. He could have died. The threat, the fear… He made calls to strengthen his security. There'd be a seasoned protector with him 24/7 from now on.

Four hours after his ordeal his private jet flew him out of Ostend Bruges for Boston. A resilient man, he lost himself in briefings for the contract discussions and winning a big deal. Every now and then he thought about revenge on a big, hard Frenchman. He'd find him, by God he would. The fear and discomfort refused to go away.

153

Xavier's lungs filled with surprise.

'Scary, isn't it? Maybe next time you'll get the sharp side.' Xavier shuddered. 'Heads on spikes, indeed!' The man searched him, took his phone, satchel, wallet and watch; sat him down and pressed his back to a tree. 'Stay here for five minutes. Move early, and you will die.'

His assailant rose from his squat, looked at him for a moment with intelligent brown eyes then walked away up the line of trees, and disappeared. He saw his attacker pull the balaclava off medium length curly dark brown hair before he went out of sight.

Xavier started to cry with fear and rage. The rough bark of the tree abraded the balding area at the back of his head. He remembered feelings of alarm and anger from childhood. He couldn't tell the time and didn't dare move. He cried some more.

* * *

Walking away, Sam switched off the iPad and iPhone to avoid remote erasure. Indira's guys would have some fun with the contents.

* * *

The damp of the grass seeped through the seat and legs of Xavier's trousers. He was still sobbing with shock ten minutes later when an old couple found him and helped him to a taxi, which delivered him to Bruges station.

154

'General Charlton, good to meet you at last.' The words lacked both warmth and sincerity; the limp handshake, a gesture to politeness. 'I think you had a call from the Minister.'

'Yes, Mr Wardle.' Charlton gestured to a seat at the coffee table. 'Drink?'

'No time.' Wardle sat back in the dark fabric seat, relaxed to the point of cockiness – legs apart, his genitalia in the apex pointing directly at Charlton.

'Thank you for making time for me.'

Charlton gazed into concerned eyes. 'Nothing more, thanks, Indira.'

'Your number is up, I'm afraid.' Hard, gloating eyes.

'Coming from you, I can't say I'm surprised.'

'Wheels within wheels, and so on. In three or four days' time you'll be gone, and the core of this excellent operation with you.' Wardle started to play with his left-hand cufflink. 'There's a man I want you to release.'

Charlton sat head erect, then bent forward. 'Not today, Mr Wardle. Wait until you're anointed.'

'Heads will roll.'

'Twas ever thus.'

'The minister required certain codes and data from you.'

'Delivered, as requested.' Charlton brushed imaginary dust from his blotter.

'Send them to me too.'

'Have you clearance?' A snooty scowl froze on to the colouring, thin face like a child's sticker. 'I see you can't provide it. Ask the creature you call "master"; he can provide it.'

'You'll wish you had treated me more civilly, General. You, Colonel Duncan and a few more. I've got a little list, you see, and you're climbing to prominence. I never forget.'

'How's the arm?'

'Much better, thanks. The men who hurt me will get the black spot.'

'I'd take care. Lord knows who they are, but I'd be surprised if they don't have some black spots of their own.'

'You're in denial, Charlton.' The cufflink twisted back and forth. 'You are where we want you. I've tried to be nice, but you'll pay for your insolence.'

'If you have the authority, remove me.'

'The next meeting of the committee will see you removed.'

'Exactly. Three or four days is a long time in politics, Wardle. Anything more?'

Wardle's thin lips compressed to a gash. 'In the face of such uncooperativeness, which I will report to the Minister, this has been a wasted journey. We won't forget. When I'm back from the north, I shall expedite your departure.'

'Good. Now, take the stench of your evil little self out of my office, and off the premises.' The door opened, Charlton's two minders entered. 'See Mr Wardle to the door.'

'I need to wash my hands.'

'Pity. See Mr Wardle to the door and give him directions to the nearest convenience.'

'That is unconscionable!'

'Walk out or be dragged out: all the same to me.' Wardle left, white-cheeked, without a word. A worried face appeared at the door.

'Awful man, Indira.'

'Coffee, Mr Charlton?'

'No thanks. Just a glass with a couple of fingers of water in it.' She returned, concern on her face. 'No, my dear, not for tablets, for this.' He showed her a blue-labelled bottle of malt whisky. 'Best of the best. Want one?'

'No sir, thank you.' Her beautiful black hair gleamed, almond eyes still luminous with concern.

'Get yourself something you do drink. Come back. We need

a catch up. A lot has been going on and, in Quentin's absence, we've some things to discuss.' The exotic symmetry of her face enhanced the warmth of her smile. 'Bring a notepad.'

155

'Run!' Eilidh bolted.

They'd been in the The Business Bar in Dunfermline for an hour. The visit with Shirl had been happy and emotional. Mission accomplished.

She loved the old smoke-stained bar. It served some of the best beer in Scotland. Cal and she enjoyed a beer, while the minders, none too happy, nursed cokes a few tables away. Outside, the rain teemed down, and, with the mist, it seemed like dusk had arrived a couple of hours early.

Leaving the pub a gang of perhaps eight men came at them. Cal yelled at her to run as he and the two minders engaged in a fierce fight. She hared away hearing shouts as larger feet slapped down the brick-clad surface of the pedestrian precinct in pursuit. She rushed towards the High Street, past a cash shop, a sandwich shop, a coffee outlet and the mobile phone shop on the corner.

She made a hard left turn, slipped on a fast food wrapper, greasy with rain, as well as a couple of chips. She skidded, but didn't fall. With a forty-yard lead she dashed diagonally across the High Street to a small pend. She dashed down the little lane. Local knowledge, she smiled to herself. Leaning back she avoided going too fast down the hill.

She caught her breath and heard a loud 'Down here!' She wasn't the only person who knew the territory.

The police would be watching the show on their surveillance system, if they could make it out in the dank rainstorm. She ran left and through the car parks at Abbey Park Place. She tried to jog, but her fear wouldn't let her, so she pushed her pace.

Behind her a voice called. She ran across the street by the smooth sculpted walls of the library. A car coming up the hill blasted its horn and hissed to a stop. A metallic bang and shriek told her one of her hunters had been downed. She burst into the Abbey grounds and turned left past a row of tombstones. How could she think the Abbey was beautiful when she was running for her life?

She hurtled down the flights of steps and round the garden on a path. Next, down some more stairs to an opening. She paused, peeking each way before running up towards the arch at the palace. No sound of pursuit.

'Got ya!' A hand grabbed her hair. His snigger had plenty of snot in it. The man had hidden near the cobbles close by the archway. Lean and spotty he looked at the wig, stunned that there wasn't a screaming girl attached. Shock and perplexity compounded when her foot slammed into his scrotum. He made a slight whistling sound as he crumpled. There were no people visible ahead. A shout from behind made her move. She raced past the Pittencrieff Park gates, two or three voices joined in the chase. She bolted down and over the bridge past the old fort.

156

Kurt Lederer had an uneventful journey back to Brussels and was relaxing in his living room with his wife when the call came.

He stood and strode through to his study. How he loved the pine-clad walls and ceiling. He hung up his phone, switched on his computer and started some highly specialized and secure video conferencing software.

'Sorry to bother you, Herr Lederer. The Villa Morentsi was overrun by special forces this afternoon.'

'Whose?'

'Italian and French.'

'The helicopter?'

'Taken, along with the crew.'

'To where?'

'The chopper has been returned to its unit and two Italian officers arrested.'

'The crew?'

'Last seen at Nice Airport.'

'Have you any concerns about us being compromized?' Lederer said.

'None, sir. There was never any evidence. All computing and other communication services were removed after the attack.'

'How silent will our people be?'

'I'm confident there will be no leaks. We pay them well. Their families are looked after. They say nothing and, after the legal process, I'd be surprised if they are convicted of anything.'

'Only one concern then.'

'Sir?'

'The legal process. The French have got hold of them. If Cassanet is involved they'll be interrogated, and soon.'

'I'll start some habeas corpus action with the French. We have insiders who'll help.'

'Excellent. Don't let me detain you.'

* * *

As Lederer logged off his system, his phone rang once more. He picked up, staring at a picture of *The Graf Spee* in a stormy sea, the bow forging through a wave. How the ship graced the wall: strength, presence and purpose. He loved the symbolism. 'Herr Lederer?'

'Yes.' A clipped response

'Kurt by name, and curt by nature.'

'What do you want?'

'You. As you can tell, we have your number.' The phone disconnected.

Ten minutes later, he left for his office.

An hour after that he learned that the call could have come from anywhere.

157

Smythsone felt a tingle of fear, as she climbed out her taxi and into the foyer of her apartment block in London. New security arrangements meant no one would get near her like that again. It didn't change how she felt about the idea of going back there, running a bath, remembering a balaclava and an American accent.

He had never actually hurt her, but the pain inside, the sense of someone being able to get to her, the awareness of fear … that would never go away.

She picked up the phone and called Anthony. He was little more than a name, but he had rowed for Oxford and they had exchanged phone numbers a week before at one of those interminable evening receptions so prevalent in the financial world.

'Anthony, here.' The voice was impersonal, strong.

'Gemma Smythsone.'

'Ah yes, wonderful. The lovely lawyer.'

'I'm free tonight.'

'Just a moment.' She heard a muffled conversation at the other end. 'I'm free too. Where would you like to meet?'

'She suggested a Michelin two-starred restaurant several blocks away from her place.'

'Eight o'clock?'

'Ideal,' she said. 'Been there before?'

'No, but they tell me it's good.'

'I'm just back from a trip. It'll be nice to meet you again.' She leaked a warm smile into her voice. She could almost experience the powerful body squeezing and touching her.

'I'm heading for the gym and this'll give me time to shower, shave and all that good stuff. Do you want me to collect you?'

'See you there.'

'Can't wait.'

With the date in mind she felt better. Her phone rang, she picked it up.

'Hi, Gemma. Good to know you're home safe.'

She recognized the American accent. She needed the bathroom.

158

'Hello, hello, Sam.'

'You look happy.'

'Ah yes, arrogant Americans aren't my favourite people.'

They talked, swapping notes and observations over an early dinner.

'Those Belgians were a real help, Mo. The hotel keys, moment-by-moment intel. I've never had such a sense of things fitting together. We've rattled every cage in EuroBizz,' Sam said.

'The whole box of tricks. You did call Lederer?'

'Of course. Word is he went to his office straight afterwards, probably running some trace software.'

'He'll find nothing. And he'll experience the squeeze.'

'How about Justine Corlay?'

'Interesting, Sam, I think she's the weakest link. The threat of revealing her sex life scared her. I think she may phone.'

Sam nodded. 'The pressure is on, and who can they tell?'

'You keep telling me they don't like it up 'em. But, apart from being unbearably suggestive, you never tell me what *it* is.'

'Something that breaks their sense of control, their security. Xavier is very unhappy and shocked. He's been knocked hard, in a way bullies can't handle. Not by a savaging, but by being powerless. Same with the others, they'll be fizzing. What we can't afford is to have them sit tight. We must keep the pressure on.'

'You think something will give?' Cassanet's accent was almost a parody.

'*Mais oui, Monsieur Choux.*'

'How many times must I tell you not to call me a cabbage?'

'Every time you fail to buy your round on time. *Choux* to

you.'

'If we didn't have the Auld Alliance, I'd have you shot.'

'A shot? Thanks. Make mine a malt.' Sam put his hand up. 'Seriously, Mo, we can't rattle their cages any harder.'

'No. Now we have to wait.'

'Patience is everything.' The mobile buzzed in Sam's pocket. He looked at the display. 'Uh-ho.'

159

Stay or not? Decision time. *Gotta go*, she decided, the longer she stayed in the park the more likely she'd be caught leaving. She broke cover and crossed the Glen Bridge. There was no one about, torrential rain hissed down and slapped the tarmac. The path between the toilets and the coffee house at the pavilion lay empty.

Moving at an easy pace, she stalked behind Pittencrieff House, then round past the greenhouses until, finally, she got to the far path at the edge of the trees.

She paused and took her bearings. Five deep breaths later she moved on, trying to look relaxed. Chill water ran down her back and into her pants. She'd be cold when she stopped and, with that thought in mind, started to jog.

Near the lower gate, three men burst from the bushes. The first grabbed her from behind and the other two laughed with joy. She kicked out and managed to deliver an abrasive foot up an attacker's shin. That earned her a smack in the mouth. 'Bitch!' Her lip stung, she tasted blood.

'Don't harm the goods, Willie.'

'She's lucky she's worth money.'

'Nothin' to stop us givin' her the once over,' the third man said.

'Down by the swings.'

Eilidh knew what was coming. 'Just a little lovin', honey.' The man holding her reeked of beer, cigarettes and take-out curry. He farted. His mates laughed.

They dragged her down the wet bank to the fenced-off play area, and pushed her towards a park seat. 'We're going to hang you over that and fuck your brains out.' He thrust her forward, banged her hip bones against the seat-back, the painful collision making her bend over. Next he pressed up against her buttocks and ground away with clear intent. Another man held her by the arms. Her upper thighs and lower abdomen ground painfully against the wood.

'Get that belt undone and her kecks off.'

Rough hands started to work at the top of her jeans.

'Stand her up. I can't get at the buckle.'

They dragged her upright, still pressed against the seat, rain pelting down. One of the attackers released her belt, undid the trouser button and tugged at the zip. The third reached over to grope one of her breasts. *Ned!* She screamed and struggled, her captors lost their grip in the rain. One of them punched her stomach. She flopped forward over the wooden seat-back, winded for a moment. They struggled with her wet jeans and couldn't pull them down. Catching her breath, she wriggled and writhed. She screamed again.

'Shut it or I'll cut that pretty fuckin' face of yours.'

'She's goin' to give me a blow job,' another voice said.

The drama became surreal. Was she back in the barn? Would she wake up? The kitten would come. Ned would be there. Not him, please, not Ned.

'Come on, lads, give us a hand.'

She recognized a snot-filled snigger.

'I'll help,' a deep voice rumbled.

'Thanks.' The speaker managed a momentary quizzical look before a large dark fist put his lights out.

The man holding Eilidh's arms received several severe blows to the face and body from a Special Forces operative. The third assailant had only just managed to get his willie out of his trousers when Cal got to him.

Two of the minders worked hard to drag Cal off the third man, by which time the aggressor had become the victim, with battered ribs and a broken jaw to contend with, on top of his crunched knackers. He would be hospitalized for a while and spend a long time recovering from a ruptured testicle.

* * *

The Range Rover was forty metres away at the Park Gates. They drove to a safe house, Eilidh wrapped in a blanket and sipping from a hot coffee picked up at coffee shop on the New Row. For all the adventure, she remained self-possessed.

'How'd you find me?'

'GPS in the phone and a link to the mapping in this car,' Cal said.

'Wow, that's good.'

'That and some platinum-blonde hair.'

Her eyes popped open. 'No wonder they found me.' She explained how she'd lost her wig. The men laughed. 'Thanks, lads. This damsel is officially not-distressed. You're a bunch of heroes.'

'Tell 'em about the bear, Eilidh.'

'Don't you start, Cal. It's private.'

'No way. When you're a warrior, the laughs and stories go with the turf.'

Eilidh nodded, gave a tight little grin and told the story. When they finished laughing she sensed she'd joined an exclusive club.

160

'I'm glad she's safe.' Cassanet signalled to the barman who came over with another whisky for each of them. The bar fittings were brass on warm wood surfaces. The lights on the wall, with their red shades and tassels, suggested a sense of style lost in time. The table, in a quiet corner, bore two half-empty beer glasses.

'Near thing.'

'We don't want too many of those.'

'No.' Sam said.

'You only get so many near misses before you get the hit.'

Sam nodded. 'The situation reeks of the drug connections that got the shooting started in Ireland.'

'Ah, the rumble with your family.'

'Right. I had a serious word with the godfather who set that up a few days back.'

'Mmm, some egos can't handle a kick up the bum. They have such vulnerable little minds and such minimal self-esteem.'

'You're right.'

'Tough world.'

'I was pretty harsh. Probably harsher than I needed to be.'

'He deserved what he got.'

'Sure. But he'll never forget. Not sure I want to tip him over the edge.'

* * *

They met in the morning and planned the next steps and how further surveillance would be. 'It's good to be in their faces.'

'Powerful criminals can be dangerous. Scared people think badly. They also act with viciousness,' Cassanet said.

'Omelette time, Mo.'

'Spare me the cliché.'

'Can they tell each other? Are they brave enough to share the load?

'I understand the idea, but I'm not sure so many powerful cages have ever been rattled in such a personal and simultaneous manner.'

'Thoughtful stuff, Mo, and only one more to go.'

'I thought we had them all.'

'We have, but there's a banker to meet in London.'

'Ah, you're wanting to lock your horn with that Gemma woman.' Cassanet's eyes brightened.

'No, she's been seen to. I'm thinking of another person, a male, who might benefit from a few words. It may be a few days, but I'll get round to it.'

'What about Eilidh?'

'She's in Scotland. They'll bring her back in a day or two. I'm going over to London on the next train.'

'I will miss you.'

'It ain't over till it's over, Mo. I think we'll be seeing more of each other over the next wee while.'

'Excellent.' Cassanet raised his whisky glass in salute to Sam. 'I must get back to France and push a pen. We'll drop you at Calais.' They stood, nodded to the barman and went into a waiting car.

* * *

Three hours later, The Eurostar neared London. Sam's mobile vibrated and Charlton's ID appeared on the display.

'Hi, Ben.'

'Successful trip?'

'Yes. I'll brief you when I get back.'

'Cassanet has saved you the trouble. You're booked on a flight from Gatwick around seven. One night's R&R in Edinburgh with your wife, two on Arran and then back to the drawing board.'

'What brought this on?'

'Some words from you an eternity ago, and a phone call from Karen this morning,' Charlton said. 'Mike will meet you at

St Pancras and brief you on a few things, then accompany you to Gatwick.'

'Anyone else?'

'The wee hard man is off home, and the others are in a safe house. Feet up, Colonel. Catch you later.' The phone clicked off.

Mike grabbed his bag and pushed his way to the car. The two security men nodded to him. They were in the traffic in moments.

'Not your usual happy self, Mike.'

Mike pressed his finger to his lips. 'Glad you're back, Sam.'

161

In Gatwick, Mike sat back in a faux leather chair, his Americano untouched and face serious. To the right of the central escalators, they sat in a quiet corner at the rear of a coffee shop.

'Thanks for sorting the booking and stuff,' Sam said. He sipped his mocha.

'No problem.'

'What's on your mind, Mike? We've got half an hour before I go through security.'

Mike sighed. 'Guess who Mr Charlton is reporting to within the next three or four days?'

'I hope you're going to tell me.'

'William Wardle.'

'Ooh,' Sam pouted. 'Weasel features.'

'That's not all.'

'You're angry.'

'Yeah. They want to end the secondment for Cal and me.'

'Who?'

'Senior people. We've listed them for investigation.'

'Anything else?'

'The two men who gave themselves up in the North-East were released. It never got to court. They recanted. No evidence.'

Sam leaned forward and rested his left fist against his mouth. He thought for several minutes, pouting while a finger played pizzicato on his lips, as if trying to pluck out some words.

'So, Charlton is still in the driving seat for a few days?'

'Yes. Some bloody committee has got to meet.'

'Mmm, right. A transfer of power, before the transfer of power.'

Mike brightened. 'Yeah.'

'Good to know the lights aren't out yet.'

'No, but soon.'

'Soon is an eternity, Mike. Options galore while we still hold power.' Their eyes met. 'Get me on the last plane, Mike. I'm going to call Charlton.'

Mike stood, 'I need a leak,' he walked off. Sam pressed a key on his secure phone.

'Charlton.'

'Sam. Where are you, Ben?'

'Embankment.'

'We need to meet.'

'Can't, ordered to resign.'

'Screw that.'

'You're being assertive.'

'How long have you got?'

'Three days, I suppose, if I dig my heels in. Wardle's up north on what he calls business. He wants scalps when he gets back, mine especially, and he's going after the team, too.'

'What happened?

'Minister Mundial called me and demanded my resignation. He promised leniency for the rest of you.'

'Guaranteed?'

'Not if Wardle has his way.'

'Are you coming here or am I heading back to town?'

A short pause. 'Be with you in half an hour.'

162

'Not good enough, Ben,' Sam said.

The secure office in Gatwick smelled clean, but the sense of stressful meetings permeated the atmosphere. Mike made sure the surveillance cameras and microphones were off and left them to it.

'Sometimes, the head goes down, Sam. Maybe I should retire.' He sat back rubbing his face. The pale green of the walls added no warmth to the atmosphere.

'Here,' Sam handed Charlton a tissue. 'Dry those dripping eyes.'

Charlton chuckled. 'You remind me of me.'

'We're up against it in the midst of a battle. What would you say to an officer who lost interest?'

'That's enough!' Frosty at first, Charlton's head dropped. 'Sorry to let you down.'

'We all have doubts, Ben. You've let nobody down. Tell me about Wardle.' The ageing green plastic seat squeaked as he leaned forward.

'He'll be reinstated. One of the junior Ministers appointed him to supervise the Agency.'

'I thought the PM appointed you.'

'Of course, but there's always a government mandarin in the loop. Wardle's the man. He came to the office yesterday to chance his arm.'

'And?'

'I chucked him out.'

Sam laughed. 'And then?'

'An unpleasant and threatening call from an old Etonian, one Percy Mundial. I'm to deliver my resignation to him about now, in person.'

'Bad show, Ben. Or should I say "no show"?'

'In your friend Fuss's vernacular, *fuck him!*' Charlton's eyes glowed. 'I don't think the Minister has the power to demand my resignation without a few more niceties, especially if they are trying to achieve a low-profile result.'

'Anything unusual in the appointment?'

'PM's on holiday, number two isn't in the loop. They can pull our teeth if they're quick.'

'Meaning we can be gone in a couple of weeks, before the PM gets back and, a week being a long time in politics, forgotten and buried …'

'Or replaced by something toothless that looks the same.'

'Two things spring to mind, Ben.' Sam paused, noted the pallor and the shrewd eyes. 'May I?'

'Do, please.'

'We've got to stop the rot immediately.'

'Right.'

'We must snooker Wardle, at least one Minister and buy some time.'

'And then?'

'Protect ourselves against a similar attack.'

'Hmm, operational stuff that, Colonel.'

'Tactics, sir.'

'Not for generals.'

'No.'

'What's Mike up to?'

'Arranging the erasure of certain video surveillance footage.'

'Not everyone is against us,' Charlton said.

'Of course not, and we needn't make things easy for the Evil Empire. The troops are good people, especially in their respect for the Mikes and Cals of this world. Bizz and EuroBizz aren't the only players.' Sam said.

'Our strength is on the ground with people of moral rectitude. They observe what's going on. They're not fools.'

A knock at the door, and Mike came in. 'Privacy

gentlemen?'

'Sit down, Mike,' Charlton said.

'You're on the 20.50, Sam. Thomson at security will take you through. Your pistol's checked.'

'Thanks, Mike.' Sam's eyes turned to Charlton who nodded. 'We're taking 'em on, down and dirty. Choose: in or out.'

A yard wide smile and, 'I'm with you, sirs.'

'This won't be tidy. We're up against some nasty people doing horrible things,' Charlton said. 'Tactical action means certain activities may not always be procedurally or politically correct.'

'Understood, sir.'

'Colonel Duncan has my full confidence and, in my absence, must be treated as if he were me.'

Mike nodded. 'Right.'

'Good, a spot of strategizing is in order. I want you to cover our lines and do some digging in town when Sam here heads north.'

'Will do.'

'The overview is simple. We have three days, four at most, to protect the Agency. Otherwise the Bizz lot take over and neuter us,' Charlton said.

'The people who killed Douglas.'

'Yes, led by Wardle.'

'Unbelievable. Wardle?'

'Believe it. We found our mole a couple of days ago.'

'Who?'

'Quentin.' Charlton's stiff upper lip quavered for a moment. Mike paled. 'He's in special accommodation.'

'Right at our heart.'

'Guess who now has access to the codes for our database?' Mike grunted and shook his head.

'Shit.'

'Mmm, Indira, God bless her, managed to move key data and content. The work started as soon as Quentin was exposed. We passed significant misinformation for the casual enquirer.'

'Who found him out?' Mike said.
'Sam.'
'Nice one.' Mike nodded.
'Now, Mike, Sam will task you.'
'No sleep for the wicked, Mike.' Sam said.
'Who needs it, sir?'
Charlton stood up, went to a corner and made a call.

163

'Go to town, get Indira and key people you'd trust with your life together,' Sam said.

'Commander Mitchell will give you support, resources and so on. I've spoken to him just now.' Charlton's renewed energy sparkled in his eyes. 'His links to counter-terrorism bypass Wardle. Many important players are on the side of the angels. For all that, keep consequential information close.'

'Thanks, Ben. Now, Mike, I want you to locate the key enemy we're dealing with. That's Wardle, and Jenkins' people, including those two who were released. The first task is Mundial.' Mike nodded. 'Keep me updated, by text, on his whereabouts.'

'Will do.' Mike raised an eyebrow.

'Don't ask.'

'Secure Eilidh's information.'

'She knows where the stuff is, but won't tell until Mr Charlton guarantees confidentiality and security for her sources.'

'Bloody risky. If she dies her secret dies with her.' Sam said.

'In hand. The legal people are going over it; the form of words is important,' Charlton said.

'Questions?' Sam said.

'Why Jenkins?'

'His fingerprints are all over the recent attack on Eilidh.'

'The Minister?'

'We need to find out as much as we can about the Junior Minister and his contacts, the constellation around Wardle. You'll find some answers floating about.'

'Off you go, Mike. Keep us posted,' Charlton said.

'And Sam, sir?' Mike looked at Charlton.

'Of course. He has some private time to enjoy with his wife, but keep him in the loop just the same. I'll be in my office.'

'Right, sir.' Mike glanced at Sam, face impassive, eyes bright.

'Sam?'

'Keep the pressure on.'

Mike stood, pushed his well-used chair under the wobbly table and left.

They watched Mike go, the urgent tension and energy rippling through his strides.

'I'll speak to Parker,' Charlton said.

'I'll ask Pete Molloy to tickle our newshound.'

'He was a bit nippy at first. Molloy's an excellent man and has him eating out of his hand and enjoying the cloak and dagger stuff.'

'Excellent, Ben, I'll call Molloy when I'm airside.'

'How secure are these mobiles now?'

'They're fine. Indira moved them off the radar when she sorted the access for the crooks. We own a whole set of numbers and lines running through what she calls a "switch"; some sort of secure private connection. You'll find new numbers on your cell.'

'Good stuff.'

'Fuss Cathel went north the other day. He will liaise with you.'

'No doubt. Fancy a whisky before your plane?'

Sam looked at his watch. 'Time for two, Ben.'

'Excellent.'

164

'Mr Mundial, Minister? Jamie Carron.'

'Delighted to meet you … eh, Jamie.'

'Firstly, Minister, may I congratulate you on your promotion.'

'Thanks so much for that,' the baritone gushed.

'You must be delighted.'

A knowing laugh. 'Of course, but it's not called a greasy pole for nothing. What can I do for you, Jamie?'

'I hope you don't mind me contacting you. We had a tip-off about some changes at the covert place down Westferry Road; the Agency, isn't it?'

'How did you find out?' The temperature dropped.

'Talk and, as a reporter, sniffing around, the usual thing. William Wardle entered the building yesterday. What can you tell me?'

'Are we off the record?'

'If you wish, Minister.'

'In answer to your question, I wouldn't know. Directors do visit places under their control.'

'So he *is* in charge?'

'Soon … eh, next week. Perhaps he popped round to introduce himself.'

'Pretty good show: from criminal proceedings to promotion.'

'He's innocent.' The laugh punctuating the conversation betrayed discomfort.

'Of course, he's a free man, and, as you say, extending his remit. Rumours abound.'

'Rumours?'

'A vendetta.'

'I know of no such thing.'

'No more changes in the offing?'

'Sometimes performance warrants change. We always aim to achieve optimal service delivery. A man with Mr Wardle's track record is expected to demand and achieve the highest standards of performance.'

'Are you saying Westferry Road is not performing?'

'No,' the Minister stuttered. 'We simply practise continuous improvement.'

'Thank you, Minister, this is most instructive.'

'Anything more?'

'One or two more questions. Won't take long.'

'This morning I spoke to Directeur Cassanet of the *Département de Lutte Contre la Corruption*, the DLCC in France. He was effusive about the excellent performance of the Agency and work we do supporting Europe. Similarly, representatives of the United States Government report a strong alliance and cooperation in sometimes difficult situations.

'We have strong links with our allies.' Mundial's voice resonated pride.

'I ask again, is General Charlton being replaced?'

'How did you get his name?'

'Privileged information, Minister. I would like to go on the record now.'

Silence. Then, 'A simple reorganization. No criticism of anyone. We aim to improve already good performance and ensure best value for money.'

'So the Agency is performing well at the moment and this is simply a continuous improvement exercise?'

'Yes, and widely respected, as you say.'

'So, Mr Wardle is taking over the Agency at Westferry Road?'

'Beyond confirming we expect Mr Wardle to broaden his remit, I couldn't comment further, even if we were off the record,' he checked his notepad for Jamie's name, 'Jamie.'

'I must enquire, if it's one of those things that everybody

knows.'

'Doubtless, and, if I may say so, you are highly respected for your work.'

'Thank you, Minister.' *Greasy bastard.* 'My job is to be the ear to the ground.' Mundial nodded. 'Are things going to be shaken up?'

'I'm unable to comment on a Director's decisions. Mr Wardle will follow due process as leader of a top secret group.'

'A source says senior police officers have been told to prepare for a return from secondment.'

'I can't say. Perhaps Mr Wardle can clarify things when his appointment is confirmed.'

'It isn't confirmed. I understand, thank you. I'll contact him once his feet are under the table.'

'Do that. Anything else?'

'Not really Minister. Thanks so much for your time.'

'Always a pleasure.'

Jamie smiled as he shook hands and left the room with the Press Officer. Who was it who said they don't like it up 'em? He giggled and stroked his bright green tie as he walked down the corridor.

165

A four star hotel and a swift check in. The concierge confirmed bookings for an excellent Chinese restaurant in Leith and a taxi. Sam went up and let himself into the room.

The scented steam fogged the mirror. 'Typical! Woman in the bath when I get in from a hard day.'

'What's a girl to do?' Soapy toes wiggled at him; a nipple peeked out from the bubbles.

'Stand aside. The hero wants a dunk.'

'I'm only prepared to move over.'

'We've got a meal booked for eleven thirty.' His belt clanked as his trousers hit the floor.

'So, you'd better get moving.' He did; water and foam slurped to the sound of giggles and sighs.

A shower removed the rest of his tiredness. Karen sat on an easy chair, so beautiful, relaxed and happy he had to smile. Her slacks and dark red silk top hinted at her figure.

She'd brought along clothes for him: clean jeans, a black leather jacket and matching brogues. The yellow silk shirt was a tad bright for his taste but fitted well; no complaints. He put on the rig, with the .45 snug below his left armpit.

'Must you wear the cannon?' She sat in front of a dressing table adjusting her necklace.

'Yes, I'm operational, and we're heading out. I left the armoured vest off.'

'You need a less chunky weapon.'

'I thought you liked chunky weapons.'

'All you can think of is sex.'

'So what was that stuff in the bath?'

'Love. Bloody men.'

'Of course, *love*. What's that?'

'The emotional, sensitive stuff that goes along with sex.'

'What's emotional stuff?'

'Listen buster, you're cruising for …'

'What? Go on, I dare you.'

'Some tough demands when we get back.'

'You want emotional stuff?'

'Sod that. This woman has needs.'

'They're sorted.'

'You wait till after dinner. We've only just begun.' They hugged, she nibbled his ear. The phone rang to announce the taxi. Sam like the way Karen's charm bracelet bounced against his wrist as they walked out holding hands. Eyes watched them from the car park.

In the taxi a text arrived. Sam read the words, replied and sent another.

'Something serious?'

'No, a helpful journalist. I'm enlisting some help to cool a difficult situation.'

'Can't you stop working?'

'That's it until tomorrow, barring disasters.'

She squeezed him. 'I can think of one disaster you can do without, Samuel.'

'I hear you.'

166

Sam's mobile vibrated, on silent, at 07.35. He went to the bathroom. 'Mo.'

'Hello.'

'You sound pleased with yourself.'

'Job done.' The pride reminded Sam of a preening cat. 'From your lips to the ears of Godot.'

Sam smirked. Crazy man. 'No violence? No police?'

'You are talking to a French pro, Samuel.'

'Sorry.'

'He's okay. No physical damage, but I think he was a bit flushed.'

'Flushed?'

'I chose the metaphor for this awful, anti-France, government minister. We put him and his corrupt colleagues down the pan, no?'

'Yes.'

'Your Minister had the head start.'

'You didn't!'

A laugh of pure childish delight burst from the phone. 'We did.'

'In the toilet?'

'*Oui*, at a station, a bit smelly but a success. Our operative talks about the previous occupant having eaten curry. '

'Oooh.'

'We detect like Sherlock Holmes.'

'We read tea leaves.'

'A threatening note in his pocket and a hair wash. My man couldn't speak. He's too French for that.'

'How come a station?'

'He went to the *pissoir*. He was alone. The operative,

opportunistic, jumped him and flushed him down the toilet.'

'What about surveillance?'

'We don't think so. Anyway, a rubber face, Merkel's, no problem. Job done. The turd is uninjured.'

'Thanks. That'll move things along.'

'Yes.'

'Where are you?'

'On a break with my wife.'

'The adorable Karen?'

'Yes.'

'Why talk to me when you could be snuggling up to such a glorious example of womanhood?' Some intense laughter ended in a click as Cassanet's phone disconnected.

Sam shook his head and grinned. Karen stood in the doorway. He told her. They lay on the bed and sniggered.

167

Around 08.00 a message pinged into Sam's phone. They were in robes and enjoying a full cooked Scottish breakfast, the sun had managed to get through some trees nearby and splashed like egg yolk over the white linen. The butter melted in its dish. The toast had softened; the coffee stayed hot in a black vacuum jug.

'That was good,' Sam said.

'Why did we have to get up?'

'Check-out is eleven. We're going back to Arran and the kids.'

'I'm still hot.'

'Mmm. Keep the fire going until tonight.'

'I can hear you snoring already.'

'How can I snore beside a randy, middle-aged woman?'

'Just like you did last night, Mister Snoozy.'

She took her gown off, kissed him … and Sam read the text at 09:15. Karen was in the shower and he poured a final coffee. Then he remembered the message.

Call. Urgent. C.

* * *

'They've got her, Sam.'

'She was covered, Ben. Cal and operatives.' Sam gazed out the window blind to the view.

'The team were called off by an administrative error for one hour.'

'Bullshit.'

'The person or people concerned will be dealt with later. The leader called me and I managed to get them sent back. Cal's battered and Eilidh's gone.'

'When?'

'Seven this morning.'

‘How’s Cal?’

‘Battered, bruised, mobile. They checked him for concussion. To all intents and purposes he’s fine.’

‘Fuss?’

‘Probably another forty minutes until he’s with you.’

‘Is Mike handy?’

‘Yes. Can we hook up for a conference?’

‘Of course.’

‘We need information. I’ll take a shower and call in ten minutes. The task is figure out what’s going on and move fast.’

‘Wardle?’

‘Him. Jenkins, God knows who else.’

‘One thing.’

‘Yes.’

‘A team is waiting to take Karen back. She’s been covered since she left Arran.’

‘So she didn’t shop on her own?

‘No. Covered all the way.’

‘Thanks.’

168

Eilidh made do on whiffs of exhaust for breakfast, her surroundings anything but luxurious.

She rolled around in the back of a transit van, wrists tied, breaking her nails trying to grip the sides. The three men in ski masks kept their backs turned and created a fug of cigarette smoke.

They spoke in rapid-fire Scots, oblivious to her, munching crisps and chocolate bars which they didn't share.

She switched off to the journey and thought of poor Cal. She remembered the thwack of the baseball bat on his head and his bloody, semi-conscious face on the floor, then the kicking of his ribs. Where had the protectors gone?

169

Karen finished wrapping herself in a towel as Sam stuck his head round the door. 'What's happened?'

'They've got Eilidh.'

'I thought she was in Fife, in a safe house.'

'So did I.'

'And?

'Someone called off the minders and sent in the bad guys. Cal had a pounding, but he's okay.'

'What now?'

'People are here to take you to Arran. I'm going to shower and take part in a conference call, while you sort yourself out.'

'I'll dry my hair while you wash, and keep quiet when you're talking.'

'Thanks.' Sam stepped in the shower and turned the power on. The motor buzzed. Karen shook her head and, snug in her fluffy white robe, sat on the stool at the dressing table, and dried her hair. She finished before Sam's call started.

* * *

'Right, Mike, what about Wardle?'

'Newcastle. Visiting a computer centre and the university: important government work and meetings with some security people.'

'Any holes in his diary?'

'This afternoon, after 13.00 he's on private time. Back in Newcastle tomorrow.'

'Jenkins?'

'Out of town in his big Rolls.' Mike snorted. 'Makes tracking easy.'

'Could be a blind. Where's the car?'

'Just past Doncaster on the A1(M).'

'The two yoicks who held Eilidh?'

'On their farm to the best of our knowledge. The surveillance isn't constant, but we're pretty confident they're in.'

Sam wrote in his pad on a cleared area of the table, head bent forward in concentration. Karen listened in silence.

* * *

'Any thoughts about Eilidh?' Sam said.

'None. The gang who took her were Scottish thugs.'

'Right, let's start there.'

'Who set up the attack on Eilidh?'

'Billy McSween, an East Coast godfather type—hard, mean and harsh would describe him pretty well.'

'Where's he live?'

'A fancy house on the south coast of Fife.'

'Where is he now?'

'On the platform at Aberdour station, waiting for an Edinburgh train'

'Keep on him,' Sam said. 'Ben, can I have a chopper?'

'Why not? We're in the mire as it is. When?'

'Available, soon as, for the rest of the day.'

'Where?'

'Edinburgh Airport, but ready to drop by.'

'Anything else?' Charlton said.

'Had an apology from Mundial yet?'

'As a matter of fact, yes. How did you know?'

'Informed guess.'

'Catch up on that later.'

'Fair enough.'

'A chopper will be close by in thirty minutes. Indira should have a link in your phone shortly.' The mobile pinged and a link appeared. Followed by a text:

Helicopter call sign: Bravo 326, your handle: Vicar.

'It's in. Excuse me.' He disconnected and pressed the link.

'Bravo 326.'

'Vicar, ETA Edinburgh?'

'Twenty-seven, two seven, minutes.'

'Copy, stand by, contact soon.'

'Roger.'

'Out.' Sam clicked off.

'Any troops available, Ben?'

'None. The pushback is starting. Black spots are hard to shake off.'

'Okay.'

'You'll just have to do it with what you've got.'

'You mean me, Fuss and a fuckin' pilot? There'll be a few of them at the place.'

'Cal's on his way,' Mike said.

'A significant percentage increase. Aren't stats fantastic?'

'Sam?' He turned to Karen. He knew the look. 'Can I come?'

'No.'

'Who's going?'

'Me. Fuss and Cal. We're strangled for manpower by the shenanigans in London.'

'What about the four special forces supermen in the black Range Rover outside?' Karen said.

'What about them?'

170

'They've got Jason.' Sam checked his watch 09.27.

'So why are you calling me?'

'Don't make it any harder, Vicar.' Jenkins voice had no energy.

'Talk.'

'They're taking your sister to the farm where she was held when they had her before. Jason went up at Wardle's request and I got the call last night. Show up or he dies. I'm on my way.'

'What makes you think it's that farm?

'Wardle called me again this morning and told me to get a move on. He said they'd be solving the journalistic problem and silencing the brothers grim ... like they should have done before. Smug bastard.'

'What do you want me to do?'

'Protect my son.'

'I will, if I can. Good luck, Bill.' The phone disconnected without reply.

* * *

'Just popping out for a moment.' The door closed behind Sam before Karen could speak. He went along the road to a pay phone. He entered it, picked up the handset, shook it thoughtfully beside his face and tapped the ear-piece on his lips. He didn't make a call and left after two minutes. He returned to the hotel. It was 09.40.

171

'We know what you've been up against, sir. The lads are up for it. I've requested permission.' His knife fight sparring partner stayed business-like in easy fitting non-descript clothes. 'Chopper too. You've got clout.'

'Friends in some places. Thanks.' Sam said.

'I'll follow up and come back as soon as I can.'

'Appreciated.' The man left the room.

'Where are you, Fuss?' The connection hissed and wavered.

'Just passin' the airport.'

'We may get help.'

'Trust me, Sammy, the fuckin' bampots down the road will put their fuckin' oars in. Expect fuck all.'

'There's a chopper on standby.'

'I'll believe it when I see it.'

'What kept you?'

'A useless fuckin' squaddie, who claims to have been a regimental boxing champion.'

'Any major injuries?'

'Nah, just a bit of bruising to his body and a fuckin' ego that's strugglin' to find excuses.' An indistinct murmur sounded, 'I don't care if you're a fuckin' Rupert now. You'll always be a fuckin' squaddie to me, Calvin.'

'See you in a few minutes. Room 235.'

'Roger.' The phone disconnected.

* * *

Sam's mobile rang. 'Bravo 326.'

'Vicar.'

'Ordered off, Vicar. Sorry, good luck.'

'Bravo 326, acknowledge.'

The communication ended. Sam stood motionless for a

moment, fists opening and closing. He looked out the window.'

'Bad news?' Karen said.

'No chopper.'

'What do you think?'

'Time's running out.' He gazed into her eyes. 'If we get this wrong, Eilidh dies and the Agency's work dies with her.'

* * *

The knock on the door sounded hollow. Sam let the close support team leader in. 'Bad news sir. We've been pulled, The Brass don't like it. We're with you, but orders are orders.'

'Understood.' Sam's mouth remained straight, somehow sad.

'Mrs Duncan, we are instructed to escort you to Arran and ensure your protection.'

'I'm packed.' Karen's eyes were bright as the sunshine wrestling with the clouds outside. She looked at Sam and nodded. 'They're trying to kill you, Sam.'

'There's Eilidh, the truth and the mission.' He sucked his upper lip into his mouth, covering it with the lower. He reached inside his jacket and handed Karen an envelope. 'Not for now, toots.' She hugged him and pulled his head to touch her forehead. 'Do unto others.' She whispered.

'Right, love.'

'And the letter?'

'Arran is soon enough.'

'Excuse me, sir? A private word please.' Karen walked into the bathroom and closed the door.

'Our instructions are to return to Arran with Mrs Duncan. The four of us *must* go.'

'I hear you, and thanks. I know you'd be with us if you could. Follow orders and keep the missus safe, I wasn't that keen on taking her along anyway.' The rueful smile said a lot. 'DCI Swindon from London will call you later. Give him the chain of command around this order.'

'Sir.'

'Report any unusual links,' The soldier nodded, 'and try not to draw attention.'

'One other thing, sir, our Close Protection Vehicle has been assigned to you and we've no instructions regarding it. The team believes the CPV remains at your disposal at the present time. What are you orders regarding the vehicle, Colonel?' The half-smile got a response.

'Take Mrs Duncan to Arran. Leave the vehicle and surplus equipment.'

'Very good, sir.'

'I'll arrange car hire for you. People carrier okay?'

'Perfect.' Sam called Karen in. She called reception and made arrangements.

* * *

Another knock at the door and Fuss came in followed by Cal. Fuss walked over. 'What the fuck are you up to, son?'

'Save your RSM bristles for someone else, Mr Cathel,' Sam said.

'Is this a fuckin' helpful person?'

'He truly is. Don't you remember him from Arran?'

Fuss smiled. 'Now you mention it. What's he done?'

'Supplied wheels.'

'Well done you.' The sunshine of Fuss's smile won a return nod.

'We best be off, sir. Mrs Duncan.' They escorted her out.

172

'Is this all it'll do?'

'It feels fast enough,' Sam said. 'We know where the action is likely to be. We've enough time.' The road opened up into the overtaking lane at Soutra. Three forty-tonners were left behind as they charged upwards. The blades of the turbines on wind farms on both sides of the road rotated in quiet disruption of a rugged view.

Sam listened on his phone and turned back. 'Wardle stopped for a break at 13.00. Jenkins changed to a rental car about an hour ago. ID confirmed, two men with him,' Sam said.

'Mike's doin' a good job.'

'Not everyone's against us.' Sam sighed

'And if it isn't the right place?'

'Eilidh's gone. I don't think Jenkins was kidding.'

'Then what?'

'Shut up, Fuss.' The hard edge was worth paying attention to.

'Sorry, boss.'

'We're all jumpy,' Cal said.

'I know.' Sam eased back in the leather seat, adjusted the rake and raised the front.

Traffic held them up as they charged down the far side. Fuss swore. Cal concentrated.

'The road widens in a few miles,' Sam said.

'Take over, Sam. My ribs are hurting.' They pulled into a lay-by and drove out before any vehicles caught up.

'Got a bit of a thumping, Cal.'

'Yeah. Some of the bastards were familiar. More enthusiastic than dangerous. God, Eilidh is feisty. She fought like a tiger until one of 'em bopped her.'

'Badly?'

'Up the side of the jaw. She wobbled and they secured her. Someone said she wasn't to be hurt.'

'The bashing on your face looks painful.'

'Had worse. The ribs are grumbling. I'm okay for a rumble.'

'That's it, Cal, ready to rumble, you muckle great bruiser. What's this I hear about Jason Jenkins gettin' a seeing to from you?'

Cal managed a lopsided smile, 'Yeah, no moves: a fuckwit of the first order.'

'He went to Cumberland Street,' Fuss said, 'Glasgow.'

'What are you on about?' Cal said.

Fuss sang, '... if you're down the south end of Glasgow don't venture to Cumberland Street, unless you're a heavy-weight champion, or one hell of a quick on your feet...' All three laughed off some tension.

'Shit!' Sam said. 'We've picked up Mr Plod. Sorry, Cal. They're all lit up and coming after us.'

The shuffling click said a weapon was armed. 'They'd better be real.'

Cal called Charlton, as the policemen walked up the sides of the car.

'They'll have called in our plate and know we're the real deal,' Sam said. 'Let's talk to them.'

* * *

'Tell me, Wing Commander, were you taking off or landing?' The policeman smiled.

'That fast?'

'Flying down the road, sir.'

'Yes. We're operational.'

Cal produced his warrant card. 'DCI Martin. My colleagues and I are members of a covert Government organization. We need your assistance.'

'Tell me more, sir.'

'My colleagues are from a less visible part of things. We are rushing to a potential incident in the North of England.'

'We checked you out.' A Borders accent thick as butter. 'You are in an official car and as far as we can tell, on official business. Our sergeant has had a call from General …' he looked at his pad, 'Charlton, your boss. He mentioned your names.'

Sam nodded in gratitude. 'Excellent.'

'Can I see that warrant card, DCI Martin?'

'Of course.' The constable made some notes.

'Mr Duncan, was it?'

'Yes. Samuel.'

'ID?'

Sam handed his over. The officer read the ID and stiffened to near attention.

'Thank you sir.'

'And you, sir?'

'Francis Cathel, Former RSM. Fuck-all ID.'

'Thank you, sir. With these two gentlemen vouching for you, we'll let you be on your way.'

Cal nodded. 'Thank you.'

'Good luck, gentlemen. Kick arse and take names.' A smile and a nod from Sam, 'One other thing … you've got blue lights. Use them!'

'Forgot.' Sam shrugged and found the switch.

'There aren't many pursuit cars between here and the A69. We'd be surprised if you see any more. Drive safely.'

'Give me your numbers.' Sam said. They were written on a pad and handed over. 'If this works out, you'll be hearing from me.'

'And if it doesn't?'

'Try and forget about this. The people we're after are powerful and decidedly unpleasant.' The policemen nodded, returned to their car and let the big black machine leave. They watched it accelerate down the road.

'Reminds me of a song,' Cal said, "The Road to Hell".' They accelerated and in twenty-five minutes were on the steep twisting bends up to the English Border.

Cal picked up is mobile and listened. 'Mike says Jenkins is

twenty minutes past Scotch Corner. Wardle is near Barnard Castle. He looked at the map. 'This is going to be a bloody close-run thing.'

173

'Ms Eilidh Duncan! Delighted to meet you at long last. We're going to ask you some questions, but first, I want to prepare you for what's to come.' Two muscular men grabbed her and manhandled her round the building. 'Awful smell, isn't it. A slurry pit is a sad place for a burial. Best we can do at short notice.'

Her silence started to irritate him. 'You can't negotiate. We need to determine where your documents are, and I can't risk you lying. Don't have time, you see?'

The man with an acne-covered face glowered and squeezed her arm hard enough to make her eyes water.

She took the pain without complaint. 'What are you telling me?'

'I'm telling and showing you where the bodies are buried. Excellent help for a journalist. We've one more … ahem … *resident* to create before it's your turn.'

'You must be William Wardle.'

'And you know where the bodies are buried.' The men laughed. 'I've showed you where mine are and …' his face gleamed with perverse power, 'I will find out where yours are.'

They dragged her through a back door and into the barn. They passed two men tied to wooden columns which supported the roof. Both were gagged. The older one was fat and pale, with marbled skin. His stomach had a flap almost down to his groin. His eyes were wild. He wore his hair short.

'You'll regret this, Wardle.'

'Not really, Mr Jenkins, just another competitor biting the dust or should I say crud.' 'As for you, rude boy, Jason. The line dies with you, doesn't it?' He smiled.

The younger one stood pale, twitching with fear, yet

attempting to be brave; stripped to the waist; bruises and abrasions covered his body. His nose wore a dirty plaster; the lips round the gag showed bruising; blood leaked out. The way his arms were tied locked him, standing, in place. His eyes rolled towards her, bulging and red-veined.

Eilidh recognized the names.

Wardle walked up close to her. ‘You’ll be so glad when the time comes to end your life. We’ve plans for you.’ He turned to his men ‘Tie her to the board and leave her by the trough to contemplate.’

174

'Lewis Hamilton's got nothing on you, Sammy.'

The bends and switchbacks on the A68 tossed the men about as they neared Hexham. The satnav told Sam to turn right on to the A69. They hurtled under the dual carriageway, charged round the roundabout and made the left at pace, racing up the hill to the main road for Carlisle.

'We'll settle down for the next few miles.'

The next roundabout came up quickly. A car pulled out, not seeing the blue lights and nearly ran into the car beside it when he spotted the flashers.

They raced on, past the end of the fast road and on to the A69.

Before long, they were heading up towards the fells on a country road.

'This looks a bit lumpy,' Cal said.

'Nothing like the hills in God's own country.' Fuss managed the arrogant Scot with aplomb.

'This used to be Scotland,' Sam said.

'Now I know why it's somewhat prettier than I first thought.'

'We're nearly there,' Sam said.

'Mr Charlton on the blower, Sam,' Cal said. 'Sounds important, you better pull over and take the call.'

They drove into a scooped-out area bearing old marks of quarrying. Sam took the phone from Cal. A wind-whipped drizzle blasted his window. The rock glistened.

'Ben.'

'I must ensure you are clear on a few things, Colonel.' Charlton sounded like someone had wound his spring.

'Go for it, Ben.'

'Please listen and act appropriately. You are about to be given rules of engagement.' Sam laughed. 'Not funny.'

'Someone's pulling your putter.'

'Big time.'

'With you?'

'Affirmative.'

'Can't hear my end.'

'Exactly.'

'Politician? Yes or no.'

'No.'

'Military? Yes or no.'

'No.'

'Mandarin, Civil Servant?'

'Precisely.'

'Please tell all.'

'The DG tells me they have reason to believe that Mr William Wardle, one of our top anti-terrorism people, has been kidnapped by criminals.'

'How awful.'

'He must be protected at all costs.'

'Excrement from on high.'

'I'm glad you appreciate the situation.'

'I'm not to slot him, Ben.'

'No.'

'There's a firearm team on its way from Carlisle. Expect it to be with you in twenty minutes.'

'Do they know where we're going?'

'Yes.'

'Do they know about the risks to innocent civilians?'

'You say you have reason to believe there are innocent civilians caught up in this?'

'Yes. We must go in. If the young lady is mobile and sane I'll refrain from killing the odious bastard.'

'The DG wants me to put you on the speaker.'

'By all means.'

'You're on.'

'How dangerous is the situation?' Sam made a signal to Fuss to go outside with the HK. He went thirty yards away.

'Who am I speaking to?'

'Anthony Thomason, Cabinet Security.'

'Fine, sir. How may I help you?'

'I want you to wait until the police arrive.'

'Are you sure, sir?'

'I'm ordering you to wait.' The tone of a martinet squeaked from the phone. Sam pointed at Fuss. He fired two bursts. 'What's that?'

'Gunfire, sir. There's mischief going on. Wait! That was close. We are holding position.' Sam pointed, another burst. 'We think there's a firefight going on ahead.'

'What are you doing?'

'Awaiting instructions.' Another point, another burst.

'Go in now. Protect Mr Wardle at all costs.'

'Very good, sir. General Charlton?'

'Get moving, Colonel. Protect Mr Wardle and any other person in danger. Godspeed.' Sam clicked off.

'Well, boys, you heard the Director General.' Sam waved Fuss over. 'Rabble to the rescue!'

175

They left her pants and tee-shirt on, removing everything else. 'They keep in the cold. Breaks you down more quickly.' Wardle said.

Next, they tied her to a rough plank, with her hands lashed to her sides, and bound her to the length of the board in sections: by her ankles, just above her knees, across her thighs, around her waist, chest and neck. They left a smelly cloth on her head. Wardle came in.

'Enjoy a rest, my dear. We'll deal with you in a little while. I must punish a rude boy. Two down and three to go. I'm going to use a garrotte. Exciting, isn't it?'

Wardle went into the area where the two men were, his voice echoed from the rusty corrugated roof. 'Thanks for coming, Bill, and here's your son and heir, too.' A man mumbled and groaned, and the volume increased to a strangled, muffled wail, a throbbing, blunted shriek. 'When we met and Atwill died, you were meant to join him. Then the Duncan girl's brother ruined my day.'

Another horrible sound burst from the man. 'Brave boy this. He is going to receive a lesson about spitting on my silk suit. No manners.'

She could make out the older man yelling and indistinct 'Please, no! or 'Pleesh, nuh! Pleesh, nuh!' He kept it up.

'Twice round his neck, and then by heck I turn the handle.' Rope creaked several times until a sound like a hollow protracted cough was followed by abrupt silence. A cotton-wool wail erupted and tailed off.

* * *

She thought a finger touched her cheek and heard Tonka's voice: 'Don't worry, love. Be brave, bear it.' It might be a fantasy, but she felt empowered. Under the stinking towel, she closed her eyes and started deep breaths: in with the good air …

The sobbing started again and deepened to horrific howl of emptiness.

Wardle's voice came through the partition. 'Ah, he's trembling … but he's gone. Look at him dance, jolly boy.' The scream from the gag had a depth of emptiness and loss new to Eilidh's experience. She screwed up her eyes. 'Well, Bill, your time is coming. Before then, I have a date, with a beautiful storyteller, and I'm saving my sweet little garrotte for you, too.'

176

'Nearly there.' Sam said. 'Remember the plan.' A text pinged into his phone. 'What's it say?'

ED in large building, four enemy. Some outside. No time to clear area. Take care.

Cal read the message out and slipped the phone back into Sam's pocket.

'Who was that from?'

'No idea. Okay. There's the building, I'm going to get us in there.' They were on the hillside approaching the farm. 'Clear the car and the transit!' Sam pointed at a van parked five yards behind the Mondeo. 'Suppress fire. Hold those bastards up; help the police when they get here.'

'Will do.' Cal and Fuss spoke simultaneously.

'Vests protect up to a point. Take care.' Sam slapped Fuss's chest.

* * *

'We're at the road end.' They turned on to a rutted track pushing its untidy way among bushes, clumps of heather and lanky grasses. The splatter of gunfire burst across the windscreen and driver's side.

'Bastard!'

'Lucky this is armoured, Cal. A normal car would be full of dead and dying,' Sam said.

'Keep yer eyes on the fuckin' road! Tune in.'

'Thanks Fuss.'

A lanky man ran out.

'Grenade, grenade.' Cal's shout startled his companions.

The big car accelerated towards the assailant who struggled with the pin. 'As long as they haven't got a .50 calibre, we should be okay.'

The man had the pin out and smiled in rotten-toothed triumph as he released the lever. A tattooed arm swung back to throw the bomb and the Range Rover went straight over him. The sound of the man being crunched under the big car seemed surreal in the luxurious environment. More bullets struck.

Sam glanced in the mirror and watched the man, a distorted lump on the road. He peeked again as the grenade exploded. The body jumped in a parody of life. Some parts seemed to detach. *Fuck him.*

* * *

Fifty metres more and they entered the farmyard. A Ford Mondeo was parked with a man struggling to get out. Sam drove over and crushed the door against his leg. The man started to scream and flap around like an animal in a trap.

'We're past the ambush.'

'Yeah.'

Bullets smacked into the rear of the Range Rover. 'Goin' in the front door is risky.'

'They'll be too excited to aim straight. See you on the other side.' Sam jumped from the armoured vehicle and sprinted for the door. Shots thudded into the barn side.

177

'You can't escape, Eilidh, you'll talk, and then the man over there, the one with the machete, is going to keep a promise to your brother.' Wardle's eyes glowed bright with excitement.

The scar of Acne-Man's skin condition glistened. He slapped a long blade on his hand. 'I've given him your head. Never seen a decapitation before. Your choice is: talk quickly, and he'll chop your head off; take too long, and he'll saw slowly. I hope you'll be quick, as I've a call to make, and it's late already.'

She wondered if Tonka had been real.

'Imagine, part of you can watch as we send old Bill, next door, after his boy. You see, I have to provide photographic evidence of your death.' He laughed as two of the men wrestled the board around. They tipped her over until her hair touched the water. They laid the dirty cloth over her face and upper body.

Wardle's face straightened. 'Right, chaps. Let's see what she's made of.'

178

The quiet and thoughtful atmosphere in the meeting surprised them. No exuberance, grandstanding by Xavier, or conflict.

'Wardle has the Duncan woman and is interrogating her. He will report answers soon and provide evidence of death. We'll interdict her papers, and she will sleep,' Xavier sniggered and wiped his lips with a tissue, 'with the shits.'

No one laughed.

179

Sam rushed through a ramshackle door, cobbled from broken planks of differing ages and colours. He went in low, but not low enough to stop two heavy bullets hitting him just above the navel. Two others missed to clang and ricochet. He fell, kicking himself to the right as another burst of fire flew into the empty space.

His head banged against the tine of a hay turning machine, rusty with age. The metal grazed his scalp and a tickling trickle of blood dribbled down behind his ear. Sam's feet struggled for traction on the cobbled floor. Even though the vest did its job, his stomach hurt from the bullets' impact. He flipped on to his front. The smell of old sacks and manure suffused the air. The place was like a junk yard.

'Looked a pretty good shot.'

'In the gut.'

'You were all over the place.'

'The recoil sprays 'em around. Single shots are better.'

'Find him and make sure he's dead.' Sam, winced with the pain and thanked God for the vest. He slipped into a stall behind the machine. Two old axe handles leaned against a wall, covered in cobwebs. He picked one up.

'Sure.'

Wardle talked as his man approached. 'Well, young lady. A few questions, and we'll send you off to join your brother.'

Sam stood behind wooden upright in the stall and raised the axe handle above his head. The gun barrel came in to view, moving with caution. One chance to get it right.

Blood dripped into his eye. He let it trickle. The shooter cradled the Mac10 like a pro, left hand holding the suppressor and, at last, the right holding the the pistol grip. Sam chopped the stave down. His enemy sensed the movement and started to pull back but not fast enough. The club crushed the fingers on the suppressor and crunched the weapon from the hunter's hands so it swung round on a its webbing strap.

With a strangled grunt the injured man watched Sam follow the blow out from behind the post and swing the stave from a baseball stance. His mouth opened as the reverse blow smashed into the right side of his head. The killer flopped down, out cold, maybe dying. Sam secured his wrists, elbows and ankles with baler twine. A snore-like breath, out for the count. Goodness, Acne-man from London. Firing crackled outside.

'Don't, don't. Pleaseeee.' Pretty good for a non-actor. 'Aaargh!'

'Got him?'

'Yeah, pitchfork! Nearly gone.' A muffled faux-American voice. 'Still want the head?'

'Bring it through.' Wardle called. Eilidh's scream tore at Sam's heart. 'I'm going to put a brotherly head right here, so you answer my questions under his watchful eye.' Wardle spoke to other people. 'Do her again.' The sounds of Eilidh's struggle ratcheted pressure. Sam wiped blood from his eye.

He crept to an open doorway, wide enough for a tractor, and glanced past vertical wooden beams. Two men were water-boarding Eilidh over a trough, less than ten feet away. Her feet kicked, her body jerked against the bindings. Wardle stood close by, touching himself, immaculate in his silk pinstripe, shiny shoes reflecting light from a hole in the roof.

* * *

The machine pistol hung down Sam's back, the Colt secure in its holster. The man nearest him held the board Eilidh was tied to. The rough stone edge of the trough acted like the fulcrum of a see-saw. The operative counter-balanced her. Her short hair touched the greenish water when they tipped her to the correct angle for the torture. The man at the other end poured dirty water on to the material covering her face as she writhed, coughed and made strangled screams.

Wardle gave his full attention the procedure with sadistic excitement. Sam stole out and hit the nearest person a savage blow to the back of the head. The man dropped, straight down and splashed unconscious into the trough with Eilidh underneath him. Her dainty feet quivered and strained against the bonds.

Sam swatted Wardle aside with a backhand blow to his ear. The skinny figure crashed on to the hard-packed earth, stunned.

The man pouring the water dropped the bucket into the trough where it clanked on his partner's head. Stepping back, he reached for the pistol on his belt. His hand touched the grip as Sam reached him. A first double jab of the stave pounded its way under his right eyebrow and then squashed his nose. He gripped his weapon. Sam swung the axe handle back and crunched his collar bone. He groaned and let the pistol go. A last swipe, delivered like Babe Ruth, bashed the side of the man's jaw above his ear. Unconscious, the torturer dropped backwards on to a clipping stool and lay supine, feet in the air. Sam picked up the pistol.

Wardle, covered in dust and dung, staggered to his feet.

'Quick choice, Wardle. Help get her out or die.'

Wardle went to the trough and pulled at the man, Sam yanked hard in support. They dragged him out and let the unconscious man topple to the floor, blood running out of his nostrils and mingling with scum and dung. Next, they tipped the board up and Sam ripped the fabric away from Eilidh's face and body. Her strangled breath gurgled as if an alien was about burst from her chest.

'Face down and spread-eagle, Wardle.'

'You know who I am?'

'Oh yes, and I know *what* you are!' Sam slapped him hard, spun him round and threw him to the floor.

Eilidh's eyes swam into awareness. Fighting knife in hand, Sam cut the bonds. 'Don't even think about it, Wardle.' Wardle froze on the floor. She coughed, retched several times and vomited greenish fluid.

Sam secured both unconscious men with frequent glances at

Wardle.

'You came.' Eilidh half-smiled. 'I thought they'd killed you.' She teared up, but none fell. Her pale face managed a twisty smile. 'When the board dropped in and the man landed on me, it had to be you. Saved again.'

'You just can't get the staff these days,' Wardle said.

Sam and Eilidh cackled. 'I don't think you'll win the wet tee-shirt competition today,' Sam said. Her eyes smiled, as she shivered.

'Had some orders, Colonel?' A muffled voice from a filthy floor.

· 'Yes.'

'Are the police coming?' Wardle turned his head sideways and spat out a length of straw. His hook-nosed profile and skinny lips remained unattractive at the angle.

'Any time now.'

'You're a hero. You saved me again.'

'Really?'

'There'll be another day for reality to catch up. Wait and tremble.' The chuckle blew up dust. Wardle coughed.

'Okay, Wardle. Get up. I won't kill you.'

'What happened to Hank?'

'Not sure. He was out cold last I looked.'

Wardle stood up and dusted himself off with both hands, head looking downwards, when Eilidh landed on his chest with a scream. She raked his face with broken nails. Sam caught her round the middle and pulled her off. 'Come on, babe.'

'He's evil.'

Wardle sat back down on the floor with a groan, red weals like thick lipstick on his face. 'He's got a get-out-of-jail-free card,' Sam said.

'I can't believe it.'

'I won't kill him.'

'You're a bloody idiot.'

'Calm down.' Wardle made to speak, Sam's raised hand silenced him. The door crashed open.

180

Four black-clad police entered, weapons at the ready. The lead officer lifted his goggles.

'Inspector.' Sam smiled and offered his hand. The handshake was brief and friendly. 'Joyce, isn't it? Inspector Joyce.'

'Well remembered, sir.'

'This is Mr William Wardle of Counter Terrorism.' He made an open-handed gesture, 'and Eilidh Duncan, who you protected in Carlisle some weeks ago.'

'She won't remember me, Colonel Duncan.' He turned to the scruffy pinstriped man.

'Mr Wardle.' Did Sam detect a touch of frost? 'Ms Duncan, you are much better than when I last saw you, if somewhat wet.'

'Colonel Duncan saved me for a second time today, Inspector.' Sam took Eilidh's arm and restrained her. 'Ms Duncan and I were in grave danger when the Colonel entered and rescued us.'

'You'll find two men near the trough. Best call an ambulance.' Sam pulled the Mac10 off his back. 'This belongs to a man round the corner,' He pointed and handed the machine-pistol to the policeman. 'Safety's on, it's loaded.' The weapon was passed to a constable nearby. 'The two men by the trough were water-boarding Ms Duncan. I intervened forcefully to protect both her and Sir William's lives.'

'Quite so, Inspector. I owe Colonel Duncan my life, as I say, for a second time.' Wardle gazed at Sam. 'I'll not forget you, sir.' The evil glint in his eye matched the smoothness of his tongue.

Eilidh quivered with anger. She stared at Sam, eyes flashing, but heeded the gentle shake of his head.

'Where is your car, Mr Wardle?' The Inspector asked.

'Barnard Castle. I was kidnapped by Bill Jenkins, the London crime lord.'

'Where is he?'

'Over in that direction somewhere,' Wardle waved his arm towards the left. 'He fell out with his henchmen, I think they hurt him and his son.' A moment later a call from a policeman confirmed Jenkins had been found alive and another corpse nearby.

'Were there some people here? Two brothers, farmers by the looks of 'em?'

'I recall seeing two men running off when I was brought here. They were heading back towards Hexham, I think.' Sam marvelled at Wardle's smooth dishonesty.

'There's a car outside with an injured man.'

'I'm responsible for that, Inspector, we trapped his leg when we drove in.' Sam said.

'Constable.' A large man came over looking like a Doctor Who villain from the eighties. 'Take Mr Wardle to one of our cars and we'll get him out of here.'

'No, no. I wish to leave without my face being seen. They had a bag over me when I came here. It's important I'm not recognized by criminals or lower echelons.'

'What do you suggest, sir? We have to sweep the area.'

The inspector spoke into his shoulder mounted radio. He pressed the ear piece, attentive. 'The back of the building is clear. There's a door. I'll send someone with you.'

'Not necessary, I have some calls to make. I'll have a cigarette at the back. Send a car and driver round for me in fifteen minutes.'

'Sir, there may be danger.'

'You have cleared the area. Now get on with your work while I step out.'

'As you say, Mr Wardle.'

'Good!' Wardle stalked away. 'See you soon, Colonel, Ms Duncan.' He snickered as he left.

181

'You're lucky you had a Close Protection Vehicle, Colonel Duncan.'

'Yes.'

'The man with the hand grenade is dead. The driver of Jenkins's car has a badly crushed leg. The man you disarmed is critical, and, we mustn't forget the two men by the trough.' The Inspector's voice carried controlled shock and horror. The smell of blood and fear rose acid, mingling with cordite and manure.

'You've seen the CPV?'

'Well shot-up.' The Inspector said.

'Believe me, I didn't want to kill or harm anyone. Sir William thinks I did the right thing.' Sam wore a serious face.

'We can only do the forensics, weigh up the evidence and pass our information to the Crown Prosecution Service.'

'Of course.'

'The men you incapacitated were armed—one with a machine gun, all with pistols and knives.'

'Probably mercenaries, if past experience is anything to go by.' Sam said.

'And the people outside?'

'The chap with the hand grenade didn't appear expert. I had to drive over him. He stood in front of the car pulling the pin. I couldn't drive off the road, there was nowhere to go.

'As I say, we have people examining the scene. They'll report back.'

'We were all at risk. In an ordinary car we'd have been dead and gone,' Sam said.

The Inspector turned to Eilidh. 'How are you, ma'am?'

'Angry! How could I be kidnapped when surrounded by close protection? And the only man left, Cal, was …' emotion made her face twitch, 'hurt.'

'Cal's okay, Eilidh.' Sam said. She inhaled down to her feet and sighed as Sam spoke to the policeman. 'DCI Cal Martin was assaulted during Eilidh's kidnap. He travelled down with us.'

'If you'll both excuse me for a moment I need to finish inspecting the scene and approve the investigation plans.'

'Please arrange protection for my sister, and I'll come through with you. I know Bill Jenkins.'

Joyce assigned two officers to guard Eilidh.

* * *

Sam and the Inspector walked through the partition. People milled around: paramedics, a crime scene specialist and others. Jason Jenkins hung down from a vertical wooden beam dotted with woodworm holes. The garrotte clenched his neck, eyes bulging, red and half-closed in death. His tongue, dark and protruding, lolled from a twisted mouth. Organic matter was leaking into his trousers, not a pleasant smell.

Past the dead man, paramedics strapped Bill Jenkins onto a wheeled stretcher. His face and demeanour were lifeless. Sam walked over and stood above Bill, who recognized him.

'Vicar.'

'Bill, what happened here?'

'That bastard Wardle murdered my son.' The flat, emotionless voice lacked strength.

'How did you come to be here?'

'A deal with a devil. He promised me Jason's life.'

'For what it's worth, I'm truly sorry for your loss.'

'Is your sister okay?

'Just. Yes. I'll visit you once you've laid Jason to rest.'

'Why?'

'We've things to discuss: peace.' Bill lay impassive, 'payback.'

Jenkins gazed at Sam for a moment. A dim light came on in the depths of his eyes. 'Call me.'

'I will.'

* * *

Sam returned to the large room. He and Eilidh went over and leaned against a wooden column with two old horse collars on either side.

'How are you?' Sam said.

'A little shaken, but okay.'

'Good for you. Most people would be hysterical.'

'I thought Tonka spoke to me.'

'There's no sign or report of him being around.' She studied him.

'The voice said I was safe. My fear stopped.'

'Tonka appears like a ghost and you feel great. I show up and you start drowning.'

'Beats waterboarding.' Her face twitched.

'Some comparison.'

'There's something you're not saying.' Eilidh stared at Sam and held her peace as Inspector Joyce returned.

'Not a pleasant sight.' Joyce walked past them. 'Back in a minute.'

'No, a tragedy.' Sam said. 'Wardle may have something to answer for,' Sam said. 'I wonder what the crime scene people will come up with.' He turned away, walked over to the trough, took the SIM card out of a phone in his pocket and broke it into several pieces which he sprinkled on the dirty water.

'What did you do?'

'A spot of vandalism.' He fitted a new SIM. The phone was back in his pocket, still switched off.

182

Wardle stepped out of the building humming to himself. His enjoyment at watching the killing of the ghastly brothers provided a warm memory which he replayed. The garrotte round the pole provided excellent entertainment. The enjoyment and sense of divinity he experienced when he sorted out Jenkins's son gave such a rush. The creaking of the rope and the gasping … Aroused, he smirked.

He plucked a rather crushed cigarette from his jacket pocket, lit it and inhaled with a deep sigh. Lost in thought, he puffed until half the tobacco turned to ash. His hatred of Sam Duncan burned in his chest.

He sighed and took his secure phone from an inside pocket, pressed the button and watched the display light up, the vibration signalled readiness. He selected a number and dialled.

'Ah, Xavier, Jenkins is sorted, Duncan and his sister …'

The hand that grabbed his possessed superhuman strength. The phone fell on to dirty concrete, a boot crushed it and kicked it under some broken pallets.

Before Wardle could speak a hard hand clamped on his mouth. The smoke he exhaled as he struggled leaked past strong fingers. He couldn't stop himself being dragged away. In moments he knew the destination. He strained hard.

His muffled voice squeaked as he tried to plead. He managed to hang his weight down and his shiny black Oxfords scuffed against the rough surface. He broke partially free for a moment and landed on his hands and knees. Spikes in the concrete cut his palms and he could feel the abrasion of his knees. His collar stayed clamped in an iron grip. He opened his mouth to scream, and a rough hand filled his mouth with manure and other debris.

They reached the gate and went alongside the low wall, his feet dragging against the pull. He whimpered and tried to spit out the rubbish blocking his speech.

He inhaled deeply through his nose. The stench was awful. His head hung as his rear was lifted off the ground.

With a muffled shriek, and a momentary sense of release and sudden lightness, he splattered into the crusty mess face first. He surfaced and tried to scream. A mouthful of slurry blocked the sound. His eyes cleared enough to see a dark figure, silhouetted against the sky, watching him to the very end.

He imagined a hand from below dragging him down. Oxygen-less, he slowly sank back into the sludge.

A minute later, Death switched his lights out.

183

'Strangled in front of his dad.' Joyce said.

'Evil, Inspector, no other word for it.' Sam said. They came out of the barn's front door, Sam in the middle, Eilidh on his left hugging him and Inspector Joyce on the right. An officer came over with a reflective blanket and a flask of hot tea. Eilidh leaned against the Range Rover, shaking.

'I'm glad I didn't see him.' Eilidh inhaled the fresh air.

Cal and two or three policemen herded some prisoners down the track towards them. One constable carried three or four weapons. To their left, near the end of the building, perhaps thirty yards away Fuss strode with a much larger constable in black. Fuss waved. 'Everything okay, Sammy?'

'Mostly.' Sam said.

'Did I hear bullets?'

'Mac10. The vest worked. He missed with the rest.'

'I can fuckin' see that.' Fuss neared the edge of the building to an almost conversational distance.

'Great to see you, lass. You're tough like your big brother and worth the trip.' Sam watched the exchange of smiles. It warmed him.

'That fuckin'... oops sorry... lump, who you wanted to protect you is...' The blast hit him just above hip height and he seemed to bend sideways, face expressionless at first. Sam drew his big pistol as he started to run. The policeman with Fuss opened and closed his mouth like a fish, his gun didn't move, held still by shock and inexperience.

The click of a pump shotgun preceded a second blast which raked across Fuss's chest throwing up puffs of fabric and blood.

Another click. The next blast, square on his armour, blew the policeman off his feet. Sam reached the end of the building,

.45 at the ready. The man jacked another round as the first bullet ripped through his sternum; the barrel headed skywards as the twelve bore discharged. Cloth fragments flew from the shoulder of Sam's Harris Tweed jacket. Sam's second bullet took the gunman just under his chin as he fell backwards; brains, bone, scalp and blood sloshed on to the muddy path beside the building. As the gunfire stopped, Sam realized he'd been screaming.

* * *

Sam returned to his friend, as armed cops went past with purposeful caution. They dragged out a man who, under shouts and nodding guns, dropped spread-eagled to the ground for a thorough search before being led away. He protested he hadn't known his mate was going to fire.

Sam knelt by Fuss.

'How's it look, Sammy?' The gurgling wheeze told its own story.

'Sore.' Blood welled from Fuss's hip area.

'No fuckin' pain.' A weak voice and a much-loved smile. A policeman dashed over with an emergency bag. 'Tell him to fuck off.'

Sam moved aside, 'no.'

'Last rites, Sam. You know the words, you Proddy pastor?'

'Yeah.' The policeman, a paramedic started to work.

'I need 'em.' The smile leaked blood.

'I don't think so, we need to stop you leaking.'

'Unction from you. Mr Fixit can plug the holes.'

Sam made the sign of the cross over his friend, *'Through this Holy Unction, and the great goodness of His mercy, may God pardon thee whatever sins thou hast committed.'* Sam marked the cross on Fuss's forehead, leaving a red trace from his blood smeared thumb. The paramedic worked.

Inspector Joyce came over. 'There's an emergency helicopter on it's way. ETA fifteen minutes.

* * *

'Did you get the bastard who shot me?'

'Dead.'

'Good.'

'Now shut up and we'll get you sorted.'

'You're supposed to talk to me and be reassurin'.'

'The medic wants me to apply pressure to your hip. You may be shriven, but I want you alive.' Sam pressed a large pad above Fuss's hip bone.

Fuss groaned. 'Easy.'

Sam and the paramedic worked away until the helicopter arrived and a doctor and her team took over and stabilized Fuss. Loaded with morphine, the Glasgow warrior lost consciousness.

Sam watched the process, quiet. Thinking of other times and other helicopters. When the medical team stood up he spoke to the medic. 'How is he?'

'He'll live. It's more bloody than life threatening. He'll need an operation to tidy up and remove external matter.'

Sam nodded, 'Good stuff.'

'His vest saved him.'

* * *

'Charlton.'

'Fuss is down.' A clenched voice tight as a funeral drum's skin. 'The doc says he'll live. Close run thing.'

The silence said it all. 'Eilidh?'

'Safe.'

'Martin?'

'Bruised and operational.'

'Wardle?'

'Alive last time I looked. VIP treatment.'

'Stay away from him.'

'The police are here. He's safe from me.'

'It hurts.' A frosty English accent.

'Always. I killed the assailant.'

'The chopper you were denied will become available to us, no doubt.'

'Bastards…'

'Yes. *Bastards!*' Charlton's snarl made Sam wince.

* * *

The emergency helicopter flew Fuss away.

Another chopper landed for them twenty minutes later. The pilot met them.

'You wouldn't be Bravo 326 by an chance?'

'Vicar?'

'That's me.'

'Nice to meet you.' They shook hands. 'Did we win?'

'Only just.'

'Thank God,'

'I have.' Sam said.

Eilidh, Cal and Sam boarded. A crew member shut the door and they took off.

184

On the boat to Arran, Karen read the note from Sam. A scattering of raindrops landed on the window where the mountain, Goatfell, grew larger, as they sailed onwards.

Dearest Karen,
I woke up with an inescapable feeling that something bad is going to happen today. Not sure if it's for me or not. I have to write this in case I won't be home. I want you to know how I feel.
You are the best thing that ever happened to me. Your courage and quiet support make me bigger every day. I love you. I love our kids, and I want to come home.
Duty called today. I wanted to stay, but I couldn't. Eilidh's at risk, and I'm needed to look after her. So, I'm away and we are separated. Remember, whatever happens, love endures.
Yours Aye
Sam

'Are you okay, ma'am?'

A practised smile. 'Just thoughtful, thanks.'

The minder stepped away. She wondered if they'd made love for the last time. The ache ran deep.

Her mobile rang.

She couldn't find her phone at first, fingers clumsy in a rush, with purse, tissues, diary and everything else in the way. Lifting the mobile, she didn't recognize the number. Her heart sank.

'Yes?' Even a warm greeting couldn't come out.

'Karen?'

'Sam.' She hiccoughed as tears started down her cheeks. 'Eilidh?'

'Safe.' He heard the trembling sigh of relief.

'You?'

He struggled with the words, starting twice and stopping. She waited. 'Fuss is down. They sent a chopper. He's away to Newcastle for an op. I'm going to Glasgow to see his family. Charlton's on his way.' Ragged breathing told her to talk.

'You can't say any more?'

'No.' One little sob.

'I'm with you.' Her voice soothed his soul. 'I'll be back on the next boat.'

'Meet you in Glasgow.'

'Right. Is Eilidh there?'

'I'll put her on.' He handed the phone to his sister and stepped back. From a distance he recognized the maturing person and the child inside. He admired her strength, determination and resolve.

In moments, both she and Karen were crying. They sobbed comfort to each other for a while. Sam and Cal locked eyes then moved away.

* * *

They flew west before turning north. On a moor road, between Hexham and Brampton, Sam saw a motorcycle with two people aboard. The passenger wore an oblong pack on his back. He nodded to himself and half-smiled. Cal and Eilidh didn't notice.

185

'Are you a man of your word, Mike?'

'Mostly, Eilidh. What's on your mind?'

'To tell you where my dossier is, so you can collect it.'

'And?'

'Promise me you'll secure it until the legals are done.'

'I promise.'

She gave him the address and location. He shook his head, Dot's flat, in the airing cupboard to the side of the hot water tank. Nine men in three police cars, Charlton's minders in a Range Rover, and an ARV collected the material.

Within an hour, all of Eilidh's information was secure at Westferry Road. Three hours later, Indira had scanned the documents, collated files and transmitted everything to three separate secure locations. Neither she, nor Mike, released copies for study or review.

'Some good people have died for this.' Mike said.

'I hope Fuss is Okay,' Indira wiped her eyes, 'he's such fun.'

'Yes. One of ours.'

186

Sam didn't have to say anything.

'He's hurt.' Sadie stood on the doorstep, grey-faced, curlers in and a head square on. 'I've been waiting forty years for the knock.'

Sam nodded, 'They say he's not too bad, and in very good hands.'

* * *

'Come in.' She led them through to the neat, unpretentious lounge.

'You're hurting, Sammy.'

'I was there, Sadie.' He'd bought fresh clothes, showered and scrubbed off dried black blood at a hotel before coming round. He'd stood in the spray, head down, watching the dirt and gore swirl away with soap suds.

'I need to go to him.'

'A car will be here in fifteen minutes.'

Sadie made tea, bringing Sam and Cal a mug each. 'Help yourself to biscuits. Was he in pain?'

'No, he was all morphined up. He took the time to say he loved you and the family before he … er … relaxed.'

'What else?' Her terseness surprised Sam. 'Did he ask you to bury him?'

'Yes, and me a Proddy.' They both sensed the humour, a guttering wick in a storm of concern.

'I'll have a wash and change.' She left and clattered up the stairs.

They finished their tea and helped themselves to another. Sadie was back in ten minutes in a swirl of perfume.

'Bless you, Sammy.'

'Did he receive the last rites?'

'Yes.'

'You?' Sam nodded.

'He insisted. He didn't look like dying. I learned the words a while back.' She came over, signalled for him to stand and hugged him with a fierceness his mother would have admired. With a sob she held him for a few seconds, then back under control. 'He admires you above all men, Sam. He was sitting around, lost, then you called and he went to protect your family. I'm glad he did that…' she struggled for a moment '… duty.'

'He only left this morning.' The wave hit the shore, and she bellowed her fear and pain.

Sam hugged her. 'Time to get to Newcastle. The car's outside.'

The sobbing and heaving slowed, stopped. Cal appeared with kitchen roll. Sam pressed it into Sadie's hands. 'I'll call the kids from the car.' She picked up a handbag and grip she'd brought down.

'I wish it was different, but at least he's still with us.' Sam said. He noticed a tear running down Cal's cheek.

Sam's phone rang. He listened. 'Good news. They've operated and he's doing well. Lost a lot of blood. Mainly minor injuries, shock and bruising. The vest saved him.' There was a sizeable in-breath from Sadie. She exhaled a large sigh and pushed away from Sam. 'I'm ready.'

'There'll be people to support you.' Cal said.

'Maybe, but not now. I've got my family.' She hugged Cal, rubbed Sam's arm and walked them to the door.

A police car, lights flashing parked in front of her car. A man stepped out of the Jaguar and opened the rear door. 'They're ready when you are.'

187

Bill Jenkins spent time in hospital, heavily sedated and under guard, both for his own safety, and prior to his arrest on suspicion of kidnap and murder. His distress took days to subside enough to allow proper questioning. He shrieked when coming out of his drugged sleep, begging Wardle to spare his son.

Jason's corpse was removed to a hospital in Newcastle for a post-mortem. His mother and sister came to support Bill and meet the police. A week later they travelled back to London with him.

The search for Wardle stopped when they dragged the slurry pit, working under floodlights after dark. The first body to be recovered was Ned's "nice" brother, one of the pair who had held Eilidh prisoner. The next, William Wardle and, finally, Ned. The search continued until they were sure no other bodies remained. A crushed phone was recovered from a puddle, beside some pallets, during a fingertip search.

The brothers' bodies were removed for autopsy and forensic examination. Coated in stinking ordure, the protruding tongues and ghastly expressions suggested strangulation, which was later confirmed. Wardle's silent scream was comfortable by comparison. The coating on his wide open eyeballs made his face appear as if carved from excrement. All three joined Jason in the morgue.

Two days later, the police were satisfied the search had been thorough and complete. The scene-of-crime specialists had days of forensic work ahead. Senior officials and some politicians were demanding answers, with the usual cynical roar of anger, power, fear and publicity needs.

188

Breakfast with Charlton at 07.00 and straight to business. 'Rough one, Sam.'

'Yes. Time for some R&R, Ben.' Sam said.

'Have a few days. I'm glad Waberthwaite's back on the radar.' Charlton stared into Sam's eyes.

'Yes. Tonka has been doing his thing in Wales, so he tells me.'

'Excellent. We need him.' Charlton paused. 'I can't think how Wardle fell into the slurry pit.'

'Maybe he was overcome by the fumes.'

'After jumping up and down on his phone?'

'Who knows? I wasn't there.'

'How are things at home?'

'Good. I'm popular with all the girls in my life, aside from the occasional hormonal outburst from daughter number one. The little one is getting over her broken leg.'

'Going to do physical jerks with the guardians?'

'Yes. It's painful at times, but it gives me an edge.'

'I'll expect you back inside a week, sooner if needed.' Sam nodded agreement.

'A private question, Sam,' Charlton said. 'You say Jenkins phoned you and told you where Eilidh was?'

'That's right.'

'You went to a call box that morning.'

Sam gave Charlton an appraising glance. 'Yes.'

'You didn't make a call.' Charlton searched Sam's eyes. 'You're a good tactician, Sam. You plan well.'

Sam stared back and said nothing for a moment. 'Some days you're the lamppost, some days you're the dog.'

Charlton half smiled. 'I see. They checked your mobile,

nothing.'

'No. They took it just before the chopper flew us to Glasgow.'

'Cleanliness is next to godliness.'

'Perhaps.' They gazed at each other for a moment. 'And we've got Eilidh's evidence,' Sam said.

'Yes. Mike collected it after her call. He gave her his word that it won't be released until the legals are done. She has mine, too.'

'When they grabbed her, she decided it was more important to have the information secure than hold out for a legal document.'

'Good girl.'

'Let's get the legals done and keep the pressure on.' Sam's eyes glinted, icy sapphires.

— THE END —

Have you read ***Angels' Cut***, first in the series? Use the links on the very last page to find a copy.

Devil's Due

A preview of the next book in the series, *Devils' Due*, begins on the next page.

Devil's Due

PREVIEW

next in the series…

1

'I need more time.'

'Time is a luxury you're fast running out of.'

'We must organize better. The Agency is—'

'You think the Agency is the only problem?'

'They cause most of the trouble in our European operation.' Xavier leaned back, the dampening cloth of his shirt clammy against his skin.

'What about the other players? Cassanet, in France, for instance?'

Xavier paused, thinking of the big man, 'he's Duncan's French poodle. Eliminate Duncan and the poodle is brainless.'

'Duncan scares you.'

Xavier mopped his forehead. 'We have options for most problems.'

'He scares you.'

'Yes, yes, he scares me.'

'And a reliable agent is compromised.'

'He was unlucky.'

'Unlucky? And now he's yet another risk.'

'They have him locked up in their building.'

'More pressure.'

'Yes.'

'You bully your colleagues.'

'I only … only want the best results. I don't mean to hurt them. I demand excellence.' Perspiration ran down his face.

'We don't need enemies inside our operation. There are plenty outside.' The woman's voice remained cold, single-paced, scary.

'They have complained?'

'We know your style.'

He sensed expectation at the other end. 'Perhaps I have been too aggressive.'

'Win them back. Get them involved. Less arrogance, more

listening.'

Relief. 'Of course. Of course.'

'We expect you to consult, and that includes me.' A firm Yorkshire accent brooked no contradiction. 'We'll solve our problems together.'

Xavier squeezed his eyes shut. 'Of course, we will.'

'We are loyal, Xavier, we value your skills and commitment. Like all of us, you need to learn and grow. I'm sure we won't need a chat like this again. Speak soon.' She hung up.

Xavier stabbed… and stabbed … stabbed … and stabbed the notepad on his desk. The pen snapped with a crack. He groaned, rested his elbows on his knees, propped his head on the palms of his hands, and let out a deep sigh.

After five minutes, he returned to his work station, threw the broken pen in the bucket, and settled in his seat. *Duncan is a dead man.* He made notes. Thirty minutes later, he picked up the phone.

2

'Jeannie was due back an hour ago.' Sam checked his watch. 'It's nearly 10.30.'

Anxiety furrowed Karen's face. 'She is 14, *darling*, she needs to get out and meet boys.'

'Of course she does. She also needs to keep her word.' Sam said.

'Didn't you ever fail to come home on time?'

'More times than I care to admit. But I'm the parent now.'

'There, you see? Hypocrite.' The brightness in her eyes warned him.

The phone rang, he crossed the lounge and picked up. The carriage clock on the mantelpiece twirled in silence, winding up, and winding down, similar to their arguments. 'Duncan.' He listened, a slight smile on his face straightened and he looked into his wife's eyes. 'On my way.'

'What's wrong?' Karen said.

'They crossed the perimeter.'

'They need a little darkness for a cuddle.'

'Jeanie's in a unique situation.' Sam said. He left the room, returning moments later with his Colt 1911 and a shoulder holster. He worked the action, holstered and secured the gun. 'I'll find her.'

Karen fixed sad eyes on him. 'How long will this go on?'

'Not much longer. We're squeezing them. They're unlikely to target kids. But I'm not taking chances.' He nodded to her, adjusted the gun, went into the hall and lifted his leather jacket from its hook. Porch light off, he eased into the twilight pulling the garment on as he walked to a shed, under some trees, near the driveway.

* * *

A man stepped out to meet him. Karen contemplated their silhouettes. A dark car pulled up, Sam got in and the vehicle drew away.

'You guard the perimeter?' Sam said.

'Yes, sir.'

'They went over the bridge, by the church?'

'Yes, followed the path, round the church and into the trees.'

Sam nodded and fixed his gaze on the line of the track. He knew the terrain well. He remembered the walks with Barney and, for a moment, the intense pain of loss, and a joyous dog's killing. 'I'll find them. Please drop me up there, by the bus stop.'

'Right, sir,' they drove 200 metres beyond the crossing. As the car stopped, Sam leapt out and trotted up a narrow path between two cottages. Within ten seconds, in the descending twilight, he vanished.

3

Her iPhone's old-fashioned ring tone saved Gemma Smythsone from a nightmare encounter involving a man in a balaclava and a tepid bath. She lurched forward in her chair. 'Hello.' Soaked with clammy sweat, her baggy T-shirt clung to her.

'We must talk.'

'Xavier? A bit late in the evening for you.' His angry intake of breath made her feel more in control.

'Sorry to disturb you. We need to talk, in person.'

'In person?'

'You are in London. I'll be over mid-morning.'

'So, we must meet in person, as soon as possible. I'll check my diary.'

'In person, it's very urgent and serious.' His Belgian accent managed to sound mournful and beseeching.

He didn't start shouting. *Unusual.* 'Where will you arrive?' She sensed an arse-kicking, and enjoyed the thought.

'London City.'

'When?'

'Around 10, I'll confirm.'

'Someone will meet you. I'll arrange a secure room.'

'Thank you, er, Gemma.' He'd never called her Gemma before. Hmm. She ended the call.

4

The lane split the grounds of two houses, took a sharp left-hand bend, and straightened up. It entered a gravelled space along the length of a row of wooden garages. Sam walked between the second and third lock-up, keeping straight on where the path veered to the right.

Within a few steps he stood on a little beach with fifteen metres of burbling, rock-strewn water between him and a near vertical bank. He stole across with no regard for wet feet. At the far side he grabbed the base of a sapling and swung his left foot up to a protruding rock. Sole planted, he kept upward momentum, reached high and gripped another outcrop. One quick pull, and he stretched up to several small ledges, and leveraging on them, surged to the top of the bank.

He moved into cover, leant against a tree, and peered back. No sign of a follower.

Easing himself round the trunk, he stepped on to the twisting and turning path which followed the stream all the way down to the Dark Esk. He enjoyed the buzz of activated muscle, calmed his breathing and crept down the path. In the gathering gloom he made for a stand of tall trees where he hoped to find his daughter. A quiet murmur of young voices carried to him, he half-smiled.

* * *

Sam closed in silence, and saw the pair whisper, kiss, hug and murmur some more. Their hands stroked and squeezed. He experienced a tinge of embarrassment …

The romantic pair jumped as *Dad* materialized beside them. 'You're running a little late, young lady.'

Jeanie checked her watch. 'Oh, God, we lost track of time.'

'That's for sure,' Sam said, 'time to go home.'

'My fault, Mr Duncan.' Jeanie's boyfriend said.

'Fair enough, Robbie, you head off and I'll walk Jeanie back.' Both young people were downcast in an instant, they hesitated. 'Off you go, lad, there's always tomorrow.' Robbie turned, and, head down, walked off in the direction Sam came from. He'd be at the farm in about 15 minutes.

Sam recognized the glint in his daughter's eye. 'We're not usually late, Dad.' Her angry whisper hissed in the gloom.

'I know, Jeannie, we're not making anything of it.'

'Why can't he walk me home?'

'The perimeter, silly.'

'We're only a few hundred yards from the mill.'

'That could be the difference between life and death, Jeannie.'

'It's unfair.'

'The perimeter is patrolled by people who protect us. You step outside it and you put us all in danger, and that includes Robbie. I explained this. I'm here to protect you.'

'You're just playing cowboys and Indians.' Teenage petulance increased in volume.

'I wish … then I wouldn't have seen your uncle Fuss in hospital yesterday.'

What started as an angry in-breath ended as a sob. 'Sorry, Dad, I love him too.'

'Let's get back, love.' They moved down the hill towards the main path by the river. Within five paces, a button taped to Sam's upper arm delivered three silent buzzes. He grabbed Jeanie's arm. 'Shhh.' He moved his lips close to her ear. 'Maximum danger. Time to vanish. Let's take the hedge line along the field. We'll talk by the falls; until then, quiet.' She nodded.

* * *

'Dad. I'm stuck.' Jeannie kept her voice low, but he heard her tension and pain. Sam explored where the barbed wire pierced her leg at the back of her knee, his touch as gentle as darkness allowed.

'Right, here we go.' Half lifting her, hip to hip, he reached round and eased her off the barb. She hissed as the wire came out.

'That wasn't so bad.' Sam said.

'I'm okay.' They moved on.

Ten minutes later they sat on rocks by the waterfall halfway up the hill. Sam checked her injury. 'You're not leaking.'

'How do you know we're in danger?'

'There's a tiny receiver taped to my arm. It vibrates. Three buzzes means: *utmost-get-the-fuck-out-of-there!*' Hilarity exploded between them in wheezing, whispery snickers. He'd never sworn with her before.

'Now what, Dad?'

'Plan to get home alive.'

5

'Did something happen to you at our last meeting, Jack?' The length of the pause surprised her.

'Yes. I was mugged in my room after you took my jet to London.' Jack Samson's voice was stark, measured.

'I was attacked in my flat after I got back.' Gemma paused, encouraged yet discomforted by the disclosure. The fear remembered like the smell of cigarette smoke. 'It was an American.'

'My attacker was French.' They were both silent.

'I wonder if we were all attacked.'

'Makes sense. Destabilizes us.'

'I'd like to destabilize Xavier.'

'Easy now, Gemma.'

'He's a slimy toad and a bully.'

'But he's not the enemy.'

'No. You're right. Sorry, Jack.'

'Who are we up against?'

'Scary people, with the reach and ability to be there when we're together, and attack us individually.'

'Is it that Duncan guy?'

'Might be. We have an eye on him.'

'We or Xavier.'

'Xavier has watchers.'

'We best have a chat with him.'

'Okay. He's coming to see me in the morning.

'I'll find out what he knows and any news of a frightening encounter in the morning. He's trying to be pleasant.'

'Pleasant?'

'Yes, the bullying little bastard's turned courteous.'

'Courteous you say?' Jack barked out a laugh.

'I hope he's not up to something.'

'He's made some blunders. He's done some fine things. All in all, his account will be in credit.'

'Pity.'

'I'll call Justine and hear what she has to say.'

'I'll brief Ken.'

6

He pressed his lips to her ear. 'We'll climb the fence by the straining post. Hunker-down until I'm beside you. When we're ready, we'll dash up the track to the main road, and left onto the Bridge.'

Her breath tickled his ear as she whispered back. 'Thank God. I'm tired of wading down all the streams, Dad, we've crawled along every hedge in the county.' A heartfelt sigh welled up, 'It's tiring. Why couldn't we make a run for it sooner?'

'Invisibility. We see dimly by the light of the moon. People with night-vision see much more.' He rubbed her back. 'Now you get your wish.'

'Some warm up.' The humour in her tone made him smile. *Morale good.*

'Okay, over you go.' He pushed her bottom up to help her climb the post's angled support. Her hand scraped on a barb. She winced, yet remained silent. Sam squatted beside her. She sucked a finger. 'How bad?'

'Sore. I'll live.' He gazed all around them with care. 'What are you looking for, Dad?'

'Movement. Haven't spotted anyone yet, but it's hard to tell.'

'Take a chance.'

'We'll have to.'

'I'm ready.'

'Okay. When we get to the bridge, we're heading for the right hand side. We'll use the midway marker where it's safe to drop into the big pool, like they do at the Summer Fair.'

'I know it.' She said.

'Good.'

'Crawl all over the countryside and now jump in a *bloody* a river.'

'Romance isn't all it's cracked up to be, my girl. *Go!*' He slapped her backside. They jogged round the corner and up the track. He pulled back on her jacket to slow and direct her. They hugged the bridge wall.

* * *

A car passed from the north side, over the bridge, and turned south. The tail lights dwindled. Headlights coming up from the south became intense. 'Eyes down.' He said. The beams swept over the wall. The sound of the engine moved on, northwards, soon lost in the river noise. 'Okay?'

'Okay.'

He pushed her forward. They raced across the bridge. The roar from the water removed the need for whispering. He found the marker and pulled her towards him, remembering his first jump from a plane. The less thinking time, the better. 'Up you come.'

The parapet was about two feet wide. He helped her slide over, holding her wrists tight. She let her right leg go down whilst her left knee and calf rested on the bridge. Her breath hissed in fear. 'I've got you. Let your other leg dangle.'

She dragged her knee off the bridge, with a little squeal, and hung from her father's hands. 'I'm okay.'

'That's my girl.' He leaned forward, belt buckle grinding on stone, forearms locked on the rugged surface, and held her clear of the wall. 'I'm going to let you drop. Remember, knees bent when you hit the surface.' Their eyes locked. 'Swim clear, I'll be right behind you.' Trust and love glowed from her gaze. Sam's heart ached as he let her go, watching her pale face fall away to vanish in the gloom and roar of water.

Sam put his knee on the marker. Gripped the edge of the stonework and pulled himself forward. His toe scraped free of the loose gravel as he swung his other leg up; mind preparing for the drop. As he turned to complete the move, a rough hand grabbed his collar and dragged him back towards the road. His mind screamed for Jeanie, as he tumbled backwards onto hard tarmac …

Available soon…

About Mac

Hi, I'm Mac Logan, Scottish and British by birth. Thanks for reading my work.

They say stress happens when you resist the natural urge to do violence to bad people who hound and traumatize you. In the movies, you can erupt on to the vengeance trail and, with your .45 in one hand and a gorgeous partner in the other, wreak pyrotechnic revenge on the evil people who harmed you.

In real life, short of spending a lifetime in jail after exacting retribution, there are few acceptable options to murder and mayhem.

I chose writing as my recourse for a 'pop' at the wicked, corrupt, and vicious people and cadres who screw us and steal our money. Such people have hurt me in the past, yet I wouldn't want to harm them, far better to do it in fiction with a satisfying robustness.

This then is the basis of The Angels' Share series, fiction rooted in grievance and amplified by a surging imagination.

I love family, cooking, good company, banter, sport, fun, and an occasional drop of 'The Cratur'.

With many articles, and now, books published, it's great to build a relationship with my readers. I'm always delighted to hear from you.

Acknowledgements

The only thing I do on my own is the writing. With the willing help and support of wonderful people, life gets easier.

Thanks to my dear wife **Meg** for her patience, cooking and support as I wrote and re-wrote *Angels' Cut*. Thanks also to:

Alastair Macfarlane for his early help.
Joe and **Ian Flynn** for early feedback.
Gale Winskill of Winskill Editorial for her forthright feedback and fast turn around. She's as professional as she is helpful.
Mariana Sing for permission to use her picture 'Keep Breathing'.
Helen Lloyd, **James Warrior** and ***Choice Voices*** for the audiobook production. Their diligence and commitment shows.
Andrew L Phillips for his interest in taking the project to the film and TV world … *watch this space!*
Hanne Partonen for her love of books, reading and feeding back with English as a second language.
Maryann Ness for her diligence in reading and feeding back from an American perspective.
Steffan Gwynedd-Lewis for his practical help with video, editing and connections … and designing the covers.
Phil Wadsley (audiobook) for his encouragement and audio and visual technical expertise (one of the best in the business).
Polly St Aubyn and her eagle eye.
Michelle Wood for tackling the Marketing and Business Plan.
Thanks to everyone else: **family**, **friends** and **helpful strangers**.

Connect

Twitter: @MacLogan_writes
Blog: http://www.macsbook.wordpress.com
Website: http://www.macloganwrites.com
Facebook https://goo.gl/Jl7uO7

Made in the USA
Columbia, SC
09 November 2017